THE FINAL CURTAIN CALL

An historical novel

THE FINAL CURTAIN CALL

An historical novel

Hector Christie

ATHENA PRESS
LONDON

THE FINAL CURTAIN CALL
An historical novel
Copyright © Hector Christie 2005

All Rights Reserved

ISBN 1 84401 436 3

First Published 2005
ATHENA PRESS
Queen's House, 2 Holly Road
Twickenham TW1 4EG
United Kingdom

Printed for Athena Press

This book is dedicated to my mum and dad.

Acknowledgements

With thanks to Mau Mau for the pictures and Daphne Lovelace for putting up with my appalling handwriting.

Who Owes Who?

Five hundred years ago today
Western Colonialists made us slaves
They stole our silver and our gold
You must not believe what you have been told
Bristol, Birmingham and Liverpool
Were built by slaves you thought were fools
You are rich 'cos we are poor
Yet still you keep us pinned to the floor

Chorus
So who owes who? Who owes who?
What we want to know is who owes who?

A message to all in Africa
I'm Monsanto's boss Mr Shapira
We have some crops for you to plant
Do what you're told you'll get a grant
You may go hungry and be ill at night
Give us your land, don't try and fight
Cruel to be kind is the way I'll bet
To help you reduce your Third World debt

Chorus
So who owes who? Who owes who?
Why all the fuss when you are us.

Exploitation and Third World debt
Milk us all for what you can get
You are rich 'cos we are poor
Drop the debt get out the door.
Just one percent of interest
For our gold, diamonds and the rest
And you'd owe us 1,000 times more
Then we'd be rich and you'd be poor
Yes we'd be rich and you'd, be poor

Chorus
So who owes who? Who owes who?
What we want to know is who owes who?

We corporate folk are to here assist
Turn your shabby lands into realms of bliss.
There'll be no more wars and no more sorrow,
Provided you give us your oil tomorrow.
We give you dams and GM crops
Our charity knows not where to stop
Homogenisation of our cultures
Will stop you all behaving like vultures
We're here to help, don't you get
It's *good* for you to pay your debt

Chorus
So who owes who? Who owes who?
Why all the fuss? I'm ordering you to keep paying us

You control our foreign policy and take our land
To help pay a debt we don't understand
You dump your subsidised maize and cotton
Into a land the world's forgotten
This all in the name of globalisation
Which is tearing the heart out of our nation
Africans starving in their millions
As Corporate profits soar into trillions
You are rich 'cos we are poor
You have 'our' blood on your hands, that's for sure.

Chorus
So who owes who?… Who owes who?
Who owes who? Why all the fuss? We don' t owe you,
YOU OWE US

Amanda

Contents

INTRODUCTION

Well, it's happened: the collapse of civilization, as predicted two years ago. My name is Annie, and I'm now thirty-two and am fortunate to be one of the ones to have survived and be witnessing the death and rebirth of the world with a totally new set of values. My dad died with millions of others as a result of fighting to minimise and soften the impact. It's hard to know if they succeeded, the collapse has been so horrendously awful, beyond any of our wildest dreams. However, I like to think the activists back then paved the way for the world as it is shaping up now.

My awakening, for want of a better word, to the ways of the world occurred in 2001 when I was ten. I was living with my dad in a big house with a small farm and garden in North Devon near the coast. Life was great fun. We had chickens, goats for milk and an organic permaculture garden for our vegetables (the one bit I didn't like at the time), pigs, sheep and a few wild Highland cattle. Self-sufficiency was our objective, and the main reason I've survived until now. For fun we used to play all sorts of games and go down the coast in what became known as 'The Battle Bus', dancing in the back to reggae music on our way to surf the Atlantic rollers.

My dad and his friends thought they could create an oasis independent of a debt-ridden world controlled by the large corporations. At this time big businesses were fast getting a grip on all aspects of life from education and medicine, to whatever food supplements we put into our bodies. However, when the foot-and-mouth disease struck North Devon in 2001, followed by the potentially devastating effects of genetically modified (GM) crops, they felt like rats trapped up a drainpipe. The Western world had become a society ruled by feelings of apathy and hopelessness, and people moaned a lot. However, some, especially those whose livelihoods and lifestyles were directly threatened, moved rapidly from a position of long faces to one of passionate activism. Not that I wholly liked it, but my dad and his cronies certainly came alive at this time.

Many people now talk about the new energies that engulfed the planet in the late 1980s and early '90s. Those who were alive at the time say it was like a higher vibration sent down from the heavens to open the door to the new Age of Aquarius. Man, in a way, was being moved on to the next rung of the evolutionary ladder in the same way as happened at the start of the Piscean Age with the help of the likes of Christ, Buddha and Muhammad.

The dawning of the Aquarian Age was often very muddling, apparently, for those who opened up to it. Many flipped out with or without the help of psychedelics such as magic mushrooms, convinced they were Jesus Christ. King Arthur was another favourite, especially around Glastonbury. The energy seemed to shine light on people's weaknesses, for them to work on – provided they chose to. However, many became confused and chose to let their pampered egos take control and blissed out in the cosmos, channelling everything from Queen Guinevere to God's Father. The simple fact was that embracing the new energies and secrets of the universe and why things happened as they did, available to all who chose it, was not easy. The polarisation then really kicked in between those holding on to the old and those stepping blindfold over the cliff into the new. It was all so perfect in the great scheme of things. We would never be where we are today had it not been for the rapid raising of global consciousness over this period until now.

Most had intuitively known for ages that the orthodox religions provided only part of the picture, and far from all the answers now embraced by all of us left in the world. The churches, mosques and ashrams are all now part of history when it comes to places of worship. Now that no one needs a priest, guru or orthodox religion to connect him or her with the limitless love and power of the unseen means life is so much better. It only seems such a shame that the earth and most of the people had to go through so much death and destruction before finally waking up.

It was during the foot-and-mouth days of 2001 that I was first dragged out to protests. Initially it was the MAFF (Ministry of Agriculture) HQs. We were protesting against the unnecessary and illegal (according to EU law at the time) killing of perfectly healthy animals. It was then on to anti-war/anti-capitalist (for anti-capitalist, read anti-corporate – nobody was against hard-working individuals making an honest buck other than the mindless few) protests, with carefully planned pieces of Direct Action in between. There were, what seemed to me, more and more depressing items on the news which was always on in our house. I was an oversensitive girl, and the sight of so many kids of my age – and younger – starving, suffering and fighting with guns in most parts of the world got to me. Even more so, since my dad said it was due primarily to our blinkered drive for economic growth and profit in the West. For this the key was *oil*.

The result was I took it personally and wanted to do something about it. However, I needed to find out more, but was too young to travel to the Middle and Far East. With the help of my forward-thinking history teacher at school, Mr Thomlinson, I managed to get correspondence with two pen friends on the other side of the globe. It was just after the horrendous second US and British destruction of Iraq in 2003, where to get rid of one tyrant they killed many thousands of civilians, as they did in 1991, that I was put in touch with Ishmael.

Ishmael lived with what remained of his family on the outskirts of Baghdad. Ishmael's mother and baby sister had been killed by one of the many stray American bombs whilst on their way back from collecting vital groceries. At least, Ishmael says, they didn't live in the areas that were carpet-bombed. I was amazed when he told me this but not entirely surprised. My dad was constantly on about press gagging during foot-and-mouth, that freedom of speech only existed between certain boundaries decided upon by Big Brother, for want of a better term. These boundaries got tighter and tighter in the dark days leading up to 2020.

Ishmael said he and his family and friends never recovered from the onslaught. Not only were foreign soldiers everywhere shooting people on suspicion, but also the depleted uranium used in the 1991 war was – incredibly – used again. Ishmael's grandparents had both died of cancer in 1993. He claims this was due to depleted uranium residues and the cruel sanctions imposed by us, which meant medicines couldn't get through to those who needed them most – the poor. Ishmael went the same painful, unnecessary way in 2007. He died bitter, even hating the West, who destroyed his country, friends and family just to get their oil. He wasn't the only one.

The West used the supposed terrorist attacks on the World Trade Center on September 11, 2001, to bombard, even destroy any country that didn't lie down and embrace its imperialistic empire. Ishmael felt it was that they'd watched too many cowboy and Indian, and James Bond films, but who was the real Spectre? He was most bitter at the double standards and hypocrisies. He said they happily sold the tyrant Saddam Hussein conventional and chemical weapons (plus the material and technology to make their own) in the 1980s. A blind eye was turned when these horrendous weapons were used on Iran and even on the Kurdish people in Northern Iraq in the late 1980s. Saddam was no threat to oil supplies at this time, plus it was in the West's interests to bring the then Iranian regime to its knees. However, when two years later Saddam *did* threaten the flow of oil to the West, they bombed him and his people to pieces, as they did again twelve years later.

My second pen friend was a very sweet Indian girl called Neela. Neela's family had been subsistence farmers in the region of Andhra Pradesh in India for four generations. They had been lucky to have a forty-acre site. On the low-lying wetter land they had grown rice, and, on the three terraces cut out from the hillside, they had grown maize and fruit such as pineapple, papaya and kiwi. They grew wheat for milling and they even had three dairy cows. They produced enough to feed themselves and the surplus they sold in the local market using the proceeds to buy 'luxuries', as Neela called them. It was a family business and was carefully controlled so it didn't have to support more than it could. Many grandchildren were encouraged into other businesses such as the rag trade, or became potters, snake charmers and so on. Two of Neela's aunts had become well-known pin-up pop stars. More importantly, even though life was tough at times, they were happy. However, the new millennium was to shatter all of this.

Neela, who like so many in her part of the world had an amazing grasp of what was going on, said it was in 2000 that the policy of physically booting families off their land escalated. She said in one of her letters:

> *The main problem is that our country is in such big debt to Western banks we can barely pay the interest on our debt. However, everybody here knows the IMF (America) lent money to corrupt*

governments knowing it would either be laundered or squandered. Now we are in huge debt, your governments can control our foreign and even our domestic policies. The policy which is destroying us is the massive introduction of genetically modified crops. It started happening to our neighbours in early 2000. Those smallholders, without official paper documentation, were literally just chucked off their land with no compensation – to further swell the overcrowded, disease-ridden slums of the cities. The same massive displacement of my people happened where, with the backing of the World Bank, they built those horrendous dams.

This is eventually what happened to us in 2003. The compensation we received my Pappy feels will barely see us out for the year, but at least we have something. We do have a tin shack, not the same as our farmhouse, and a fresh water tap which sometimes works. It's funny, but we saw our cousins on the plains of the Sardar Sarovar Dam being displaced and never thought it would happen to us. They fought to keep their land but the soldiers came and raped the girls and took my uncle off for a week of torture saying they would slowly kill off his family. He moved voluntarily, but due to his stance received no compensation, and has already lost his wife and a son to disease in the slums. He now works twelve hours a day for a dollar an hour for an American company.

When my Pappy heard some lady in your Government called Clare Short was giving aid of some £65 million via the Department of International Development (DFID) to the Andhrah Pradesh Government he went mad. We had to stop him from killing the local soldiers. The US was, of course, giving much more mainly in the form of GM seeds and chemicals. In early 2002 he took out his life savings and joined with a group of farmers to go to Europe and the US to beg them not to give money to their governments. He said the reason was that practically every penny was used to pave the way for big agribusinesses to invade our land, displace our farmers and create huge fields of often inedible GM crops such as cotton and feed for your animals on the other side of the world. The reason, they tell us and you, is to help solve the starvation problems of India, and the foreign income generated will filter down to all of us. It's now 2005 and none of us have seen a rupee; even the World Bank admitted the chances of this happening were remote – the shareholders must be paid, after all. Also, if they grew anything edible we'd raid it like locusts.

On returning from the US, Pappy was broke and suicidal, but Grandmama dying has made him resolve to stay alive for us. I hope you are OK and your Pappy is set free soon...

This is an excerpt from my third letter received from Neela on May 1, 2005.

For us in the West, the breakdown in society took a little longer. However, when it happened it was just as severe and testing as anywhere else, and was life-changing for each and every one of us who survived. Most of us couldn't understand why our Government couldn't see that the more they bombed those who didn't submit to their ways, killing millions of innocent people, the more so-called terrorists, normally just desperate grieving relatives, were created. The extraordinary thing was they were actually amazed when millions upon millions rose up and stopped the lifeblood flowing to the West – the oil.

Part One

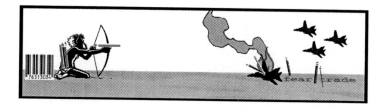

CHAPTER I: LIFE ON THE FARM

The foot-and-mouth crisis in 2001 was to be our first real taste as a family as to where the world was heading. The West hadn't sorted out how to deal with its own people at the time. If we had been a Third World country my dad would have received far more than a short prison sentence and a huge fine for his antics. However, September 11 came to the Government's rescue: In the aftermath of the attack on the twin towers in New York, anti-terrorist legislation was rushed through, allowing the state the freedom to lock up anybody they even just *suspected* of being a terrorist for an indefinite period without a trial. A similar law was also quietly sneaked through with regard to farmers resisting the slaughter of their healthy animals.

My dad is sadly no longer with us. Even with our collective spiritual awareness I still can't quite forgive the actions of the state towards him. Fortunately he left detailed diaries of this period. My mum and dad were divorced but I spent most of my time living with him. Even though I was just ten, I remember it vividly. Those eight months were the first taste of living in a war zone, never knowing what the day or the morrow would bring. The only difference at that time was that it was animal's lives we were dealing with; but the next time and the time after that, it would be humans.

A short summary as to the state of food production and consumption might help further clarify the impact foot-and-mouth had on farmers and farming practices at this time. When Dad originally set up his smallholding in 1986 on a beautiful hillside at Saunton, overlooking the beach and the stunning Braunton Burrows, farming was, on the surface, good. However, it was only good because the farmers had given away their power to market their produce. 'Intervention' prices were implemented by the Government some years before, to artificially top up or subsidise the price paid to farmers for their produce. Big food-processing companies bought the produce at the market price, which was variable, and the Government, via taxpayers' money, subsidised farmers by anything between an extra quarter to a third of the market price. Thus farmers received a steady price per ton of wheat, barley and oats, and the same for their sheep and beef. Meanwhile manufacturing industry looked on, green with envy.

Farmers maximised their profits by maximising their output per acre. With the seed of wheat, for example, hybridised to increase yields from one ton per acre up to four tons in a ten year period in the 1970s, profits skyrocketed. Many people disliked the 'greedy' farmers, and then had little sympathy when intervention prices were slashed in the 1990s, and BSE, swine fever, then FMD ravaged livestock farmers.

The bigger picture shows it was the way the system was set up. Environmental damage was barely recognised by farmers, or the average person, when a massive increase in herbicides and pesticides were used to accompany the huge yield increases during the 1970s. Money was God back then, and farmers were simply maximising their profits, as most people were in those days.

Another consequence was enormous grain, meat and butter mountains, stored at enormous cost rather than given away to the starving millions through fear of causing a big drop in the world market price for these products. It was for this reason that Dad tried to set up and farm in Zambia before moving to Devon. He couldn't see the point of simply contributing to the mountains of stored food.

With regard to livestock, it was the same. All the farmers

had to do was fatten or part-fatten the farm animals, then take them to the local abattoir or market. Market demands meant enormous price variations but farmers were largely protected by intervention subsidy. Again, the farmer did not have to concern him or herself with regard to anything beyond the killing of the animal. Historically it is now recognised that this was the root cause of the farmers' downfall. More and more the supermarkets were buying up the meat and other produce as they insidiously took more control of the food chain. At the time, the farmers weren't bothered who took their produce. With intervention it made no difference.

It was the dairy farmers who first really felt the brunt of the ever increasingly powerful retailers. Dairy farming, propped up by the Milk Marketing Board, had been for years about the most profitable form of farming. However, things went pear-shaped when the increasingly large supermarket chains decided, seemingly randomly, to use milk as their number one loss-leader in order to attract customers into their stores. When the Milk Marketing Board was disbanded in the 1990s, many of the small- to medium-sized dairy farmers found it was actually costing *them* three pence to produce a litre of milk. Bottled water was more expensive than milk on the supermarket shelves, and with the consumers quickly hooked on this cheap product, there was apparently nothing small- to medium-sized farmers could do. Most went bust.

As with the dairy industry, meat production was becoming ever more centralised. Traditional small livestock farmers in the West Country, Wales and the North especially were struggling with the closure of small abattoirs and the local butcher, as more and more of us flooded into the supermarkets. It quickly became economically unviable for small farmers to transport the odd fat bullock or few fat sheep sometimes hundreds of miles to the nearest (enormous, centralised) abattoir. Added to which, supermarkets chose to buy from big farmers rather than small, due to the economies of scale.

As more regulations come flooding in, especially from Europe, many small farmers lost out to the big farmers with regard to the subsidies – some simply unable to understand the vast amounts of paperwork. It was even made law that farmers were no longer allowed to kill their own livestock on farm for personal consumption. This was because it was feared that some naughty small farmers were selling off the odd joint to friends and neighbours and thus avoiding paying tax. Oh, and folk could get poisoned from ill cured-meat! (Not that there was ever one single recorded case of this, in contrast to the toxic muck sometimes found on supermarket shelves. The phenomenal damage done by herbicide and pesticide residues in the pristine, clean-looking food, and cancers resulting directly from 'additives' such as Sudan 1, Para-red and so many others, were never really documented until now – for obvious reasons.) Every aspect of our lives had to be controlled.

Dad was livid. He, like many others, recognised the importance of respecting the spirit of the animal. He would always spend time with the pig or bullock the day before it was due to be killed and talk to the animal's spirit about what was about to happen, giving thanks for its life. To most of society, which had all but lost total contact with the soil, this would have seemed bonkers. Yet in most traditions across the world, there was always some kind of a ritual before sacrificing or taking the life of an animal. Respect for the land, nature, water and air was no longer necessary – man could control all this after all. Dad went to prison (for the third time) for rightly refusing to obey this law and send any animal sixty miles to the nearest abattoir. I remember going with him once to a large abattoir in North Devon with a load of fat lambs in the back of a horsebox. The lambs smelt the death and, clearly terrified, packed tightly together in the back of the horsebox. Dad had to drag each one out individually. The pigs, waiting in pens for slaughter, squealed and fought incessantly to relieve their fear. Dad was always upset for a good week after this.

Whenever he could, he would use a much friendlier, smaller abattoir. However, the best for the animal was to be 'dropped' on farm when it had no idea of what was to come. The meat tasted so much better as well, since it didn't contain the vast amounts of adrenaline released due to the stress of impending death in the abattoir. Tragically, most people in the supermarket saw a rasher of bacon in the same light as a bag of seedless grapes. They no longer cared about the fate of an animal, or even saw meat as once having been part of an animal, so long as it was... *cheap*. Thank heavens, things are completely different again now.

Dad was known locally for being an above average semi-professional footballer rather than living in a big house. On February 3 2001 his leg was badly broken when he was bearing in on goal away at Paulton Rovers. He was rushed to Bath Hospital, where he said he spent (according to him) the happiest three days of his life in excruciating pain, without sleeping at all (other than during the five-hour operation, presumably). He said he thanked God constantly for taking the trouble to directly intervene in his existence to lever him onto his true life's path. This he said he knew, because the day before he spent hours showing his friend, Biff, precisely how to feed the farm animals, for no apparent reason. When his leg snapped his first thought was, 'That's why I showed Biff the feeding routine,' and immediately relaxed in the knowing it was 'meant to be'.

It must have sounded crackers to most people he told this to at the time. What excited him most was the sensation of being propelled totally into the moment with a blank canvas; having to put his trust and faith in some higher power. This of course is old hat to us who survived the collapse. We live our lives in this state automatically now, and no longer, thank heavens, need the suffering to propel us there.

After three and a half weeks of recuperation he had a dream. It was one of those ones where it clearly felt so real you remember every detail even when you're awake. Many people were waking up at this time to the fact that memorable dreams carry important messages from the spirit world. His dream went – and I quote from his diaries:

> *I was sitting in the kitchen at Tapeley looking out of the window and noticed a large tornado – F2 or F3 near to the Monterey Pines on the horizon. I ran to the top of the house and noticed another five at least; two were F5's, half a mile or more wide each. The most worrying thing was they were heading our way, for some reason. I was the only person who noticed them. I also knew there were many more out there. I rushed downstairs, grabbed the children and led them down to the cellar. The problem was I had too many keys on the key ring, and whilst fumbling around, trying to find the right one, the first tornado hit, shredding the house around us like matchsticks. I could have been prepared – but just wasn't, and that's what hurt.*

He says that he didn't get back to sleep that night, then had the 'Saul on the road to Damascus' blast whilst watching the lunchtime news the following day: the foot-and-mouth around Holsworthy and Hatherleigh in mid-Devon was spreading northwards. Coincidentally (everyone now knows beyond any doubt that there is no such thing as coincidence), some fellow popped around half an hour later with a page of sheets about vaccination he had downloaded from Sheepdrove.com off the Internet. He felt it would be of interest.

To my dad this was manna from heaven. With time on his hands due to his broken leg, he got his head down and learned everything he could about the benefits and potential dangers of the foot-and-mouth vaccine, along with

European law on the subject. The reason soon became clear to him why his leg was broken. Had he been playing football, often twice a week, his focus would have been dissipated and he'd have put only fifty per cent of his energy into the next eight months rather than the one hundred per cent needed for maximum impact. Also, defending himself from the police and the MAFF men on (and sometimes with) crutches, looked far more stylish on local TV.

The first of many protests that Dad organised that year – The Pro-Vaccine Rally – was on Instow beach. He kept a fairly thorough diary of the events of that period, with some typed sections for press release or just general interest. I have used a few of the pieces as they were written since they best capture the mood of this time. For us it was a time of transformation and preparation for the major fallout which was to come. It was a big wake-up call as to precisely how the fear-oriented global powers operated. The massive difference between us and the Third World at the time was that we were fighting for our animals' lives but they were fighting for their own lives.

I had never seen anyone so stressed as Dad in the lead-up to that first rally. Like everything he did, he did it with such urgency. I suppose he had a point as the number of new cases was rising every day and he was convinced that vaccination was the only way to stop the disease from spreading completely out of control. Every other country in the world vaccinated, after all.

The situation totally preoccupied him. He clearly wasn't sleeping, was very short with me and even forgot to pick me up from school one night – something he had never done before. However, when the day of the rally came, he had it all together: A sound system for the speakers was set up by some so-called 'crusties' more used to setting up for open air 'free parties' popular at the time, and two thousand leaflets (see below) were printed in time to be circulated in the local towns the day before and at the rally.

CULL MAFF

PRO-VACCINE RALLY ON INSTOW BEACH
1PM SATURDAY APRIL7th.
FREE PARKING. EXPECTED FINISH 2-2.30PM

cost infective farming

FORMAT:
Opening talk by Hector Christie at 1pm sharp! Then one or two talks from a hotelier or small business whose future is uncertain and possibly Peter Kindersley or Richard North. Friends will be mingling in the crowd during the talks with pen and paper to get YOUR feelings which we or you can relate.

THE MAIN POINTS: to clarify the FACTS and MYTHS of MAFF.
1) FACTS: Current slaughter policy could take one year to bring under control and 18 months to 2 years to stop sporadic outbreaks i.e. 2 seriously disrupted tourist seasons to survive ...or not! In the first 18 months of the 1967 outbreak 400 000 animals were slaughtered, but in the first six weeks of this one, of the one million culled or due to be culled, only 5% are infected.
2) MYTHS: a) "vaccination is inefficient" - RUBBISH, it is 99% successful.
    b) "vaccination means we lose our right to export" Again untrue.
Regionalization of unaffected areas is accepted for export of stock. Even herds etc in affected areas can export once the disease is under control and they can prove their animals and land are FMD free – as happens now in N. Ireland and Holland.
    c) "vaccinated animals are FMD carriers." There is not one case proved as to the validity of this. Also many animals, such as sheep, will get FMD and recover unnoticed - the disease is literally everywhere.

Please bring placards, signs and all your friends. OUR LIVELIHOODS ARE AT STAKE. Help in the fight for mass vaccination of ALL livestock in affected areas now!

The most striking aspect about the sheet is obviously the picture. This was knocked up by a cool friend of my dad's with dreadlocks reaching down to his thighs, hence his name – Dreadlock Dave. His two kids became good friends of mine. We used to go surfing together in the years leading up to the collapse until those Great Whites set up a breeding ground just off our favourite point break and a friend of ours had a chunk taken out of his left buttock.

The barcode, supermarket bags over the blistered feet and a Nazi-looking MAFF slaughter man summed up most people's perspective of what was going on. My dad was never big on conspiracy theories, which naturally abounded at this time; he liked to stick with the facts. However, he was convinced that it was due to the supermarkets that the movement of animals all over the country was allowed to continue for three days after this incredibly contagious disease was spotted. This, coincidentally, was the exact amount of time needed to sort out the import of meat from abroad to substitute for British meat. Empty shelves meant loss of revenue. It's extraordinary to look back now but money was revered above all else back then.

The day went OK. However, for all the efforts, of the hundred and thirty people the majority seemed to be sympathetic friends – most prominent his old mates from the Bideford Football Team in their spanking red tracksuits en route to a home game. Dad had spent Wednesday and Thursday sitting on the phone to the guest houses and hotels in a thirty-mile radius. He explained that vaccination was the only way they'd sort out the problem and get the hoteliers some much needed business that season. They nearly all agreed. There were, after all, next to no tourists in Devon due to the disease. Eighty per cent said they would come but only two people turned up. This was his first encounter with the greatest British disease – *apathy*. It was this attitude that made the eventual collapse so much worse for most people.

It wasn't long after this that Dad chained and padlocked us in. This was not just to keep the public and their vehicles out that could be spreading the disease, but more importantly the MAFF vets. There was one farmer in Chumleigh, mid-Devon, who was convinced beyond any doubt that the only way his animals could have contracted FMD (foot-and-mouth disease) was via the vets. He had chained himself in, much as we had, and not allowed anyone in or out of his farm. The risks of airborne transfer of the disease weren't nearly as bad as the early scare mongering suggested – plus his neighbours did not have animals. When MAFF threatened him with a very expensive High Court Injunction, he let in a Spanish vet. She, unmasked, looked into the mouth of a cow which two weeks later contracted FMD and he lost the lot. Vets were in such a hurry that they didn't disinfect properly unless a farmer made them. Move hastily from a FMD infected farm to inspect a non-infected farm and the results are obvious.

Press interest went up a couple of notches on the back of Dad's stance and articles began appearing in the national press and on TV. The large wrought iron gates at the bottom of our drive with big chains around them made for a perfect photo opportunity and helped my dad get the message out as to what was really going on. However, the experience gained over this period also showed him the extent the press were gagged by big business and the Government.

By mid-April there were outbreaks occurring on neighbouring farms. Under the crazy so-called Contiguous Cull Policy, whereby anything within two miles of a case was earmarked for slaughter, an English Bull Terrier spirit descended over the place. Each time MAFF vets turned up at the premises, with the customary police escort, they were aggressively turned away.

I had never seen my dad lose his temper before other than on the football field with the referee, which is not quite the same. Hobbling around on his crutches with his eyes glazing over in an 'I'll stop you at any cost' sort of way, he looked pretty formidable. He was tall as well – plus those crutches doubled up as weapons. I think that dragging me down aged ten, plus his little army of strong strapping men, clearly determined to defend the healthy animals, it must have looked pretty scary as well as a little dotty to the authorities. The most powerful weapon of all was, however, knowledge: knowing EU law, he would tie the remarkably ignorant vets up in all sorts of knots. EU law categorically stated that it was 'illegal to kill a healthy animal without blood testing that animal first'. Therefore, according to their law, the Contiguous Cull Policy was illegal. This fact he ferociously bellowed out from behind the chained wrought iron gates.

When the MAFF booklet called 'Vaccination – the Facts' with MAFF covering fifty-one questions from the NFU was leaked into Dad's possession, I've never seen anyone so excited. He called it his 'Jewel in the Crown', and felt he had the evidence from the horse's mouth to change government policy. His main concern was to get vaccination for the 240,000 cattle in Cumbria and 180,000 in Devon before turnout into the fields. They should have been out already, but farmers were keeping them in the sheds where they were not as likely to contract FMD – one of the many facts confirmed in the MAFF booklet. The following small piece of writing from his diary/press release sums it up:

THE ALTERNATIVE: VACCINATE. The MAFF booklet on 'Vaccination – the Facts' states pretty much the same facts as we, the pro-vaccine lobby, have been saying for months: that the FMD vaccine is as efficient as a vaccine gets (point nineteen states that it is ninety-nine per cent efficient); that livestock in Cumbria and Devon could be vaccinated in between ten–fourteen days (Cumbria has had sixty vets, including Bob Shaw, all being paid £100 a day on standby to vaccinate for the past month) and cattle would be immunised after three–five days and could then be mixed with non-vaccinated animals after a week at literally no risk. (Countries such as Macedonia, Tunisia and many more who vaccinated during FMD outbreaks in the 1990s have not had a single outbreak since, and the Danes freely mixed vaccinated animals and livestock which had simply got over FMD with 'clean stock' during their last outbreak without one new case of FMD!). It talks of FMD free status returning twelve months after the last vaccination or Cull and mentions the zoning areas. This is where parts of a country which have no cases of the disease can be declared FMD free and continue to export. Exports are worth a mere £400 million – peanuts compared to the cost to business so far.'

It's hard to believe now, but in those days – just twenty-one years ago, and continuing and getting more extreme pretty much up until the Collapse – countries such as the UK were importing almost the same as they were exporting with regard to the likes of lamb, pork products, milk and butter. The vets were obsessed with regaining export status. All this meant was that a few of the bigger farmers received a premium when they sold their animals abroad. The culling policy had already cost the country £2 billion up until this point, and ended up costing six billion with the eventual deaths of over ten million animals registered and at least a further three million unregistered as part of the so-called 'Welfare Cull'.

With the export market worth just £400 million per annum, the economics just didn't add up. Put this with other hidden costs – phenomenal human suffering, suicides and the unregistered loss of thousands of small businesses in the countryside dependent on farming and tourism, and you can see why conspiracy theories abounded at the time. As I have said, my dad resisted this temptation, preferring to stick to the facts. Here is another piece from his diaries:

WHO STANDS TO BENEFIT? In Canada, small farms are getting squeezed out and snapped up by large corporations and multinationals in ever increasing numbers. 3.5 million animals have been killed (including a few labelled for cull) so far in the UK of which 1.2 million have been slaughtered on simply welfare grounds. Many more will go unless we vaccinate.

Tony Blair announced a few weeks ago a plan to vaccinate housed animals in Cumbria and Devon due to there being twice the risk of contracting FMD when turned out ∟ FMD being rife in wildlife, the ground, etc. (It was also a good bit of political spin for when the truth about the vaccine is widely known.) However, a senior official of one large multinational supermarket chain has just announced they would 'have to label all vaccinated produce as a safeguard for their customers', effectively kicking any chance of vaccination way out into touch. Another MAFF document released on March 29 states 'there is no risk to human health from meat or other products which have FMD, or which have been vaccinated against it'. Neither they nor the Government mentioned this at the time of the supermarket chain statement.

This whole episode has sadly shown how little power the Government has in the face of the multinational billionaires. Globalisation of the meat industry alone means livestock being transported vast distances across the UK and Europe, packed into huge lorries – welfare is not a consideration to these people. Cheap meat is flown or ferried around the world more as small abattoirs, farms and localised trade become unable to compete – the environment/global warming and spread of disease from massive import/export is also not a consideration. Also if we turn our countryside into a theme park we will become wholly dependent upon cheap imported food, and any control over our destiny we still have will be gone. Remember the crucial self-sufficiency policy from the two World Wars.

There was an EU White Paper, an ex-senior member of MAFF told Dad that he'd seen, stating that it was planned to rid the UK of practically all livestock by 2010. This was because Eastern European countries such as Hungary, the Czech Republic, Slovakia and Romania were due to join the EU soon. He said that the report stated that meat and milk products could be produced cheaper in these countries, due to cheaper labour and better growing conditions, and transported to Theme Park countries such as the UK. By 2004, the supermarkets had bought up large tracts of land in Eastern Europe, and were importing milk from Poland, for example, at nine pence per litre compared to the twenty-one pence farmers were paid here (which was still not enough for most to make ends meet). The main reason East European milk could be purchased so ludicrously cheap was because of vast EU subsidies given to the farmer on joining the EU, sourced primarily from the pockets of British, French and German taxpayers. This at the expense of dairy farmers in these countries. My dad said at the time of FMD that they would destroy small farmers with disease and economics. There was swine fever and mad cow disease before FMD hit us. Sadly he has been proved to be right.

The change in subsidy legislation in 2005, which made farmers better off getting rid of their livestock and leaving their land fallow, proved another massive step forward for the big corporate goal. Nobody was saying the existing subsidy system was just. Historians today now state that had the Government simply given some subsidies to Organic producers and imposed an Environmental tax on the use of damaging artificial fertilisers and sprays, this would have instantly resulted in the desired drop in production of some twenty-five percent certainly with regard to livestock. But... ICI and other spray and fertiliser manufacturers may well have gone bust... Oops! The fact that we were so dependant on other countries for our food meant that there was so much more unnecessary death when the collapse struck. If only people had known how much damage they were doing by shopping at supermarkets instead of local shops back then!

A striking memory of those times was, when it looked odds on the housed cattle at least would be vaccinated, with the prime minister's blessing, to prevent the spread of the disease rising almost exponentially, my dad's reaction when that supermarket chain owner stamped on the issue once and for all. Dad was on local TV in tears and when he picked me up from school the tears were still streaming down his face. He'd put so much energy into this he was utterly exhausted and on the verge of giving up.

One of the most frustrating things for him had been that the day the 'Vaccination – the Facts' booklet landed at his feet, so did Phoenix the calf. Phoenix was a white fluffy little thing that crawled out from a mass of dead bodies. Such occurrences happened frequently: there were many reports of lambs sticking their heads out from under the canvas on lorries stuffed full of dead carcasses (often with blood flowing out from the back, further spreading the disease).

The government, with an exceptionally clever piece of spin, set up Phoenix as the beacon at the end of the tunnel. They very publicly (and hypocritically) stepped in and stopped MAFF from killing the cute, cuddly, fluffy little calf, announcing that the end of foot-and-mouth was now in sight. They said the disease was now under control (it wasn't), new cases were falling (officially yes, unofficially no) and there would be no more contiguous culling (utter nonsense; nothing changed). They'd moved the election forward a month to June 6 to deal with the crisis and set about, successfully, reducing (fudging) the number of new outbreaks to practically zero by the time June 6 arrived which helped sweep them in again with an overwhelming majority. The opposition Tory Party was just as much in the pockets of big business as they were, so they needn't have really bothered. Phoenix was the one animal my dad would have gladly pointed the gun at, and willingly pulled the trigger!

Dad's entry below gives an insight as to how they fiddled the figures:

FUDGING THE FIGURES, or simply keeping quiet at strategic moments. SOS – slaughter on suspicion. Any animal not blood tested (with positive FMD) but slaughtered when FMD is suspected, does not have to be declared a new case- just another 'contiguous'. I have struggled to understand how new cases in Devon could go from twenty to zero within a few days, but there is an election looming and FMD is 'yesterday's news'. An article in the *Telegraph* 2/5/01, page ten, focuses on a farm in Essex where two culled sheep were shown to have FMD antibodies and not registered as a case. The article says MAFF said, 'it was dealt with as a dangerous contact under our contiguous cull programme.' The farmer said, 'I don't know what to believe from the ministry anymore. The fact that those animals were showing antibodies means that they were in contact with the disease. We, and other farmers, have had a lot of difficulty getting clear information about that case from MAFF.'

The Funeral Pyres

One of the worst consequences of the disease at the time were those dreadful funeral pyres. It was stressed above all else after the last outbreak in 1967 that the most important thing of all was not to burn the carcasses out in the open. This was primarily due to the highly carcinogenic dioxins released from the treated hardwood, mainly railway sleepers, needed to make the pyres hot enough to burn the sodden, decaying carcasses. It seemed, back then, that the Government hadn't read the '67 Report, or they just didn't care – it was a long way from London after all. Two months before the first outbreak there were lorry loads of railway sleepers saturated with creosote, imported from Eastern Europe – just yet another fishy fact.

This next piece from Dad's diaries gives some idea of what it was like with these pyres burning everywhere:

27/04/01 It's 4.30 a.m. I am down at Westward Ho! Beach, smoking a bidi and drinking a beer. Dawn is about to break. I am feeling that same alive presence of timelessness I last really felt in the Forest Brown ward in Bath Hospital just after I broke my leg playing football. I can just make out the surf through the first dawn light. Reckon it's about three foot and offshore but a little early to tell.

'Offshore' – that's the problem. I awoke at 2.30 a.m., choking with a headache and stomach pains. My room was full of the acrid smell of death. I could hardly breathe – and certainly didn't want to breathe. The tornadoes have hit! (A dream I had two months ago.)

It was the end of yesterday when I had thought that the Army might come up with a police escort to arrest me, as they said they would. I've had the padlocks and chains on for six weeks to keep the bastards out. They're getting very fed up with me, but I don't care. They are suddenly making out that it's all over, but I know it's not. The Government has 'eased' their ruthless contiguous cull policy, having directly intervened to save the life of baby Phoenix amidst a wave of media emotion and heartfelt thanks from the farmer's eight-year-old son. Mind you, they had killed the remainder of their perfectly healthy livestock! I was slightly disappointed in a way, especially in the light that the leaked, potentially explosive MAFF booklet only fell into my possession the day before.

They've said dioxins, which are highly carcinogenic, are not really an issue. Yet they have advised those downwind of the huge pyres in Holsworthy to move to a site in Bude if they can. I've read that a scientist reckons twice the amount of dioxins have been released in the first three months of burning as the legal maximum annual limit that all heavy industry is allowed, and it is concentrated primarily in Devon and Cumbria.

Surely the authorities know what is best? Yet these are the same authorities who are saying and doing the opposite to what their pamphlet preaches. Remember the lies, deception and hush-hush surrounding the recent Gulf War Syndrome? I would love to believe them, but sadly I have no faith or trust in any of them. All I know is vaccination works and the policy of burning (outlawed since the '67 outbreak) is making me, a very healthy person, feel very ill, and if there is a large concentration of cancer patients in Devon and Cumbria ten–fifteen years down the line when FMD is a distant memory, it will no doubt be the same 'brush it under the carpet as quickly as possible' as we have just seen with Gulf War Syndrome.

A policeman recently asked me from the other side of our padlocked iron gates why I was being so stubborn. I pointed to the air around us thick with smoke and told him what I knew about dioxins. Then I said if my daughter was dying of cancer aged thirty and turned to me and said, 'Dad, knowing what you knew then about those pyres, why didn't you try to do something about them?' I'd never be able to live with myself. I then told him she'd come home from school saying her school chums subjected to the pyres had huge bags under their eyes. They'd had headaches and stomach aches all night, and been physically sick. There was one Mum who'd had a baby at Christmas. The baby had been the epitome of health. A month earlier the smoke had enveloped their house and the baby had had chronic asthma ever since. The policeman said nothing and even looked sympathetic.

The fact is, it is not as if healthy animals will no longer be slaughtered. We have been told they will only be killed if it was felt there was a good risk of them contracting FMD. In other words nothing has changed much. It's yet another clever bit of political spin to diffuse the heat in all of us. There is a cull of healthy animals due behind us today, and I would be surprised if my animals don't get FMD from the virus carried on the bits of hair and hide floating in the air from the fires all around us. FMD is, sadly, far from 'yesterday's news'.

The surf is three feet and offshore. I wish I had my board and no broken leg, and was in another society.

There were about four or five pyres that directly affected us. The landscape looked similar to the pictures shown when Saddam Hussein set light to all the oil wells in Kuwait in 1991 before being captured in 2003. On our kitchen table the picture on the front page of the local newspaper from the town of Barnstaple showed a huge pyre just half a mile away at Bickington – again illegal, due to its close proximity to a town, but no one cared. With the thick black smoke swirling high into the sky it looked just like an F5 tornado according to most people who saw it. Dad felt it gave further credence to his dream.

The next night at 1 a.m. Dad woke me. Our house was thick with the smoke, the likes of which I had never smelt or tasted before or since, thank God. He bundled me into the car and took me down the coast. We had to go further afield towards Hartland because the wind had gone north-easterly, and Westward Ho! was engulfed. Dad took his bidis and a six-pack of beer – he didn't care if he was breathalysed; he was up for any sort of confrontation.

Sitting on a headland, gazing out to sea in the darkness, he kept saying the tornadoes had hit. But this time he was ready unlike in his dream. He spent the next few hours psyching himself up for what he planned to do the next day. Another piece of writing he did at this time might help shed a light as to why he upped the stakes on that day in Bideford High Street. Much of it repeated stuff he'd mentioned before, but one paragraph concerning the pyres from a national newspaper sheds more light on his rapidly disintegrating mood:

OUR TRAGIC LOVE OF MONEY OVER AND ABOVE LIFE

The *Mail on Sunday* 29/04/01 had the headline 'Smoke from burning pyres will kill humans'. The official report made by 'a team of nineteen government scientists' they found 'posted on an Internet page which is difficult to access'. It reported 'pollution levels in some areas three times higher than during the winter of 1991 when smog which enveloped London was linked to a hundred and sixty deaths in just four days'. The report suggested that asthmatics should be publicly warned before pyres are lit and carry at all times sufficient medication to help with breathing difficulties. Department of Health Chiefs warned that vegetables close to the pyres should 'be washed thoroughly and the outer leaves stripped before use'. Environment Minister Michael Meacher has conceded that 'dioxins produced by the fires were a health risk'. Tests by the Army have been done on smoke from the pyres, but, like everything else in this sad, sick saga, don't expect to find anything official... yet!

★

After yet another near sleepless night, judging from the state of him, Dad took me to school the next morning. He had on his blue mackintosh with 'CULL MAFF' emblazoned on the front and 'JAB DON'T CULL' on the back. My chest heaved with pride when I noticed a look in his eye that I hadn't seen before. Wearing his skatey red skullcap with crutches and loudhailer, he looked so different from the very nice but conventional parents at my school. I also saw that he had with him a bag of water bombs, which, along with the crutches, became his two favourite weapons during this period.

Fortunately, a friend in the house took a video camera to record the proceedings. He clambered out of the car with all his paraphernalia looking tired and a little nervous, but defiantly declaring that he was looking forward to getting arrested. He had been saying to me the night before how there's two ways to get attention: one is sacrifice, the other is violence. Dad wasn't really violent, not just because he was a bit of a lanky weed, but it just wasn't in his nature. He never condemned others for choosing violence due to the violence bestowed on people everywhere one hundred thousand times more by governments and big business. He always said, Who of us knew what was best according to God's will, to help minimise and reverse the disruption and pain over this period of evolutionary transformation?

He hobbled up the High Street in Bideford and into the middle of the road outside Barclays Bank. Here he started spouting his prepared speech about vaccination, the pyres and so on. The car drivers being held up seemed a little agitated but there was a group of lads on large motorbikes hooting their horns in delight.

A large crowd started to gather, made up of passers-by and shopkeepers coming out to check on the disturbance. He then started hurling water bombs on the road calling for revolution on a massive scale and asking people to come and join him and sit down in the busier Quay Road running alongside the Torridge Estuary. The young skatey kids were the first there saying excitedly, 'Our parents are always telling us not to get arrested and here are you saying just the opposite… cool!'

After a while the police arrived in the form of two policewomen. The policemen were up at Deep Moor, a landfill site in Torrington being used to dump carcasses. There, the locals were holding a feisty protest, blocking the lorries. The policewomen seemed very reluctant to arrest Dad, but he and his rent-a-mob army of skatey kids were clearly not going to move. It was only when the traffic had banked up for two miles in both directions and drivers were becoming very irate that Dad was handcuffed and arrested and pushed into the police car.

There was a great photo in the newspaper that week of a small policewoman trying to push Dad's head down into the car. Dad had his fist raised in defiance to all the cheering skatey kids in the background. The next time he saw the same policewoman (which wasn't too long obviously), she said to Dad she could have killed him, because when she went into the police station the afternoon the paper came out, her colleagues had bought hundreds of papers and stuck the pictures all around the station. I think it was her first arrest of a hardened criminal! Dad managed to keep a very healthy relationship with the police and courts at this time. He was very polite and always stressed they had a job to do and there were no hard feelings.

I heard that there were meant to be other, slightly more aggressive, protesters turning up in support. However, what Dad hadn't accounted for was if he held up the traffic for two miles in each direction, everybody would be stuck – including the protesters. It was when Dad was being driven away in the police car that they saw what must have been a motley-looking bunch of banner-waving farmers who'd had it far worse than us so far. Dad said that the police then called for back-up.

According to his diaries, he was put into a police cell for five hours. The irony was that the smoke from the Bickington pyre – the very thing he was protesting about – was billowing into his cell. This time he couldn't go down the coast. The court date was set a week later.

In the meantime he was still blocking the MAFF vets from coming up to check his animals. He was only too aware that once you let the vets in and you were in a contiguous cull zone, your animals were earmarked for slaughter. The threats from MAFF and the police of arrest, a long spell in prison and very expensive High Court injunction costs were increasing in intensity.

MAFF said that if he didn't let them in on a certain day he would be served an injunction and possibly be arrested. They warned him that such an injunction, allowing the police, the Army and vets to enter his property by any means necessary, cost a farmer near Norwich £20,000 in a similar situation. The day was set at four days before he was due to appear in court for his other offence.

I was ill at home when the day came, and the phone didn't stop ringing. Everybody was told not to answer it. The messages on the answer machine were crammed with calls from the police, MAFF, and the Crown Court in London from where the injunction was issued saying that if they were not allowed in by 5 p.m., the order would be taken and Dad would be in real trouble. Knowing this is what they were saying Dad didn't listen to any of the messages until after 6 a.m. – in case he cracked. They also said that they would be up in force the next morning at 10 a.m.

True to form, Dad dug in. He came up from the chained gates to the house at 7 p.m. with the injunction. He tore it up and said he wouldn't be able to sleep again that night, so he was off to the beach again to prepare himself mentally. He stuck a note to this effect on the wall saying he was 'Off to war!' the next day. Then our friends in the house wrote messages of support all over it – such as, 'Follow your heart', 'May God be with you', and 'Fight to the death.'

By this time a close relationship had been forged with the local TV station. I think they liked Dad because he always put on a show, having quickly learned the power of visual impact to make a political point. He was lent a video camera for the next day and went to the gates an hour before MAFF were due to arrive. He had with him his main 'comrade-in-arms' – his friend Biff. After much trial and error, they managed to find the perfect place for Biff to conceal himself and film the entire proceedings. The roof of the house next to the gates behind the chimney provided the ideal spot.

Having said he'd meet the vets at the gate, they arrived without the anticipated massive back-up. Dad defiantly carried out his plan, lost his temper and opened up with a barrage of water bombs. He told them in no uncertain terms that he wouldn't let them anywhere near his animals. Clearly exasperated, the vets said they would be back soon with the police to arrest him for Contempt of the High Court (a very serious offence) and Assault. The main reason Dad used water bombs was that when he was done for assault and the judge in the courtroom asked how the vet, the policeman or whoever was assaulted, they would state it was with water bombs. There would then be a good chance that if the judge had a sense of humour, he'd simply laugh.

I was still not well and stayed at home warned not to open the door for anybody. I was quite excited until I saw him coming in. He was looking very tired and visibly shaking. He went upstairs above the back door sitting next to the window armed with a pile of water bombs awaiting his comeuppance. I must admit I thought he was going too far at this point.

We waited and waited, then caught a glimpse of the vets and the police in the fields. 'Expect the unexpected!' Dad always said. We did it to them, now they were doing it to us;

it was a bit like a game of cat and mouse. Dad immediately hobbled out, with Biff following with the camera, and chased them off the property whilst hurling water bombs at them.

It was on the evening news. He caught one vet smack in the face with a water bomb from thirty metres – those excruciatingly boring games of village cricket had their uses. He struck another one with his crutches, yet amazingly the police didn't try to arrest him. It seemed they felt that due to all the adverse publicity Dad was conjuring up, it just wasn't worth it. It may also have been because they knew they were on shaky ground. Whatever, I was relieved not to see him being dragged away. Dad had made it quite clear that he was prepared to be locked up and the key thrown away.

Three days later and he was off to court. He and Biff decided to put on a show to help get their message home. They both shaved their heads; Biff leaving a small tail on the back and Dad with a bright red 'CULL MAFF' cut out of a patch of hair he left on the back of his head. The pretty picture was completed by the addition of their smartest Oxfam suits and gas masks in reference to the pyres they were protesting against.

Excitement and uncertainty levels in the house were high at such times when the canvas was blank. There was no knowing whether they'd fall flat on their faces – get into more trouble or make some sort of progress. It helped tremendously that everyone was prepared to make fairly major sacrifices if necessary. It was, as the Americans called it, 'Showtime'!

At school, I had been struggling to get on with my classmates. They were all a bit cool and sophisticated, and I just wasn't. I couldn't even pretend to be. However, due to the publicity that Dad, Biff and the gang were getting, my schoolmates were quite intrigued. It didn't quite upgrade me into the 'cool' bracket, but it certainly helped. That morning when Dad and Biff dropped me off at school on the way to court, I insisted they carry my kit bag and books into school for me past my schoolmates, their parents and the teachers. My chest heaved with pride as everybody stared at them. Biff, a big muscly man, looked especially resplendent in his black suit with briefcase (empty) in his hand. He had a briefcase because he was pretending to be Dad's solicitor.

The story goes that they arrived at Barnstaple Magistrates' Court where the local newspaper and TV and a few protesters were waiting. The protesters were bearing banners inscribed with things like 'JAB DON'T KILL'. Dad was representing himself obviously with his 'solicitor's' help. On arriving, the guy doing the prosecuting ushered them into a small room to discuss possible terms. He offered them the bare minimum fine and was amazed when Biff asked what his 'client' could do to get the bare minimum prison sentence. The whole point was Dad felt if he could get a prison sentence, the national news would be interested in what he had to say particularly with regard to his 'Vaccination – the Facts' booklet. The local news was carrying the whole saga wonderfully, but policy decisions were made in London – and that was the target.

The prosecutor could not believe what he was hearing. He said he had never in all his career come across anybody asking how best they could get into trouble... 'normal' people being prepared to do almost anything to minimise the fine or sentence! Biff told me later that the prosecutor found it hilarious and probably a blast of fresh air. He no doubt dined out on the story for months.

Dad entered the courtroom wearing his gas mask and turning his back to the three magistrates pointed with both hands to the 'CULL MAFF' on the back of his head in the same way footballers pointed to the back of their shirts after scoring a goal. He and Biff then went and sat down at the allocated table in the middle of the courtroom, Biff slamming his (empty) briefcase down in front of him. The scowling magistrates hissed at them to stand up and stay standing until they were told they could sit down. They duly obliged and Dad took the oath. I wished I could have been there to see it, but Biff gave me a blow-by-blow account when he picked me up from school that afternoon; Dad, as expected, was back in the police cell.

Biff, who had managed to remain more detached than Dad, and therefore managed to see the funny side of things more easily, always kept me closely in the picture. He had a daughter two years younger than me. We got on OK, but she was a real wild child – hardly surprising, with a dad like Biff who had nothing but disrespect for man's laws. Looking back now, I see he had some valid points. Having spent five years in a cult settlement in Burma he had no fear. This made him a potential threat to the authorities. They had good reason to be worried. When our society started breaking down, it was people like Biff, the survivors and the strong-willed, who came into their own, in much the same way as many Islamic and Hindu people had become long before.

Dad's news update, with the usual title, is written below. However, Biff said the magistrates didn't quite know what to do with Dad, as they made a five-minute hearing last two hours. As Dad put his case, within five minutes the scowls on the magistrates' faces had apparently turned into looks of sympathy – with tears even welling up in one lady's eyes. When they fined Dad – the bare minimum since they were just desperate to get rid of him – he refused to pay 'now or at any time in the future', challenging them to deal with him 'there and then' and whispering to the prosecution to suggest they send him to prison. They didn't want to do this, and Dad refused to leave so they recessed for twenty minutes.

On their return they announced they were going to continue with the next case, and in came a fellow being tried for GBH. I know the only thing Dad felt guilty about was for the people in the queue of cases behind him and having to hang around to wait for their trial; however, by this stage he'd come to expect the unexpected and so as not to disappoint the galleries, he stood up and announced loudly, 'Clearly you are still interested in what I have to say about vaccination.' He then proceeded to read the fifty-one questions and answers from the National Farmers' Union to MAFF from his booklet. He was threatened with Contempt of Court (a reasonably serious offence), which pleased him causing further confusion and another recess.

Eventually the police were called and he was escorted out of the courtroom, apologising for the inconvenience he'd caused to the bemused yet sympathetic magistrates. However, after a couple of minutes outside the courtroom, the police started to go. Dad asked why they hadn't arrested him – Contempt of Court was, after all, very arrestable. They were obviously desperate to get rid of him and said he would only be arrested if he went back into the courtroom. So that is precisely what he did.

From Dad's diaries 5/5/01:

I had an unsatisfactory, hollow, empty feeling after yesterday's victory in court and fine of £120, which I've refused to pay now or in the future. The police all fully understood and agreed with me, as did no doubt the magistrates, prosecution, and whole courtroom. Everyone from this area has suffered from the acrid, toxic smell of death. The result was I got some accurate, objective, well-reported coverage in the local press and TV; but there was still a nasty niggle I couldn't pin down.

On getting back to Tapeley I learned that MAFF had been up in their numbers with a large police escort. I knew they were within their legal rights, having served a High Court injunction on me from London the day before (at huge cost to me, according to them!), but they didn't tell me they were coming. I was really angry when I heard three of them went into the field where my three Berkshire pigs were. When questioned on this by a friend they said they could arrange one visit per week and just one person could enter the field to 'cut the risk of spreading FMD' – acknowledging that there was a risk! They claimed they were showing everyone in Europe how to deal with FMD effectively – even when faced with their 'Vaccination – the Facts' sheets, and when it was pointed out the FMD virus can live in the throat up to four days, they joked about gargling whisky. If my pigs get FMD now watch this space!

One thing I've learned from my very personal spiritual quest (by far the most important thing in my life) is that to move on or up a rung of the spiritual ladder, a risk or a leap of faith is involved into a void or a blank future canvas of total uncertainty. It also involves listening to the very subtle inner intuitive feelings. That evening my stomach was tight, my heart was heavy and hollow and I wasn't being very nice to my girlfriend. The next morning following yet another near sleepless night I was focused and fully alive again, even though I was scared at the seemingly bottomless pit looming.

I realised that I have achieved barely twenty per cent of my task and done little more than build a platform, and really only locally if that.

All I have been is a slightly irritating thorn in MAFF's side, but have changed nothing. They will continue to slaughter animals both healthy and affected, and pyres will be back after the election if and when the outbreaks increase again (remember the FMD virus has a break until June 7). The same deception, lies, confused information, figure fudging and spin are set to continue into the foreseeable future. They know that even after the event when more of the truth comes out we'll all be bored and forget it quite quickly, and should a further outbreak occur, it will be dealt with in the same way. This must not be allowed to happen! *With any luck for them, most of us and our children, along with our animals, will have died of cancer by then.*

Currently 'they' are on course to win. I have huge respect for the police and the legal system but have absolutely no respect for MAFF, the NFU, any government party and most particularly the large business corporations and multinationals, supermarkets etc., who I believe are behind this outrage. However, I believe that with the information I have got such as the MAFF document from Nobel House, called 'Vaccination – the Facts' in which they say the opposite to what they are preaching now, I have a chance. I know it can only work if I strike now and strike hard without any expectations for my future. The thought of my ten-year-old daughter wheezing, telling me about her school friends coughing all night in their mothers' arms, with stomach pains and headaches and being sick, keeps me going.

★

Dad arrived home at teatime looking haggard but still determined. A few days later he wrote the following piece. I think he was aware that if he carried on as he was he would be taken out of the picture and most importantly lose the animals he'd be fighting so hard to keep.

I have just spoken to the MAFF vet I bombarded with water bombs and struck with my crutch yesterday to try to strike a deal. The reason being 'having slept on it', is the increased threat to my animals of lots of vets and police coming up and my having no control over their precautions. For example, two vets walked the fields yesterday without wearing facemasks. I pointed out the recent case of a swab taken from a vet's nostrils showing live FMD virus. He said that in 1972 some vets did an experiment inhaling deeply over an infected FMD animal, and then half an hour later all coughed and spluttered until 'their throats were sore' over four calves – and only one of them contracted FMD… minimal risk? For once I managed to keep quiet, knowing that if I lose my control again lots of vets will be walking amongst my stock ignoring my pleas for what I consider essential precautions.

He agreed to come up once every four days (due to my pigs, mainly), disinfect in front of me, wear a mask and just one vet enter the field. Understandably he will come with a police escort in case I pull another trick – though to be honest I'm running out of ideas and energy, having been on this madness solidly for the past two and a half months. He also said he expected yesterday's visit to be amicable, but I had become incensed that they had lit another pyre just behind us at 4 p.m. on 7/5/01, four days after Blair had said the last pyre was lit. Yet more smoke billowing across us; and yet another blatant, carefree lie from the Government doesn't help the mood. Also we had constant phone calls from smallholders, such as a lady nearby who, coming home from work, found her gates open and heard a barrage of shots as her eight healthy sheep, all named by her children, were being mown down. This keeps the horror 'in yer face' so to speak. So much for 'no more contiguous culling'!

I am playing ball because I have to for the sake of my animals, plus being crippled with a badly broken leg. However, it's far from over as I still have the costs of a Crown Court injunction hanging over me as well as the fine from Barnstable Magistrates' Court – both of which I currently have no intention of paying. This feeling was strengthened this afternoon when clouds of acrid smoke wafted into our house making me and the children wheeze and have headaches again – seven days after a MAFF vet said the last pyre was lit on May 3! Even Anthony Gibson of the NFU was saying on the lunchtime news today he feared MAFF were fudging new outbreak figures. Add to this MAFF saying they would not talk to the media until after the election (i.e. unanswerable to anyone), and to me you have the chilling icing on the cake.

The feelings we have must be similar to what it's like fighting a war. There's a constant tension in the pit of the stomach, which keeps me ready for action or the unexpected at a moment's notice. Even the dogs sense it as we prepare for battle and become agitated and restless. Trying to anticipate the next move of 'the enemy' is not easy especially under the present political climate. I have packed, then later unpacked an overnight bag at least four times so far, for an overnight or extended stay in a cell. It is strange when it doesn't happen or I get time on my hands, because I have sorted arrangements for my daughter, feeding the animals and other business.

As well as distraught calls, I am getting calls from an ever increasing group of militants, many of whom (not even farmers) have lost their jobs due to MAFF and the Government. One offered to be concreted in at the bottom of the drive. I have been warned by more serious legal people to watch my back for the faceless bully merchants doing someone a 'job' if it's felt I am becoming more than just a thorn in the system's side. Don't get me wrong, I desperately want out; but every time I relax a new outrage hits me in the face. For example, when I grudgingly did a deal with MAFF, then that afternoon my house was full of smoke again and I was getting calls all night that Instow was 'choking' due to a fire lit within the last two days. These lies, the contiguous cull lies and the threat to my and other people's children force me to keep the adrenalin pumping, near-sleepless nights and so on. What's happened to honour, integrity and the noble gutsy art of humility in holding your hand up when you have made a mistake?

★

The funny thing was, whenever the vets turned up, they would be visibly shaking, unsure about whether and what stunt Dad would pull next. However, Dad was (nearly) always very polite. He always stressed the importance of good manners, but would talk a lot to the vets about vaccination, the relative unimportance of the wretched export market and so on. His objective was to fan the fires of revolt within MAFF itself. There were a lot of discontented MAFF officials, policemen and Army around.

At the same time protest marches were beating a path to the MAFF HQ at Exeter. The first one was organised by the Green Party and was described by a Channel 4 cameraman, who had covered most modern day protests from Mayday to Prague, as 'the most focused march he'd witnessed'. We wouldn't have known – Dad and I were only first-timers at this kind of thing.

Dad asked me to draw a banner for myself of whatever I wanted. I drew and coloured in a picture of a slaughter man with a huge happy grin wearing a First World War helmet, pointing a gun at a pile of hapless sheep. At the top I wrote; 'Don't Cull the Animals' and at the bottom, 'CULL MAFF', with blood dripping from the words. Dad was quite shocked at my perspective of foot-and-mouth.

He kept saying that young children shouldn't have their heads filled with such images. For me it was upsetting, but not nearly as upsetting as seeing my dad get into such a dreadful state. However, being a child I accepted the reality of my environment, good or bad, more easily than a grown-up. I knew exactly what was going on and always gave my opinion on the subject of vaccination, Direct Action, the next battle, tactics, and the like, which took place around the kitchen table. The water bombs were my idea. Rightly or wrongly, I couldn't not get involved because for that eight-month period they spoke about nothing else in the house. When it came to an end that fateful day in Gloucester, I can't begin to explain how relieved I felt.

One thing it did do was to help prepare me for the Collapse, and I suppose give me an unfair advantage over those of a similar age in the towns and cities. Very simply, my eyes were open to the bigger picture. I learned that you couldn't trust any large body of authority. Money and power were ultimately corrupting in those days. Many were awakening to the Universal Spiritual Forces – largely due to that blast of cosmic energy in the late 1980s and early '90s. However, those seemingly holding grimly onto power represented the majority, and had their eyes and ears shut, worshipping money and power above all else. Everybody intuitively recognised this, which is why fewer and fewer people in the so-called democratic world would turn out to vote. When they were chanting, 'Say no to culling for the export market' on that march, I knew exactly what they meant.

It helped me hugely living in a spiritually-oriented environment. Fortunately, Dad had experienced those four years when a cult bedded in and nearly took over and destroyed the place. This meant he could spot the dodgy, manipulative, freeloading (lazy work-shy, as Dad put it) New-Agey types a mile off. The result was there was a mixture of all sorts of people, some in the house, others in travellers' trucks, yurts and low-impact sustainable turf huts around the grounds. They were labelled as hippies by the outside world, which was unfair; or anti-capitalist activists, but the latter ironically only applied to my dad in the early days. Everybody worked hard to produce beautiful home-grown food, including, luckily for me, things like pizzas, or it would have been a little too holy for my liking. The basic philosophy, stemming allegedly from some channelling in the early 1990s, was for the place to be occupied by a bunch of hermits. They were allowed their own space and freedom to be individuals and grow at their own speed. People sought help and advice from others as and when they chose. Nothing was forced on anybody, although respect for others and their ways was paramount while at the same time working for the shared dream.

Even though they were trying to expand into the new ways, they were still very much learning. They were still of course a part of the overall global mentality and energies. The universal law whereby the greater mass will always dominate the lesser mass meant it was impossible to totally step into the new way. Now that the balance has shifted, there is no need for money, with everybody eager to give and to help because of the personal reward this brings. This may sound selfish, which I guess it is in a funny sort of way. Also, anybody in power is in effect a servant to the rest of us; but our job is made easy now due to the love that is everywhere. The puffed up ego and 'power corrupts, absolute power corrupts absolutely' dilemmas are, thankfully, becoming distant memories.

Initially Dad set things up as a community. He allowed decisions to be made democratically by the vote. However, due to egos and the human failings of those times, he found that when the minority didn't get their way they would take it out on him, hence his energy was constantly being drained. I remember being present at some of those gatherings where decisions were being discussed and voted on – often on the pettiest and most unnecessary details. Heated debates would ensue and an uncomfortable atmosphere generated which spilt over into daily living, creating frictions between people.

Like everything in those days, people had to find out what it wasn't all about before they had the conviction of their actions to live by what it was about. 'What it was about' of course always had the same bottom line: that of Love (without conditions), Truth, Integrity, Respect, Understanding and Forgiveness. Dad realised after a difficult year that even his world wasn't ready yet to be totally free as it is now. He reluctantly imposed himself as leader. However, he did it in such a way as to make it as easy and free as it could be in those times. Whatever deal or agreement he did was between himself and an individual. Likewise, if anybody wanted to do anything such as something creative, even a bit wacky, they'd go to see him. As he always said, ninety-nine times out of a hundred, he'd say, 'Yeah go for it' and give his full support. Thus many things got done so much quicker and without all the aggro. Luckily, Dad had some integrity and wanted to give freely whenever he could. He was far from perfect though and very much had his 'stuff': He was hopeless at relationships, for example, and had a string of girlfriends after leaving Mum before finally settling down. Plus he'd force me to eat some disgusting vegetables such as onions, leeks and kale.

For me, growing up in these surroundings was fantastic. Those weird and wonderful people often had children of their own who had time to play. They all had a wonderful array of crystals – from rose quartz, lapis lazuli and obsidian, to amethyst and moldovite (my two favourites). I loved learning about their energies and how they worked, along with the medicinal value of the herbs they collected from hedgerows and the forest floor. It was fortunate that I did. This knowledge saved my life during the Collapse.

The highlights of my year were the Health and Harmony Festivals we'd have throughout the summer. They had a strong spiritual focus, though Dad would use them to rally support for his anti-globalisation antics. I would help build labyrinths on the lawn made out of pine cones and old branches, for example. Within the maze we would make a sacred space for earth, fire, air and water at the four poles, with a set of tarot cards at each point to play with. We'd put one huge marquee up where there would be therapies such as aromatherapy, reflexology, Indian head massage and so on, with a harpist strumming beautifully in the corner. There would be t'ai chi, belly dancers and small bands playing on the lawns where people had their refreshments, plus drumming workshops and meditation in the outbuildings and yurts, and didgeridoos being played to the spirit of the oaks and the Monterey pines around and about. The place came into its own at such times. My favourite was the fire-walking.

The idea about walking on fire was about personal empowerment and discovering that anything is possible. Our education system back then centred upon our limitations and weaknesses, can'ts and shouldn'ts. Likewise, religions were based on fear and the need to go via a qualified priest or established system to attain salvation. These powerful systems moulded the way we thought, without us realising it, into a bunch of semi-happy, often miserable slaves who could be easily controlled by the system and the elite minority. 'Reality TV programmes', all too common at the time, such as 'Big Brother' reflected this mental state perfectly. Avoiding taking personal responsibility often so we could blame others, and giving our power away i.e. burying our heads in the sand, were the norm in those days.

Fire-walking removed the blindfolds. As small children we were told to be careful of fire. It's hot and it burns. By walking on burning hot coals and feeling nothing other than a slight tingling, everybody who did it had their so-called reality challenged. It made all of us who did it aware that much of what we had been taught to be reality was in fact illusion. That being the case, how much more could be achieved if we could just break the limiting illusions of those times? 'Dangerous thinking' as far as the establishment powers were concerned. However, this is what the Awakening was all about; a switch from a feeling of helplessness to one of 'anything is possible'.

Marion, who was the organiser of the fire-walking, would start the workshops three hours before the fire walk to enable each person to get into the right mental space. She learnt the importance of this after the first fire walk when everybody got distracted by family and friends whilst walking out to the fire. The result was eighty per cent of those who did it (including my dad, ha, ha!) got burned – some severely, to the extent that they ended up in hospital with third-degree burns. Dad said he started off fine, but when he was halfway across, the thought that he was actually walking on fire suddenly popped into his head, and instantly the pain was excruciating. He ended up with huge blisters.

I wasn't present at the first one but was determined to do it. Dad was not happy about my decision, nor did he want to do it again himself, because he was scared! But, under pressure, he compromised and decided to do the workshop with me. He insisted I didn't do the 'glass walk' however. The glass walk was part of the preparation designed to demonstrate the illusion of mans so-called reality. Marion would scatter a sack load of broken bottles and glasses over a rug on the floor the length of the room. We were then told to tune in, have faith and walk over it barefoot. Glass of course cuts, and there are big arteries in the soles of the foot.

Luckily for me, Dad was late for the workshop. I was first to do it in case he caught me. He was a little cross when he found out but relieved I hadn't cut myself, but I was still not to do the fire walk. To most people, the glass walk seemed more scary. Some people would look down and pick their spots very gingerly through the minefield of upward facing jagged pieces. Others just froze and couldn't do it. I, being young and not plugged in to the fear of glass, would toss my head back and skip across it without feeling a thing – as did my dad, to give him his due. It was really just a good game to me.

Other games we did as preparation included arm bending. People of similar strength were pitted together. One would stretch their arm out sideways, the other would grab their elbow with one hand, and wrist with the other, and try to bend the arm. No matter how hard the one with the arm outstretched resisted, they couldn't stop their arm from being bent. Marion would then tell the person with the arm outstretched to visualise small blue crystals filtering into their arm from the universe for thirty seconds or so; at the same time you would be telling yourself that your arm was unmovable. If you were the one with the arm outstretched, it felt like the person trying to bend your arm wasn't trying at all. In fact it seemed so pathetic you realised that your bicep was totally relaxed. The proof came when you did it the other way round; no matter how hard you tried, that person's arm felt like a log.

My favourite was the riot assimilation exercise, whereby two people would crouch and lock together holding one another's shoulders. A third person would build up their energies. There were lots of chants of 'I am powerful', then you'd look beyond the obstacle as if it was nothing and walk through it. It was their job of course to try with all their might to stop you. I remember, then aged ten, scattering two fully grown burly men across the room. In the Far East this was called the chi energy. Marion, who was a no-nonsense protester on the side, said she used to use this energy when sitting in front of bulldozers or carcass lorries. She said that she would visualise a root going through her body into the centre of the earth – and four policemen couldn't budge her. It wasn't as if she was a ten ton Tessa either. Nowadays this knowledge and practice is part of daily life. For example, walking on water is no longer a big deal.

Eventually I got Dad to agree that I could do the fire walk as long as he didn't burn himself. He went first and looked horrified when he finished (unscathed) as he turned round to see me four paces behind him. I had decided not to make his choice an issue. I did the walk about five or six times, and whenever Marion did the walk in the future. I never burnt myself even when the coals were white hot. Those who hesitated, had fear or lack of respect and focus, always burnt themselves. I seemed to be the only child to take it in this way. However, I used to spend whatever time I could in the woods with the fairies, elves, pixies and animals. Birds and butterflies were always landing on me, and I was perfectly happy just watching Biff's Alsatian chasing his tail round and round all day.

★

The chi energy came in useful on the march to MAFF and others. For example when we arrived, there was a line of policemen blocking the entrance to keep us out. We were having none of it and with focused anger someone announced that we were going in. 'Looking beyond the obstacle as if it were nothing', we brushed through the police with Dad at the front on his crutches.

About two hundred of us had met at the 'Park and Ride' in Exeter and marched two miles chanting things like, 'What do we want? Cull MAFF! When do we want it? *Now!*' Dad had his loudhailer. As we neared the MAFF HQ, I could feel the tension building up. Even though I was only ten, I was loving every second of it. There were a lot of hurt, desperate people and no one knew what was going to happen.

Having got into the grounds, banners saying 'Vaccinate don't slaughter' and suchlike were erected everywhere facing the building, along with a microphone for the speakers, of which Dad was one. The tone was set when Dad pointed out that those working in the MAFF building were looking out of the windows pointing at us country yokels and laughing. Bob Harris, a friend of Dad's for twenty years from his days at Agricultural College, now farming in mid-Devon, grabbed the loudhailer. Shaking like a rattlesnake, he let rip at the MAFF workers, yelling, 'How dare you laugh when you're causing so much pain, suffering, death and destruction in the countryside!' They rapidly disappeared, quite literally like rats up a drainpipe.

The anger levels were high with all the speakers. At the end, to stop the angry mob from storming the building itself, MAFF agreed to allow a delegation of six into the building to meet the boss and the leading MAFF vet. Dad went with them, as did the Channel 4 cameraman. Channel 4 featured the whole of Bob's rant that evening. Bob Harris looked a real ruffian. His trousers and working boots were plastered with mud and 'CULL MAFF' was emblazoned all over his white T-shirt in black marker pen. The most striking feature was how tired, thin and stressed he looked. When he told his story it was easy to see why.

For the past two months he had been fighting to save his herd of organically reared cattle and sheep. The valley he lived in near Chumleigh had been all but cleared out, with the exception of his animals. This was due to a reported case on a neighbour's farm. MAFF had killed all the animals and, as was typical, left them to rot on the side of the lane and in gateways, some for three weeks and more. Bob and Sandra, his wife, had four small young children and had toxic effluent from decaying carcasses from up the valley floating into their yard and through the back door into their kitchen. He made this point with his finger pointing at the bridge of the MAFF boss's nose from three inches.

He shouted at them that on top of this the slaughter men were ringing up at all hours of the day and night (a commonly used intimidating tactic) to say they would be up the next day to kill his animals. He had nine tractors banked up on his single-lane track to keep MAFF out. At the same time he was constantly asking MAFF if they had the test results of the neighbouring farm, which supposedly had foot-and-mouth. He was also asking for his animals to be blood tested for FMD – an EU stipulation for all healthy animals before they could be slaughtered. When the results eventually came back after six weeks, during which time all the animals had been slaughtered within a five-mile radius except Bob's, they came back negative.

Another frequent occurrence was that in their haste to kill as many animals as possible to stop the spread of the disease, they would kill animals which looked like they had FMD. This was called 'slaughter on suspicion', or SOS. The problem was that other very common diseases looked very similar to FMD. For example, a common viral disease in sheep called orf produced blisters around the mouth very similar to FMD. It was also frequently forgotten that FMD was little more than a bout of flu. In the days before vaccination was available, animals were treated by applying Stockholm tar to the blisters on the feet, and salt water to the same around the mouth. Most animals would recover within about two weeks and contain enough antibodies to never contract the disease again. Some of the older and weaker cattle would sometimes die, as with flu.

Bob, his whole body shaking, yelled at the officials that even when the results came back negative, they were still trying to kill his animals. The vet responsible, in the firing line of Bob's fury, had already visibly shrunken to three-quarters of his normal size. When he mumbled to Bob that negative can sometimes mean positive it was like a volcano suddenly erupting.

'Negative is negative. Positive is positive. How dare you move the goalposts yet again to suit your policy?' he exploded. He hadn't been able to get his children to school and demanded that the vet call his bullies off.

It was quite clear the officials, like most white collar workers, were blissfully unaware as to what was going on in the field, safely locked away in their cosy warm ivory tower.

All they could talk about was 'The Policy'. Like other corporate and governmental slaves of those times they'd learnt the ethics of 'see no evil, hear no evil' tunnel vision. They were like robots – slaves to their masters. The one thing they did know was that if they started thinking for themselves – and, God forbid, acting on it – they'd be out of a job, not able to afford the mortgage and other debts they had to pay, and their world would collapse. It was for this reason, and the fact that the whole education system was geared up to mass-produce people of this ilk, with the spectre of fear hanging over them, that you couldn't really blame people for complying. The irony was that it was this very mentality that made the Collapse so extensive, painful and destructive for so many. To step out from the herd was scary, and many brave individuals perished in the years leading up to the Collapse, trying to minimise the impact and suffering for themselves, their families, and for those persecuting them or trapped in the system.

Even then I remember feeling sorry for those bureaucrats humiliated in the evening news across the country. Even worse than Bob was seeing a fiery, bright sixteen-year-old called Dale rubbing their noses in it. Dale, like so many others, soon moved in with us.

Dale lived at Petrockstowe, where a series of giant pits were being dug to bury thousands of carcasses. Dale had brought the community together and set up 'STAMP' (Stop The Ashmoor Pits). For the previous six weeks they'd organised a round-the-clock vigil to stop any carcass lorries from entering, and they intended to do this for as long as it took.

Dale said to the MAFF officials that they 'obviously did an environmental risk assessment before embarking on such a project, so as to ascertain the potential viability of the site'. They said 'yes'. He then said they completed the assessment 'on such and such a date' to which they agreed. He then asked why the bulldozers had moved in and started digging the hole two weeks before the assessment was completed? He lured them in and then hit them between the eyes, and there was no way out for them. He then quoted the results of the assessment which said the clay was liable to move, and the nearby river, providing many villages with water, was likely to become polluted and toxic due to the leachate. Leachate, meant in this instance, is liquefied carcasses. He asked if, in the light of this, they would abandon this site, to which they waffled unconvincingly, and the word 'policy' crept back in. The great news at the time, millions of pounds later, was that the site was eventually abandoned due to the dogged determination of 'STAMP'.

While all this was going on, I led the march back to the Park and Ride. I had Dad's loudhailer and chirped away the same chants we had on the way: 'Say no to culling for the export market', and so on. Dad was very proud when he heard.

★

What seemed quite extraordinary was it was Dad and two of his very close and long-standing friends who were in a way leading the resistance in their respective areas. They only found out when they saw each other on the news. Bob Harris, as mentioned, was one. The leader of the resistance in Cumbria was Tim Luxton, or 'Tupper Tim', as Dad called him. I never quite got the joke but they farmed together for two years in the early 1990s. They had sheep, beef, courgettes and 'pick-your-own' strawberries (my favourite) so presumably it had some reference to the rams, known as 'tupps', being allowed out with the ewes in the autumn. Hence, this was known as 'tupping time'.

I was very young but remember poor Tim being teased a lot. By all accounts this was because he was somewhat accident prone; overturning trailer-loads of round bales downhill onto and through neighbour's farmland was not uncommon. He also demonstrated eco-friendliness to levels not even seen today. For example, there was always a small pile of hay sitting beside the toilet which Tim insisted on using instead of toilet paper, which he would then put on the vegetables in the garden. The rather high price to pay, beyond us having to eat the vegetables, were the grass seeds left behind and embedded after wiping, which caused Tim some fairly major irritation.

The farm was half an hour away from the big house. Mum preferred the big house because the farm was quite extraordinarily messy with four boys living in it; with a goal, ping-pong table and surfboards everywhere. For these reasons girls never stayed very long; but their parties, by all accounts, were the things of legend. Dad, however, loved it and would drag us over whenever he could.

When Tim left Devon he went to help his mum farm cattle and a flock of hefted sheep on the fells in Cumbria. Dad used to take us up at least once a year to stay with Tim, which I loved. It was very beautiful and they had lots of cats and fluffy Pekineses which hated our big sheepdogs, Melvin and Roughage.

Cumbria was worse hit than Devon by FMD and the farmers didn't come together in the same way. Tim, like us, shut MAFF out for two months whilst all around him animals were being slaughtered. He was regularly on the BBC News talking about the tragedy of Cumbria losing hefted sheep, and that no amount of compensation could replace their loss.

To the outsider it seemed that some lucky farmers were getting disproportionately large amounts of compensation. In many cases this was true, especially with regard to dealers and businessmen who played the intensive farming game, often with no regard for the animals' welfare. It was these farmers who gave the industry such a bad name. They would milk the subsidies; for example, twenty per cent of big farmers received eighty per cent of the subsidies back then. A few rogue farmers were buying up any old stock so as to obtain FMD compensation up to three times the value of the animals. Such actions did huge amounts of damage to our industry. However, as mentioned, these people with their attitudes were little more than a product of the way the then system had been set up. They were not 'bad people'.

The small- to medium-sized farmer with blood-lines in cattle sometimes stretching back many hundreds of years felt very differently. Also, the fewer animals you had the more the farmers generally loved them. They were not just a business commodity. Dad got very cross with people who said, 'What's your problem? They are all going to be killed anyway.' Killing any animal is not nice, or easy. However, not only were these animals killed under extreme brutal circumstances, with many only wounded, but the meat was all wasted by being burnt, incinerated or dumped in landfill sites.

Hefted sheep were unique in as much as they'd been bred over centuries. They would spend most of the year on the massive, unfenced common ground of the Cumbrian fells. Here the flocks would not only stay together but would not stray off their patch. The ewes (mothers) would somehow teach this law to their lambs which would become the breeding ewes of the future – and people call sheep stupid! Tim's point was that with these sheep gone, the only way they could be put on the fells to graze in the future would be to erect a mass of hideous, very expensive fences. This would have been unviable, due to the low price sheep fetched. Tim doggedly held out until one very nasty late spring evening.

He was looking out of his kitchen window and saw a brand new Land Rover with no number plates speed past his farm. It pulled up briefly on his outermost field on the edge of the fells before whizzing back. He told Dad he had a bad feeling about this, and went up there first thing the next morning. To his horror he found a sheep riddled with FMD just over the stone wall adjoining the road, with his sheep sniffing it. He said the most sinister thing was that it was unmarked; all his sheep were marked. He felt the sheep, judging by the teeth, was from the other side of fell. But no matter, he knew he had to then allow MAFF to kill his livestock. Tim had no doubt his sheep would contract FMD after this sneaky episode. If that happened, his neighbour, who had a pedigree herd of Blonde d'Acquitane cattle, would lose his as part of a contiguous cull.

Tim's neighbour had been getting nervous and frustrated by his stance with regard to his sheep for this reason. Tim knew, as did the person who planted the sick sheep, that if Tim's sheep contracted FMD and his two neighbours went down as a result, his name would be such dirt in Cumbria he'd have to up sticks and move elsewhere. He couldn't be totally sure it was MAFF. It could have been another farmer with a grudge. When Dad came off the phone to him, after two hours, he was genuinely concerned that his friend would join the rapidly growing list of suicide cases.

It was around this time that the Resistance Movement in Devon was growing. During that first march on the MAFF HQ there was lots of exchanging of phone numbers. From this, the beginnings of a tree grew whereby any farmer could ring up one of a few numbers if they suspected an attack by MAFF officials and slaughter men, backed by riot police and the Army.

Dad got a mobile phone. He hated the things and all they stood for in the Western world. He got it purely for protesting. Along with Bob and one or two from STAMP, the Deep Moor pit and the Green Party, his number was circulated to all farmers in the area if they needed help. The piece below written by Dad at the time seems to demonstrate a typical day on the farm gates:

23/05/01 The Battle Of Brent Oak Farm

Described by one relatively hard-nosed journalist as 'his bleakest day in twenty years of journalism', and by Major James Ackland as 'the pride he had felt in serving the Ghurkhas for fifteen years has now, in just one day, turned to shame'.

Brent Oak is a stunning farm on the edge of Exmoor with a family that embraces everything that's good and pure about rural Britain. Geoff and Jane Harknell, aged sixty-eight, and their two daughters, Sarah and Jessica, simply lived for their animals consisting of seventy near-pedigree Charolais cattle that Geoff had proudly bred over his life. He had had his best ever start to the year, as his first two cows gave birth to large healthy twins. Two weeks earlier he and his wife looked out in horror as police and Army personnel were in a nearby farm mowing down terrified fleeing livestock, killing some and wounding others. Some stampeded onto neighbouring farms where the stock were then quickly slaughtered as dangerous contacts resulting simply from the slaughter men's crazed butchery.

No animals touched Geoff's land, but MAFF wanted his animals as part of a contiguous cull. Even though he was very worried about his wife, he started to hold out. He loved his animals dearly – they were his life; plus there were no more animals for as far as the eye could see all around his farm, except for a few manky sheep belonging to someone else at the bottom of his drive. One MAFF official had even suggested that they needed to kill his cattle to protect the sheep. Oh, and a dozen or so unmarked sheep with FMD had materialised in a nearby field a few days earlier.

On May 22 I received phone calls from the wonderful Melanie Coates – a solicitor who has worked nineteen/twenty-hour days for months on behalf of small farmers – and from Bob Harris, wanting protesters. I said I'd be down with four others at 5.30 a.m.

However, that night I had that bad niggle and couldn't sleep, so got up at 2 a.m. and got to Brent Oak just after 3 a.m. prepared for battle mentally if not physically (broken leg!). The previous Saturday we'd stormed the MAFF headquarters in Exeter and staged a loud angry protest, and I've been arrested twice so far but this felt like a different ball game, and so it proved.

In the headlights I recognised Bob's Volvo blocking the drive (and his feet sticking out of the back!). The Harknell's daughter Sarah and her friend Mark were also sleeping soundly. I felt guilty about waking them up. Soon after dawn just before 5 a.m. a police car pulled up and two policemen approached us. They announced they happened to be 'just passing by' and asked 'how we'd slept'. We simply turned our backs on them and prepared for battle. Melanie Coates had warned us of a 'leaked' likely dawn raid by the slaughter men. It was a major political hot potato and in MAFF's interest to 'bury the beast' before the press arrived and the appeal against the High Court decision the day before (which ruled in favour of MAFF) came through at about 10 a.m. that day after which legally, we were told, they could not slaughter the animals until the result of the appeal.

Two aggressive, bullish vets turned up with a small police escort at about 8.30 a.m. and literally tried to bulldoze their way through, even though the cameras were on them. They failed, but left laughing and mocking us, a pattern we were to see from so many MAFF people throughout the day – as we had from those inside the MAFF HQ at the weekend. I was going to read the legal rights angle from Melanie when they next arrived, and draw it out as long as possible to get into the safety zone of post 10 a.m. I had a busy day lined up, erecting a marquee and removing my Highland bull from his wives – a near impossible task – but that was out.

There was a sigh of relief when the 10 a.m. deadline was reached. However, soon after a local man from Knowstone drove down to tell us that Army trucks full of servicemen and riot police vans had pulled up at the service station on the link road, where police were putting on their bullet proof vests. They said the same slaughter men were there who butchered the animals in the field two weeks before. They were still coming in!

We brought more vehicles in to block the driveway. Two guys with chainsaws felled a tree across the drive further back. I was worried about the Army coming across the farmland at the back of the house and sent a local woman off to keep an eye on them. In my experience MAFF often do the unexpected. With mobile phones not working in the bottom of the valley, she returned to say they had disappeared. We walked, quickly, the mile to the farm so we could see the animals (the felled tree proving an obstacle to us), only to get a message that the military trucks had collected in Knowstone and looked like they would descend on the drive, and back down we went.

It was weird, because the echo in the valley bottom made even a small Mini sound like a large diesel truck, and from 5 a.m. on we'd 'leap to arms' each time a vehicle came down the hill. It's important not to forget that these people are paid by us to protect us – and here we were, frightened, jumpy and prepared to fight them!

The next message we had was the Army and slaughter men were heading for the back fields, and the police and the MAFF officials were descending into the valley to the driveway. Heavily outnumbered, we had to make a rapid decision and chose to go back to the farm in case they opened up on the animals.

From a vantage point at the farm we saw the riot vans descending into the valley and within twenty minutes the MAFF heavies (including the smug officious ones we'd blocked earlier) approached us, escorted by bullet-proof vested police. We had a plan: It was my turn to read them their rights and hold them up for as long as possible whilst some of the others, including Bob and Mark, went to the fields to hide in the hedgerows. I was not to get arrested yet (not easy being utterly drained and emotional) because I was then to join the others in the fields and get amongst the cattle so they:

A) couldn't get them into the yards; and B), if they opened up as they had two weeks earlier, they'd have to shoot us as well.

I told them this and appealed to their humane side (nonexistent) as they pushed past us. They were all hell-bent on seeing Geoff Harknell – knowing he was near to cracking under the pressure in concern for his ill wife, who'd lost half a stone in the past week and barely slept. As the police and MAFF converged on the elderly couple, one MAFF vet silently sloped off to the cattle and was caught reaching out and touching one on the nose. Another friend, Brent Johnson, confronted the vet and asked him to get away. The official had something in his hand he was trying to hide. We reckoned it was a phial of FMD virus in case of a reprieve – remember the unmarked FMD-diseased sheep that appeared a few days earlier? My best friend in Cumbria had an unmarked FMD riddled sheep put in his outermost field on the fells to finish him off after holding out against MAFF for two months. Dirty underhand tactics are a part of war!

As they were talking, Jessica excitedly came running out of the house holding a phone saying MAFF legislation had changed the day before – that healthy animals could now only be killed after a blood test was taken and proved positive (this is after all EU law anyway). I was sent back, on crutches, by the Harknells to get the TV crews in standing at the gate some five hundred yards away. I told them the latest, but they felt they couldn't cross the line of red restriction notices even though there was no FMD on the farm – a MAFF vet had even given the animals the All Clear the night before.

Any excitement was cut short as we saw the Valuer (the exemplification of the Grim Reaper who prefigures Death) approaching us, protected by more riot police. I desperately tried to stop him and appeal to his spirit, saying things had changed and couldn't he at least ring the MAFF officials with the Harknells to safeguard any more stress and pressure being applied to the elderly couple. I read him his rights and asked if 'he was legitimate and clean'. He just said he was 'legitimate' and climbed over the gate, unmasked and undisinfected, with the police holding me back; 'clean' was not now nor had ever been an issue.

He hadn't been at the house for long when the protesters and Sarah (who'd been sent away by her shattered father) approached us, looking drawn and tired. They were soon followed by Major James Ackland, of the Freedom in Action pressure group, who had been a huge support and help to the family. Major Ackland, a man in his mid sixties, announced to the TV crews that the Harknells 'could not go on in the face of merciless pressure', and how 'this is a terrible day for freedom and democracy in this country'. He was right, because this had effectively undone the work of the Anglesey Six two months ago, and puts MAFF above the law. They now have a license to kill whenever and whatever they want – answerable to no one, not even EU laws. Even the Labour manifesto states that a public enquiry will only involve a 'Scientific review of animal welfare and a new farming commission to examine agribusiness practices'. There is, currently, to be no official enquiry. The final card MAFF threw at Mr Harknell was to say if he persisted with his appeal and lost, costs would amount to £30,000. It's already cost him £1,500, which I'd like to pay – hence buckets out for donations and a special fund-raising day for protesters and protest costs at Tapeley next Saturday, June 2.

At 4 p.m. we saw Mr Harknell herding his animals into the yard for slaughter and we let rip, verbally (Mr Harknell had especially requested that our protest to be peaceful, without arrests, and we maintained that out of respect for him – just!), at the MAFF officials and police around us. I now have no respect for bodies of authority at all. I told them if they'd looked sincerely at what they were doing on all levels, moral and otherwise, and genuinely believed it was in the best interests of mankind, the environment, and for the animal kingdom; i.e., when they were on their deathbed their minds, hearts and souls were at peace and they'd done their best, I'd respect them. Their eyes dropped. Our tragic love of money over and above life… 'It's more than my job's worth' – trouble is, the big corporate boys pave the path with gold for those who carry out and comply with their wishes. But what about our souls?

Policemen tell me they agree one hundred per cent with what I'm doing, yet they are protecting MAFF vets, officials and slaughter men from the protesters. I say, 'Make a stand! Leave the Force, making it clear as to why, and encourage those who feel the same to do likewise.' We don't have to obey orders we believe to be morally and humanely wrong – we all of us have free choice.

To the small shopkeeper and Guest House owner who can now see they will be swallowed up by the large hypermarkets and hotels belonging to big businesses, I say to them, 'Get out and actively *protest and fight! Take a risk!' The same message goes out to all small farmers in rural England who feel their livelihoods are under threat, and their treasured land will become just another plot in a large amalgamated farm or theme park.*

Sarah Harknell phoned me last night. She had witnessed the slaughtering of her father's animals. She said she couldn't stop crying and she still couldn't sleep. She was desperately worried about her mother, whose condition and state of mind were worsening. Her father was being brave for his wife, but inside – who knows? As if this wasn't enough, two MAFF officials clad in their all white, alien, soulless space suits went up to the farm the next morning and slapped an 'A' notice on them, effectively stopping them from getting away from their farm until further notice, and thereby keeping the hideous memories and misery fresh in their minds. They, MAFF, claimed one of the stampeding beasts fleeing the trigger-happy gunmen had run across one of Geoff's fields.

a) He was watching and said none did.

b) He was an excellent farmer, his fencing was of the highest standard, so if one had got in it wouldn't have been able to get out.

Another cruel MAFF lie.

Cumbrian friends mentioned earlier on about the holocaust. MAFF officials and vets have said to us, 'They're showing the rest of Europe how to deal with FMD efficiently and effectively.' They believe in what they're doing. Now I know if those same people were told to dispose of us they would certainly do it without question.

It really is time to say 'No' to culling for the export market.

★

Knowestone, a small, tranquil farming village on the edge of Exmoor was to become the shining example of just what our government bodies were capable of. The word 'extreme', 'fascist' and 'Gestapo' were frequently used when describing our (official) fellow countrymen at this time. This sadly turned out to be a forerunner of what was to come on a far bigger scale.

Unfortunately for MAFF, the police and Army, they created the epicentre of resistance in the South-West. I remember the whole village of Knowestone – shopkeepers, farm workers, grandparents and their grandchildren, rising up and fighting back. After their own bloody fight, they would travel around en masse to assist other farmers in their fight. Dad felt sure this was the main reason MAFF left Devon and went back to concentrate on mopping up the relatively easy pickings for them in Cumbria and Northumberland. The Devon 'Resistance' started winning more battles than it was losing.

Fortunately, an amateur cameraman videoed the bloody massacre on Mr Godfrey's farm. It showed the sixteen Limousines panicking and stampeding through fences onto other farms, and other cattle writhing, partially wounded on the spot where they were shot. Given the fact that this was shown on local TV, and MAFF then tried to kill everybody else's animals on the back of this, it is easy to see why the village rose up. Sadly, the Harknell episode was not the worst case.

To summarise Dad's writings of this time, the Worthington's case and that of Phillip Berry stand out the most. Dave and Martha Worthington had a small herd of cattle that they had proudly built up over their lives on a seventy-acre plot of land. They were in their seventies, and as with the Harknells' stock, MAFF wanted to slaughter all the cattle on the back of a potential 'dangerous contact', due to the naughty stampeding Limousines.

The Worthingtons exercised their right by law to demand their healthy animals had a blood test to show FMD antibodies before being slaughtered. MAFF, as usual, ignored their pleas, and threatened them with the usual massive court costs, possible arrest and so on – and ringing them up at all hours of the day and night. Dave, on a friendly solicitor's advice, chose to go to court to appeal against the slaughter.

The day for the appeal happened to fall on the twenty-first day after MAFF wanted to first steam in. EU law clearly stated that once neighbouring farms had survived twenty-one days after the slaughter of infected animals they were in the clear and there was no need for further slaughter. On the surface it appeared the appeal was therefore unnecessary. However, MAFF had set a precedent at the Harknells', overriding all law and legislation.

The appeal day was on a Monday. By this time everybody was used to MAFF's dirty tactics, whereby they would launch their biggest slaughter onslaught at a weekend, and on Sunday in particular. This was when the courts were closed and solicitors much harder to get hold of. It was our fund-raising day that Saturday for protesters and small farmers with huge legal fees. Dad was so run-down, with a high temperature, that he couldn't make it down to the Worthingtons' farm gate on the Sunday. However, fortunately many did, locking arms against the determined intruders. Powerful pictures appeared in the local paper the next day of folk in their eighties and children under eight doggedly standing firm with the burly farmers.

Many thought that was it – a victory – and went home. The appeal was due at 9 a.m. the next morning at Exeter Crown Court, where the damaging precedent set at Brent Oak would be reversed. Six protesters thought otherwise and chose to sleep at the Worthingtons' farm gate. They were foiled by an all too familiar dawn raid at 5 a.m. and were simply brushed aside as the authorities stormed up to the Worthingtons' front door and banged on it loudly.

A bleary eyed Mr Worthington was seen, tired and scared, eventually signing a bit of paper thrust before him.

Some of the protesters claimed that the MAFF officials had said the signature was to help him in his appeal, but whatever, the poor man was well into his seventies, and by then was weak and broken by the constant, merciless pressure. It was, of course, the valuation document, otherwise known as the death certificate. Many farmers were told that the more they protested, the more their compensation would be cut. By 8.30 a.m., half an hour before his animals were due to receive an almost certain reprieve, they lay dead all around his yard and fields.

Phillip Berry's sheep and his two store cattle were next on the list. He lived just up the road from the Worthingtons. His partner of ten years, whom he loved dearly, died one day and MAFF turned up the next day to kill his animals. Phil, however, was a different bag of potatoes altogether. He was not in his seventies like the Worthingtons, but in his forties. He had seen what had happened to his friends and colleagues and as a result hated all authority with every fibre of his being. He did not hesitate to resist them. He moved his flatbed trailer outside the gate leading to the field where his sheep were, on top of which he placed an effigy of a hanging Tony Blair, fully clad in a set of white MAFF overalls, with blood spattered all over it. Next to this he placed his favourite armchair, on which he sat, keeping a round-the-clock, twenty-four-hour a day vigil.

I turned up with Dad and the boys in the Battle Bus, Bob Marley blazing out, 'Don't you worry 'bout a thing' when there seemed the likelihood of an attack. Dad asked Phil if he was all right and bearing up. Phil turned and said, 'Don't worry, I have lost the one thing that I love the most, there ain't no way I'm gonna lose the only other things I love.'

The police had labelled him as 'unstable' and were scared, maybe with good reason. Underneath his trailer there was a Hessian sack with odd protrusions. Word had it that it was full of guns, which he would use on the authorities if they tried to storm his farm then probably turn one on himself. Dad was always saying that sooner or later there was going to be a gun battle. The number of suicides were going up and up on the back of the illegal Gestapo-style tactics being imposed.

It was so bad that Phil didn't dare bury his partner. The day for the funeral came and went. Phil feared that MAFF would take the opportunity whilst he was burying his wife to kill his animals in the same way they stormed our place to see Dad's animals when they knew he was locked up – possibly with a phial of FMD ready to hand, had Biff not seen them off. It was weeks before he felt safe enough to have the funeral, during which time the anger and determination burnt brighter by the second.

Meanwhile, to 'keep busy', MAFF homed in on other smallholders nearby. One such family, Sally Thomas and her daughter Tamsin, had just fifteen sheep. Dad said that even if they were offered £1 million they wouldn't have sold out. Many of the ewes, now with lambs, were hand-reared as pets. Pet lambs were those that came from ewes with no milk or were rejected and couldn't be adopted for whatever reason and had to be bottle-fed. As such they were a time-consuming liability for the farmer, but effectively became pets for those feeding them.

Mum and daughter slept in the fields with their sheep, with one or two protesters at the gate in contact with Phillip Berry and other protesters just up the road. They were, quite literally, under siege, not knowing when they would be attacked. It was due to circumstances such as this that Dad got incensed when ignorant outsiders harped on, saying, 'The animals will die anyway'…and, 'The farmer gets fat compensation payments, so what are they whingeing about?'

Knowestone was clearly getting under Dad's skin. He wasn't the type to get depressed, but this was the nearest I'd seen him get to it. He seemed to have lost interest in his own business, which was becoming a mess. He took no interest in my school life and what I was up to, and wouldn't speak to anyone unless it was connected with how to best go about 'fighting the bastards'. It was at that time he decided to launch his own 'attack' against the enemy.

In earnest, another visit was organised to the wretched MAFF headquarters in Exeter. The objective was to threaten and genuinely scare the enemy. Sadly, I wasn't there for this march, because I had to be at Mum's that weekend. A piece from Dad's diaries best sums up the events of the day:

We all met at the 'Park and Ride' at midday as usual. On the way there, having listened to the rousing music of Manu Chau in the car with Biff and the boys, we all got the revolutionary fighting spirit going. We played this tape on the way to every protest, farm gate blockades or whatever, and it always pressed the right buttons.

There was a rather sombre funereal theme to the day; many people dressed in reference to the millions of animals that had died unnecessarily, and the farmers who had committed suicide. By 12.30 there were only a hundred-odd people compared to the three hundred expected. This was because I'd changed the time and failed to alert everybody. Some were furious with me, but in retrospect it made the whole day more potent. This was because people continued to turn up for the rest of the day, laying their funeral wreaths with the others and sitting in sad contemplation for ten minutes or so.

Another reason there were not more of us was that we had to leave a hundred or so to protect a number of small farmers at Knowestone. I received a call the night before from a tearful Sally Thomas, terrified that if we were all at MAFF, they would take the opportunity to attack – which, based on previous form, was true. I promised her we'd leave enough people to protect her, Phil and the others and would have mobile phones, so if they did turn up we'd be with them in half an hour. For this reason we chose to drive to MAFF rather than march.

This time we hadn't alerted MAFF as to our plan and there were only two policemen on the gate. We asked politely if we could come in. One policeman said he'd have to check with MAFF and started to call them on his phone. Nobody had any intention (or interest) in waiting for MAFF's reply and, led by Biff, claiming to be pushed, we barged through the gate.

It never occurred to us that at the time we must have appeared quite a rough-looking bunch. Most of us were masked up mainly in death masks or along that theme in reference to the funeral focus. However, with the exception of me, everybody from our pad wore black balaclavas with just three little round holes for the mouth and eyes in the style of Islamic fundamentalists or anarchists. Biff looked the best with a bandero wrapped round his head and neck and a grinning pink pig mask around his eyes and nose.

(Masking up had already become illegal on protests by then. This was mainly so that the police, instructed by 'Big Brother', could record everybody's faces on video cameras or CCTV. Unfortunately, such people were subjected to special treatment from the authorities when society really started to collapse.)

While the police disappeared for back-up, we shut, padlocked and chained the huge wrought iron gate so as to spend some uninterrupted time with the enemy. The vibe was angry and heavy- reflected in people's banners. One read: 'This is WAR. We will fight to the DEATH'.

Tens of thousands of bits of paper with swastikas on one side and 'Nazi' written on the back were stuck on the bushes around the garden. Biff had brought a big banner with 'MAFF OFF' written in red across it, which he was going to hang from the roof of the MAFF HQ. Angry words were blasted out via the loudhailer at the officials in the building. This time there was no one laughing at us through the windows.

The Nazi theme dominated: Bob was on the news that night explaining precisely why we were calling them the modern-day version of the Gestapo. My whole rant was based on the same theme, finishing with a poem that came to me at 3 a.m. the night before:

> *The Hidden Agenda paves the path with gold*
> *To those it employs, both young and old.*
> *Whether killing cows or Jews,*
> *Who gives a damn, if it's on the news?*
> *Give us a thousand pounds a day and more*
> *We'll shut our ears and eyes – you know the score.*
> *For our love of money more than life*
> *I'll kill your cows, your sheep, your wife.*

There then followed a two-minute silence with everyone giving a Nazi salute to the MAFF HQ. We found out later that this protest really put the wind up MAFF. At one point a Trading Standards posse appeared behind a fence round the back of the building. The group was led by a fat squat little Hitler whom we recognised as the person who had been very aggressive on the farm gates with us. Half the protesters ran down to the fence yelling obscenities at him especially.

In the meantime fifteen vans full of riot police had arrived, only to find the gate heavily chained so they couldn't get in. They sent for bolt cutters and blowtorches. Once we'd finished with MAFF, Biff went over and undid the padlock. The riot police burst in, clearly upset and nervous about what we'd get up to. We'd made our point, so there was no point in our getting arrested; so we put out a peaceful 'We're going home now' vibe to the police. They were especially keen to get everyone to remove their masks. Everybody obliged – except, of course, Biff. He was too light on his feet for the police who tried to corner him. Outnumbering Biff thirty to one at one point, even the police sensed it wasn't worth their while to forcibly insist Biff remove his mask.

★

Two days later, Dad went to London. He'd been invited to the Public Inquiry Conference in a big posh office in the centre of the city. It had been organised by a serious group of business people with solicitors and barristers present to try to force the Government into a vaccination programme and a full Public Inquiry – something the Government was strategically sidestepping, for obvious reasons, like a slippery eel.

The main purpose of Dad going was to drum up the national news into giving the real picture about what was going on. He had had articles in most of the national papers, but was frustrated that each one omitted the bullying Gestapo tactics being used to eradicate the small farmer in particular. He kept going on about how he felt such information came outside the parameters of what people were allowed to know, as directed by the government and big business shareholders who owned and controlled the editing of the Nationals.

Again, based on his diaries and what he told me, he arrived in London early afternoon the day before the conference. He was due to meet up with the Channel 4 cameraman, Carl, to go to the Camden Centre that evening where José Bove, a much celebrated revolutionary French farmer, was over to launch his new book.

However, because Dad had arrived so early, and being literally like a duck out of water in London, he went straight to a pub in Camden. Here he settled down for the next few hours in front of the TV watching what he described as 'an extremely exciting one-day International between England and Pakistan'. He was talking about cricket. The words 'cricket' and 'exciting' have never been remotely connected for me. Football was boring enough but cricket was in another universe. Apparently, due to the 'excitement' he managed to down six pints of lager.

He eventually met up with his Cumbrian mate, Tupper Tim 'The Boy' Luxton, and Carl and staggered, presumably, into the Camden Centre. The room was packed with 3,000-odd so-called left-wing extremists dominated by the SWP, the Socialist Workers' Party. I think if Dad hadn't had all that lager he might have been a little nervous. There were one or two other speakers, including the legendary statesman Tony Benn, a good old-fashioned socialist.

After the talks, people were allowed to ask questions, and a mike was passed around. Dad said the questions directed to Bove were so hero-worshipping that they weren't achieving much, though quite what he expected I don't know. Bove had become famous for dismantling a McDonald's, the epitome of revolting nutritionally toxic Corporate America taking control of the global food chain, in his local town, and going to prison for it.

Dad and Tupper Tim held up placards with 'Devon' and 'Cumbrian Farmer' written on them respectively. The mike was brought over to them immediately, and Dad grabbed it. He boomed out that it was all very well what they'd achieved in Seattle and Prague but now it was happening on their doorsteps. He spoke of the Gestapo tactics being employed and asked for protesters to come to Devon and Cumbria to fight the riot police, Army and MAFF officials on farm gates. He finished with an angry rendition of the poem he had fired at the MAFF HQ two days earlier. Following a short (probably rather stunned) silence, a huge cheer went up.

During all his ranting, Dad found that he was having a minor battle with the guy holding the mike who kept pulling the mike away from Dad's mouth. Being angry, and somewhat drunk, Dad probably didn't realise how deafening it was when he held the mike so close up. He had a very loud voice anyway and had become used to bellowing into his thirty-year-old loudhailer. The fellow turned out to be Terry Yeo, the leader (or 'dogsbody', as Terry preferred to be known) of Globalise Resistance, who was to become a great friend of Dad and the rest. He became a frequent visitor to North Devon. Their friendship was to become a key link between the countryside and the city when things really started to hit the fan.

Everybody now clearly sees the tactics of 'divide and rule' used by those in power at the time and throughout history. The powers that be knew that if they kept people divided and at loggerheads and fearful of each other they could be easily controlled. People united were a big problem.

The politicians and big corporate leaders pulling the strings from behind the scene had, however, started to become careless at that time. The leading parties in the so-called democratic 'free world' in the West had all pretty much begun to merge into one and were all very obviously under the control of big business. This meant that fewer and fewer people even bothered to vote in the elections. Countries were selling off all their industry including their public services such as water supplies, schools, hospitals and public transport. The problem was not only did the workers have to be paid, *but* also the shareholders who'd invested their money. The shareholders' sole motive was to make money, preferably more than was being made than from a long-term deposit in a bank account. If they could make more money elsewhere, they'd pull out and reinvest.

The Government's reasoning was that money would be more efficiently handled with the tight overseeing of businessmen with a personal interest. In other words they felt there would be less wastage than when industries were nationalised. It seemed to fail to take into consideration the huge profits that needed to be generated to increase share prices and pay huge dividends to investors to stop them pulling out and investing elsewhere. Pitting, for example, a non-profitable rail service against a, say, profitable computer company on an even playing field, and you get… disaster.

When British Rail was sold off in order to turn the subsidised deficit around into a fat enough profit to feed the shareholders, railway maintenance was slashed, staff numbers were reduced where possible – by computers controlling signals, for example – and workers wages kept to a minimum. The previous Conservative Government had all but destroyed the power of the unions so the threat of strikes were minimal at that time, but oh boy – how quickly things went downhill! The result was horrendous accident after horrendous accident and huge amounts of public money being pumped into PFI, the Private Finance Initiative, to save the whole rail network from total collapse.

The same was happening with the hospitals. To cut costs, old hospitals were being pulled down instead of being repaired, leaving fewer, supposedly more efficient hospitals. The result of cost-cutting to make profits was that patients were being sent back home sometimes too soon after operations to free the beds, many others were being left in the corridors, and some poor surgeons were doing thirty-six-hour, round-the-clock shifts. Again all hospital staff were paid as little as could be got away with. In Coventry, for example, three hospitals sold off to PFI soon became one at the Walsgrave site (smaller than the one that had been there before). Our tax money was used to kit the whole hospital out. The NHS, with our tax money, rented the hospital at huge costs from the PFI on a yearly basis on a long index-linked lease. The costs of this to the taxpayer was far greater than if the Government had paid for the repairs for the three hospitals originally and subsidised them as it had been doing. Likewise, a consortium that built the Altcourse Prison in Liverpool broke even after two and a half years into the twenty-five-year contract. It then enjoyed, via our taxes, twenty-two years of pure, no nonsense profit.

The situation then was so much worse in the so-called developing countries – daft name since the Western powers did all they could to maintain and increase the horrendous poverty for control purposes. Just how bad it really was only became clear to me once I opened up correspondence with Ishmael and Neela.

It was becoming ever clearer back then that it was the multinational corporations that were in total control of global politics; their sole objective was to maximise profits in the short term, in the same way as it was here. Regard for human health, life and the environment were nonexistent. As mother earth cried out in pain – in the lead-up to the Collapse, due to human greed, some of the natural catastrophes were horrendous. The corporations had placed themselves beyond accountability, controlling the global policy makers such as the International Monetary Fund (IMF) and the World Trade Organisation – WTO (Dad called it the 'World Terrorist Organisation'), who created their own laws. One example being the international code of law passed in the 1990s to forbid the multinational corporations based in the UK with set-ups in the Third World from being sued. Expensive health and safety requirements could thus be bypassed so when, for example, a disaster struck, as in a South African asbestos mine, terminally poisoning 3,000 workers, there was no comeback. Similar situations arose in Tanzania, Kenya, and frequently all over the world.

Tax was never a problem. Offshore accounts and bank accounts in obliging countries often contained hidden billions in cash. For example, at this time, most of the top eighty-odd companies in the US did not pay all the thirty-five per cent corporation tax. Over 1,000 corporations with assets of more than $250 million paid no tax at all, and some, such as General Motors, juggled the figures so that the Government owed them. If a country gave them grief they'd threaten to up sticks and move elsewhere leaving massive unemploy-ment in their wake if the Government didn't back down – not a problem.

Abraham Lincoln saw it coming when he wrote:

> I see in the near future a crisis approaching that unnerves me and causes me to tremble for the safety of my country. Corporations have become enthroned and an era of corruption in high places will follow.

Indeed, when the stock market was set up in the late 1600s the potential for abuse was recognised right back then. It was a device set up to safeguard national institutions such as churches and schools from potentially crippling inheritance tax. The importance of non-profit was clearly recognised and implemented by the highly moral shareholders. However, a few traders found a loophole in the government legislation and began trading in shares in other businesses 'for profit'. The infamous East India Company was such a business. People quickly cottoned on to the fact that they could get a far greater return on their capital from such investments than by leaving it in the bank. Then came the South Sea Bubble in 1721, when the East India Company collapsed and everybody lost their money. The stock market only recovered properly toward the end of the 1700s – with a vengeance.

Looking back, I find it hard to believe how people couldn't see even twenty years ago the evil they were fuelling and enhancing from such investments. Maybe they didn't want to see. The problem was even money invested in banks was invested in turn by them into the stock markets. Debt creation by the banks was another criminal control device. All this made it unnecessarily hard for everybody.

The whole education system was designed to produce clones for the system, whereby success and respect was based on how much money you made. The way you made it, having ever more expansive boundaries, further increased man's avarice, greed and distorted ego. Spiritually, physically, and emotionally, this reached its peak appropriately in the year 2000. The spin, lies and deceit then started exploding like a giant boil as some of the world's most respected corporations and banks collapsed. Too many had become overconfident, greedy, smug and careless... as had happened to all imperialist powers throughout history.

It is clear now that this will never have to happen again. We all feel today so blessed to have lived through earth's transformation, even though it seemed (and was) so destructive at the time. Now that the Spiritual Awakening has occurred, it is easy for everybody to see that money was an energy, and as such was designed to be spent for the betterment of all and the planet. Even then when people did this the universe rewarded them threefold, but how hard this was for the majority to realise in a world so governed by fear. From 2000 onwards with the new energies firmly in place, whereby anybody hoarding or saving money for the sake of it, it simply rotted away – pensions, stocks and shares – you name it!

*

Unbeknown to Dad at the time, I think, but he had stumbled across the main group of like-minded people who saw the bigger picture and, like him, wanted to actively do something about it. He was to go on many boisterous, passionate marches with them, but there were two that looking back helped pave the way for global change, for very different reasons. They set the tone for polarising and eventually isolating those holding on to the old way and those desiring the new. One march was the one in Genoa later that year, the other was 'that' march for peace, rather than war against Iraq, on February 15 2003.

Dad's angry outburst meant he got a lot of attention afterwards in the bar, including from one or two journalists. I can just see him gleefully knocking back the free pints on offer. I am ashamed to say he was a bit of a session drinker, whereby he used to get blind drunk, remember nothing and claim to have enjoyed every second – not very 'spiritual'. To give him his due he never became aggressive, just very loving towards everybody, and, he claimed, never got a hangover. He put such behaviour down to the 'footballer' inside him, but I think this is a bit feeble. One journalist from one of the more liberal national papers said he'd come down and do a piece on what was really going on, so I guess it was mission accomplished, outwardly at any rate.

The next day he trotted off, hangover free of course, to the Public Inquiry Conference. The highlight for him seemed to be getting uncontrollable giggles with Carl in the back of the posh office when his mate, Tupper Tim, was speaking. When Tim used to phone for up to two hours at a time, Dad said he'd get onto the subject of 'the milk lorries' spreading FMD over and above all else, and there was no stopping him. Dad said Tim had just been asked to wrap his talk up when his voice became quieter and quieter, culminating in the words 'the milk lorries' in a barely audible whisper. He then spoke for another twenty minutes on the subject. Having known Tim since I was born, I could see how funny he was. With specs and short curly hair he was the spitting image of the Sixties pop idol, Buddy Holly, and when he got onto a subject was like a bull terrier with a bone.

Mid-morning, Dad sneaked out for a bit to visit Noble House in Smith Square. This was the MAFF HQ for the UK where José Bove was hosting a small protest. It was organised by a small environmental lobby bearing organic fruit and veg for the MAFF officials. I think it was meant to be peaceful so the last thing they needed was Dad turning up – angry.

After hanging around outside for ten minutes or more for some junior officials to come out, say all the right things and not mean a word of it, Dad, disrespectful as ever announced, 'What are we doing out here? This is a public building which belongs to us, which means we can go in.'

Two security guards closed ranks on the top of the steps, but apparently as a result of a few chosen words from Dad the guards parted and in they went. With Bove on his heels, the environmental lobby, who evidently were doing wonderful work at the time without Dad's input, followed. They were asking for peace and (understandably) denied Dad an organic raspberry when he asked for one. They were furious at the time, but probably didn't understand what it was like in the field. After a few months, however, they softened and did valuable work with Dad for the cause.

Whilst up in London, Dad received fantastic news that there had been two victories where the whole village of Knowestone with other protesters had turned up on farm gates and blocked the officials and slaughter men from taking yet more healthy animals. The main reason for more victories than defeats from here on was the Protesters' Tree had become very well organised and, just as significantly, the police had decided to stop supporting MAFF soon after the election. Whether this was due to all the words the protesters had had with the police and giving them documents of EU law proving that MAFF were the lawbreakers, not the protesters, who knows... Educating bodies of authority, MPs and so on, became a major part of the protesters' campaign on all manner of issues. They certainly weren't getting much of a picture from the Government-controlled information being handed to them.

Dad did one or two more protests when he got back. One was to protect some sheep and 'Grunty' the pig, star of a film back then, presumably about a pig. It was the other side of Exmoor in Somerset, so a fair way to drive. The owner, Dave Armstrong, had yet another typical story: he'd been protesting on a friend's farm nearby to save six pet alpacas. The farmer was having his animals killed as part of a contiguous cull but it was pretty much as unlikely for alpacas to catch FMD as it was for humans. Dave's friends loved the alpacas like their children, so Dave tried explaining to MAFF the facts stating that they should just be monitored on the incredibly unlikely chance that they contracted the disease.

MAFF were having none of it. They called the riot police, presumably afraid of losing yet another battle. When it became clear that MAFF were going to go ahead with the slaughter, Dave made for his friend's house to phone his legal team to prevent another illegal tragic cull. The riot police and slaughter men tried to stop him physically. Dave broke free and broke into a run. They chased him but he managed to get into the house and slam the door.

Dave's friends were a sweet couple of small farmers in their eighties. They had their two grandchildren staying with them that day, aged nine and twelve. As Dave reached the phone in the kitchen the door burst open and a bunch of burly riot policemen and slaughter men wrestled him to the ground. The grandchildren bravely leapt on to the attackers, pulling their hair as Dave was being roughed up and handcuffed. He was dragged out screaming in pain and hurled into the back of the riot van while they killed the alpacas.

The police had, on purpose, put the handcuffs on so tight so as to hurt him. He kept telling them this but they ignored him. When he came up to our house three weeks later to tell his story to the journalists, he still had massive bruising going up his forearms. They locked him up and released him in the early hours from Exeter police station, letting him find his own way home. This story reminded me of the lady up north who to save her six sheep took them into her kitchen. The police and MAFF then lured the lady out on the pretext of a friendly chat... and then she heard the shots ringing out.

The problem for the authorities with Dave was that he was a professional man, a land agent, and not intimidated by police brutality. He, with a little help from the protesters, managed to hold on to Grunty and the sheep and force a High Court hearing in London. There was huge excitement that if he won this it would knock the wretched contiguous cull policy on the head once and for all. He did win but the case was deemed a one-off, an exception. The big boys pulled the legal strings as usual and the contiguous culling continued unabated.

It was around this time that the journalist came to stay to 'get the real picture'. Dad took him everywhere. He met Dave, Bob, all the Knowestone fraternity, the Ashmoor and Deepmoor protesters and the rest. He told Dad that in twenty years of journalism this was one of the most pokey stories he'd covered in the UK. However, just as Dad expected, when the story came out, it contained not one mention of the Gestapo tactics used in our 'police state', as it had sadly become. It was the police drafted in from the cities causing the problems. The local bobby was as good as gold.

In September, MAFF started pulling out of Devon, returning to the easier pickings in Cumbria and Northumberland especially. The protesters felt this was largely due to the tenacity with which they fought, though it left many in financial, as well as emotional, ruin. They were convinced that many of the so-called 'positive cases', many of which they didn't even test for officially, were simple cases of orf and other related diseases which looked like FMD.

Rumours abounded of the EU White Paper planning to rid the UK of sheep by 2005 and cattle by 2010. The rumour that scared the farmers most was the 'scrapie thing'. Scrapie is a viral infection of the sheep's brain which makes them go round and round in circles. The vast majority tend to recover, as with FMD, and contain the antibodies to fight it from happening again.

Scrapie became famous when farm animal offal, including sheep's brains, were *legally* allowed to be incorporated into cattle feed as a source of cheap protein. It showed how bad things had become that non-meat-eating herbivores were being fed on other animals. The result was BSE (or mad cow disease) in cattle, and the potentially deadly CJD in humans. If you mess with nature (as here, for profit – the usual story), nature fights back. We didn't learn even then after this experience. We still pushed ahead with genetically modified crops. With regard to scrapie, the meat of the sheep was still fine to eat, the same as if they had FMD.

Yet on the back of this the authorities were murmuring about killing all flocks in which scrapie was found. Things went quiet until that mad year of 2007 when it again reared its ugly head. It was felt that they killed our animals with disease (FMD), and then even more through simple economics – fat lambs fetching nearly half what they did fifteen years earlier. Put this with the scrapie thing, change in subsidy law in 2005 and you get the picture.

CHAPTER II: GENOA

I might have been only ten, but it was clear from the build-up on the news that the Italians were preparing for big trouble during their G8 Summit in Genoa. They showed huge fences going up everywhere and I think had 18,000 Italian riot police on stand-by, plus other specialist riot police from elsewhere. I for the first time wanted to ask Dad not to go, but knew it would be a waste of breath. His excuse was, having failed again to get anything of significance out in the national press, that he had to try anything and everything. He was ridiculously overexcited, spending far longer than usual packing all his trinkets for 'battle'. Dad's press release, a little disjointed as it is, best captures the picture:

The Spirit of Genoa at War – A Protester's Experience of Direct Action

18/7/01

The train has been cancelled. I drove from Devon to Glyndebourne yesterday in the pouring rain and spoke to Jane Angus, who works as the Green Party press agent at the GLA. She said she'd had 'one hell of a day' since rumours had been flying around that the Globalise Resistance train, which she'd helped organise, had been cancelled by none other than Berlusconi, the Italian Prime Minister. The authorities are worried about this G8 Summit more than any other, especially in the light of Bush's presence, and that he'd turned his back on the Kyoto summit. The largest security operation ever at such events is being launched and three hundred coffins are on standby – the Italian riot police are a different ball game. Missile launchers are in place in case Islamic suicide bombers decide to attack the G8 Summit boat.

19/7/01

Received a call from Jane at 8 a.m. to say the train had now definitely been cancelled, and do I want to still go? I said I want this more than anything in my whole life, having seen first hand the devastation multinational corporate businesses are causing animals, humans, our freedom and the planet through their unabashed greed and blinkered grabbing of every last dollar. I know if we don't do something now we will soon be in a world where our destiny is totally controlled by a few unelected, faceless, ruthless businessmen. She booked us two tickets on Ryanair from Stansted for the next day at 5 p.m. as we were on the phone, and hired a car. We were still going.

Later that morning Jane rang back to say armed Italian police had escorted thousands of protesters out of the football ground where they were camping and out of the country. She said to me to not wear anything 'Bohemian', as anyone with beads was being turned away at the border. I went to the wardrobe at Glyndebourne where they lent me a magnificent cassock and a dog collar from the *Barber of Seville*. I suggested to Jane I'd fly as a 'member of the cloth', sneaking my secret mistress (her) out of the country, where I was having to maintain the illusion of celibacy, for a naughty weekend. The idea being that they wouldn't look in my bag and discover my pig mask, balloons covered in burning pyres and slaughter men shooting cows, a vinegar/lemon juice mix (against tear gas) and loudhailer – crucial as this was the tool I needed to deliver my talk on foot-and-mouth. She loved the idea, even though my dad warned me I could get into trouble for impersonating someone I was not as opposed to being in fancy dress. That afternoon I went to see *Othello* by Giuseppe Verdi – got me 'in the mood'.

At 11.15 p.m. Birgit rang – the train was back on! There had been a massive outcry from the Green Party in this country, Germany, Italy and France about losing our democratic right to protest that the French and Italian authorities had buckled. Also, the French railway union workers promised an all-out strike! The *Anarchist Express* as it's described in *The Times* was ready to roll! My dad came into the kitchen and asked if I knew what I was letting myself in for. He'd just seen the news and said 18,000 *carabinieri* (Italian armed police) were there, plus the Army, plus special riot police from other European countries and the town was already swarming with anarchists. My mum tried to stop me going, knowing how passionate I am and that I might get carried away – she's right! I've never felt so much support or respect from my dad.

After just three hours' sleep I drove to Dover. On arrival I was approached by two men who turned out to be undercover police who took my passport and particulars to check me out. At 8 a.m. Jane arrived with Noreena Hertz, author of *The Silent Takeover*, and very active in getting the anti-globalisation message out in the press, with Alf, a Channel 4 cameraman filming her every move for a documentary.

The 'Globalise Resistance' party numbered some four hundred – impressive since we only found out the train was back on at midnight the night before. We were ushered into a cold corrugated shack in which you wouldn't even house your cattle over winter. Most people checked for evidence of showers. A civil feeling of being made welcome was non-existent.

Once in France we were herded off the boat into a number of buses. The energy levels had tangibly gone up a notch or two whilst we'd been on the boat. However, following a five-minute journey, we arrived at Customs where we were inevitably subjected to a thorough search. The main worry was the threat of police dogs snuffling around our baggage under the bus and eating the sandwiches we'd just bought on the boat! We knew the train didn't have buffet facilities and there was no guarantee we'd have time to buy food. I was subjected to the most thorough search on our bus – not sure why, but they didn't like the look of me.

It was then on to the train station for a few hours with no sign of the train and still no guarantee we'd actually get on it. When it did arrive a huge cheer went up and everyone piled in. There was singing and dancing and waving of flags out of the windows. Many of us had foregone our plane tickets and the cars – the train was everything, the Grail. There was a media feeding frenzy – I put on my pig mask and scarf and spoke about FMD.

The train was not the Orient Express, though ironically it was parked next to it at the station. However it was great – basic couchette facilities and two large open cars – one for the disco/bar, the other for discussing 'tactics'. There was a fascinating debate on violence; whether ripping down the fence was deemed violent – it wasn't. The fence is a symbol of our lack of democracy, and we were all angry at the increasingly selectively regulated capitalist world designed to favour big business and Western banks as opposed to the people. All agreed not to start the violence but many said they'd fight in self-defence. Their bravery, dedication and focus impressed me.

No sooner than we'd got to sleep than we woke up to a banging on the side of the train. It was fully clad riot police shouting to us to get out of the train. It was 4 a.m., somewhere in the Alps, and unbeknown to us we were at an unscheduled stop off the beaten track. Everybody recognised it was the CRS riot police, a nasty bunch, and we were told not to provoke them in any way. The favour was not reciprocated. We were funnelled out of just one door with all our luggage, and jostled and pushed into a line against the wall of the station. There were four hundred of them (armed) and four hundred of us, and it felt like they were waiting for the merest excuse to hammer us. We, inevitably, got the giggles.

Following another painstakingly long search, we found ourselves at dawn stranded somewhere in the Alps. We were all quite chuffed we'd made it this far, but just as we were discussing how we'd get home a fleet of buses miraculously just turned up. We really were a hot potato. We breezed through Italian customs and armed up at a service station in northern Italy.

The 'Anarchist Express' was now entering Genoa in the form of a fleet of coaches – the Italians wouldn't allow the train across their border. The adrenalin was pumping. We'd heard there was a massive non-violent protest last night by 50,000 people about protecting immigrants' rights. The message is not to hurt or damage the people or property of Genoa, but the fence is not part of that category. The police are everywhere – they're stopping all the elderly people, yet the protest coach goes ahead fearlessly!

We were dropped off at the Piazza Acqua Verde and took a number 33 bus across town passing many colourful peaceful happy demonstrations. That was the one and only time we were to see that because as we arrived near the station things 'kicked off'. Plumes of black smoke were raging over the buildings, we could feel the tear gas stinging our eyes. We'd had barely three hours' sleep in two nights, we didn't know where we were and there were two police helicopters whirring overhead. The worst thing was lugging food and drink – caskets of water – enough provisions for two days, all over town… and it was hot!

We decided to drop our kit off in *Guardian* journalist John Vidal's hotel room. We had a hotel and street name and one useless map. We had to go under a big bridge where clearly it was 'going off' the other side. We weren't disappointed because on reaching the other side there were lines of riot vans and thousands of riot police lining the road entrances three or four layers deep on all the roads in a large square. I felt we should go right, and John's hotel was somewhere in the cordoned off yellow zone in a street called Via Saulli. You could taste the tension.

I was the only one of us who spoke a little pidgin Italian so approached a line of riot police, who immediately motioned to me not to come any closer. I continued pointing to the ladies weighed down with baggage – it helped that they were pretty, especially in Italy! After some persuasion that we were journalists they reluctantly let us through but told us to 'take long strides, it very tense'! We did.

Then we came to the second line – a host of riot vans blocking a small gap in a huge menacing fence, with hundreds more riot police. The police here were positively hostile and told us to leave quickly. Luckily an Italian journalist was passing and said we needed a large yellow press pass like he was wearing, but we needed to get it from across the square where rioting was by now in full swing. As we turned to walk back into the fray, however, our pathetic appearance clearly got through to the police and they let us through.

The contrast was amazing. Empty streets, and a luxury hotel and shower! We then turned on the TV and watched open-mouthed the huge riots taking place some few hundred yards away. After two hours, we took to the empty streets, aware that if we got out we wouldn't get back in without official press passes. However, we followed a couple of Italian journalists, nipped over a wall and were in the streets – you can't block everything in a big city.

We spent the rest of the day 'looking for action' for the Channel 4 documentary and found nothing but empty streets with the odd convoy of riot vans screeching past to the fray. However, our disappointment turned to relief from what we saw on the TV on our return to the hotel. The scenes were truly horrendous – innocent people being beaten senseless, tear-gassed and shot. We'd been divinely protected.

On our way back to the hotel Noreena decided we should ask the police if we could go into the red zone. I was reluctant because it felt like a pointless stunt. As I was walking past the police they said they wanted to search my bag. I felt I was being singled out having been the most thoroughly searched at Calais and by the CRS police. Also, my bag was full of riot protection gear and loudhailer – which I didn't want to lose! Surrounded by ten burly, non-smiling riot police, I breathed deeply and emptied my bag.

I smilingly, calmly blagged my way through the contents they questioned me with: 'The loud-hailer?' I pointed to the pretty paintings on it of flowers and mermaids stating they were done by '*mia bella figlia*' (daughter) – '*artista*'; then the goggles (essential against tear gas), I made breaststroke movements and said as if like a goofy lost English tourist, '*per nuotare*' (swimming) '*in voi bella*' (beautiful) '*Genovan mare*' (sea), '*ma il non possibile perche*' (but its not possible because of) '*the fences*'; 'The pig mask?' (masks meant an instant beating and arrest) I replied with, '*Mia figlio*' (son) '*e un po di'* (a little) '*pig*,' and I made accompanying piglet noises to get the message home and confuse them more.

All the time I'd been worrying about how I'd blag the final item, the jar of vinegar and lemon juice mix. We'd soak our banderos in this liquid to protect our lungs when tear-gassed. When they found this they grunted and held the jar up to my face, then raised their batons. They clearly felt they had me at last. From out of the blue I said, '*Lo Inglesi e in Inglaterra noi amare*' (we love) '*chips, ma in Italia il vinagra no buono*' (but in Italy the vinegar is not good), 'so it's vinegar for my chips.'

Fortunately, by this time police cars and riot vans were storming past us – the main riot had begun. I was very relieved to walk away.

My main fear was losing my loudhailer, which I had because my objective was to boom out a talk on behalf of the small farmers in Devon who had lost their animals due to the merciless brutality of the multinationals and the state. I'd planned to do it dressed in my cassock and dog collar in front of a fence during a riot. The idea was that halfway through Jane was to attach some hooks and the tow ropes we'd brought in an Italian service station to the fence, which we then hoped people would have pulled, with me continuing my sermon as the tear gas and water canons blazed away. However, seeing the scenes that night made me drop that idea. Dying was not part of the plan – my daughter had made me promise not to get shot just as I left.

The next morning Jane and I hit the streets at 8 a.m. and headed for the convergence centre on the coast. The scene had a Glastonbury feel to it. Soon after 9 a.m. thousands of lively Italians chanting and waving red flags passed through us and we all joined in. We were led to a forum in a massive tent where inspirational talks were given by a host of international revolutionary speakers. The most poignant message being put out was that the past was irrelevant, as were people's political leanings. Our sole purpose was to destroy permanently the corporate multinational takeover of our world… 'Our world is not for sale – put the G8 into jail. Divided they win, united we will win!'

Surveys had been done in countries such as France and Greece where the vote averaged at sixty per cent against globalisation and ten per cent for, with thirty per cent not understanding.

I believe if the governments did not pay the anarchists to cause mayhem then fifty to a hundred times more people would turn up at these summits for very powerful peaceful protests. I always put myself in the shoes of the 'enemy'. What do they stand to gain by subterfuge? Firstly, it focuses the whole press on the violence, and the peaceful protester gets tarred with the same brush; and secondly, as mentioned, it keeps so many more people away – it is seriously scary. The hard core Black Bloc and Blue Bloc anarchists (many paid) infiltrate peaceful protests and hurl missiles, Molotov cocktails and petrol bombs at lines of riot police, who then storm the protesters – who in turn fight to protect themselves; meanwhile the anarchists move to the next one. This happened to the 'comrades' – those on the train, but they, out-numbering the anarchists, beat them up and took their weapons from them.

After blowing up our balloons, depicting smiling slaughter men shooting cows, and sheep burning in pyres (drawn by my daughter), we joined the biggest, most colourful, noisy march seen in Europe for decades. The buzz was electric – not even the terraces at Brighton's Goldstone Ground could compare. Seeing riot police on the hill watching us and the helicopters whirring menacingly above inspired angry chants of '*Assassini!*' – plus a few hand gestures! The chanting was deafening throughout, and comprised the repetitive yet very powerful 'One solution… Revolution', and '*So-so-so Solidarite*' with fists raised, thumping the air. The more comical ones included things like, 'George Bush we know you – Daddy was a killer too.'

The mood on the march was one of togetherness and defiance. Most people realised that the orders for excessive violence came from Berlusconi supported by Bush and Blair. The idea was to scare the anti-capitalist/globalisation movement into submission once and for all. The day before thousands of innocent protesters had, without provocation, been beaten senseless, some of them men and women in their sixties.

One Italian, Carlo Giuliani, had been shot and killed. The authorities didn't seem to take into account the presence of the world's media. On the Friday night there were pictures of Carlo nearly being run over by a speeding van. A fire extinguisher had fallen out of the van. He picked it up, no doubt angry at the speeding van. As he was putting it down he was shot twice through the head. The van then ran over his head then reversed back over it to make sure he was dead.

It took two hours for the march to get into town, when at 1 p.m. the most deafening roar went up I'd ever heard. I checked the escape route in case the riot police were attacking in their thousands. But the message was the G8 Summit had been cancelled, the protesters had *won!* The message was that 'Bush, Blair, Berlusconi and the rest had gone home because they didn't want any more violence and death'.

Then there ensued the biggest most amazing street party, with all the old people leaning out of their windows clapping and shaking their fists in victory with the marchers responding. It was the happiest moment of my life: 'They make misery, we make history.' It felt like something major. An impromptu stage was set up and wonderful revolutionaries such as José Bove gave powerful speeches – even our very own utterly charming Terry Yeo, of 'Globalise Resistance', spoke. He was shaking like a leaf afterwards and humbled to have shared a stage with the likes of Bove.

After three hours of celebrating, an eerie silence descended over the masses. They'd lied to us: the G8 Summit was still going ahead. I'd had a funny feeling at the time, because putting myself in their shoes, when it was quite clear that 300,000 of us were going to pull the fences down, I thought about sending some stooges out into the crowd to say they'd given up.

Needless to say, riots broke out again. (We found out later that the police actually attacked the march.) You could smell the tear gas in the air, and the helicopters whirred menacingly. On the long way back we heard explosions and Jane and I fired up and angry, went to check it out. There were five cars overturned, burning and exploding, and the Black Bloc and other anarchists were fighting amongst themselves. As rocks then started raining over us and the riot police ran in firing tear gas, I felt it was time to leave – at least we found the goggles and vinegar/lemon juice mix to be effective.

I then hit the 'zone', whereby I no longer cared what happened to me and following a strong intuitive feeling found myself putting on my cassock and dog collar, slipping the loudhailer over the shoulder. I was going to fulfil my Genoa objective. Jane, who'd briefly wandered off, smiled broadly as she saw me cassocking up; then off we went, following some riot vans hurtling under a bridge.

We came out in the same square where the riot had occurred, and with the cars still blazing I went and stood in front of twenty or so riot vans. Here I boomed out, '*Buongiorno, Genoa! Sono piccolo agriculturo in Inghileterra in Devon,*' and delivered my prepared talk through the loudhailer about the human and animal rights abuse surrounding foot-and-mouth. After five minutes, two hundred or so riot police with shields, gas masks and guns appeared in a line on a street across the road. Behind them were fifty or so riot vans crammed with riot police. It couldn't have been stage managed better by the great man in the sky. Under Jane's direction I strode out into the middle of the riot-torn streets, turned my back to the police and continued my twenty-minute talk.

I went on about Monsanto's takeover of land and water in the Third World and how they were about to start fifty-eight new large GM trial plots in the UK; the horrendous sneakiness of the authorities in pretending the G8 was cancelled (I shook with anger at this point); and stressed the need for a spiritual awakening to accompany the revolution, otherwise we'd just end up down another blind alley of human weakness – ego, deceit, greed and so on. Many in the crowd were nodding their heads at this last point. The foreign photographers lapped up the scene of a mad English priest defying the riot police telling them how pathetic they and the authorities were. All the time I was prepared for a bullet in the back or barrage of cracks from their truncheons – Italians don't take kindly if they feel the mickey is being taken out of their religion! For this reason I kept leaning back in case the riot police saw I was wearing trainers. I finished with 'the poem' then walked purposefully off to … the pizzeria, where I lined up six Becks and let out a yell of delight! I felt I'd risked my life for the cause – and boy, was it empowering!

That night we left hearing that riot police had stormed the convergence centre and a school, unprovoked, and seriously beaten up hundreds of innocent people. On the train we heard that one of our 'comrades', Mark Harrison, had been set upon within an hour of arrival, whilst innocently labouring with his luggage. Riot police had beaten him senseless, put him into prison and made him stand for eight hours with a huge gash in his head until he passed out in his own blood and was carted off to hospital. The jokes were flying on the journey home, but our thoughts were with those hospitalised or gone missing over the past few days. I felt wholly accepted by the comrades – a real honour.

On getting home on Sunday night my mum gave me the biggest welcome I'd ever had. My sister and sister-in-law said the dead man looked like me. Both looked at the shoes – they were smart and they'd sighed with relief. Back to Tapeley on Monday night – shattered from so little sleep – and the bailiffs arrived first thing Tuesday morning.

I was up unusually early the night Dad got back. We met in the kitchen for breakfast around 7.30 a.m. Considering he'd barely slept for four nights, he looked better than I'd seen him looking for ages. His furrowed brow had smoothed out and he was calm and not angry, which made a nice change. This lasted all of half an hour then there was a knock on the window. Dad, guard down for the first time in ages, motioned the sturdy-looking visitor to go to the back door.

The bailiff said that if Dad didn't pay his fine he'd come in and take belongings to the equivalent value. He then moved as if to come in. Dad pushed him back, but the bailiff explained that now he'd put his foot over the threshold he legally could break in if Dad refused him entry. Dad slammed the door on him and exclaimed, 'Over my dead body!' No peace for the wicked, I thought. The furrowed brow was back and I was sent upstairs and told to keep away from the doors and windows. I was, by now, tired of living like this and just wanted to have some fun for the last bit of the summer hols.

Dad went straight to the phone, not to ring the solicitor but the local TV station. The bailiff had said he'd be back within fifteen minutes with a locksmith. When he returned with the locksmith and policemen he wasn't overly pleased to see he was on Candid Camera (I'd sneaked down to see what was happening). The bailiff said that because he'd put his foot over the threshold this gave him the right of entry. Dad, leaning out of his favourite window above the door, said he hadn't seen him do it, so it was his word against

Dad's. They quickly sussed that it wouldn't look good on the local news, breaking into a big house with children in it, and then having to fight to get whatever articles they could.

They then left saying that they'd be back within five days and have Dad locked up and me taken away and then put into care. The tension was back. Dad went ballistic if anyone left the door unlocked and unbolted; our car was hidden a mile away, and I was only allowed outside with what felt like a bodyguard. Roll on term time!

They might have said they'd be back within five days, however, as was par for the course, they never did what they said they would. This was no doubt because they knew the extra pressure this exerts. We couldn't plan anything knowing we could be carted off at any time of day or night. On day seven Dad packed me into the car and we did a runner to stay with some friends up country. Dad's mood was hardly helped in that he'd just had to pay DEFRA – the 'Department for the Eradication of Farm and Rural Assets' – £3,000 for the privilege of keeping his animals. DEFRA was simply by then the disbanded MAFF – same wolf, different clothing, or whatever the phrase is.

For nearly four months the bailiffs paid regular visits, increasing Dad's fine by £90 each time. Dad had felt for some time, like so many others, that his phone was being tapped. Mentioning words like MAFF seemed to trigger a background clicking noise. This was as good as confirmed to Dad because he frequently said on the phone that he had had to hide his car in the woods. Because the bailiffs couldn't get into the house, the car was the only thing outside they could take.

We were all hoping they might try to take a Highland cow or two. The cattle had all become so wild it was like farming buffalo. This was due to a rogue steer called Hugh Hugh, who had charged me and Dad around Christmas time when we were trying to move them. He caught Dad in the side twice before Dad leapt over a fence, but he missed me. I'd learnt in netball practice to drop a shoulder then go the other way; Dad was a footballer, unfortunately for him. Anyway, whenever the bailiffs came they combed the woods thoroughly, all bar a sneaky little spot they passed regularly but amazingly never checked. Definite divine intervention, Dad felt.

Each time a white Skoda van was seen coming up the drive it was action stations. The bailiffs seemed to get bigger and burlier each time, but by now we were used to being under siege. Mind you, what with Biff 'the Tank' and the odd feisty, young, aggressive yet intelligent protester who had become friends on farm gates, and since moved in, pound for pound there was no contest. One day, whilst I was playing with the peacocks, two bailiffs were seen having tea on our Tea Room lawn. They didn't need the Skoda to give them away. Biff came out with the boys and asked, very loudly, if they were bailiffs in front of other members of the public. They cowered and pretended, very unconvincingly, they weren't. Biff simply said that unwanted visitors up here could end up with six-inch nails through their tyres, and worse. They got up and left quietly.

By December the bailiffs had given up. Dad thought he'd got away with it, but during the early part of the following year it all caught up with him.

In the meantime as the slaughter men and carcass lorries were moving back up North, a nasty little sting in the tail was left behind. This was that all the movement restrictions were left in place, even when Devon was given a clean bill of health. The problem was that it was one set of rules rigidly applied across the board. This proved to be the final nail in the coffin for many smallholders, as we found out when we tried to sell some piglets.

Like so many other farmers our animals had been breeding – yet there was nowhere to move them. Overcrowding was a real problem; hence all those crazy pictures of a flock of sheep with their lambs packed into a muddy field, with a field bursting with untouched fresh green grass next door belonging to the same farmer. This in the light that it was proven that healthy animals with a strong immune system were far less susceptible to FMD than unhealthy animals. For this reason, there have always been far fewer organic livestock that have contracted the disease historically. In the same vein, many farmers were giving their animals homeopathic borax – illegally. The authorities claimed it disguised the disease, thereby admitting borax worked. It in effect reduced a type of 'flu' to no more than a common cold.

To move animals, you had to pay for a DEFRA vet to inspect the animals and give the all clear. Over and above this you had to have your transport vehicle disinfected on the way *and* after picking any animals up. DEFRA, in their wisdom, contracted this business out to private companies. They, having a monopoly, in turn charged a small fortune. Smallholders used to deal in ones and twos. I remember Dad saying that to move two weaners (ten-week-old piglets) worth £15 each was going to cost £210, taking into account veterinary costs and disinfection – plus the nearest depot for disinfecting was in South Molton, half an hour away.

Due to overcrowding we felt we had no choice but to have two batches of weaners put down. He wasn't the only one to lose animals as part of the so-called 'welfare consideration'. Smallholders were disappearing by the bucket load due to appalling legislation *and* the policy of supermarkets. Our next-door neighbour had a hundred fat lambs carted off and *incinerated* because the supermarkets refused to buy British. They preferred to continue buying on the global markets from New Zealand and so on. Our farmers were getting £10 in compensation for fat lambs, normally worth £30 to £40 each, which were getting burnt. Supermarkets were paying £30 for foreign lamb, presumably having settled in to their new markets. The Afghan war was about to start, and food aid was needed around much of the world – and here we were burning good meat. Hatherleigh abattoir, like so many others countrywide, killed 250,000 animals on welfare considerations. Hence, millions more animals were killed on the back of foot-and-mouth over and above the official ten million.

Dad saw red (again) and decided it was time once more to hit London. He was inspired by a practical joker who pulled off outrageous stunts and would get front page news. This he managed to do without offending or upsetting anybody. For example, he wandered out on to the pitch before an apparently important Manchester United game in Germany. He was dressed in the same kit as the players, who didn't seem at all happy when he managed to join in with their pre-match team photo. Dad felt it was a shame not to combine this with a powerful political message.

The Last Night of the Proms at the Albert Hall in London with a live audience of 5,000 and beamed live throughout the UK and across the world, was Dad's chosen target. The plans were meticulous. A plan of the backstage area was acquired and I had great fun joining in the shopping trip. We went to all manner of charity shops and bought a magnificent dinner suit with long tailcoat, huge brown shaggy wig (good contrast to Dad's thinning hair), loud glitzy white collared shirt, paint, a small stick and some corks. We also went to the local printer to get 5,000 sheets with the hymn 'Jerusalem' on them with the words slightly changed as shown below.

JERUSALEM

From the first verse of tonight's version, please sing with full gusto:

> 'And did those feet in ancient time
> Walk upon England's mountains green;
> But now the cows burn in the pyres,
> This is the mul-ti-nat(sh)ion-als' desire.
> without the dung from animals
> To grow our crops needs more chemicals;
> And were more supermarkets builded here
> On England's once green and pleasant land!'

Second line of next verse:

> 'Till we have RE-built Jerusalem...'

May God help us save the unnecessary, unlawful killing of healthy animals and rescue our small farmers and rural communities from EXTINCTION.

BUY LOCAL – BOYCOTT SUPERMARKETS

The plan was to circulate the sheets of Jerusalem to every prom goer as they arrived at the Albert Hall. By writing 'Jerusalem' and keeping the first two lines the same, it was felt the punters would gladly accept the sheet and that most would only read it fully whilst actually singing it. The fact that the conductor walked off stage between every piece of music for a little breather, and the extra applause, was perfect for the plan. This was when Dad planned to boldly stride out onto the conductor's podium, from another entrance, tap his stick and announce in a German accent, 'I'm afraid Mr X has had to leave on urgent business, so I, Frank Fürther his understudy, am filling in.' He then planned to remove his jacket revealing the red painted words: 'BUY LOCAL – BOYCOTT TESCO, SAFEWAY, SAINSBURY' – with the supermarket's names written in the style of their logo's; and proceed to see how far he got conducting 'Jerusalem'.

I think he lost quite a lot of sleep in the lead-up to this stunt, but I've never seen anybody so desperate to pull something off. The supermarkets were, after all, ruthlessly destroying so many people's livelihoods and indeed whole communities. Dad clearly felt people needed to look at the huge damage they were doing by shopping in these dreadful places.

The plan, sadly I think, was kicked firmly in to touch with the obliteration of the Twin Towers a few days before. Even Dad realised it would prove a huge damp squib if he pushed ahead with it. However, he decided to go up anyway, and with the help of some activist friends hand out the sheets. Everybody happily took them, as expected, though apparently a few suited corporate-looking types rather angrily returned them having read past the first two lines. Dad said the noise noticeably dropped a few decibels after the first two lines and most people were holding the sheet, the noise level rising again for the last verse. He also said he went into a cold sweat at the thought of standing up in front of all those people. One thing's for sure, if it hadn't been for September 11, he'd have definitely done it.

On getting back to Devon, Dad decided the only option left was to try to organise a full-scale farmers' revolution in the style of the French or the recent fuel protests: blockading motorways, ports and so on. However, before getting to this we heard that our then Prime Minister, the now infamous Tony Blair, was coming to Devon and then to Cornwall for his holidays.

'Dreadlock Dave', so-called because his dreadlocks reached down to his thighs, had become a good friend of ours. His daughter, Jasmine, had become a good friend of mine. We made cakes together, both loved all the animals to bits (even the ones we were going to eat), and played with the fairies in the woods. Dreadlock Dave happened to be one of the most respected spray can graffiti artists in the country. Dad and he set about designing, spraying and erecting the three billboards shown below. They had five days to do everything before Blair was due to go to Cornwall. Everything, as usual, had to be done in a hurry.

This billboard obviously refers to the mindless slaughter of ten million animals just to get the wretched export market back for a minority of farmers. Also, the fact that the export market was worth some £200 million p.a. and the cost of the FMD slaughter policy to the Government, and hence us the taxpayers, was in excess of £6 billion, suggested something else was afoot. Hence, the 'faceless multinationals' looking down, without expression, at the proceedings; transactions such as those of 1996, with forty-seven million tons of butter imported and forty-nine million tons exported, served only to line a corporate businessman's pocket – and further expand the hole in the ozone layer with the burning of the extra tax-free aviation fuel.

FACELESS MULTI-NATIONALS
THE LOVE OF MONEY IS THE ROOT OF ALL EVIL

It didn't help the mood that everybody knew about the abundance of incredibly efficient cheap 'o'-type vaccine at 50p a shot, available from Pirbright and Europe. The hypocrisy of Nestle and ASDA (Wal-Mart), who had the vaccination issue kicked out for good, had extremely sinister undertones in light of the facts. Firstly, vaccinated meat was, contrary to what they were implying with comments such as 'we want to safeguard our customers...' *totally* safe to eat. The vaccine was an inert protein designed simply to stimulate antibody production in the animal. Farmers in those days were forever shoving live vaccines in to their livestock such as Heptovac P and antibiotics which even with a withdrawal period would enter humans on eating such 'infected' meat. Secondly, supermarket meat counters were *all* bulging with meat from countries such as Argentina and South Africa, who were all regularly vaccinating against FMD. This was not given a mention at the time.

Such facts, and the fact that supermarkets only traded with big farmers, preferably on the other side of the world, and the rest, provided the foundation for the second billboard: BUY LOCAL, BOYCOTT SUPERMARKETS had by now become our catchphrase.

Last but not least was the billboard depicting the Corporate Robocop with a vicious-looking circular blade about to cut through the skull of one of Dad's Highland cows. The cow, with seemingly no chance against such opposition, is defiantly standing its ground, prepared to die if necessary. In the background there are many gravestones with crosses in reference to the seventy-odd farmers who'd committed suicide so far that year due to the actions of the Corporate Robocop. Hence, the rather dark, tragic message: 'Our Farmers who are in Devon (crossed out)... *Heaven*' for the third billboard.

I helped to whitewash the billboards and get them up on the side of the road Blair would have to pass on his way to Cornwall. Mind you, I think he'd been in power for so long he didn't really care about the feelings of the people he was governing any longer. This would have been much like one of his predecessors, Margaret Thatcher, had become after a while. Anyway this done it was off to organise the Big Protest.

★

Gloucester was the town selected for the event. This was because it was central. It was within two and a half hours of

Devon, Cumbria and Northumberland. There had also been a fair bit of foot-and-mouth around Gloucester, where the resistance had been successful on many occasions. Again, with the benefit of my dad's diaries I've tried to piece things together as best I can. This especially in the light Dad spent most of the two weeks leading up to the march at a friend's house nearby, where a helpful girl gave her time to email every group and individual, and the relevant media. He was also allowed to make endless phone calls to try to rally as many people as possible. He spent time with the Gloucester resistance group and getting clearance from the police; where people could park, and the route of the march.

The odd time he came home and I saw him, he and the crew were putting banners together and making up new chants. The chants even to me seemed like they'd be a little too radical for farmers – things like 'One-two-three-four, Margaret Beckett is a whore, five-six-seven-eight, this is now a Corporate State!' Maybe it was the Genoa influence, who knows. Dad's banner read: 'WTO – The World Terrorist Organisation. Buy Local; Boycott supermarkets'. This was a message he was to use at other marches, such as at May Day the next year.

He had a special axe to grind with regard to the World Trade Organisation (WTO). He blamed their policies for the fact he had to have his piglets killed – the only time in the whole proceedings he said he actually felt suicidal. A few years earlier, the WTO had revoked the Rome Agreement with something called 'Article 44'. The Rome Agreement allowed countries to shut their borders to imports on welfare considerations, and make supermarkets and butchers buy locally. It was all done under the banner of so-called supposed free trade, and resulted in millions more animals being mindlessly slaughtered, as imported livestock continued to flood in through our ports. The hypocrisy was further heightened in that Western countries imposed tariffs of up to four times the value on Third World produce, and in turn dumped their heavily subsidised surpluses back on them. This destroyed most small farm businesses in the Third World, where the WTO ensured such countries imposed no such tariffs on Western goods. The effect such policies, plus debt and patenting laws, had on Ishmael's and Neela's family defies belief when we look back on them today.

Dad certainly seemed to be on a bit of a suicide mission when he left. I think he'd made his mind up if he didn't get a groundswell of support to get the tractors to blockade the motorways and more importantly the ports, he was going to chuck in the towel. His diary at the time again says it better than I can.

A carload of us set off to stay with Sheila and her husband Burt near Gloucester the night before the march. There had been an accident on the motorway and we were caught up in a thirty-mile tailback turning a two hour journey into five. It became known as the 'Zen Traffic Jam' because we honed our chants and plans. The longer we spent in the jam the more extreme our plans became. We decided to go into the dreaded Asda after the march. Midge was going to dress up as 'Edward Bottle-hands', paint his face white, dye his hair black with shoe polish and spike it up and have ten empty beer bottles on his fingers and thumbs. We then planned to sing 'Ten green bottles sitting on his digits... And if one green bottle should fall on Asda's floor, there'd be nine green bottles, sitting on his digits, etc.' ... and drop a bottle. We then planned to fill up trolleys and leave them (slightly unoriginal, but bear in mind the likes of Asda were destroying our lives) ...oh, and burn the American flag which had 'WTO, World Bank, IMF, Monsanto SCUM' written on it. This three weeks after September 11.

On getting to Sheila's we tucked into her generous supply of alcohol. We thought Sheila and Burt looked a little stunned when we told them of our plans. Bear in mind we had been on this solidly for eight months, and probably quite naturally were becoming a little nutty. We all turned in ridiculously late and utterly plastered.

We rose early the next morning. Lack of sleep was no longer a problem. We were used to it. On arriving at the Park we found Biff and the others lying on the ground beside the Battle Bus, 'CULL MAFF' still emblazoned all over it. This sight made us feel all was well with the world. We found the perfect spot to set up – a bandstand on the edge of the park where a group of ten local youngsters were getting drunk on scrumpy. Folk gradually arrived as we were setting our banners up, including the Oxford contingent who brought along pantomime-style cow, pig and sheep costumes. The Devon boys nigh on fought to get into the costumes whilst Biff was practising on his stilts.

The mood was set when half a dozen policemen approached us. Dale, a seventeen-year-old staying with us now dressed as a cow, walked towards them, hands behind his back. On getting to within twenty yards or so he pulled his hands round, crouched and aimed a toy gun at the police, then made as if to shoot. The police instinctively leapt to the side. They were furious, and it took all my powers of appeasement not to have the gathering cancelled there and then.

There ended up being a disappointing one hundred and fifty people. Part of the reason for this was because the local radio station had put out the wrong time and place for the meeting. We found out afterwards there were lots of people walking through the town centre carrying banners. However, the main reason was the same old British problem: apathy. Many who said they'd come didn't bother.

We did, as ever, have some excellent speakers and even a band – Seize the Day – who had our sort of songs. One was about the 'Joys of Monsanto' as they gave more and more adults and children cancer with their GM crops. Proceedings meant that Seize the Day never got a chance to play.

The first speaker was a Green Party representative. The Green Party were the only party to actively stick their necks out in support of the farmers and were very pro-vaccination. The second was the wonderful Sheila who spoke passionately about the flip side of our own NFU, the fact they have shares with Tesco and Sainsbury's and the biotech industry (GM). She was saying how a new Farmers' Union would soon be set up and how important it was for all of us to support it, and not continue to be suckered by cheap insurance for NFU members.

I delivered my rant in cassock and dog collar. I spoke about FMD and called for all of us to block the ports. I also spoke of the evils of supermarkets and Monsanto. At this moment, Dale was soaking the US flag in lighter fuel. I then leapt off the bandstand and, making it quite clear this was nothing to do with the innocent people who'd been killed three weeks earlier, tried to set light to the flag. Many of the farmers were shouting abuse at me and telling me not to do it. Some were afraid that the press had their names, which would be passed to the police and they'd be bracketed as terrorists. The problem was the flint had gone on my lighter, so Dale got his out. However, the flint worked on his lighter but there was no gas in it, so we tried, unsuccessfully, to use the flint of Dales lighter to light the gas in mine. It really had been a late night.

The mood by now was very antagonistic towards us, and we were physically stopped from trying to set light to the flag. Spiritually, I knew that when things didn't work as planned, there was a good reason, so I wasn't too bothered. There then ensued a debate as to whether we should or shouldn't burn the flag. When we took a vote, the only ones for it were the wee band of us from North Devon.

The police then arrived en masse. They told me they had undercover police in the crowd who'd informed them I was talking about aggression and revolution. They said that Asda was heavily protected and we weren't welcome there and that the march was not to go ahead. I eventually persuaded them to let us march, promising to take full responsibility. However, when we set off, the march comprised the North Devon brigade and the ten local youngsters, who were by now absolutely plastered. The other farmers looked on despondent, some furious.

Those of us who'd studied the spiritual path knew that if we met with a brick wall with our plan it was best to let go. God, Spirit, whatever, clearly had a different path for us to go on. One spiritual law is that so long as you do your best at whatever you do you can't do any more. We felt we had and had achieved as much as we could on that particular path. Anger was another useful spiritual tool used correctly. It needed to be focused, controlled and purposeful. Channelled correctly we knew you could move mountains. Mindless and uncontrolled, and you'd always do more harm than good. I must admit I didn't feel comfortable with dropping bottles on Asda's floor, so I was thankful to the police's 'Spiritual Intervention'. Asda was obviously doing terrible things but had we carried out our plan we would have undone any words of wisdom and certainly done more harm than good to our cause. The same could possibly be said about burning the US flag. Dodgy lighters plus a noticeable increase in the wind at that moment says it all.

Anyway, I then went back, leapt on to the bandstand and boomed out through my loudhailer, 'As far as I am concerned Monsanto can have all of your land and cover it with GM crops. American conglomerates are already buying up large tracts of land round Dumfries. This is me, Hector, signing off.'

I leapt off the bandstand to jeers and boos, the happiest I'd been for eight months, and adjourned to the Battle Bus for a celebratory cup of tea with Biff and the boys.

Plan B, to create an organic oasis on our patch, beginning with a few months of wheelbarrowing ten large trailer loads of well rotted five-year-old dung into our Permaculture Garden, was well and truly in place.

Part Two

CHAPTER III: THE ELEVENTH HOUR

Following a very pleasant three months or so, Dad went on holiday to France for the New Year of 2002. Here he had another dream to see the year in.

I woke at 4 a.m. following one of those once a year rather pokey dreams that doesn't let you go back to sleep lest you forget. I was standing by some railings on the side of the road watching a small march approaching. It struck me as being rather dull and listless, to the extent there was no belief they would get their demands even listened to let alone acted upon. I, incensed, leapt onto the railings and boomed at them, via my loudhailer which happened to be with me, to have some conviction and determination. I said they must get out and do weekly protests if they were to make a change. We were then in our dining room where there was a cordon of riot police blocking us from getting to the kitchen. I led the crowd and we broke through. I woke up and the word 'TESCO' hit me across the head like a thunderbolt.

The adrenalin was pumping like it hadn't for three months and the fight was back. I'd had my rest. Tesco were sniffing around a site in our local town of Bideford. There was already a Safeway, and those of us, with our eyes even just slightly open, knew a Tesco would create yet another ex-market ghost town. This has happened at Langport (Somerset), Leatherhead (Surrey), Brecon (Wales), Stalham and many hundreds more. Local business simply cannot survive in the face of utterly ruthless big business. If Tesco won at Bideford, they had plans for ones at Braunton, Ilfracombe, South Molton and Holsworthy. This would in effect give them total control over the food chain in North Devon, destroying the last of the small farmers supplying small shops in the process.

I knew of all of this, and the rest, and had managed to suppress it for the past few months, knowing how angry it makes me. Last night, following the dream, I realised that none of us can quietly hide ourselves away even in the remotest parts of the world. The ever increasing environmental destruction, due to our highly polluting lifestyle in the West especially, means that our whole world is becoming increasingly unstable. The attitude of American politicians and big business in refusing to work on reducing carbon dioxide emissions as laid down by the Kyoto Protocol, sums us up. Closer to home, the threat of genetically modified (GM) crops coming in is increasing all the time. If we don't actively fight them, and GM crops are grown around us, then we will no longer be able to live a wholesome, independent organic lifestyle. This is because the GM gene is so dominant, it will cross-pollinate with native species and seeds such as ours, and contaminate them irreversibly.

With these thoughts buzzing around in my head and that knotted sensation back in the pit of my stomach, the headlines of the daily International Herald Tribune *the next day simply reinforced these feelings. They read: 'The world needs corporate driven globalisation.' Next to it there was a picture of a grinning Dwim Wuisenberg, head of the European Central Bank (ECB). The article was about the introduction of the Euro, stating proudly that the ECB had 'now become a serious global bank'. The ECB was run by a small group of undemocratically elected people, answerable to no one. They quite literally operated behind two-foot-thick steel doors making key monetary decisions, such as on interest rates and tax – dangerous. To cap it off another headline ran: 'In WTO… Taiwan joins'.*

A paragraph at the end spelt out the small print. It said that Taiwan would no longer be allowed to impose tariffs on imported goods, and international companies would be safeguarded and operated under WTO rules, not the Taiwanese Government's. Cheap subsidised goods would therefore be dumped onto Taiwan, destroying local agriculture. Also, independent local businesses would be swept up under the cosy umbrella of big business. There is no difference between this and being occupied after losing a war.

When Dad came home we set about getting banners together

for our weekly protests. Dale's one saying 'DETESCO' was my favourite. Each Saturday morning we'd trek out with loudhailer, banners and information sheets, which Dad would change each week depending upon location.

The first one was in the relatively cosy option of Bideford High Street – the site of one of Dad's finest hours (his first arrest). This was about informing and winning support from local shopkeepers and local shoppers. The next week we went to Safeway in Bideford, and after that the Tesco in Barnstaple.

It was great fun. We turned up, leapt out of the car and placed our banners round the entrance door to the supermarkets. Dad then gave his usual rant on the loudhailer whilst we all handed out the appropriate information sheets. Dad had done price checks for both places to show people how much cheaper (and fresher) meat and veg were in local shops. I was thrilled to see two of my teachers outside Tesco and gave them a sheet each.

We knew we were being quite controversial, but took immense trouble to smile nicely as we handed out sheets to the shoppers. Dad was adamant concerning the spiritual law of non-judgement (condemnation) and not just because it meant people would be more likely to read the sheet. It was, in those days, becoming harder all the time for people not to shop at supermarkets, with some supermarkets being open all night and most small shops simply doing the usual opening from 8 a.m. to 5 p.m. Put this with the debt-ridden masses working ever longer hours to keep their heads above water, and the reasons are obvious. It's very sinister to think of these days being like this, but it's come out that this oppression and hardship was deliberately inflicted on the masses. This reliance and dependency on big companies made people less independent and more easy to control. A world of mind-numbed robots, controlled by fear, working without question for the system was the objective. Thank God for the Collapse.

In both Safeway and Tesco, security people came and asked us to move. Dad flatly told them no. Both times they returned with a lot more security, and out came our video camera held by the nimble Dale. The idea here was to entice confrontation, from which a debate as to our reasons for being there would ensue. The big guns liked to operate in the shadows, portraying their monster as the 'Family Store'. They would do anything to avoid the light being shone upon them. A little knowledge and their lies and spin would be easily exposed as shown by Dad's 'The Truth about supermarkets' section on Tesco shown below. True to form, security, no doubt from orders from on high, would slink back into the shadows. They knew we couldn't stand outside the wretched places for days on end – and how much would it have achieved with so many people too terrified to open their eyes?

Support wasn't exactly flooding in, so Dad decided, in effect, to carpet-bomb Bideford and the surrounding towns and villages with his 'Truth about supermarkets' sheets. This was in an attempt to educate local people as to the power they had with regard to where they spent their money and the damage they were doing by shopping in supermarkets. A favourite line of ours was that the supermarkets estimated that each person spends an average of £70,000 in their stores in one lifetime. Start removing a few £70,000 lump sums and it would hurt.

The Truth About Supermarkets

Please take the trouble to read this and if you feel it warrants it, photocopy as many as you can and circulate to help save our local culture.

If a new supermarket is built anywhere around Bideford this will result in the following:

JOB LOSSES

A recent article in a newspaper, clearly a rosy Tesco press release, stated that the new Tesco would create two hundred and seventy new jobs. It never mentioned the fact that on average two hundred and seventy-six jobs are lost locally for each supermarket built inclusive of the jobs it creates. Or for one job created two are lost. This information comes from the supermarkets own research team – the National Retail Planning Forum.

THE MAIN LOSERS

The big losers are the small independent shopkeepers in the High Street and their local distributors, and the local small farmers who supply them. Many shopkeepers are just surviving, but with a new Tesco, along with Safeway, this will be the last straw. The heart of Bideford, like so many others countrywide, will become a ghost town – even more of a shame, since it really seems to be taking off with new cafes and the ceramics centre. Also money spent in supermarkets *leaves* the area rather than staying in the community: what you spend with a fruit and veg shopkeeper will circulate locally because he might then buy a few pints, the pub landlord then may use it to get local sausages and eggs, and so on.

QUALITY OF WORK/JOB SATISFACTION

Having lost their jobs, the proud independent shopkeepers and small farmers could, should they want work, soon be working on mind-numbing, spirit-crushing, bar-coded

check-out tills for some faceless multi-national boss...
'Would you like to use the points on yer savers card, sir?'

SUPERMARKETS ARE CHEAPER?

On 21/01/02 I did a price comparison with Safeway to
Patt's and Kellard's greengrocers, and GF Honey and Sons
Butchers – bear in mind this is not a good time of year for
local producers.

Safeway's Royal Gala apples, Maris Piper potatoes (at fifty
per cent off), and parsnips are 63p/lb, 35p/kg and 78.4p/lb
respectively. Kellard's for the same are 39p/lb, 31p/kg (no
discount), and 39p/lb. Safeway's South American bananas
and cucumbers are 53.9p/lb and £1.19 each respectively;
Patt's for the same are 39p/lb (plus fair trade) and 89p each.

Likewise, Safeway's unsmoked back bacon and streaky are
£8.58 and £7.16/kg respectively. Honey's is £5.90 and
£3.40/kg respectively – even Safeway saver for streaky is
£5.23/kg. For lamb chops the price is double at Safeway's
and all sausages are cheaper at Honey's. If we take that
extra half-hour to shop locally it will make all the
difference. Everything and more is available in Bideford –
for now!

THE TESCO WEBSITE

Tesco's comments are in quotes. Here are some examples:

(1) Q. Are supermarkets making excessive profits at the
expense of farmers?

A. 'No, in fact on most fresh meat and dairy lines we barely
cover our costs.' We all know that some products are used
by clever marketers as 'loss leaders' to lure the customer,
stamps selling at 1p less than cost (crucifying Post Offices)
is just one example.

A DOE (Department of the Environment) Government
report has stated that Tesco is the most guilty of all
supermarkets for accelerating profits at the expense of
farmers and producers.

Supermarket regulations demand uniform products. Any farmer stepping outside these tight bands is crucified, e.g. a local farmer recently sold a fat lamb of 25kg (slightly big) for a mere £16, the price on supermarket shelves is at least £160; a mark-up of 1,000%. We don't have a transparency clause in this country, as there is in much of Europe and the Monopolies Commission leaves the supermarkets well alone.

Once you could sell an odd-shaped carrot with a bit of mud on it; now supermarkets demand regulated sizes and shapes, resulting in huge wastage. (One third of Kenyan green beans are thrown away, rather than being given to the local poor and starving, because they are the wrong size or shape.) So now, to be a successful farmer you need high mechanisation, few workers, monoculture, high chemical input and, most importantly, a contract to distribute bulk produce around the country for processing and packaging. The Tesco website question 4 even has the audacity to ask the question, 'Do supermarkets have too much power over farmers and suppliers?' They then answer, 'No'!

Q. Do supermarkets sell cheap lower quality food from abroad?

A. 'No. Customer safety is our priority and we ensure the standard of food safety, quality and welfare are the same regardless of where the food is produced.'

For a start, it is often not cheaper (see above). The average vegetable travels six hundred miles from the farm gate to the supermarket trolley. Crude oil – for the road miles, pesticides and packaging makes up an obscene forty per cent of the UK's domestic waste. Professor Tim Lang, of the Centre for Food Policy at the Thames Valley University says that 'plant breeders have been trying to develop tomatoes, carrots and fruit that look nice, resist disease and can withstand being shipped halfway round the world.' Like many other nutritionists, he cites the resulting lack of minerals as a major cause of coronary heart disease and cancer. Nutritionist David Thomas states that 'artificial fertilisers encourage growth at the expense of minerals'.

Towards the end of the 2001 growing season, the Somerset apple growers had not managed to sell one apple to the supermarkets. Instead the supermarkets persisted in importing for example chemical ridden, flavourless Braeburns from New Zealand. To move five tons takes I huge tanker full of kerosene... ozone friendly? I don't think so. And the Tesco website has the audacity to speak of 'commitment to the environment'.

THE BIGGER PICTURE

The movement towards large, soulless, monoculture farms often corporate-owned, multinational distributors, processors, package plants and supermarket chains is growing exponentially. Food is becoming a monopoly to big business. The common denominator: *huge profit* (for them and their shareholders) is their *sole motivation*. It's time to stop being deceived by their clever political-style spin and rhetoric, and open our eyes before it's too late and all small business connected with our food, from growing it to selling it, are history. Supermarkets destroy our soil, our society and soul. They work closely with world governments – Blair's idea of developing the countryside is to develop supermarkets.

All legislation is designed to destroy the small and help the big. There is no tax on aviation fuel, hence the globalised movement of food is encouraged – diseases like FMD being another by-product, besides pollution, appalling animal welfare, human health problems and mass unnecessary starvation in the Third World. By 2035, the Arctic ice caps could have all been melted away, on current course. What sort of world will our children grow up in?

BUY LOCAL – BOYCOTT SUPERMARKETS

It's never too late to write about your grievances and fears; it's also important. Please write to me and I will pass them all on to Mr Holland, the Independent Inspector, where they will be heard at the Public Enquiry March 15–19.

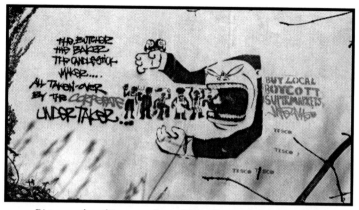

Pictures such as this appeared overnight on the spanking whitewashed walls of Marsh Farmhouse – purchased by Tesco for destruction, being that it was built on their chosen sight. The general consensus was that the greater the variety of actions, the more effective the protest.

He had 15,000 of these sheets printed and I was roped out after school and at weekends to post them through letterboxes. Cleaning chimneys, as done by Victorian children of my age, began to feel like a rosy option. It was one thing walking up steep paths to get to one terraced house, but quite another when the postman-hating dog lurked waiting and alert the other side of the door. We found where folk had put 'Beware of the Dog' signs up, the chances were it was a big loving Labrador, that at worst would try to lick your hand and nearly always barked first.

The potentially most lethal were those houses with the spring-loaded steel flaps under which were heavy duty brushes. To get the sheet inside these you had to literally stuff them through. It was here we'd sometimes encounter the silent terrier, who had learnt that through stealth, silence and unrelenting patience, success was virtually inevitable. We would picture such dogs lying all day by the door, ears pricked, listening for footsteps coming up the garden path. They probably didn't bother with the postman in the early mornings; letters and general post were more solid and could be slotted home without revealing any soft succulent flesh. With the loose, floppy A4 fliers there was no choice but to push it through with your hand. If you were lucky you might hear the patter of feet and get your hand out before the inevitable thud into the letterbox, followed by the noise of your piece of paper being shredded by razor sharp teeth. The true 'stealth bombers' leapt from a sitting position. By the time we'd distributed 13,000 sheets, Dale's and Dad's hands were pitted with tooth marks and covered with plasters.

Dad went to speak at the Public Inquiry against the Bideford Tesco and came back very upset when the so-called Independent Inspector brushed aside environmental damage and destruction of communities as an irrelevance. He said the Inspector and the Council were only interested in the effects on housing, flooding potential and traffic congestion. Dad later found out from his local MP that local planners and even MPs themselves had virtually no power in deciding whether a superstore was built or not in a chosen location. The Independent Inspectorate would simply award planning permission provided the three aforementioned criteria were satisfied. As with the ECB and so many other bodies somehow miraculously materialising at this time, they were answerable to nobody. The one common denominator was they favoured big corporations above independent small businesses the world over.

★

Around this time, Dad had an unexpected holiday – the first of a few of its kind. Again, his diary tells the story:

Date: 07/03/02 PRISON: Well, who'd've thought it! Me mum'll be soo proud. The warrant arrest officer, a charming man called Tommy Collins, issued the warrant while I was up in Glastonbury. I was shocked and stunned at the time, being that it's nearly a year since committing my traffic offence and I had not heard anything for months. Whilst the bailiffs were coming up over a four-month period last year, the fine had rocketed up to nearly £1,000. However, the fine they were asking for now was back to the bare minimum original of £120. They were bending over to help me.

I quickly resolved to dig in and got press releases out stating that I'd have happily paid the fine if they'd opened a full inquiry, said they'd vaccinate during the next outbreak and officially banned pyres as was categorically recommended after the '67 outbreak. We don't get a chance to debate things as people; there is no democracy at all, and the only way to get heard is to break the law. My way is by peaceful, harmless protest and making a sacrifice: so far this has got me a massive fine, the mindless destruction of eleven piglets, and now imprisonment. But I believe this is preparing me for what is to come.

I got back from Glastonbury yesterday, hid my car and contacted newspapers and TV. The hardest part was making arrangements for my daughter. Mum was understandably concerned but respected that I was standing up for my convictions. Slept better last night accepting the consequences.

At 7.55 a.m. today the arrest officer was outside my back door- Carlton TV weren't due until 9.30 a.m., so I hid and didn't answer the phone, which was ringing incessantly. At 9.30 they filmed me on the phone to Tommy. It looked like it was going to be a damp squib since the arrest officer said the chances were the judge would suspend sentence, get the bailiffs involved again – back to square one.

Off to court where many of those at work asked, tongue in cheek, 'Where's your gas mask?' Having taken my oath, the judge warned me if I refused to pay the fine I'd probably go to prison. My heart excitedly missed a beat but I think I managed to disguise it and said my blurb and that I respected whatever decision they felt obliged to make. They tried exploring all other avenues that hadn't worked before, such as bailiffs, direct debit from a wage bill and so on, and then very reluctantly sentenced me to seven days' imprisonment. I really couldn't believe my luck – I had my overnight bag and book (G Monbiot's Captive State*). I had done the same at least four times last year when a prison sentence looked far more likely.*

The most magical moment came when two burly prison warders came in and handcuffed me to one of them then escorted me past reception into the bowels of the building. The cell I'm now in is definitely a notch down from the luxury I encountered last year where my cells had plastic mattresses and a toilet. This one's simply got a hard bench and no window – but it's still heaven!

All the warders seem to know me; the magistrate said they'd never sent anyone to prison so politely before – a very nice compliment. They also said I did well to keep the bailiffs out for so long and if they had've got in they'd have cleared as much as they could. Also they would, for example, have taken the TV down to a shop and got, say, £500 for it and only declared £40, the rest going into their pockets. Tommy, an ex-copper, said how much he hated bailiffs.

I think they're all amazed how happy I am to be here. I do find the running of Tapeley very draining at times – a great challenge. This is because everyone lumps their problems and concerns onto me, Biff and Alf being the exceptions. It's part of the package but so nice to be away – anywhere. My piles, which reflect how wound up I feel, were hurting a lot this morning, but have now all but vanished.

After three hours or so sitting on a hard bench in the semi-darkness, I must admit I was getting a little bored. Then there was the rattle of keys and in came the police warden. 'C'mon, you hardened criminal!' he said, and on went the handcuffs for the short walk to the Black Maria. The handcuffs were removed when I was sitting (relatively) comfortably in what can only be described as a very tall slim fridge, where my knees were pressed tight against the opposite wall.

I was quite relieved to start with that we had our own individual fridges. There were two other guys on their way to Exeter Prison with me. *They sounded like the wildest, most totally uncontrollable crazy nutters I'd ever come across in my life! It wasn't the swearing, but the way they swore, that, I admit, shocked me. At the same time they were incredibly funny, most of their jokes being directed at the bus driver: 'Ah, Johnny, d'ya see that!' 'Yeah, could'a f—n killed a kid!' 'Nah, 'e's three yards over the line, never saw the red light, could'a killed a whole f—n family, c—!'*

It soon became clear they were joyriders. They were howling with laughter as we passed the insurance building still boarded up a month after they'd driven a car through the display window.

They told me the story whilst in the waiting (holding) room at Exeter Prison. They were a couple of very tall, lanky twins called Johnny and Gav, and they'd been joyriding since they were twelve. Gav said they were getting a bit old for it now, so they just did the odd one here and there to 'keep their hand in', but when it came to a buzz they said there was nothing quite like it. Their eyes lit up as they told me stories about flying over motorway embankments into fields at a hundred mph whilst being chased by the police…

Their latest venture happened whilst walking through Ilfracombe. A spanking red Montego caught Johnny's eye, and he suggested taking it for a spin. Gav answered indignantly 'Eh? Montego? Might as well nick a f—n' Robin Reliant!' They were pleasantly surprised as to how fast it went and notched up a hundred and twenty mph down the Braunton to Barnstaple dual carriageway. However, on reaching the town they hit the traffic lights (and the by then single lane) at the same speed. They had a police car on their tail. Slightly unfamiliar with the area and pumping with adrenalin, they'd forgotten the road ended with a mini-roundabout and T-junction. They saw it late, jammed on the brakes and hit the roundabout at a mere ninety mph – and were immediately airborne heading for a glass fronted shop window! Johnny, crying with laughter at the memory, said Gav just had enough time before impact to say chirpily, ''Ere we go!' The next thing they knew were computer and PVC shrapnel flying all around their eyes, ears and bodies. Then… silence.

The police took three hours of digging to get to them, convinced they would find two dead bodies. "Bout f—n' time!' was the first thing Johnny said to the police.

Gav had a grazed cheek and bruised rib, Johnny a slightly sore knee. Karma's a funny old thing! They said they'd never hurt anybody and would be devastated if they did, which is why they had an 'after midnight only' rule. I asked how long their sentence was and they told me eighteen months. I rather stupidly said what a long time that was. Gav, huge grin on his face, piped up, 'You must be joking, we did thirty grand's worth o' damage!'

We were then separated, strip searched, photographed, (I managed a broad smile), and put into prison uniform – woolly pyjamas – before being handcuffed and marched off to our respective wings. I was escorted across the yard next to another nice-looking inmate. I, out of politeness, asked if he was in for long. He said, 'Yes.' I asked him how long. 'Life.' I exclaimed, 'Goodness!' and asked him what he was in for. 'Murder.' Blimey – they were putting me on the lifers' wing!

The prisoners weighed me up as I was escorted along the iron mesh floored corridor. I was nervous for the first time. The prison was so overcrowded and it seemed disorganised to the extent they couldn't find a cell for me. The warden was literally knocking on people's closed doors and asking if they had a spare bed. Ninth time 'lucky'. He opened up a cell door and there was the most terrifying bloke I'd ever set eyes on. He was sitting on a chair, reading. He looked identical to Robert de Niro in Taxi Driver, *with a thick Mohican down the centre of his head. I said, 'Hello,' and he looked up, eyes nearly popping out of his head, veins suddenly protruding from his neck and said 'Hrhunggh!' I turned to flee and found the door slammed and locked.*

It's now about 8 p.m. and I'm banged up. Prison is quite hard core. Toby, whose cell I'm in, says it's the shittiest prison in the country [Exeter]. Inmates are locked up in cells for nigh on twenty-two hours a day – one hour exercise in a small yard, and half an hour at mealtimes when you queue at the top of the stairs before being let down to get your slop, which you then take back to your cell, where you're locked in to eat it on your bed or standing up. It's the only prison without TV, just dirty cream glossed walls. So much for my dream of becoming C-wing ping-pong champion. The comedy prison series Porridge *seems more like* Fantasy Island.

This cell's doing my head in. I don't know if they put something in the food or if it's claustrophobia, but I feel very, very weird. You can't even see out of the hatch and into the corridor. Toby says there's a blonde and a brunette who walk down the corridor wiggling their bottoms. Their job is to help detox addicts. If anyone even chats them up they're taken to 'The Bloc'. I asked what that was and he said that's where you get a severe kicking from the screws. He said in 1993 no one left the Bloc who was not in a cast – broken leg, ribs, arm, whatever. He said people still have their legs broken, but only people inside know about it. He says he hates the screws – most are ex-squaddies who see people like… us, as scum.

Toby, my Robert de Niro lookalike cell mate has, thank God, turned out to be a top man. I can hear fights in some of the other cells. Alarms are being pressed by inmates in trouble and the screws are taking an age to arrive. I shuddered at the idea of being banged up with a lifer who took a dislike to me with nothing to lose. With two to a tiny cell containing two bunk beds, a sink and a bog in the corner, there would be no escape. At least if there were three or four to a cell the other guys might help; but just two is a potential death trap.

Toby said he was brought up by his drug-dealing dad in Brixton and spent most of his childhood in youth custody. He was addicted to strong drugs aged nine. However, by the time he was twenty he decided to turn a new leaf and emigrated to Redruth in Cornwall. The drugs had made him psychotic and he was on very strong, dangerous benzodiazepines and the rest to keep him calm. One night, having run out of benzos, he went to the pub and had two pints of lager. Next thing he knew was when he woke up chained up in a cell.

The police said he was arrested for firing a barrage of bullets from a twelve bore shotgun above the Redruth police station. As they approached he laid down the gun, knelt on the ground, hands behind his back and head bowed in submission. He keeps saying how he wished he could remember what he'd done so that he could deal with things and sort his head out. I wholeheartedly believe him. He has been in prison for an incredible eight months on remand awaiting trial. Before this latest incident he'd not been in prison for seven years.

Toby and I have spent the last few hours lying on our respective bunk beds getting to know each other. I think he's enjoying having me to stay. I noticed almost all the other cells I passed were real tips, junk everywhere. However, Toby's was clean and immaculate, with clothes and towels folded neatly. I told him I felt like a stranger off the street who had just barged into his home. He sweetly apologised that the fridge was broken so he couldn't offer me a beer. We then spent a couple of hours talking about the scantily clad (nudes were not allowed) women from glossy magazines on the wall. Sex was not mentioned once, just a breakdown of their personalities based on their body language and eyes especially. We both agreed about the one we could fall in love with. It was the one who was not obviously sexy, but with soft, slightly vulnerable big brown eyes. I'm really spinning out, it must be the food…

★

Next morning – …same feeling as after I broke my leg – a rather beautiful, peaceful void. To see light coming through the small window is a joy. The pigeons keep visiting, wanting breakfast. Toby has his own regulars, which he's named; most of the long-termers are the same. The first thing that struck me when I arrived was the number of pigeons everywhere. You're not allowed to feed them 'cos they bring in lice, apparently.

The night was quite haunting with people swearing abuse through the tiny windows at each other like wild dogs cooped up in tiny cages. There were prisoners arranging to meet at certain places to fight to the death. Others swearing they'd go around to so-and-so's family if and when they got out and systematically put a gun to each one's head, describing, with all the details, what would happen to their brains and skulls when they pulled the trigger. When the anger *reached certain levels the banging of fists on the windows was almost deafening. Much of it was directed at the paedophiles in B-wing, who in turn were describing in disgusting graphic detail what they'd do to other inmates' young children on being released. Toby and the others all have one thing in common: they loathe the scum in B-wing, the nonces, not just 'cos of their deeds but they're the only ones in the prison who have TV, PlayStations and regular trips to town. Some of the paedophiles are, of course, men of the cloth – and judges! After this quietened down there was Toby's earth-shattering snoring from the top bunk – hardly surprising, with all the pills he's given for his extreme psychosis.*

Just had breakfast and I feel all weird again; listless, tired, ridiculously calm, concentration span of a gnat, no sharpness at all. I mentioned this to Toby and he said it's the bromide they put in your food, which suppresses any sexual urges as well – true, no thought in this direction. This has really fired me up; it must be against the law. I'm gonna make a big noise about this when I get out and go on hunger strike when I come back in. I'm completely brain-dead, poisoning must be a breach of f— human rights. I feel the anger deep inside.

Lunch – fish and chips. I didn't have the milky parsley sauce. I'm told the bromide's most prevalent in milk and potatoes, plus their sauces. Definitely feel less effects – but what do they soak the chips in, and why are they so hard? (They're bloody horrible, even by my broad standards, and I can't even drink the tea; it truly is the sweepings off the floor.)

Went to the CMA, whatever that stands for, and they asked if I had any questions to ask them and to believe nothing the inmates said. I asked them about the bromide in the food. The said they don't do that: 'It's illegal.' I asked why I felt so weird after eating. They said it's because the prison's full of cannabis and my passive inhaling of this is the reason I feel funny.(It's amazing how these guys take us all for complete idiots – I haven't smelt one joint, yet I'm on C-wing which is the so-called 'smack wing'.) I had been told I'd be out today because they can't release on a weekend. However, after I'd opened my big mouth, they promptly extended my release date by three days to Monday. I admit this was hard to take; it's not a holiday camp here at all, almost twenty-two hours banged up. It would be OK with a clear head, but with bromide or whatever it is in the system, it's bloody horrid.

I asked Toby what'd happen if I went on hunger strike, he said I'd be put in 'The Bloc' – twenty-four-hour solitary, no rights, no clothes, one sheet, freezing cold, no natural light, if you want a ciggy it's at the discretion of the screw, plus you have to leave your baccy outside. There's also a danger of a severe beating up. How far should I push it? I'm not eating that poison, and it is poison.

There was a fight in the exercise yard – handbags – and the guys nearly had their arms broken by the warders, apparently to discourage them from trying it again. I've also heard that if someone's due for a kicking, such as a paedophile, everyone leaves their cells with towels on their heads and the screws just stand by. Toby says that it is one of the worst prisons in the country because it's got a mixture of all sorts: remands, lifers, paedophiles/rapists and some short-termers like me, so nothing has a chance to settle. In such close quarters you can see how people become easily destabilised and flip. The mind games with me are taking a hold. I had been planning what I'd be doing tomorrow – football etc., only to find out I'll be locked up for maybe at least three more days and nights. They do try to break your spirit, but f— 'em!

★

8/3/02 RELEASE! I'd resigned myself to twenty-two hour/day bang up over the weekend, when at 7 p.m. they came and released me. I was only upset I didn't have a chance to say goodbye and good luck to Toby, but I wrote him a note. Have just had two cups of milky strong coffee with biscuits in a café at Exeter bus station. The guy recognised my 'just out of prison' bag and gave me the biscuits for free. I'm elated but muddled and a little sad, having resigned myself to staying. I think Toby really liked me. A nice warden said what a good guy he was. I'll miss him, he has real morals and lives by common law; in his own words he's 'an old-fashioned criminal, and will always hold his hand up when caught red-handed'.

★

The supermarkets weren't the only corporate body Dad engaged with. He went to Florence in 2002 with Globalise Resistance, for the first European Social Forum (ESF), to protest against the impending war with Iraq. The ESF had been hyped up by Silvio Berlusconi and the newspapers that the 'Ghosts of Genoa would destroy the beautiful city of Florence'. It was the first international march since Genoa a year earlier. Dad said, proudly, that due to no police provocation a million marched and there was not one arrest made or any damage to property. As well as the massive Peace march on Feb 15 2003 he somewhat surprisingly went on the Countryside Alliance (CA) march.

Dad and the rest had always been very scathing about the CA. He said their overriding obsession with a threatened foxhunting ban not only detracted from the more important issues of GM crops and supermarkets but simply annoyed city people. He rightly felt that divided from the city 'they' would win, but united we would win. He wanted to fight a campaign to get affordable locally grown fruit and vegetables for city folk, utilizing areas of the green belts especially, and work together to keep GM crops out, for all our sakes. I helped a delightful hippy called Beccy, who was living with us in a circus bus with three cats, make Dad's and his girlfriend, Mandy's, fancy dress for the day.

Dad went as a genetically modified square melon 'for ease of packaging' written on the side. With green strands of 'DNA' hanging off his square melon and a green hat with huge syringes sticking into it he looked like something out of *The Wizard of Oz*. Mandy went as a 'GM tomato, perfectly round, utterly tasteless' – written on the warning sign on her costume, underneath a skull and crossbones. She wore a red hat with green leaves and more syringes. They both wore white face masks, one saying 'us next' the other saying 'where will this end?' With loudhailer and a banner reading 'Total irreversible destruction of our food chain – imminent: Syngenta, Monsanto we don't want your GMOs' they went off to stir up the foxhunting lobby and distribute 4,000 information sheets about the danger of GM. It wasn't as if Dad liked foxes; they used to kill lots of his lambs and not even bother to eat them. However, he also said foxhunting brought out the inverted snob in him: 'Toffs parading around in their red jackets.' Like so many others, he just wanted this relatively very unimportant issue much lower down the list.

As was the norm back then, with just so much going on, campaigns needed prioritising. With an invasion of Iraq looking ever more imminent, war moved to the top of the agenda.

CHAPTER IV: IRAQ

There is no doubt, according to all the history books written recently, that the war against Iraq in 2003 was the main catalyst for change. This happened at exponential speed. Spiritually, morally, emotionally, materially, you name it, the world had learnt nothing from the wars and experiences of the previous century and throughout history. Dad, as usual, couldn't resist getting involved in the local protests. The following is taken from his diaries.

Anti-War Protest

Nipper and Ned planned, like so many others countrywide, to hold round-the-clock peace vigils for as long as the war lasts. The grass square in the middle of Barnstaple under the clock tower was the spot selected and agreed to by the police. The unique thing about Barnstaple is that it is five miles from two Marine bases at Fremington and Chivenor.

The peace vigil began on Thursday 20 March, the day the first bombs were dropped on Baghdad. It was the night of the equinox and my girlfriend, the lovely Mandy, wanted to camp out somewhere to see in the spring. I'm not a fan of camping, but don't mind doing anything if there's a good reason, so I was prepared to camp – provided we did it in the middle of Barnstaple. Barnstaple is a difficult town with a lot of trouble at night. It has a mishmash of different people, including soldiers and others who as such are not part of the community. As a result the town seems to have a scattered soul.

We turned up at 9 p.m. and pitched our tent amongst six or so others. There were banners saying things like 'Stop the War' hanging from the trees and planted in the flowerbeds, and 'Rogue States' written next to the US flag. The spirits of the thirty or fifty protesters, including a lot of switched-on angry teenagers, were high. Local people bought out hot drinks and food for us and there was lots of hooting of horns as people sped round the roundabout on which we were based.

There were also a lot of people yelling aggressive, often mindless abuse at us, which increased as the evening wore on. The most magical exchange happened when three young soldiers came over wanting to talk to us. They said they'd never spoken to people like us before and just wanted to hear what we had to say. Obviously they were indoctrinated by the Army into a certain way of thinking so that they'd obey orders without question. However, we had a positive debate and left shaking hands, acknowledging mutual respect. Moments later two drunk squaddies steamed across the road and started kicking in and ripping down our banners. Ned and Nipper raced over and quickly managed to calm them down. They engaged them in conversation, which just about prevented further trouble, but the tension was rising.

I was standing with them, holding Bryan, our English bull terrier with his ears pricked straining at the leash to play the 'biting game'. Bryan had 'PEACE' written across his forehead in black marker pen. He looked the same in London on February 15 when nearly two million marched against the war, and was the most photographed 'person' there. I must admit I was finding it hard to control myself in the face of such mindless violence. However, from the squaddies' point of view, their mates were in the Gulf in the firing line. They had been convinced it was a just war but were fully aware that the vast majority of the population were against it. It was the same in every country in the world except America, where the media propaganda was at least two notches more biased than our own. This is a unique situation. There has never been a more unpopular war. The politicians have told us so many lies we wouldn't believe them even if they did tell the truth now.

With emotions running high for everybody at times of war, debates often become heated as people or groups are desperate to convert others to their way of thinking. The Government and military avoided debates at every turn with an air of overpowering self-righteousness. In parliament, Blair brushed aside questions from the anti-war brigade as if they were some sort of irritating, unpatriotic claptrap.

It seems the much predicted polarisation of people, with some sticking to the old way based on the lies, spin and deception of those in power; and those saying, 'Enough's enough,' was rapidly increasing. A Labour 'rebel' politician said last night that she hoped her strong gut feeling that this unjust war would be the catalyst for decades of terror, would be proven wrong. We all hoped for this but I prayed even more that it initiates fundamental change in the human consciousness – a wake up call.

Since I was unsure about controlling myself, I retired with Mandy and Bryan to our tent in the middle of the square. We looked out at the outside world, which was rapidly deteriorating as more and more drunken people poured out of the pubs and clubs. The sight of blokes peeing on our signs and being sick on the grass as we zipped the tent up to chants of 'Bomb Iraq!' suggested it was time to turn in.

Just as my mind was turning to seeing in the equinox at dawn there was an almighty crash. A drunken prat had leapt onto our tent, smashing the poles and tearing the canvas. It wasn't my tent. The last words from the guy who lent it to me were to make me promise to look after it. This, combined with Mandy yelling that her shoulder had been damaged, meant the red mist engulfed me. Having fought myself free from the debris of canvas, I went to the verge of the island in my underpants and T-shirt. Here I yelled every obscenity I could think of, saying I'd take all of them on asking them to come over and fight. There were forty of them, drunken idiots and squaddies. The only thing stopping me from wading into them was that I didn't have my shoes on. Having not thrown a full-bodied punch since I was eleven, I felt more confident with my feet, but they needed some protection. I went back to the tent and asked Mandy for my shoes. She'd weighed me up and, thank heavens, refused to give them to me, or I wouldn't have been writing this or anything else for the next few months.

The police then arrived in their numbers and arrested the guy who'd trashed our tent, fortunately before I got to him. I then spent the next hour at the police station giving statements. It definitely was no ordinary night anyway, because some guys came out of the pubs chanting, 'Don't bomb Iraq!' This upset the squaddies, and angry fights broke out. Was this a taste of what was to come?

We got home at 4 a.m. I lay in bed wide awake, shocked at my reaction at one button too many being pushed. Ever since the foot-and-mouth I have something inside, a little furnace, that when lit I can flip with absolutely no regard for my personal safety at all. I just can't work out if this is a good or bad thing. Uncontrolled anger certainly doesn't seem very spiritual, but who knows, maybe it's an energy that could be needed at this moment in history?

It seems that the Iraqi people are using their energy to combat the seemingly overwhelming attack from us and the US. They might not like Saddam, but in their eyes we are worse. We gave them the technology and chemical weapons that have been used on their own people, with us turning a blind eye. Bush has said we'd leave after the war, then says the Iraqi oil will be used to pay for the cost of 'liberation' (so presumably we'll have to stay). Without UN support the invasion is illegal. As more and more Iraqi civilians are killed in massive bombing raids, the friends and family of the dead are understandably taking up weapons and fighting back. Bloody Sunday in Ireland, when fourteen civilians were mindlessly slaughtered, resulted in a huge escalation in IRA enrolment. How much bigger will this prove in the long term? The list goes on and on, but the two aces up Iraqi sleeves are that they're not afraid of death and we, the West, are; and secondly, the double standards we have shown in recent history is meaning the world is waking up to what a heartless, manipulative bunch we are.

Recently the Iraqi's paraded five US POWs on TV. The US Defense Secretary, Donald Rumsfeld, furiously exclaimed this was in breach of the Geneva Convention, and they would be done for

155

war crimes. However, when questioned about the 641 Al-Qaeda suspects in Guantanamo Bay, Cuba, swept up by the US from the Afghan war eighteen months ago, US spin kicks in. As POWs they would have to be treated with respect (not tortured, as they are being) and freed after the war. Alternatively if they were civilians they are entitled to a trial. The US bypassed (ignored) the Geneva Convention, just as they had recently overridden the UN, and described the prisoners as 'unlawful combatants'. As such they have no constitutional right, not even contact with friends and family at home. Some appear to have been simply working as engineers, teachers and aid workers in Afghanistan.

A recent article in a national paper wrote about the 8,000 Taliban soldiers and Pashtun civilians who surrendered at Konduz to General Dostum of the Northern Alliance in the Afghan war. The Americans had originally supported the Taliban to get rid of the Northern Alliance; now it was the other way around. This was done under the guise of killing Osama Bin Laden (who is still alive), but most of us know it was because the Taliban wouldn't let the US build a massive oil pipeline across their country. The pipeline is now being built, and the terror in Afghanistan worse than when the Taliban were there.

Many of the prisoners were packed into container lorries which were sealed and left for several days in the searing sun. When they eventually left for Sheberghan prison eighty miles away, some of the prisoners, by now dying of thirst, started banging on the sides of the trucks. Dostum's soldiers peppered the containers with bullets. The US forces told the alliance to get rid of the bodies and together they emptied the contents of the containers into ditches. The bodies, which moved were instantly shot from above. One Alliance soldier said the US soldiers were totally out of control. They administered severe beatings to the prisoners and he witnessed one US serviceman break a prisoner's neck.

The Arab world is familiar with such instances. We've broken so many promises and cried wolf too often. In the 1991 Iraqi war we promised to look after soldiers who surrendered. As soon as the war was over we left them to the remnants of Saddam's Army. The overriding hypocrisy is our promise to sort out the issue of Israel and

Palestine. Yet the US fund and arm Israel, supporting their ever increasing, illegal occupation of Palestine. With the backing of the US, the Israelis have built fortresses in Palestinian land and split Palestinian communities into the size of small towns. Here Palestinians are only allowed to travel to see friends and relatives at specific times – if they are lucky – and even then are subjected to humiliating searches and treatment. Ninety-five percent of the time their roads are used solely by the first class Israeli citizens. Any dissent is harshly dealt with, including death. The only way the Palestinians feel they can fight back is with the tragic suicide bombers.

Mankind had had so many chances to mend his ways and try doing things differently. America is the country most blamed for causing the Collapse, but I think this is a little unfair. They happened to be the dominant nation at the time and simply behaved no differently to any other imperialist power throughout history. A few decades earlier in 1963 an American president was 'preaching the Gospel of Truth'. John F Kennedy spoke of peace for all mankind via respect for other people's cultures and ways: 'Genuine peace must be the product of many nations, *the sum of many acts.*' In 1989 the US had a tremendous opportunity, with the communist threat removed, to demonstrate acts of love. For example, by dropping the devastating Third World debt, not dumping heavily subsidised goods on poor nations, not seeking to control another's foreign policy – oh, and not selling weapons of mass destruction to whoever wanted them…

Any chance of man choosing a peaceful resolution on the path to love died, in effect, with the sinister murder of John Kennedy. By the time the Iraq war began, America (like the British, Romans, Spanish, French and Germans in the past) had become so self-centred, and its reputation so corrupted, that its ability to export liberal democracy by anything other than force had all but disappeared. 'U can bomb the world to pieces, but you can't bomb the world to PEACE,' read one mural on a motorway bridge near us at that time.

History states that once the road to war had been decided upon there were no ifs or buts. I remember Dad saying in January 2003 that an ex-SAS Army fellow had told a close friend of Dad's that they'd be going in on March 20/21 come what may. The date stuck out for me because this was the spring equinox *and* a full moon – earthly cycles meant something to me even back then. The UN weapons inspector, Hans Blix, a man of seeming integrity and honour, stated afterwards rather angrily that it wouldn't have mattered how much progress had been made, they had made their minds up long before. He felt he was making good progress and with time the war could have been averted.

The result of the war was obvious. Against the mightiest Army in history the degree of resistance put up by the Iraqis said a lot for their bravery. The wording used was obscene to any sensibly minded folk. The bombing of Baghdad with enormous cruise missiles worth £1 million each was gleefully described by the Americans as 'Shock and Awe'. It was as if they were putting on the biggest firework display in history to impress the world (and press upon it) with the awesome might of their toys. Such showing off, designed as well to instil fear in the rest of us wanting another way, was conveyed with a large degree of excitement verging on titillation. Millions sat up all night in their cosy homes in the West glued to the 'show'. The odd bomb missed, of course, blowing up busy marketplaces and civilian homes. However, this was deemed worth it to oust the threat of Saddam's weapons, which would soon be used on us unless they were destroyed.

The fact they never found any weapons of mass destruction inspired and further infuriated Muslims throughout the region. This combined with Israel using the fog of war to occupy more Palestinian territory such as around Jerusalem (the city itself having been illegally seized in 1967), and the furnace was built for a full-scale Islamic uprising. What eventually caused the furnace to ignite like a wind-ridden, tinder-dry forest nobody could have anticipated in 2003.

★

There was not just racist attacks from ordinary people in the US and UK at this time but from the respective governments as well. Some mosques were being closed in the so-called 'free world', and everybody of Islamic or Middle Eastern origins was being closely monitored by the Secret Service in every corner of these two countries. Any stepping out of line including expressing despair with too much passion at the treatment of your kindred spirits in the Middle East, and they were locked up without a trial indefinitely on the back of the new anti-terrorism laws passed in the wake of September 11.

All this became much, much worse after the first suicide bomber blew himself and four others up in London in late 2005 in the Docklands. The bomber was a disillusioned Pakistani, distraught at the occupation of Iraq and the plight of the Palestinians. Young Islamic radicals with fewer mosques in which to express themselves became utterly disillusioned with so-called democracy. Having marched with the two million or so UK civilians against war on February 15, to no avail, many went underground. To add further fuel to this subversive racism, hundreds of US evangelical missionaries, disguised as relief workers, crusaded into Iraq after the war to provide for post-war 'spiritual needs'.

The relentless bombing destroyed local people's security and self-respect. The West simply didn't understand that by carving up territories, irrespective of culture, history and the rights of sovereign nations, their arrogance and naivety would always backfire at some point. The state of Israel and Iraq, the latter cobbled together by the British from three Ottoman provinces, whose people have very different religious and ethnic loyalties, are two of many such examples. Democracy and freedom were of a type bestowed upon countries provided they unconditionally agreed to specific provisos laid down by the West. After the war, Iraq was given back its oil – operated through the likes of BP, Shell and Exxon. Unfortunately for the West, such control only lasted for a short period. President Bush's promise that the Iraq adventures would make the 'world more peaceful' vibrates some ten times higher on the Richter scale than Neville Chamberlain's promise of 'Peace in our time' made in 1939.

★

Had it not been for the Peace Activists and accompanying spiritual awakening, things would have been even worse. Many Peace Activists were American. In every country outside the US, the vast majority were against war in Iraq. However, even with the appallingly inaccurate propaganda of the US press, just seventy per cent of the population were actually for the war. At the same time Americans were placing themselves as human shields in Iraq, and the West Bank and Gaza Strip in Palestine. Many lost their lives.

The horrendous bombing and indiscriminate killing by US forces in Baghdad as they tried to bring a speedy end to the war, combined with an ever more massive exposure of their lies and spin, and Pandora's box was irreversibly blown open. Our home not only became a centre of resistance, but an example of wholesome, community living. It was, in a way, a microcosm of how we live now, but often very fraught due to the times and what they were trying to achieve.

The Health and Harmony Festivals in the summer of 2003 took on a new direction. They focused on grounding the often blissy New Age spirituality into actively doing something to assist the world in its transition. The spiritual truths were stressed with more authority than they had been previously. This was possible because more and more people were waking up to the simple truths; the one most often stressed being that there is no coincidence in whatever situation or person you encountered. The potential for mutual growth and learning in each case, especially the apparently negative experiences, was becoming better documented at this time. Many were realising that the only choice we had was how we chose to respond, with more and more choosing to embrace the experience rather than keep their eyes and ears shut.

This was vitally important in those seemingly dark days, because the more folk were awakening spiritually, the more they could be used to assist in the process of Transformation. The Universe, God, whatever anyone chose to call the Universal Energy, needed as many volunteers as possible to be guided by their intuition. This often meant following your heart into a seemingly terrifying scenario with no knowing what the outcome would be. Dad's main initiation came with the foot-and-mouth, but he had taken many leaps of faith before then.

It was stressed to everybody the importance and joy of relinquishing the pampered ego and simply being in service; a tool in a way to Divine Will. The blatantly obvious example of not relinquishing ego were Bush and Blair sending their armies around the world. They genuinely thought they were doing God's work (as did Hitler).

However, what they failed to see was that their actions were based on fear, not love. The fear stemmed from a fear of not being in control. The results were legislation to keep poor countries poor, starving, helpless and dependent upon the West, combined with the ruthless killing inflicted on those who threatened their control in any way. Their delusion was made easier by having the justification, for example in the case of Iraq, based on atrocities such as torture and death being imposed on the less subservient civilians by such wicked regimes. They did, however, play more on the threat of weapons of mass destruction (even though they had been the prime donors) rather than the torture. This was probably because they were doing the same in Guantanamo Bay and their POW camps around the world.

Our Festivals were used to encourage as many people as possible to take up their sword and use it in whatever way they felt appropriate. By 'sword' it was meant their spiritual sword of truth. Dad and the others believed it was not the time to be sitting and blissing out on a mountain top or in a forest glade, but to actively get out there and do something. Sheets about GM food, mineral and vitamin supplement ban, supermarkets, war and nuclear power were given out, along with guidance about what people could do. It was always stressed that the individual should choose his or her battle and do whatever they felt comfortable with in their hearts.

It was the time of the spiritual warrior. The faith and belief of the masses, who had been suppressed and overwhelmed by feelings of hopelessness for so long, began to stir at this time. Nothing symbolised this better than when nearly two million marched on a freezing cold day in February against the war in Iraq. It had become clear to virtually everybody that the most powerful politicians and big businessmen, coming from a point of fear, could no longer tell the truth. A true spiritually minded person could only tell the truth, no matter how hard it might have been. If not they would keep silent. The world saw through the damage being done from half-truths, spin and outright lies. They even openly had such things as spin doctors in those days to help senior politicians lie and twist things to what they wanted.

There were many debates on violence at this time. In the face of such overwhelming violence, people were concerned. They knew they had to fight back and resist but were confused as to how far they could go spiritually. Many such debates on this subject were held at Direct Action group meetings at our house. Dad kept stressing the non-judgement angle: 'Could we really blame a person whose family had needlessly been blown up by armed forces, for taking revenge?' Christ's message of 'love your enemies' featured a lot. It was felt that this 'love' did not necessarily mean lying down and allowing the perpetrators to walk all over them, or else they'd just keep going, not realising they were doing anything wrong.

Spiritually, it was felt to be not good to lower yourself to the levels of the aggressor and act from a position of uncontrolled anger. This proved a huge spiritual challenge for many. Dad stressed the importance of moving like a knight on the chessboard. The knight was hard to pin down, could easily sidestep an aggressor, and could jump over unnecessary obstacles to target the core of the Beast, – the King on the chessboard. Mental energy was therefore often more important than physical energy. It was similar to the spiritual truth that for optimum results it was the purpose of the intellect to rationalise and act upon the intuitive messages received from the heart. Mankind had pretty much lost touch with this, relying almost solely on the intellect with the intuitive faculty pushed into submission.

Violence in self-defence and protecting your family was suggested as reasonable. However, if you were being persecuted and walked all over and nobody was listening to your cries, you had to listen to your heart and make your own mind up. Again, non-judgement was vital, especially in the face of such monumental violence bestowed upon the masses by big business and governments. Destroying genetically modified crops was deemed an extremely worthwhile act of so-called 'violence'. The importance of keeping going and never giving up was stressed above all else. Whether this meant breaking into nuclear missile warehouses, as the wonderful Greenpeace activists were doing, or simply spreading the word about the importance of not shopping at supermarkets, was down to the individual.

As more and more came to our place for inspiration and ideas, the secret police began taking more of an interest. The local police were wonderful and very much behind us, but it was the big boys who were closing down mosques and fighting so-called terrorism who were more than a little curious. The number of police helicopters hovering over us went up noticeably in 2003. Suspicious-looking types were often spotted in the woods and gardens taking an unusually keen interest in our activities.

★

After the war in Iraq, it very soon became clear to the Iraqi people they were in for another very rough ride. In the same way as with Saddam Hussein, they found that if they expressed anger at US occupation (liberation!) a harsh punishment was dished out. Democracy and freedom were theirs, provided they totally submitted to American will and that of the US approved leaders. Many who expressed concern via demonstrations were killed. Al-Qaeda and other terrorist organisations had fertile ground in which to further their causes.

The whole Middle East was very aware of the goings-on in Afghanistan. For most Afghans, liberation from the Taliban had meant more harsh repression, the return of rival warlords, widespread torture, the continued policing of women Taliban-style and the mass re-introduction of opium poppies and heroin. Civilians were still being killed from cowardly aerial bombings from the Americans. Children especially were still being blown up by unexploded cluster bombs. Cluster bombs were incredibly used on Iraq, even after the outcry of their use in Afghanistan, many more dying and maimed post-war as a result. Equally as unbelievable was an estimated four times the amount of depleted uranium had been used in 2003 as was used in 1991. The consequences of this in 1991 and the accompanying sanctions proved devastating for the health of the people back then, when it was estimated that one million people died as a result.

The US President, George Bush, was soon talking up war on other members of his so-called 'axis of evil'. This comprised of countries with dictators who, put simply, wouldn't allow a McDonald's to be built. Due to the universal law of like attracts like, it's very difficult not to become that which you are focused on attacking. The Americans accused these countries of all manner of human rights atrocities and terrorism, but with the rigid new anti-terrorism laws implemented after September 11, they were behaving in exactly the same way. We in a way had become global capitalist dictators. Donald Rumsfeld, the alarmingly composed US Defense Secretary at the time, who clearly lost no sleep before, during or after the war, described the war as 'compassionate'. When asked about the Peace Activists he stated, in Churchillian fashion, 'Never in our history have so many people been proven so wrong.'

It is well understood today that the human 'stupid gene' expands and dominates, the more ego and power override humility, integrity and love in a person. It became well known then that the final paper used to justify the war read out to the United Nations (UN) was amazingly no more than a twisted, hyped up version of a Californian student's thesis. Similarly, in 1991 stories abounded about Iraqi troops, having occupied Kuwait, killing and torturing Kuwaiti children. This proved to be utterly untrue.

On November 19 2003, Dad went up to London in order to welcome President George Bush on his much maligned state visit. Things had been going from bad to worse in the Middle East, and in occupied Iraq and Palestine especially. In the light of this, the question on most people's lips was, 'Why on earth was the Queen made to have such a warmonger to stay?'

★

Dad came to pick me up from school on the way back down from London full of stories, adrenaline still pumping. I was not happy; I felt I was missing out on all the action. Dad had just got back from the European Social Forum (ESF) in Paris, where there was also a big demonstration. His diaries best describe the historic day and ever more exasperated mood of the nation whose wishes were being ignored:

The night before the big day in London, I went to stay with members of Globalise Resistance, with a French lady called Maria, who had kindly given us some floor space in her flat whilst at the ESF in Paris a week earlier. There had been a few arrests in the days before and a bit of trouble which, it was claimed, had been initiated by the rather jumpy police. 14,000 Metropolitan Police officers were there for duty the next day along with the 700 US snipers brought over to protect the President. They were clearly not expecting the streets to be filled with US flag-waving members of the British public. On being presented with a supposedly leaked document of Bush's movements for the next day, I decided it was best to have a sober, relatively early night.

Maria and I arrived at Westminster at 8.30 a.m. The number of police suggested we were in the right place. There were a few protesters with banners slung over railings, but instinctively I was drawn down a narrow street packed with businessmen and women, and more important, where the vibe of the police was edgy to say the least. We ambled past some policemen in normal clothes with banners hidden.

On getting in amongst the clearly marooned business people, I undid my rucksack, and began putting on my white boiler suit. The mushroom cloud at the top spelled 'BUSH', and this plus numerous bombs falling on dead civilians and their children, with blood flowing from their mutilated bodies, proved a dead giveaway. Dozens of police swarmed around me and threateningly told me not to go a step further into the crowd. I knew we were in the right place, but where were the comrades?

I had given Maria phone numbers to call in case I got into trouble or was arrested, and looked for a gap in the police lines where I could jump the barrier and leap in front of the cavalcade. The police were watching my every move. I regretted looking like a radical and not wearing a pinstripe suit.

My banner didn't help me look any less conspicuous. On one side it read 'WMD [weapons of mass destruction] =Bush', with a painting of a panting pink poodle, (Blair) '= Mass Murderers' – with yet more blood oozing forth. I had learnt over the past two years that immediate visual impact was important, not subtlety. Having said that, on the back of the banner I had written, 'Please can I have diplomatic immunity in case I accidentally shoot George Bush.' This was in reference to the fact that the Americans had asked for diplomatic immunity in case one of their trigger-happy snipers accidentally shot and killed a protester. Of the ten or so snipers glaring down the enormous telescopic sights of their even more enormous guns, one at least had a good chuckle. It occurred to me that they must have families too.

We'd only been there for twenty minutes when the cavalcade, sirens blaring, came round the corner. The eighteen-inch thick blacked out window designed to withstand rocket-propelled land-to-air missiles in which the US President sat some twenty metres away, summed up the popularity of this man to me. The police had crowded around me – the lone protester – by then and I realised I wouldn't have even made it halfway up the barrier before being arrested, with back-up for the police from ten snipers on the rooftops. I would also have missed the rest of the day, so I resolved to get arrested at night if necessary instead. I settled for waving my banner and shouting, 'Murderer! Terrorist! Killer!' at him.

Having laid a few wreaths at Westminster, Bush was due to make the short journey to Downing Street, which is where we headed for immediately. (The leaked document stating Bush's precise movements helping enormously – security? What security?) We bumped into three charming Australians bearing banners en route who decided to join us, increasing our numbers to a scary five. I had no idea where Downing Street was, but when we saw the police blocking off a road to our left, we decided, without the need for using too much grey matter, that this was our – and his – next port of call. We nimbly walked through a gap into a street which was being blocked off. It was bristling with police vans and snipers, and once in, we parked ourselves opposite the gates of Downing Street.

The police approached and asked us to move. We told them we were led to believe we had a democratic right to protest at the atrocities being committed by Bush and his poodle throughout the world. An extremely nice, polite superintendent very nearly persuaded me to move. I was a sucker for good manners. Seconds later it was a bunch of heavies threatening us with this and that, which made us determined to stand our ground again. It was the good cop/bad cop routine.

During this period, two other protesters joined us. One began reading the rights of the protesters to the ever increasing number of police around us. The other, a small (very stoned) British Muslim wearing a mask of a horrible-looking old man, launched into the abusive lines based on human rights. The police had had enough of our games and said that they would arrest us immediately if we didn't move. One thing I've learned over my two and a half years of protesting is that it is through childish behaviour that you get the best results (plus it's a lot more fun). I told the police that we'd move, then got all of us to shuffle incredibly slowly, insisting that we were moving.

The police wanted to get us into a pen some fifty metres away. We complained that Bush would not see us if we were there. I complained even more that being a sheep farmer, I wouldn't even consider the pen on offer fit enough to put my sheep in, let alone us. The police, understandably bored of our games over the previous twenty minutes, locked arms and forced all seven of us into the enormous pen. They kept saying to us that if we didn't get there quickly we'd end up at the back of the queue of people. Seeing that they had shut the road off, this was clearly not much of a threat.

On getting into the pen, my Muslim pal – called Shia, funnily enough – and I bellowed out a series of aggressive chants such as, 'George Bush – terrorist! Tony Blair – terrorist!' And, 'Bush, Blair, the CIA, how many kids have you killed today? No more war, no more sorrow, how many more will you kill tomorrow?'

Following this, my back being a bit sore, I hopped out of the pen, crossed the pavement and lay down on the grassy verge and started doing my back exercises.

The police had an immediate discussion about this latest threat to global security. Then a few of them, including a policewoman, came over. They ordered me to get back into the pen. I explained that I would in a minute but had a terribly sore back, and asked what harm I was doing. They said that if I was there, then all the others would get out as well. I laughed and pointed out that there were just seven of us and a thousand of them, plus the snipers on the roof. The policewoman then turned particularly nasty and, grabbing at my arm, said that she was going to arrest me. I said, 'OK OK,' and proceeded to get up as slowly as I could. As soon as I got back into the pen we boomed out another barrage of angry chants at the police and snipers.

Minutes before the arrival of GW Bush, thirty or so orange-clad Amnesty International workers were escorted into the pen behind us. In the meantime, Shia was telling the police, and the policewoman with Nazi leanings in particular, the funniest unfunny jokes I have ever heard. A typical example was: 'Hey, yoo no… I like chicken… with a little chilli sauce and things. Do you know what my favourite bit is?' (At this, he'd look down, little smirk appearing, so we knew the punchline was next) '…The breast…' big smirk plus series of sideways glances knowing he'd told a classic… 'and yoo no what? …I'd like a bit of Laura Bush's breast, and…' pointing at the policewoman… 'a bit o' yours too!'

Maria and I were crying with laughter – it's the way you tell 'em. After the second of these jokes the policewoman was so angry she had to be escorted away. All good protests need a nutter or two to give a lateral edge to the rigid framework of the authorities. I've discovered a combination of childishness, focused anger and extreme politeness have a similar effect.

Bush appeared again, some fifty metres away, to our shouts and banner-waving. We had seen him twice, which was more than anyone we spoke to on the march had seen him, as it turned out, and decided we had earned ourselves a cup of tea and some breakfast.

The march was the most focused one I had been on in the UK, even more than the anti-GM march we had a month earlier. It started at 1.30 p.m. and the last of the demonstrators arrived in Trafalgar Square at 8.30 p.m. At least 300,000 people demonstrated against George Bush, the largest number ever to protest on a weekday. I had my usual rant in the street and go with the loudhailer. However, the best bit was the pulling down of an enormous twenty-foot-high effigy of George Bush in Trafalgar Square in the same way the Saddam Hussein statue was pulled down in Baghdad the day it was 'liberated'. The pictures were sent to the US, and more importantly the Arab world via Al Jazeera TV. I hoped this image, cheered on by hundreds of thousands of British people, would touch the hearts of Muslim people – extremists and innocent civilians alike – and show them 'we're on your side'.

At this time we received a message that George Bush was going to pass through Hyde Park at 7.45 p.m. on his way to take the poor old Queen to dinner at the American Ambassador's house in Regent's Park. The adrenaline immediately kicked in; this was our opportunity. The word was passed around people in the crowd, only trusted friends, so as not to alert the police, and we adjourned to the pub to discuss tactics and (for me) get some much needed Dutch courage. It was Direct Action time, my favourite bit.

Direct Action is not dissimilar to going into battle. The difference between an Army and us is that they have to go into battle, whereas we 'choose' to. I find I need to build up a certain kind of energy in me whereby I am prepared for any eventuality, ranging from a good beating, even a bullet (especially in this scenario) and arrest, to a total damp squib sort of failure. It needs a concerted build-up of the warrior type spiritual energy, because it requires a leap of faith into a blank and potentially dangerous canvas. Again, it's similar to preparing mentally for a relatively big game of football – a feeling I no longer get, having just given up. Maybe this is providing me with a substitute for the adrenaline rush I no longer get from sport – who cares? I know it's important in these times.

We left the pub at 7.30 p.m. walking briskly and purposefully. Within minutes we met with two hundred or so comrades, mainly on bicycles, coming down and blocking the road from Piccadilly. In their midst was a big sound system on a trailer behind a bicycle, booming out a beat similar to a military bugler sounding a charge to the cavalry. Within minutes, police cars and vans came speeding through Hyde Park and down the road with sirens blaring. We broke into a charge yelling, 'Bush out!' as we dodged the police, who were getting rather clumsily out of the vans. I clearly remember the look of terror on the faces of the city workers on their way home.

On arriving at Hyde Park we were outnumbered by at least five to one by police. They tried to circle us and contain us as they do during the May Day protests. I noticed a small gap and, inspired by England's impressive run during the Rugby World Cup, sold two policemen a couple of dummies and managed to get onto the main road with a few others. Having ducked and dived a few attempts to catch me, four coppers finally caught me in a pincer movement. They put me in an agonising half nelson, leaving my elbow sore and bruised for a good two weeks, then hurled me into the pack with the others. I landed on somebody's bicycle, which broke under the impact. By now I was fully fired up.

I went around telling everybody we would storm the police lines when the cavalcade approached and throw ourselves in front of it. I stressed that this was the biggest opportunity, and a potential key moment, of our lives; that these would be the pictures concerning George Bush's visit which would be sent around the world, fully expressing the disgust of the majority of the West. I told people that the worst that could happen was a bit of a kicking and arrest – reassuring everyone that being arrested was a bit of a nuisance, but not that bad. Inside, however, I knew there was a good chance of some of us being shot by the trigger-happy US snipers. I'd anticipated this and written an updated will before leaving for London, and had worked hard to build myself up to accept such a possibility.

The sound system was by then pumping out the most fantastic disco music, so good that all of us were dancing like demons. I kept breaking off to check everyone's adrenaline levels were still high, stressing that it would be pointless if just four of us charged, and that together we had a good chance. Terry kept coming over to tell me that he could hear me from the other side of the cordon and to keep my voice down because I was announcing our plan to the police. After an hour and a half of the best dancing I've ever had, in a very intense atmosphere, the police let us go. We heard later that the cavalcade did a three-point turn as it approached us and was re-routed.

The police certainly sensed there would be trouble if Bush and his entourage had tried to pass by us, thus potentially undermining the whole visit, and chose not to risk it. We embraced this on its own as a minor victory and went back down the pub for a couple more pints to celebrate.

★

This was a time when all sorts of grisly skeletons were coming to the surface and being made known to the public. For example, Somalia, one of the world's poorest countries, was targeted for harbouring anti-American terrorists after the 'victory' in Afghanistan. As with Afghanistan, the US had interfered, supporting one ruthless warlord called Aideed against the others. When Aideed then turned against the US interests he was labelled 'the Hitler of Somalia', and the special forces were sent in. Over-confident and trigger-happy as ever, they blew up a building where Aideed's clan were holding a peacekeeping mission with the UN. Fifty-four people were killed. Another of many raids on Aideed's buildings in 1993 led to the deaths of eighteen Americans and two Black Hawk helicopters were destroyed. However, by then all of Somalia had united to fight the Americans, due to many Somalian citizens from all the different factions being taken hostage, and many more carelessly and needlessly killed. Somalia was beginning to recover from years of famine and the US moved in and made a bad situation seriously worse. The Americans, as usual, cast themselves as the sacrificial messiahs on a path to deliver the world from evil.

This same scenario had played itself out so many times throughout the world that it was a wonder it took people in the West so long to realise the deception being dished out. I must confess to taking much of this information from the wonderful history books written over the last two years about this extraordinary time in our evolution. The IRA activity and the Indonesian takeover are two much quoted examples, but the list is endless.

In Indonesia it was as if the template was formulated for future conquests. The pattern was familiar – good for the West, bad for the unfortunate country in question overall. Indonesia was run by President Sukarno in the early 1960s. It was practically self-sufficient, had only small debts and was independent of the outside world. However, it was very rich in natural resources such as rubber, tin, copper and chromium ore. Equally important, it had a communist regime, and as such was deemed a huge risk to the freedom of the West. Sukarno, who like most leaders in the world was not a particularly nice fellow, was replaced by an American/British puppet, President Suharto, in 1966.

Within days of the take-over there was a meeting in Geneva comprising the world's leading multinational bosses. Here, the country was literally carved up and control appointed to various businesses. The rainforests to one; agriculture, textiles, mineral rights and so on to others. The World Bank, as usual, gave huge loans to grow cash crops for export in place of self-sustaining agriculture. In the meantime, well over one million people were murdered between the 1960s and 1990s in the name of communism. The CIA and British Intelligence ticked off the names of some of the significant 'evil commies' as they were erased. The Western attitudes to the value of the lives of third-class citizens is best summed up in the words of certain senior

Western diplomats. The British Ambassador, Sir Andrew Gilchrist, reported to the Foreign Office. 'I have never concealed from you my belief that a little shooting in Indonesia would be an essential preliminary to effective change.'

Likewise, the Australian Prime Minister, Harold Holt, demonstrated what a laugh he was when he said in the US, 'With 500,000 to a million communist sympathisers knocked off, I think it's safe to assume a reorientation has taken place.'

The historian, Gabriel Kolko, wrote that the final solution to the communist problem ranked as a crime of the same type as the Nazis perpetrated. Globalisation in Asia was truly conceived in an horrendous bloodbath. In Vietnam at the same time the chemical known as Agent Orange was carpet-bombed over the forests to defoliate all vegetation and expose the 'enemy'. The side effects on the Vietnamese were the most horrendous cancers and deformities in live and stillborn babies lasting many decades.

In 1997 the World Bank described Indonesia as a 'model pupil of globalisation'. This thanks to the fact that most workers were doing shifts of twelve hours up to thirty-six hours in the sweatshops of Nike, Gap, and the rest. They barely received a dollar a day. Access to fresh water, medicines and decent food was available to far fewer at this time than had been the case during communist times. One famous statistic at this time was that Tiger Woods, the world-famous golfer, received almost as much in annual sponsorship from Nike *as all the workers in the Nike sweatshops throughout Indonesia received put together*. Soon after the above accolade by the World Bank was made, the Asian stock market went into free fall, and it wasn't the main businessmen who went hungry. The 'booming, dynamic economic success' (another World Bank accolade) left more than thirty-six million without work.

Big businesses the world over were being equally exposed as deceitful liars. Yet most people, although becoming increasingly aware, were feeling powerless and helpless about what they could do. For example, with regard to our food, facts were coming out that the contents of the colon and intestines were accidentally cut and emptied out from one in five beef cattle, passing into the slurry of meat used for McDonald's beefburgers. Likewise, most chicken McNuggets were coming from factory farmed chicken from Thailand, with chickens reared and killed on a forty-two-day cycle. Here the mashed up (quite literally) chicken was injected with up to forty-three per cent (and fifty per cent in Holland) water called 'tumbling'. The indiscriminate use of antibiotics banned in Europe such as nitrofurans and chloramphenicols often being found. However, as in European-based factories, hydrolysed proteins were used to stop the water draining out during cooking. Hydrolysed proteins were made up of the inedible hides, bones and ligaments of old pigs and old cattle. The salty taste was then neutralised by adding sucrose and lactose. Chicken flavourings were then added to make it taste of chicken again, and phosphates added to further bind it all together. Tesco, who claimed to only accept humanely reared livestock, were the leading shareholders of Thailand's leading chicken producer, Charoen Pokphand, and along with McDonald's and KFC brought cheap birds from the large chicken houses.

A *Panorama* programme, recorded by Dad in 2003, which escaped the 'raid', shed further light on corporate greed. It was called the 'Chicken Run' after a favourite animated cartoon of mine. However, this version gave visual proof to what Dad had been going on about with regard to the chicken industry for the previous year.

It showed Dutch and German firms adding 'hydrolysed proteins' to a giant slurry pit of chicken, mixed with up to fifty per cent water. It really made my stomach churn seeing the process described above with my own eyes. Directors were openly bragging to their would-be buyers (the BBC crew with hidden cameras) that they'd buy frozen processed chicken from say Thailand, defrost it then add more water and so on and reprocess/freeze it again. This was so 'the buyer' could make bigger profits.

The most sinister part of all was an interview with a German director of the processing firm, Provico. He openly bragged that they had developed a method to break the DNA of hydrolysed protein (beef and pork mainly because they were the cheapest) into a 'base pair of genes which would be unable to recombine to its original DNA pattern in any circumstance. This makes it totally untraceable'. The *Panorama* team tested this for themselves, taking samples from bags of hydrolysed protein called Surplus 600, and confirmed the statement. The conning of the public and huge potential health risks of BSE were clearly of no concern to the 'businessmen'.

Equally as sinister was the Food Standard Agency (FSA). The FSA was set up by our Government with an annual budget of £130 million per annum to police the food industry and thus boost consumer confidence. *Panorama* utterly exposed them for what they were – just another bland, useless corporate-controlled bunch of idiots. When questioned, they tried to wriggle out by saying so long as things like 'hydrolysed proteins' and 'water' – mentioned as part of the additives – appeared on the label, this was legal. Human health was amazingly *not* a consideration… provided the label was clearly marked. The fact that practically none of the British public knew what hydrolysed protein was (until this programme) or how much they were being ripped off with up to fifty per cent water added, was not an issue. At the same time, antibiotic growth hormones were liberally being used in the chicken hutches. This antibiotic would naturally enter the human food chain and build up resistance to similar antibiotics prescribed to us when we became ill, so they wouldn't work. The same applied to an antibiotic being found in GM oilseed rape where it had been present in trial plots in the UK for three years – unnoticed!

This all sounds grisly stuff. However, I remember Dad being thrilled it was all coming out. The effect was instant, and is documented in today's history books. The vast majority of people stopped buying cheap chicken overnight. KFC and chicken McNugget sales plummeted, hitting the revolting McDonald's flagging profits yet more. At the same time the supermarket shelves serving chicken were bursting at the seams even though they were being offered for a pittance. Most people, however, as was the norm back then, soon forgot. However, awareness was increasing at every piece of disgusting news, and the tide was gradually turning.

Asda (Wal-Mart), the other supermarket Dad loathed as much as Tesco, who especially drew on cheap, illegal immigrant labour, were doing exactly the same. For example, Asda's fresh pork loin steaks with 'basted' butter were twenty-six per cent water, polyphosphates and the rest. Many used to comment 'how disgusting' meat looked in supermarkets. This was because it really was... *disgusting*. Meat in butchers' shops would have been 'hung' for a good two weeks. During this time it loses fifteen per cent of its body weight as water and body fluids drained out. To supermarkets this represented a fifteen per cent drop in profits, hence their penchant for un-hung (and thus revolting) meat.

The public were becoming more and more disillusioned with big business and the ruthless lies they told. It wasn't just food either. There were programmes about Glaxo

SmithKlein's flagship antidepressant – Seroxat. Users claimed appalling side effects such as terrible addiction, far deeper depression, nightmares and suicidal thoughts and actions. Even ex-ministers were coming out of the closets and boldly admitting their mistakes. One such example was Stephen Byers, the Trade and Industry minister who retired in 2002. He spoke of his support for the IMF, World Bank and WTO free market trade policies whilst he had been a minister. He then publicly admitted that he and these global bodies were wrong. He stated, following a holiday trip to Africa, that trade liberalisation as a part of a loan agreement increased poverty rather than reduced it. He criticised the 'have your cake and eat it' attitudes of the West, whereby they said they were prepared to open their markets (reduce huge tariffs being imposed on imports) if developing countries did the same. At the same time the West refused to drop their subsidies – so they could still undercut local businessmen in the Third World.

Such information was helping to shake a Western public out of its apathy and start people doing something. This is where we and so many others came in – giving guidance and direction to those who wanted to get off their backsides. Amnesty International were shouting from the mountain tops that human rights were being eliminated in the 'War against terrorism', as more and more were illegally locked up on suspicion without trial.

The following words of one American, with regard to the war, best summed up the madness of those days:

> I am a father, and no amount of propaganda can convince me that half a million dead children [from the first Iraq war] is acceptable 'collateral damage'. The fact is that Saddam Hussein was *our boy*. The CIA helped him to power as they did the Shah of Iran, Marcos, the Taliban and countless other brutal tyrants. The point is that George

Bush Senior continued to supply nerve gas and technology to Saddam even after he used it on Iran and then the Kurds in Iraq. While the Amnesty International reports listing countless Saddam atrocities, including gassing and torturing Kurds, was sitting on his desk, Bush Sr pushed through a $2 billion 'agricultural' loan, and Thatcher gave hundreds of millions in export credit to Saddam.

Amazingly, with all this information being ever more readily available, the vast majority of Western people continued to be, for example, fast food junkies. Psychologists put this down to things like habit, the fact people had deluded themselves into being so busy they didn't have time to think about what they ate, and that they couldn't quite believe governments would allow such filth to be consumed. It's true that most people were under ridiculous amounts of pressure to keep their heads above water, and it was scary to open up their eyes and ears and glimpse what was going on. Most, understandably, accepted the rosy rhetoric of privatised companies, who fuelled the ridiculously over competitive nature of the world. BP, for example, projected a very green environmentally friendly and humane picture of themselves. However, with a little scratching and a very different picture reared up. For example, in Turkey, when building their pipeline, farmers and homeowners who resisted were ruthlessly beaten up and displaced, often without compensation. All the big oil companies simply made the bare minimum green gestures to keep the majority of the public off their backs. Remember, environmental friendliness meant lower profits.

BP were also the British Company who invested the most into 'corporate social responsibility', and in April 2005, received approval to start developing a gas field in West Papua. The internationally recognised sovereign Government of Papua – the Indonesian Government – granted the licence. This all seemed fine and normal on the surface – were it not for BP's boast of 'corporate social responsibility', a phrase which would presumably embrace human rights issues such as mass murder and torture.

In 1962 when West Papua was being prepared for independence by the Netherlands – its colonial ruler – the CIA felt it necessary to appease Indonesia, teetering on the brink of communism, by giving West Papua to them. However, the US Ambassador to Indonesia noted that up to 90% of the population would have voted for an independent West Papua if proper democratic elections were to take place. So in 1969, the US oversaw 1,022 Papuans specially selected by Indonesian soldiers taught the words, 'I want Indonesia', then lined up at gunpoint. One person who refused to say his lines was shot and others were threatened, and the result was a celebratory unanimous vote for… Indonesia.

Human rights groups say that about 100,000 Papuans have been killed, villages napalmed and torture and murder rife. As per usual they've tried to utterly wipe out Papuan culture. The BP website stated that human rights abuses only took place under Suharto, who was deposed in 1998, and suggested the Indonesians were in the process of granting autonomy to the Papuans. This was a blatant lie, since the Indonesians were in fact dividing West Papua into three regions controlled by Jakarta. When the Papuans tried to set up their own assembly, their leader was murdered by the Indonesian army, and an extra 15,000 troops were flown into the area.

BP claimed Papua would benefit by having a share of the revenue. However, with the central, provincial and local Governments all answerable to Jakarta, it was obvious where the money went. BP did try to get local soldiers to protect their plants, but once the Indonesian soldiers attacked a few of their own and blamed the Papuan rebels (a frequently used method), control soon reverted to them. The Papuans had no assembly or say as to whether the project should go ahead or not. BP, in effect, were deriving their authority to act from an occupying power in the midst of an attempted genocide – and they had the audacity to claim to be a beacon of 'corporate social responsibility'.

In Geneva in 1967 it was the likes of Shell, BP, Esso, General Motors, British Leyland, US Steel, Siemens, Goodyear, the major banks and other giants of western capitalism who divided up the spoils of Indonesia. In 2003 in Iraq it was the modern equivalent such as Halliburton, the big oil line manufacturers, and Bechtel. Coincidentally most of the senior ministers in President Bush's cabinet were recruited from industries connected to oil extraction. The seediest of all was the then US Defense Secretary Donald Rumsfeld. Rumsfeld had been a director of ABB, a European engineering giant making nuclear reactors, amongst other things. In 2000, ABB sold two light nuclear reactors to North Korea, a contract worth $200 million. In 2001 Rumsfeld left ABB and joined the cabinet. In 2002 he declared North Korea a terrorist state and a target for regime change due to the threat of its nuclear capability.

The global capitalist dictators were turning a blind eye where some dictators, such as President Mugabe in Zimbabwe, were committing appalling human rights atrocities. This was because there was no opportunity for making fat profits. The world was waking up to the fact that the IMF, World Bank and WTO (i.e. America), were controlling their economies and keeping them poor on purpose. For example, I remember being on holiday in Port Isaac, Cornwall, with Dad for a couple of days. We stayed in a cosy little room above a pub which had a TV. We watched a programme about Pakistan with Dad making notes and getting angry as usual. The Pakistani people interviewed said that everyone knew the IMF was America, and that they were running their economy.

In 2000, with their Government investing just .5 per cent of its budget on health, 2.2 per cent on education and sixty per cent servicing the interest on their debt to the West, the Pakistani people were very angry. They said the Americans lent the money to ignorant corrupt rulers knowing it would be laundered and squandered and thereby they'd get control. Farmers were interviewed who said that to help service the debt the price of diesel had been put up from twelve rupees to twenty per litre. This meant the farmers couldn't afford to fill their tractors and sow their seed for the next season. A year or so later I believe some of their debts were written off in return for control of their foreign policy. As usual, their markets were opened up and cheap subsidised Western food and products were dumped on them, destroying local businesses.

★

In the light of all this and so much more, it is not hard to see why suicide bombings and other so-called terrorist activities escalated throughout the world from late 2003 onwards. A letter I received from Ishmael in November 2003 explains the mood better than I can.

Dear Annie,

You sound so well and happy I feel guilty writing to you of our plight. I'm sorry I haven't written for a long time. There's a feeling of such hatred towards America and England in our house my mother's even told me to break all contact with you. Mother was with my brother Abu on the banks of the Euphrates collecting water and fish when the Americans invaded our city. They got caught in some crossfire. Abu was just sixteen and finishing school. He'd never said an angry word to anybody. When mother saw the

Americans shooting civilians indiscriminately, she advised him to hand himself over to them to prove he wasn't armed or a threat. They were our liberators, after all. From his meagre hiding place in the reeds he raised his hands and walked towards the US troops. When he got to within ten metres a soldier raised his gun and shot him through the heart.

Mother went crazy, and without any care for herself ran at the soldiers, screaming and hitting them with her bare hands. They just pushed her to the ground and carried on killing. I know it's not your fault but when you write back, please write to the above neighbour's address or else I might not get the letter.

I am now eighteen and haven't been able to restart at my university since the war. We all hated Saddam but things are so much worse now. Everybody says that now the Americans have got our oil they don't care about Iraqi people. There is still sewage all over the streets collecting in small ponds in low-lying areas. The smell was so bad on hot summer days I was frequently sick. In fact we've all had severe diarrhoea and sickness most of the time since the war. The lack of fresh drinking water is the worst. Seeing children playing in the open sewage and drinking it in desperation breaks my heart.

Anarchy still rules. Ruthless bullies and their gangs steal and kill whilst the American soldiers simply stand by and watch. However, the one thing we all have in common is we hate the Americans – or at the very least want them out. There is little or no help from our occupiers in creating income earning opportunities. Huge contracts handed out to the Bechtels and Halliburtons seem far more important. My father is an economist and has only recently got his job back in the bank, praise Allah. He says most of the large amounts of aid money for reconstruction simply leak straight out of the local economy back to multinational engineering firms. Everybody here knows it would be cheaper and better for long-term development to use local independent construction businesses. Frustration is growing that reconstruction has to wait until foreign contractors are ready.

What the Americans don't realise is that their 'spoils of war' approach, leaving the majority of us unemployed, is creating ever more resentment which will backfire on them. I know of some people nearby who looted barrels of raw uranium and the isotopes from the al-Tuwaitha nuclear complex. I've heard they are building radioactive dirty bombs for use against the US military targets and oil refineries. Al-Qaeda has mounted a very successful recruitment campaign. The Americans don't realise that by keeping all of us poor and taking our most valuable asset for themselves they create the perfect breeding ground for Al-Qaeda. We're not stupid, and Al-Qaeda give many a purpose and the means to fight back against our seemingly invincible oppressors. Most importantly they give us hope. I've politely declined the invitation to join and beg of you not to disclose this information.

I've heard the Western press describes Al-Qaeda members as terrorists and scum of the earth. I don't know whether Western governments ever wonder what it is that drives so many people to the ultimate extreme of blowing themselves up in the process of killing others… It not only takes enormous courage but is an act of sheer desperation. Most of the new Al-Qaeda recruits I know lost some or all of their family to the American and British soldiers or the local thugs. Not only are they extremely angry, but it's as if they've had their souls ripped out of them and they don't understand why.

My older brother, Fashtu, emigrated to Saudi Arabia two years ago to work for a small travel business in Riyadh. He wrote to me shortly after the first suicide bombings in May. He was extremely upset, having narrowly missed being blown up himself. He was working in his office when a suicide bomber blew herself up close enough to blow out a large window facing the street. His business is now in some trouble since most foreigners (the ones who've stayed) hardly now venture outside their fortified barracks, otherwise called homes.

He stresses that discontent has spread and deepened, because even though Saudi Arabia appears fantastically wealthy the vast majority of people live in poverty. Income since the early 1980s per capita has reduced by nearly a quarter and the population more than doubled. Unemployment is twenty-five per cent as jobs have been taken by the better qualified, relatively cheaper foreigners. The result is vulnerable, desperate young people with no prospects are embracing a message of purity and radicalism. Witnessing the brash drunken lifestyle of many Westerners heaps more coals on to an increasingly angry fire.

He says that the fact King Fahd is barely alive is not helping. The princes, many accused of funding Al-Qaeda, are fighting for pole position. The Americans might have left Saudi soil (and set up base next door in Iraq), but the people see any occupation of Arab land as reason for Jihad. Anti-American feelings soared to new heights when you invaded Iraq, and the worsening situation in Palestine further fans the flames. Pressures exerted in schools to reform the curricula and teachings about Islam so as to 'treat at source the culture of extremism', is one of many other antagonising factors.

Mention by President Bush of a 'crusade' into the Arab world after September 11 has never been forgotten, and Colin Powell's statement that 'such terrorist actions are carried out for no particular reason other than to kill innocent people', demonstrate the seemingly insurmountable gulf between our cultures. Western officials never ask the question 'Why?' or show any desire to get to the core of the problem. What Saudi, Iraq and other nations around us need is far reaching economic, social and political reform. Without this America's reason for it's love affair with Saudi Arabia will go 'tits up' (as I've heard you Westerners say). The revolution or war in Saudi which could erupt at any moment like a giant volcano, would (I've heard) cause the price of a barrel of oil to rise from $40 to $150. In which case you could find yourself in the same situation as us.

Please forgive the depressing nature of this letter, but a sole focus on survival from day to day and the sense of humour I once had is somewhat overridden. However, we do appreciate the active support of you and so many in your country. Peace be with you and your family.

Your friend, Ishmael.'

When I received this letter I felt stunned and shell shocked. Being young I couldn't grasp much of it. I didn't show it to my dad until the next year in 2004 because I knew how upset he became at such news. When I did in around February 2004 Dad showed me two videos he'd recorded in 2003. One was about Palestine, the other about the Chechnyan suicide bombers in an opera house in Moscow. At this time the tragic Chechnyan civil war with the Russians was in full swing.

Suicide bombings in Chechnya, barely heard of before 2000, had escalated on occupying Russian military targets until President Putin gave the go ahead for full Russian military might to suppress the 'terrorists'. The video clearly showed why the Chechnyan 'terrorists' took over the opera house. It was the same old story. With the fall of communism, Chechnya, occupied and suppressed to become part of communist Russia, wanted their country back. The Russians refused, probably because of the oil Chechnya possessed, and embarked on a path of horrendous suppression of the Chechnyan people. The nineteen veiled female suicide bombers in the theatre had had some or all of their family killed by Russian soldiers and Russian planes, often using weaponry provided by us in the West. Thus the souls of these poor, once innocent people had been destroyed.

CHAPTER V: POVERTY

The madness of the world was encapsulated in a letter I received from Neela. I received it on August 21 2003. She was a few years older than me and her mum was now a teacher at one of the ridiculously overcrowded schools on the outskirts of Hyderabad. Neela had said in a previous letter that an aid agency had recently equipped the school with some computers. This had clearly given them greater access to the outside world and had had a big inpact on their lives. I'm not sure whether this was a good thing. The bitterness at their unjust displacement seemed to be further fuelled the more they knew:

Dear Annie,

I hope this letter finds you in the best of health. I'm so glad you managed to keep your animals, the Highland cattle especially. Riding around on the back of 'Marvin' holding his horns on a cool, sunny spring morning through green fields sounds my idea of heaven. Without I hope sounding too feeble, it makes me miss the open countryside and our farm terribly. I dread to think what that big company's turned it into. Please tell your dad not to become too great a thorn in the side of the system. We too are supposed to be a democracy, but anyone here they deem too radical seems to be taken out of the picture by fair means or foul. You still have some measure of freedom of speech, but as things deteriorate more and the authorities get more desperate, as it sounds they are, I fear things will change for you as well.

Our situation still isn't as bad as some. My mother and father attached huge importance to education. It's made such a difference not just for me and my sisters, but mother's got a job teaching English and Arithmetic at the local school. She's the only one earning a small income. Father's still so depressed about being kicked off his land and losing all his money on that trip to Europe which he felt achieved nothing. He barely says anything and just sits around all day eyes glazed, just staring at the squalor all around, smoking tobacco.

The smell of sewage piled up and stagnant in open drains on a hot day is almost unbearable. Seeing children splashing and playing in the pools drained from this sometimes makes me cry. Disease is rife. Indra, now aged six, has terrible malaria. We can't get the drugs and Mum's very worried she might not pull through. One of the hardest things is getting fresh water. There's a standpipe one kilometre away which doesn't work more often than it does. Kanga, Jose (and Indra when she's well) and I seem to spend our lives queuing and bringing home what water we can.

Mother is still bitter about how the farm was so brutally taken away from us and the fact it's destroyed Dad's soul. During break times and after school she gets on the Internet. She's helping to organise an underground movement with other displaced families to try to fight back. They're not sure exactly how they'll turn the tide against such an aggressive monster, but Mum says all we can do is follow our hearts and have faith. She's collecting as much information as she can off the Internet and circulating it around the shanty towns. To us the information is mind boggling. Your governments and big business must deeply regret not controlling computer information from the start.

One of Mother's information packages reads as follows: 'According to last year's Earth Summit in Johannesburg, there is enough food produced in the world to feed everybody and 800 million more. The grain silos in India have been bursting for years, and in August 2002 held a record surplus of 59 million tonnes. Yet 24,000 people, mainly children, die daily and one third of us suffer from nutrient-deficiency diseases.

Somebody somewhere is benefiting hugely at the expense of the world. We most of us know now that it is the large corporations, collectively known as Agribusiness, who are to blame. They traverse

*the globe, buying at the lowest possible prices, putting farmers in
direct competition with each other.*

*It is easy to blame our subsidised brothers and sisters in the West.
However, I recently discovered from the Internet that they are in
much the same boat as us. It states that supermarkets blame the
consumer for wanting cheap food. However, fifty years ago farmers
in the west were receiving between forty-five and sixty per cent of
the money that consumers spent on food. Today that proportion has
dropped to as little as seven per cent in the UK and three and a half
per cent in the US. The profits for the middlemen, taking none of
the risks of production, must be astronomical. As in India, suicide
rates amongst farmers are abnormally high. In the US, suicides
amongst farmers occur at a rate three times higher than in the
general population.*

*I have to keep a close eye on my husband, who speaks of suicide
regularly, having, like so many of us, had his farm taken away. I
make sure he hears nothing of what they have done since we had to
leave. The forests on the hills above our farm have been clear felled
by a big logging company. Mudslides have since washed down onto
our once fertile terraces below. The terraces were not being used
anyway, since they didn't suit the large machinery which is now
used, and our low-lying land has been bulldozed into one big field
together with other people's land. It now just grows genetically
modified corn for cattle feed in the Western world. I've heard they
use fertilisers and sprays to grow their crops.*

*We have been told that free trade and market liberalisation would
enrich our country and allow us to buy other food in. Yet even the
World Bank has acknowledged that the globalisation of agriculture
has left us worse off than before. It has also admitted that the
expected filter down of riches from our government from an increase
in foreign money simply has not happened. I'm afraid they love the
money too much. The free market, with a global price set for grain,
means that we cannot afford the grain in the grain silos. The
emergency aid which we get often ends up enriching multinational
grain companies whilst failing to reach us.*

It is a fact that fertilisers and herbicides have almost quadrupled yields in the last fifty years. This is another reason we are given for what is happening. Such global practices do not, however, account for the enormous social and environmental damage – deforestation, deteriorating soil and dropping watersheds. However, such statistics are primarily due to increased output from Western farms. It does not apply to us. Small farmers such as we, were achieving four to five times more output from our land than what they are getting now. In China the figure is up to nine times greater for the same. A World Bank study of north-east Brazil estimates that redistributing farmland into smallholdings would raise output by an astonishing five times the amount the big monoculture farmers are producing. There is a myth that circulates in the West that we peasant farmers farm inefficiently have more crop failures than successes and don't understand soil impoverishment. We know that nothing could be further from the truth and it is totally the other way around.

What can we do? *We were told that this more efficient, productive farming would free us for 'more rewarding activities.' However, most displaced farmers are now rotting away with no job or future prospects. We most of us would rather be producing food provided we are paid a fair price for our product.*

The reason we so many of us went quietly when they wanted our land was because we were often getting paid less for our crop than what it cost to produce. With US and European farmers getting subsidies of about $350 billion a year, this allows their surpluses to flood cheaply into poor countries, depressing world prices and undermining local farming. Rice farming in Ghana and elsewhere has all but collapsed under cheap US and Thai imports.

It is vital we as a people unite to vote members into our Andhra Pradesh government who will block the dumping of these subsidised goods, or at least impose tariffs to give us a fair chance. They will have to be strong and prepared to stand up to potential recriminations from the World Trade Organisation (WTO). We must be prepared to take this risk if we are to break free of the shackles of globalisation. Most of us have nothing to lose, after all.

Take heart, my friends, we are not alone. More and more people in the Western world are actively campaigning on our behalf. Individuals, Non-Government Organisations (NGOs) which include bodies such as Friends of the Earth and Greenpeace are getting huge press coverage, especially in Europe, about our plight. The massive multinational company, Nestlé, was recently brought to its knees by press exposure. It was trying to get millions from the near bankrupt government of Ethiopia for a questionable coffee deal more than twenty years earlier. Following exposure, there was a huge outcry from the British public and they massively reduced their demands. We must have faith for the sake of our livelihoods. We could pull off similar and more by standing up to the WTO – America. The farmers of Via Campesina actively campaign on our behalf everywhere, none more so than at the World Social Forum in Pôrto Alegre, Brazil. Their message is clear: nothing as important as food should be ruled by the WTO; and people should concentrate on producing food for themselves, not products for export.

I believe that some trade is healthy but only after countries are encouraged and helped to become as self-sufficient as possible. We must demand our rice farmers, for example, be allowed to sell their rice first before any subsidised foreign rice is allowed into our shops to make up any shortfall… Like many others I want to see a modernisation of the old system. This to be based on land reform, more investment and research into conventional crops, together with education about manuring, water saving and ploughing. This I feel could boost incomes significantly without leading to social distress. To make such education worthwhile we first have to collectively lobby our Government and fight, if necessary, to reclaim the land that is rightfully ours.

I have seen it quoted that 'it is the right of people, communities and countries to define their own agricultural, labour, fishing, food and land policies which are ecologically, socially, economically and culturally appropriate to their unique circumstances'. I believe that food is a human right, not a commodity, and that the job of producing food is fundamental to all human existence.'

*I will write again soon. In the meantime may peace be with you
and your family.*

With heartfelt warmth and love,

Your friend, Neela

★

GM

Neela told me in her less formal letters how much she
loved hearing my stories about Kelpy. Kelpy was a beautiful,
five-year-old chestnut gelding standing at fifteen hands. I
told her about my trip to pony camp during the hottest
week of 2003. Dad drove down early on the last day of camp
from London to witness the events with other parents.

I already had had the record number of tumbles over the
week, and Kelpy's mood was not helped by the searing
humidity. He simply refused to move during the dressage.
His true colours, however, really shone through during our
show jumping round. I was fourth to go, and had to follow
three perfect clear rounds by very accomplished, neat girls
with disciplined ponies and enthusiastic and determined,
equally neat mothers. My round took longer than the other
fourteen riders put together. Kelpy simply refused at every
fence. Fortunately, a powerfully-built teacher called Nell
came out to help make sure Kelpy didn't get away with it.

Nell would run behind Kelpy shouting and whipping his
bottom as he ambled reluctantly towards the jumps.
However, it was her fluffy terrier cross called Margo, that
with Nell furiously trying to kick him out of the ring,
would run up and bite Kelpy on his ankle, which made the
difference. He still did at least three refusals at each fence,
but it was the trays under fence six that Kelpy decided were
the scariest things he'd ever seen. He bucked, reared and
spun sideways until he eventually hurled me to the ground.

It hurt but I still yelled to Dad, who was proudly snapping away with his Instamatic, asking if 'he got that'. It was only when all the poles were removed leaving just the trays, and with Margo biting with all her might, that Kelpy did his biggest leap of the day. It felt wonderful, but he still managed to rear up and get me off at the next fence to make his point! To rub salt into the wound he then decided he was hungry and simply wandered off to eat some grass. Having caught him, I clambered back on and after more of the same on the last two fences, I completed the round to rather exasperated looks from some mothers – and rapturous applause from my proud dad shouting, 'Clear round!'

Dad and I then spent three hours in the heat mucking out Kelpy's stable, clearing away (and finding!) his tack and helping mums take all the fences down. I don't think Dad was expecting this. It meant he was going to miss his favourite (if rather sad) soap... *Neighbours*.

Kelpy was now so bad-tempered he tried to stamp on my toes as I was leading him into the horsebox. He did the same to my friend's experienced mum, who then decided it was time to get Nell. Dad was standing nervously to one side. Mind you, he had been chased by one of his Highland cows the week before. He had a horn mark on his back and deep cuts on his left thigh, since he had to go flat through a barbed wire fence to avoid being seriously gored.

I hadn't really noticed the size of Nell's shoulders until she approached the troublesome Kelpy. They were like those of a rugby player. She locked hands with Dad, who went white, not knowing what she was intending, as my friend's mother led Kelpy up the ramp. Nell dragged Dad round the back of Kelpy who immediately lashed out with his back feet. Dad ran. Nell then grabbed Kelpy and kicked him in the stomach. Kelpy then reared up on his hind legs and went for Nell, jabbing out with his front hooves like a boxer. Nell kicked him harder, glared him in the eyes and warned him with chosen words the likes of which were not the usual part of a horse whisperer's vocabulary, then calmly led Kelpy into the box.

I used to tell such tales to both Neela and Ishmael. Ishmael was more serious, but still said he liked to hear of these stories. Neela, who had remarkably managed to keep her sense of humour under the circumstances, really loved them. It probably conjured up happy memories for her of life on the farm.

Soon after this I wrote to tell her that I'd broken my collarbone whilst out riding Kelpy on the hills near us. I also mentioned that Dad was complaining bitterly that GM was about to be forced into our country. This was happening without the results of the three years of trials being taken into account, which suggested the potential for much environmental damage and the creation/mutation of various pests into much more virulent strains. The mention of GM touched a nerve with Neela and her family. I received the following letter in July 2004.

Dear Annie,

It was lovely to hear from you again. I'm so sorry to hear about your shoulder. It must have given you such a fright, but I have heard horses can be a bit jumpy around dogs, especially when they run up on them like that! What a bit of luck the dog sat with you in the long grass or your Mum may have struggled to find you.

Your mention of the GM thing worries me and my family hugely. Please, please tell your dad to do all he can to stop this evil from invading your land. When big agribusinesses were promoting GM crops here they told us that it would help 'defeat food insecurity and world hunger'. They then kicked us off our land and covered it in GM crops which are almost all sold to Western countries. We were told GM would 'increase food production relative to population growth'. However, there are many more starving and dying of malnutrition now than before we let them in.

The claim went on to say their GM crops would 'cope with constant climate change, continue to outpace pests and diseases and provide environmental improvements'. We believed them. They were the kind, scientific experts of the educated West, and as such, more advanced, superior beings who knew what's best. Our crops would sometimes fail, for example, when the rains didn't come or we were overwhelmed by a certain pest. Many of us would go hungry and feel desperate so when we were told this problem would be removed and we could pursue 'more rewarding activities', the less sceptical amongst us thought it wouldn't be so bad.

The truth is that their crops fail just as frequently as ours did, and not just in our country. One of the better known examples is Monsanto's new leaf potato containing the modified BT gene (BT – Bacillus Thuringiensis, is a natural pesticide discovered in Germany in 1911, which had always been used sparingly by organic growers because overuse would allow insects to develop resistance), mass planted in Georgia in 1996. Farmers lost two-thirds of their crops and more, and many went into huge debt as a result. Many then lost their land which itself was bought up – cheaply, by... the big biotech corporations.

The claim that GM technology will outpace pests has even more sinister indications once you scratch a little below the surface. Mother discerned from the Internet that a study by the Nanjing Institute of Environmental Sciences in China found that the insecticide BT gene in GM cotton, injected to kill the cotton bollworm parasite, destroyed other predators as well. They also found the pests were mutating and increasing in potency as more of the same pesticides were used. This is the same as malaria in our mosquitoes mutating and becoming more dangerous as they ingest blood containing malaria pills. In the same way GM crops have been found freely swapping their genes with native species, weeds and so on, creating increasingly invasive more virulent weeds. Incredibly we were told that GM crops 'should be used with organic agriculture to overcome problems of yield'. Yet farmers are finding with the creation of these new superbugs and superweeds they are having to give up their organic status and buy chemicals from the big companies if they want to get a crop.

The biotech companies have admitted that insects will develop resistance to BT, for example, within five to eight years. However, they boast that this is not a problem because their in-house scientists will come up with alternatives by then, even though this will deprive organic growers of their only natural insecticide.

Again thanks to hours on the Internet, Mother has found that after rigorous tests in the US the yield of GM soya is six per cent less than normal soya. Likewise, since GM crops were introduced in the US, farmers have been using more pesticides and herbicides, not less. This for the reasons mentioned, plus with crops such as maize modified to resist Monsanto's Roundup, farmers could easily spray more often to eliminate competitive yield-reducing weeds. However, we were told that 'GM crops' would dramatically reduce the need for pesticides and herbicides and reduce production costs by twenty-eight per cent or more. It claimed that in other parts of the world 'the use of toxic pesticides such as organophosphates is reduced by as much as eighty per cent'. Again we believed them. Mother then discovered that Roundup was banned in Denmark due to alarmingly high levels of carcinogenic organophosphates – incredibly a vital ingredient in Roundup, found in underground drinking water supplies.

The lie which goads us the most is: 'Genetic engineering will allow us to extend crops into ecologically challenging areas, such as those with saline soils.' The agrochemical revolution in our country has entailed a massive programme of big dam constructions. (Many of the fifty million displaced by these projects now live in the squalor around us). The initial government subsidy policy of free water encouraged farmers to use water carelessly and abandon traditional tanks. Excessive irrigation has lowered water tables and brought salts to the surface, turning much of the once fertile land into desert. We would not need crops that are genetically modified had Western business not stolen our land from us.

'GM crops will further play a role in the delivery of medicines, vaccines, and improved nutrition.' The most magical thing about

India to me has been our biodiversity. We Indians have for millennia obtained our medicines and remedies from our native plants found in our forests and countryside. Your (I'm sorry, I mean Western) corporations are rapidly removing our beautiful hardwoods, which combined with GM crops rapidly cross-pollinating our flora and fauna, and our natural plant life is being irreversibly destroyed. To cap it all off, other big companies have taken our medicinal plants, copied them with chemical equivalents which they then patent and sell back to us at huge profits for themselves.

During the last century, three-quarters of the genetic diversity of agricultural crops was lost. Out of 100,000 varieties of rice just a few dozen remain and three-quarters of the world's rice comes from just one variety. If one pest manages to outpace biotechnology on this variety, the consequences will be catastrophic. With regard to 'improved nutrition', our new 'knights in shining armour' have inserted Vitamin A into our rice to boost this vitamin for the locals to help counteract blindness. However, what we have recently found out is that it is nigh on impossible to eat enough of this rice to make any difference. Indeed the whole issue of health does seem to be a very grey area, especially in the light of so many of us being so undernourished that our bodies are incapable of absorbing most of the potentially beneficial nutrients anyway.

Our brothers in Zambia upset the Americans, I believe, by refusing to accept their aid of GM food. They feared that their farmers would use the whole grains of maize as seed and once planted would loose their GM-free status. They are not stupid and saw how this affected the export trade in other countries, even Canada. They also worried about the affects of GM food on a population whose immune systems are considerably weaker than those people in the West. Indeed it is common knowledge that Western companies work on a principle of 'Safe until proven deadly'. Because of this and the lack of efficient testing, Zambia bravely refused even maize that came in the form of flour. They felt there was only one reason why they were only offered genetically engineered aid, bearing in mind this is only a tiny percentage of the total food produced globally. This was so that US companies, once the GM-free status was gone, could get control of their agriculture, just as they have with us. You, my friend, must do as your Zambian friends are doing.

Mother downloaded a small piece which sums up just how severe the corporations policy can be. The 'control' it mentions is in reference to the likes of Monsanto and Cargill buying up everything from seed, fertiliser and pesticide companies, to grain processing and collection, here and worldwide, in the name of globalisation: 'This level of control is one of the reasons why GM seeds are of such concern. They give agribusiness yet more weapons with which to enforce total dependency on their patented seeds. Some of them require own brand herbicides and even own brand "trigger" chemicals (known as 'traitor' technology) that the farmer has to apply for before the seed will germinate.'

Once again my heartfelt love, Neela

This last point is in reference to the soullessly named AstraZeneca who had unbelievably been allowed to develop seed that was sterile unless their own chemicals were applied. A league beyond even this was Novartis (Bayer) who developed plants whose resistance to viruses and bacteria had been removed. This technology was not being applied here at home at the time I received this letter. However, Monsanto were plugging away at Mr Blair to accept their aptly named 'Terminator' maize seed. This seed was programmed to become sterile as the corn matured so that farmers had to go back to Monsanto each year to buy their patented garbage.

One extra twist in the name of control was Monsanto selling 'Roundup Ready' seed. Roundup was Monsanto's own weedkiller, which would kill everything it touched for months on end, but would not harm the GM modified soya, cotton or corn. The scam they spun was it would mean less spraying and was thus more environmentally friendly. However, the Roundup itself, marketed as one of the 'friendliest' of sprays, was so potent it destroyed biodiversity, created sterile soil (killing earthworms and vital bacteria) and eliminated natural predators. Small farmers the world over were farming sustainably, working with nature rather than against it and using negligible amounts of chemicals compared to large monoculture farms.

With regard to Neela's mention of 'Safe until proven deadly', a now much written about effect on human health was the genetically engineered hormone used at this time in the US. The Recumbent Bovine Growth Hormone (RBGh) was liberally injected into dairy cows at this time to boost milk yield. This had been shown to directly increase levels of Insulin Growth Factor 1 (IGF1) in our bloodstreams. Even slight increases could increase the risk of prostate cancer in men by seven times and breast cancer in women by five times. Tamoxifen, the main drug used for breast cancer, simply reduced levels of IGF1 in the bloodstream. As Monsanto themselves admitted in the scientific journal, *The Lancet*, in 1993, 'IGF1 can be present at up to five times normal levels as a result of drinking milk from treated cows.' Incredibly, Monsanto still maintained RBGh milk was safe, according to their sales tape, and it was still freely on sale in US shops, such was their power.

Jane Akyre worked for the Florida-based TV station, Fox, at the time. She was so horrified at discovering that her friends, family and the population as a whole were playing Russian roulette with themselves by drinking milk or eating cheese from these cows that she decided to do an information documentary on the subject. Bear in mind that one in two Americans were contracting cancer at this time, compared with one in four in Europe. Nobody said then that this was all due to GM, but they did know that you are what you eat, and a dodgy diet was the major cause of cancer. Monsanto, a sponsor of Fox, on discovering this had the programme banned. The news manager was fired, and

Jane Akyre was offered a large cash settlement for her resignation and silence.

This was far from the only example of such underhandedness. When profits could be affected by something everyday, like human health, it was all guns to the fore. The Government scientist, Dr Apad Pusztai of the Rowett Research Institute in Aberdeen, was doing tests on rats fed both GM and non-GM potatoes in the late 1990s. He found the rats fed on GM developed a thickening of the stomach and intestinal linings which could have been a prelude to certain cancers. Pusztai, having printed his findings in a scientific magazine, was then vilified and hounded out of his job. His studies were deemed flawed, but what angered Dad and the rest was that he clearly found something which posed a potential health risk, and as such it should have been checked and rechecked. Likewise, at Newcastle University, a single meal of GM soya was fed to volunteers. It was found that GM DNA was transferred to bacteria in the gut which, it was said, could compromise antibiotic resistance (antibiotics or viruses were used to 'carry' the GM gene) and even alter the genetic layout. As per Pusztai's work, no more checks were done. Michael Meacher, the Environment Minister for six years – sacked because he started speaking the truth about the environment, was furious. He claimed that this was a very serious discovery, and checks and rechecks should be done over many years to discover the true health implications. The whole tragic mess was summed up in the words of Prof. Bob Orskov OBE, Director of the International Feed Resource Unit in Aberdeen: 'As a scientist, I wouldn't drink milk from cows fed GM maize with the present state of knowledge.'

Around this time, December 2003, Dad did a debate with an 'independent scientist' from CropGen (a very pro-GM body, considering they were meant to be 'independent'

– Dad found out afterwards they were largely funded by the likes of Monsanto, Syngenta and Bayer), who nailed Dad very slickly. It was the first time Dad had encountered a well-paid professional who was trained in exactly the right way to play an audience. The Professor dismissively brushed aside Dad's claims about Pusztai, for example, stating that, 'This is what all the antis throw at us,' adding that Pusztai's work was flawed. Dad was by this time agitated, having lost his temper earlier (big mistake) when the Professor dismissed the contamination of organic produce as 'being just one per cent of food consumed, and thus irrelevant compared to the ninety-nine per cent of people who wanted affordable [GM] food, which is what they catered for'. In retrospect Dad realised he should have stressed that Pusztai was a Government scientist, and flawed or not, further checks ought to have been done to satisfy the public.

The example CropGen and Monsanto always used to preach as to the success of GM was BT cotton (even though this would kill natural healthy predators, and immunity in the cotton bollworm – the most virulent predator of all for cotton – soon built up). The sense, and sensitivity, of the cotton example was summed up by Bill Dyer, Dad's friend from the Small Family and Farm Alliance, on returning from a trip to India. Here he attended a meeting organized by Syngenta in a large warehouse to explain the benefits of GM to thousands of small farmers. He spoke for half an hour using cotton as his example, after which he took a question from a little old lady in the front row who had her hand raised within five minutes of his talk. She simply asked, 'Excuse me, sir, but how much cotton do you eat each day?'

This defeat demonstrated to Dad how easily farmers would be persuaded to accept the 'environmentally friendly, more profitable GM crops'. He also never got caught out again – he did his research properly after this. Dad set about carpet-bombing most individual farmers across the UK with an information letter (which I've used to glean much of the information here, plus I did a project at my school with regards to GM at this time – I got my first ever A!). He said that had he not lost this debate he probably wouldn't have bothered with the letter. He made sure that the 6,000 envelopes were handwritten to give the message a personal touch and make it more likely to be read. More importantly, they were all addressed to the farmer's wife. He believed she would take the health and environmental threats more seriously than her husband. Most farmers, having had a tough time for a while, were understandably only interested in their profit and loss accounts and keeping the bailiffs out.

The attitudes of big business make for unbelievable reading now, yet it was only eighteen years ago. In retrospect, we see such extremes of greed and depravity as necessary. The world had become such a mess with profit being so much more important than people, it sadly needed the biggest possible kick. This was so as to wake everybody up once and for all and have the experience so ingrained in our history that mankind will never have to go down this path again. The examples in this book of agriculture and the use of war to boost flagging economies and get more control were just two of many such things happening at this time.

The world had had so many opportunities to make a change and thereby avoid the devastation we've just experienced. It's common knowledge now that spiritually speaking mankind had been given a seemingly unlimited number of wake-up calls. The two World Wars in the previous century, and endless bloody local wars, especially in the Third World, from Angola and the Congo to Tibet and Indonesia, should really have been enough. However, with the relatively comfortable yet hard working debt-ridden Western people burying their heads in the sand, and their politicians and big businessmen milking the situation for personal gains, it's easy to see how there was very little choice.

It's also clear now that the world situation was a macrocosm of our own individual lives. The spiritual workings are so damn simple and obvious it amazes us all now how the vast majority of mankind failed to see it when it was staring them in the face on a daily basis. We all know today that every situation we are presented with is here to help us. The Universal Energy is so loving it never gives us anything we cannot handle, if sometimes only just. However, it got to the stage when the world had so overwhelmingly chosen greed, selfishness, corruption and fear over and above love, that millions had chosen a short, sharp life of suffering. This was so as to hit home at the conscience of the influential global forces to try to help make a change. It also held karmic benefits for the brave souls themselves, yet the spirit of the person was doing it selflessly as service to the mind-boggling universal love of the cosmos.

It's again common knowledge now that an individual's spirit chooses its family and circumstances for maximum potential growth for both parties. They know it's a risk due to the law of free will on earth, whereby it's solely down to us how we respond to each circumstance presented to us – we can always 'choose' to do more harm than good, and add to our karmic load. At death, we get escorted by all our old friends and relations to our appropriate environment. Here the light is shone brightly on our experiences for us to work through with the relevant person or people. This can be painful, depending on what we have done. We may decide we need another life to learn, come to terms with and release, say, jealousy, greed and the need for security or whatever. The fact that we gravitate to a level of light that reflects and matches our own inner light is now common knowledge. We know if we tried to push our way into a level of light too bright and pure for us we'd feel very uncomfortable, so what's the point? The concept of going either to heaven or hell is a load of codswallop. It was simply a controlling device used by some of the major orthodox religions.

★

During the remainder of 2003 and into 2004 Dad laid down the gauntlet to the System. It was his relentless, aggressive anti-GM campaign which eventually drew the Big Boys out from the shadows a few years later. The attack in the early hours by fully clad, armed riot police was straight out of a violent American movie and the most terrifying experience of my life up until then. It was so over the top. Dad was not a violent person. When they dragged me out and shot our dog for no reason something changed in me at that moment and a strength and resolution exploded into my heart which I can't put into words. But, after that, I was never the same again.

The stakes had been upped when Dad went to the farcical Public Debate on GM foods at Taunton in early June 2003. His message was clear at the debate. He said, 'Agriculture and the global food chain are under threat like at no time in our history. Our message to Blair, Monsanto and all big agribusiness is that we will destroy *all* GM crops grown in Devon. We are here to collect names, phone numbers and emails of those willing to help us and will fight you all the way…' He then gave his reasons why.

Typical Dad! He got this message out on Devon Radio, Carlton TV, and the headlines in the *Western Morning News* read 'GM Campaigners vow to destroy all GM crops', with a picture of Dad dressed as the GM melon and the words 'Square Meal' written underneath.

Anyone with their eyes even slightly open could see that the GM debates, held in obscure places, were a feeble smokescreen by a nervy government at pretending to the public that they had a say. The first of the six debates at the NEC in Birmingham didn't even mention the debate in their events list. Add this to the fact that the debates were held three months before the results of the dubious GM trial plots were due, and it's not hard to see why activists were planning for the next stage. The Government had already put its money where its mouth was investing £52 million on research into GM biotechnology in 1998 and £13 million in 1999 to 'improve the profile of the biotech industry'. At the same time a mere £1.7 million was spent on research into organic farming in 1998.

Evidence was abounding at this time that weeds were acquiring herbicide resistance. In Canada some oilseed rape (OSR) volunteer weeds had all but become resistant to Monsato's Roundup (glyphosate) herbicide. The result was farmers were using the environmentally poisonous 2,4 D. Anybody with a miniscule bit of scientific knowledge knew that by using the same spray year in year out, the weeds naturally build up resistance. It was for this reason farmers rotated the wormers they administered to their sheep or cattle, and doctors restricted and varied antibiotics given to patients. (2,4 D was so powerful it could destroy brambles and gorse. It was banned in Europe where it was used on roadsides, because it was associated with miscarriages when inhaled by pregnant women and the Councils didn't fancy footing the compensation claims.) Not only were some farmers mixing glyphosate and atrazine (an equally toxic nasty that would sit on the soil and kill any weed foolish enough to germinate), but one biotech firm also took out a patent on a tank mix of the horrendously lethal glyphosate, atrazine and 2,4 D. This on its own was an admittance their GM crops were creating superweeds. It also meant that any farmer caught mixing his own spray tank with their combination could be heavily sued, something with which Canadian farmers had become all too familiar.

Monsanto's Terms and Conditions, which had to be signed by all farmers who took their GM seed, stated that they were 'allowed to drop in on farmers for three years after growing a GM crop, if possible in the presence of the grower'. In Canada the inspectors simply turned up when they felt like it. A friend of Dad's spent six months with Canadian farmers in 2003. He said he found hundreds of them battered, bruised and nearly broke as a result of GM. If traces of GM were found in seed bins or fields, the farmers were prosecuted, successfully, by Monsanto's well-paid lawyers, even when they swore the small amounts were due to cross-contamination. Inspectors turned up one day at Percy Schmeiser's farm and took samples of his canola (OSR). They found a percentage of GM canola and sued Mr Schmeiser. Mr Schmeiser vowed that he had never sown GM canola, but he'd been saving his own seed which had been severely contaminated by his neighbour's crop. The courts ruled in favour of Monsanto and fined Mr Schmeiser $120,000. Some farmers refused such injustices and went to prison. The situation was made even more absurd and obvious by the fact that when 'blue' maize was grown next to 'yellow', up to fifteen per cent of the yellow corn was turned blue by the dominant pollen from the neighbouring field.

It also became clearer to all and sundry that the reason there was no (apparent) evidence available of damage to human health from the chemicals used on GM crops, was that the clinical trials and epidemiological studies were 'still to be conducted'. Even without these studies, other than the two mentioned earlier, the journal of the US Cancer

Society reported in 1999 that Monsanto's Roundup led to increased risks of the cancer called non-Hodgkin's lymphoma. In 1997 the UK Government had quietly raised the permitted safety levels of Roundup in soya destined for humans by twenty thousand per cent. This on the back of a hugely expensive advertising campaign by Monsanto promoting its favourite weedkiller as one of the safest herbicides on the market in terms of the environment and human health.

Monsanto, like Enron and many more, epitomised the corporate corruption so rife at the time. It was reported in *The Financial Times* on 7/1/2005 that: 'Monsanto is to pay $1.5 million in penalties to the US Government over a bribe paid in Indonesia in a bid to bypass controls on the screening of new genetically modified cotton crops.' The Justice Department (DOJ) stated that the company paid $50,000 to an unnamed senior Indonesian environmental official to, 'repeal the requirement for the environmental impact statement for new crop varieties.' A senior Monsanto official in the US approved the bribe and tried to disguise it as 'consultant's fees'. Once found out the company admitted it had paid over $700,000 in bribes in Indonesia between 1997 and 2002. They only 'admitted' this because they were caught. This was the tip of a very murky iceberg and should have, on it's own, been enough evidence to Governments world wide to pull out all GM crops on the market. When profits were at stake, environmental and human safety issues were clearly of no consideration whatsoever to these irresponsible big companies.

Everybody in the know knew the UK Government had buckled before under pressure exerted by the US via the WTO. European ministers didn't need reminding of the astronomical fine imposed upon them when they refused, by a vote of 366–0 in the European Parliament in 1996, to allow imports of hormone-implanted beef from the US. Other crippling recriminations from this were that the WTO allowed huge tariffs to be imposed by the US on local businesses such as Roquefort cheese and specialist mustard farmers. However, Dad was buoyed up by being part of the anti-Tesco campaign in his home town which had recently been won, and used the Health and Harmony Festival on that magical June weekend to launch the battle plan.

★

So what of the rest of the world? I overheard Dad talking to a corporate businessman in 2004 about the utterly destructive exploitation of the world's resources in pursuit of short-term profit for the few. The businessman said flippantly, yet quite seriously, 'Sure but when the oil does run out or there's a major catastrophe, man will have colonised another planet and the richest of us will be able to move there.' This when there were sixty million actually starving in Africa alone.

What amazed me about this attitude was how such a person couldn't see the mind-blowing beauty of this planet and desire to help preserve it. Living in a bubble on Mars with other rich people was the most depressing scenario I could possibly think up.

By the spring of 2004 things were going horrendously wrong for the US in the Middle East. Attacks by the Nationalist/Islamic camp on the occupying (sorry, *liberating*) forces had steadily increased in ferocity and results. There was lots of talk of Vietnam in the papers but the Americans were never going to back off this time – not with oil and their pride at stake. Arabs from Jordan, Syria, Iran and pro-US regimes such as Saudi Arabia and Egypt were increasingly flooding in to join with Arab 'freedom fighters' against the 'imperial aggressors.'

I received a letter from Ishmael in the spring of 2004. Here are some snippets:

Dear Annie,

I'm glad to hear your dad is blowing his top at the American-backed student demonstrations in some of Iran's major cities. We too have heard George Bush and Tony Blair say these people have a right to demonstrate for 'Freedom and Democracy' yet as your dad rightly says when he was demonstrating in Genoa for 'Freedom and Democracy' people were shot and thousands injured. The point is it all depends on how you define 'Freedom and Democracy'.

In Iraq we are demonstrating for the same thing, our own democratically elected President and party. Yet here the Americans kill us for demonstrating. We believe we can't start sorting our lives and businesses out until the Americans leave. Big American companies are flooding into our country, unashamedly carving up the spoils from our state industries and parts of government, to reconstruction, hospitals, schools, agriculture and, of course, our oil. We've never seen anything like this before.

My father, in the now American-controlled bank, says we must sit tight for now for our own safety and that our time will come. It really is no different to when Saddam was here, and we are fed up. When freedom fighters successfully blew up an Apache helicopter killing Americans, I, like most others, let out a huge cheer. The recriminations are, however, as usual, horrendous. The US planes literally blitzed Falluja, where they claimed the terrorists were hiding, killing many more women, children, farmers and innocent people.

It seems to Iraqi people that the US Army and Government think they are doing us a favour. One thing is for sure and that is they are very insensitive – and, we feel, rather stupid. How could they think we would accept their continued occupation and exploitation of our country? It is clear to all of us that they were never interested in Saddam or our weapons. These were just a smokescreen for them to create unprecedented wealth and boost their dwindling economy.

My father says that the American governors are now selling terrorism insurance to corporate personnel as they come into Iraq.

Our Arab brothers in Iran have not got a particularly good ayatollah in charge. However, they don't want the Americans going in and sorting them out, having seen what's happened here. The sewage and lack of drinking water are still a huge problem, and my brother has had a fever for four months. More and more of our neighbours, many armed only with rocks and wearing flip-flops, are joining the freedom fighters. However, what hurts every Iraqi Arab the most is the knowing that when Bush wins the next election he might use Iraqi bases to attack Iran from. I don't think the US has begun to realise the reaction this will ignite in all Iraqi people. My father, however, does not think this will happen. He believes the noises Bush is making against the terrible mullahs in power is simply hot air, to show he cares for the human rights of the Iranian people. He says that whilst Iran continues to let big business in, the US, secure behind their military threats in Iraq, will turn a blind eye. We will see, my friend.

With warmth and peace, Ishmael

The US economy was by now in quite serious decline. The cost of global domination was beginning to look a little less fun. As well as more and more American soldiers being picked off, the reason for their being there was coming under increasing attack. The exposed oil pipelines in Iraq were easy targets for the freedom fighters and hit the US right where it hurts. The continuing arming of Israel's forces and their inability to get Israelis out of the illegally occupied areas of Palestine was not helping matters much. Indeed, when President Bush tried to introduce his 'road map' for peace it simply helped to escalate the violence to new levels in the short term after the initial ceasefire. The assassination of Ariel Sharon, shot twice in the chest by Jewish right-wing extremists unhappy at his pulling out settlers from the West Bank, did little to ease the tension in the Middle East. Terrorist attacks continued, but were controlled in a kind of stalemate. This suited the Americans.

One of the sickest things were the US were still using so-called 'aid' to the Third World simply to try to boost their balance of payments. Other countries normally gave cash, which if used correctly (it often wasn't) could boost the local economy and employment. However, America simply tried to flood as many countries with GM food, for example, to bolster its by now near crisis-ridden corporations; eighty per cent of money they did give went directly to their own multilateral service industries and big consultancy firms.

Soon after my last letter from Ishmael I received another. It is well documented that the situation was by now out of hand. Laws were enforced by the US that outlawed all gatherings, pronouncements or publications that focused on opposition to US forces. Those involved were classed as 'subversives' and 'terrorists' and simply shot.

Dear Annie,

I'm glad you are still managing to get some news of what is going on out here. The propaganda war is a key factor now. The US have total editorial control over what goes on TV and into our newspapers, just as it was when Saddam was in control. Brave Iraqi writers, loyal to their country, are risking their lives circulating fliers delivered through letter boxes. US servicemen are now watching for this and using torture to make delivery boys tell where the sheets were written and printed. Many are losing their lives but Iraqi people are determined to keep this service going. It is the only source of information of any truth or substance for most of us. A recent one posted through our door reads as follows:

'Iraqi brothers and sisters, I would like for you to know of the plight of our Arab brethren in Palestine. This to warn you of what befalls the Islamic people in the hands of Western infidels and might. For those who are familiar with these facts I beg forgiveness. No matter, the point is we must all shut our eyes and ears to the US led

propaganda we are being fed. As always we urge all of you to risk your lives and die if necessary to remove the Western military occupation from our country. In the name of Allah.

'In 1948 Palestine's indigenous people were evicted, terrorised or fled from their homes. A Jewish population, mainly from Europe, seized their property and land. Six million Palestinians were displaced. They were not even compensated for their losses.

'The international community ruled against this act and the UN passed Resolution 194 requiring Israel to allow the displaced Palestinians back. Israel, backed by the US and Britain especially, to the tune of $4.5 billion of subsidy each year with all manner of up to date military hardware over and above, refused to comply.

'Israel wriggled out of recriminations by offering that Palestinians return to a new state. However, like George Bush's recent botched road map, the wording was totally ambiguous. The area recommended was so small and infertile it was simply not feasible. Bear in mind most Palestinians originate from what is now Israel.

'The result is today, one million Palestinians live in Palestinian-owned Gaza. The vast majority live on less than $2 a day with unemployment running at eighty per cent in some places. One third of their land is, however, occupied by 5,000 Israeli settlers. They are protected by the Israeli Army and live in luxury houses with liberally watered gardens. With eighty per cent of all water in the West Bank and Gaza being directed from the Palestinians to the Israelis, water for drinking or otherwise is sporadic to say the least.

'Palestinians sometimes wait for days at a time at Israeli checkpoints when trying to find work or get access to essential medical care. UN Resolution 242 states that Israel must withdraw from all land occupied since 1967. Yet Israeli soldiers continue to drive families from their homes, confiscate property and demolish whole neighbourhoods. The residents are sealed off from each other and live under curfew, being picked off by marksmen in the watchtowers for the most innocent of misdemeanours. With authorities viewing torture as acceptable, and using collective punishment and withholding essentials such as water as a means of control, and you get the picture of what to expect from long term Western occupation.

'Already we can see the plush mansions being built around the most expensive hotels for the US corporate bosses moving in to carve up the spoils of war and increase the size of their bank accounts tenfold. Those large walls with barbed wire are to keep us out. As with the Palestinians and our Arab and Muslim brothers throughout so much of the world, we are to become subservient second-class citizens to our superior masters from the West. We will soon form a massive underclass and be as slaves to our imperialistic rulers, as has happened throughout history.

'My friends, I ask you not to believe the American propaganda being fed to us and our brethren in Iran, Syria and throughout the Arab world. I implore you to rise up, as our brave brothers Hamas have done in Palestine, and rid our sacred land of this evil foreign power. It is now the time for the Iraqi intifada on an overwhelming scale.'

With love and respect, Ishmael

It's heartbreaking to know of the bloodshed on such a massive scale in that part of the world. What a waste of so much life, especially in the light of the remaining Palestinians, Israelis, Iraqis and so on now living side by side in wholesome harmony, balance and love. Who would have ever thought those religious barriers were so fraught with fear, hatred, anger and death?

I remember Dad coming back from big protest marches chanting 'Victory to the intifada!' The loss of any life unnecessarily upset him, but he said he could easily identify with the suicide bombers.

Society in the UK, and elsewhere in the West, took a noticeable downturn from 2005 onwards. It was gang war in the cities especially that took things onto the next level of desperation. The debt culture meant many families in low income brackets were simply breaking down. Paying mortgages and rents disproportionate to their earnings left little or even nothing for people to pay other bills or even buy food. This combined with an ever tightening Welfare State, with the Government claiming there were simply not the funds available (they always seemed to find enough for their war machine), and capitalism was in free fall.

As family life broke down, many parents had no time for their children. Children as young as eight were joining gangs taking crack and committing gun crimes to get them accepted by their new 'family'. For some it was the first bit of real security they'd experienced in their lives.

The punters in the street, private houses and shops were, for the gangs, their DHSS dole money and housing benefit all wrapped up into one. Folk living in constant fear of gang attack had been localised to the poorer parts of cities until 2005. In 2005 there was such an increase in gang numbers that these areas were not providing enough to go around. Gangs hooded to protect themselves from CCTV were making raids into every part of all the major cities. Many gang members were shot and killed. As shortages and desperation rose so did the stakes. However, if they made it back to their turf with the loot they were safe. Police rarely entered these areas at all by then, unless as a band of a hundred or more fully armed riot police going after a particular target. As more police lost their lives in such raids, the raids themselves soon petered out.

As had become the norm in occupied Palestine, most of Africa and much of the Third World, where rich folk lived within reinforced, often electrified gates, so it became in the West. Even then these houses were attacked as things became ever more desperate and the underclass grew exponentially. The armed guards and occupants were often killed, sometimes for just a loaf of bread and some fresh fruit. It was in 2011 and 2012 when it became a free-for-all throughout all parts of the country. By then there were no safe havens.

★

Much, however, happened in the years leading up to this time. The polarisation, first seen on a big scale with the hugely divided results of public opinion before the 2003 Gulf War, increased in intensity from 2004 onwards. There were folk from all manner of cultures and creeds, rich and poor and those in between who were actively waking up to the evils of global capitalism. (Dad and his friends always described it as 'Capitalism gone wrong' – they were not against anybody making an honest buck through hard work.) Millions the world over began doing their bit.

It was clear to anyone who wanted to open their eyes that this system was rapidly leading to economic, social and environmental breakdown as at no time in recent history. Millions worldwide played a part in a manner best suited to them depending upon their circumstances and capabilities. My dad went further than some, getting a longer prison sentence than he deserved for destroying GM crops in France, and blockading ports where GM animal feed was flooding in from the US and Canada. However, the authorities deemed his antics too much when he began making disruptive inroads into their implementation of compulsory ID cards and the rest. The man who helped more than any other reduce the destruction and death during the Transformation was the American politician, Harold Smith.

He was an independent who managed to raise funds from rich American individuals especially and provided the model for the world as it is today. There is no question that he managed more than any other to help the world avert an environmental and social catastrophe that would have wiped out the human race apart from a few. By the time of his inevitable assassination, the template was already in place. The beauty of it all lay in its simplicity.

★

Dad very kindly picked me up for the launch of his Anti-GM campaign at the June Health and Harmony Festival 2003. I had been pestering him in every letter and phone call about these festivals. I looked forward to them more than anything else in the year.

I'm not sure if Dad appreciated the five-hour round trip as much as I did. This in the light of the fact I spent every penny I could get out of him and all my savings on my addiction at this time... crystals. It wasn't just the pretty colours I loved, but also the magical properties. For example, the dark blue lapis lazuli was said to work on your third eye to help increase your intuitive perception of things; green moldovite – a stone from outer space, worked on opening your heart chakra (energy point) and filled you with love. My favourite crystal from that weekend was a piece of translucent blue calcite, which was said to help give clarity of thought and speech. This was exactly what I needed at the time. I had just been off to do an interview for a potential new school where they asked me what I'd like to do when I grew up. All I could think about was to 'be a housewife'. However, I realised this was somewhat unambitious and might not help my chances, so I tried to think of something else. As many of us have experienced, the more I tried not to think about being a housewife the more I thought about it – the pink elephant scenario. After looking around the walls and ceiling for three or four minutes, out popped, 'When I grow up I'd like to help do a little work in the garden.'

On my way back to school I was showing Dad my crystals and he was amazed at how many I had. I said I'd left some of the more valuable pieces at home and mentioned one was particularly valuable but I couldn't resist it. He immediately asked me how much. I told him that it was probably best if he didn't know.

Dad delivered his hour long talk/debate on GM to about two hundred mainly, I feel, unsuspecting visitors on the Tea Room lawn where people were having their lunch. 'No point preaching to the converted,' he'd always say. The numbers were far greater for the July and August Festivals which were part shared with a Globalise Resistance posse and a fund-raising campaign for Iraqi children respectively.

He'd had some sheets printed up on which there were two columns front and back for people to get their friends to put names, phone numbers and email addresses. One was for those who were prepared to slash all GM crops if they came in, the other was simply for those who wanted to accompany the protesters in support but not slash. Sixty sheets were taken up that weekend and over two hundred the following two weekends. The campaign was underway.

Dad spoke with so much passion at times his eyes filled with tears. It was when he spoke of the recent arrest of José Bove in France I became concerned. He said that Bove was asleep in his farmhouse having previously been arrested for slashing GM trial crops, biding his time before his trial. In the early hours, eighty armed riot police broke into his house, grabbed him and took him off in a helicopter to an unknown destination. Dad assured everybody that this wouldn't happen to them, but if they targeted him he 'no longer cared.' He'd learnt from foot-and-mouth and other experiences the spiritual fact that if you wanted to achieve something, you sometimes had to take that leap into the void and pray that God would catch you.

Dad, his friends and I, were handing out two information sheets with his 'recruitment' sheet. The gist of the first I've mentioned in bits and bobs throughout this book. The second was more urgently stressing the importance of getting ready for what he believed to be the imminent invasion of GM in 2004. His main thrust was to demonstrate how the biotechs' claim of no proven health risks, increased yields, improved nutrition and a reduction in spray from GM use was totally wrong. In fact the opposite was true.

With regard to human health and yield, he quoted the examples mentioned earlier. 'Improved nutrition' – he gave the example of vitamin A in rice and the nutritionally enhanced GM 'wonder' potato. This was interestingly named the 'Protato', maybe because it made the word sound like protein. The gene was said to boost protein and amino acid levels by thirty–fifty per cent to help the nutritionally deficient poor. The angelic aspect was further enhanced when Dr Manju Sharma, head of the Biotech department in India, said that the protato would be given 'free' to millions of poor children for their midday meal.

A counter-argument, provided by some Greenpeace 'smarty pants', questioned why India's traditionally grown pulses could not be further encouraged rather than being replaced with the Protato. The pulses contained between twenty to twenty-six per cent protein compared to the two and a half per cent in the GM Protato. They also fixed nitrogen in the soil and needed little or no artificial fertilisers and sprays to grow it. Oops, (Dad says), where's the profit for the biotech boys in this? This in the light that the global potato market was worth £116 billion and India was exporting potatoes to twenty-nine countries at the time. Another 'bonus' was that potatoes required more sprays and fertiliser than almost any other crop. The relatively small investment into the distribution of the fifty-nine million tons of corn, being eaten by rats and weevils in the grain silos in India, apparently did not occur to agribusiness at this time.

With regard to pesticide and herbicide claims, he gave the example of the tests on the BT insecticide in China and the disastrous consequences of GM OSR weed species in Canada. Even the US Department of Agriculture admitted in 2000 that 'there was not a noticeable drop in herbicide use since the introduction of GM crops in 1996'. This from a body whose workforce operated a revolving door set-up with the biotech industry's workforce.

His sheet continued with a mention that NFU Mutual, the main agricultural insurers in the UK, would not insure farmers who grew GM. This was because they knew the mass of claims and counterclaims would send them under within six months. Incredibly just before the arrival of GM, which happened considerably later than the big GM seed companies would have liked, agribusiness managed to sneak through the law of all laws to demonstrate the tight control big corporations had over Government. The law stated the biotech companies to be 'not subject to legal liability with regard to possible health and environmental impacts of the crops or for any genetic pollution'.

The sheet encouraged guest house owners, hoteliers and smallholders to write to their Councils and neighbouring farmers to keep Devon GM-free. Then to promote the area as such to state that local Restaurants and Hotels stocked all local, fresh food where they could. This proved non-viable, because Upper Austria had their request to be a GM-free zone flatly turned down by the European Parliament – under huge pressure from the WTO. Obviously if Austria had succeeded then every European country would have followed suit because nobody wanted GM.

During the foot-and-mouth epidemic, the reason stressed the most for destroying a quarter of our healthy animals was to get the export ban lifted quicker than if they had used vaccination. Yet in the lead up to the GM invasion, there was no mention of the export crisis in the GM nations. In 1996, before GM crops were introduced in the Americas, US maize farmers made a profit of $1.4

billion. In 2002 they lost $12 billion. Likewise, hugely profitable exports of corn and soya to the EU from the US dropped from millions of tons to almost zero. The US farm sector entered a period of record levels of bankruptcies. The cash-strapped Argentinean Government spent $200 million it didn't have to help farmers to try to switch from GM crops back to non-GM to recover export markets. The 'export' argument was helpful in destroying our livestock to pave the way for cheaper imports, but quite the opposite when promoting the other corporate delight – GM food. The irony was that Dad first went to prison when fighting in effect against the policy of re-instatement of the export licence. The next time he went to prison was for fighting against a policy of ultimate destruction of the export market.

It's awful to think how the world could have been so two faced back then. What did the corporations do to compensate? They invaded GM-free countries such as Brazil where they destroyed vast areas of rainforest in a process called slash and burn. Trees dating back to Roman times in the Amazon Basin were simply eliminated. GM free soya for export was then planted in the bare soil. An area the size of Belgium was destroyed in the Amazon in 2002 alone simply to meet their needs.

His sheet ended by stating that the legal loopholes found by the corporations were enormous. Firstly, in the States GM soya and non-GM soya was mixed together in the vast silos. Hence, any processed food from the States such as the cheese in supermarkets, was contaminated. The same applied to commercial cattle feed containing soya. Interwoven with this was dodgy labelling. Meat containing the GM food livestock had eaten didn't have to be labelled, and processed food was only partially labelled. Countries such as Japan, which wanted full labelling of all GM food containing GE products, were threatened with massive recriminations from the WTO.

★

Dad and I had a good chat on the way back to the school. He was exhausted and it wasn't just because of the usual party on the Saturday night. He said that he had had an uneasy feeling on the Friday night and didn't sleep much; Biff and Biff's new girlfriend had felt the same.

On the Saturday night I was wandering through the grounds and came across a gang of kids my age and a bit older pulling at the wrought iron bars of our grotto. The ceiling of the grotto was made out of beautiful shells, hence its name: the Shell House. The bars were there because some children in the past had mindlessly bashed a section of the shells down with large sticks.

I rushed to get Dad, and when we got back there was a fourteen-year-old boy with a large rock in his hand aiming it at the shells. I was worried Dad might really hurt the boy. The year before there had been a 'Free' party and a gang of about fifty or so young teenagers were tearing around the garden showing off to each other. They smashed cold frames and trampled some of the flowers, even when they had been told to stop. However, when they started tearing up Dad's newly made hay, which he'd made himself, and ignored him when he told them to get off, the red mist descended. I'd first seen this during the foot-and-mouth and it was scary (and luckily rare). His anger was such he'd lose all sense of self-preservation for himself and his opponents. On this occasion he grabbed a child and hurled him across the concrete into a wall, then stood there yelling to the shell-shocked parents to take him on. The child wasn't too hurt. Dad said he had thrown the child flat so as to minimise damage. However, Dad felt remorse for days afterwards, and sad that so many parents couldn't teach their children respect.

This time he took the children down to meet their parents and talk to them. He said the parents camping in a field clearly did not care, and one even threatened him when he mentioned the previous year's incident. It turned out that some of those camping were simply festival freeloaders, not stallholders as they were meant to be. The same children had earlier in the day chucked the niece of a lady in the house into the lake – she couldn't even swim and nearly drowned. I didn't tell Dad at the time.

At the same time the (special) 'Brew Crew' turned up. These were big burly wasters from the local town who spent their whole time drunk and causing trouble. They then headed for the woods where Biff was doing the traditional barbecue for the stallholders and close friends. There were six of them, and the biggest one of all ran into me, sending me flying. I bruised my ribs and twisted my ankle quite badly, but was more shocked than anything else. I was taken up to the house, given some chocolate and watched *The Italian Job* on video, which helped me feel much better. I asked everybody not to tell Dad, who was dealing with the dodgy campers at the time, because I felt he may go berserk. That night they were repeatedly asked to leave and they said they would, but instead they went around trying to break into the outbuildings and threatening individuals. Three of the girls in the house even confronted them with baseball bats at 3 a.m. in the marquee where they were peeing on the floor and lying on massage tables.

All this was deemed extremely positive next day by Biff, Dad and other long-termers – spiritually speaking. It was difficult in those days when most of the world felt so alone, powerless and spiritually impoverished. Such tragic lack of any fulfilment made many feel like, 'What's the point? I'll simply look after number one, and sod the rest of you…'

Dad and his close friends knew that this was an important spiritual warning and message. There was absolute minimal damage, but they also knew next time if they didn't listen then the lessons would be much harsher in intensity – again a fully understood truth today. The message was clear to them that they couldn't look after all of the lost souls everywhere, many of whom had become freeloaders. Whenever they tried to do this their friends would come up, and the wholesome alternative they were trying to create would simply crumble away into ashes, as all the decent folk would leave.

The vibe in the woods was tense that evening and people didn't have as good a time as usual. However, thanks to the experience, when the Brew Crew turned up for the July Festival, Dad had all the ammunition needed to send them peacefully away. He simply asked them what they would do if he came into their house, drunk and uninvited, and sent their child flying down the stairs, and then proceeded to pee on their kitchen floor and help himself to whatever he wanted.

To compound the intensity of this experience, Dad had had a dream before the May Health and Harmony that money would go missing on the Sunday when he was away. When he returned he heard that it had been the best day ever with record takings. However, when Dad checked the money it was just over £500, about £400 short of the previous best. The sheets bearing details of the takings had been over-calculated by £400 by the lady on the gate that day. When Dad asked her about this in June, she said there were people hovering around the area who might have helped themselves when she was dealing with a carload of new arrivals. More was made on the June Sunday than that in May, yet the lady on the gate said there were about three times more people in May. Dad said it was yet another lesson to follow up on his dreams rather than just thinking

Naah! He said the guy he asked to collect the money from the lady on the gate was the one who stood out the most in his dream. The day after his dream he had felt the need to ask him to regularly collect the money on the Sunday but didn't bother.

★

Harold Smith broke into the public eye during 2005 and 2006. He was a tall, wiry man with a depth, honesty and compassion so obviously radiating and touching all those who dared look into his piercing blue eyes. However, what truly set him apart from any Western politician over the previous forty years was that he was not only a man of genuine integrity but wore a refreshing air of humility.

When questioned on a subject on which he was not fully up to the mark, he would have no problem in saying, ' I am sorry but I don't have enough knowledge on this subject to make a genuine or worthwhile appraisal, but if you would like I will study it and give you my opinion when we next meet.' He would however sometimes give his gut feeling if he had a little knowledge on a subject, always making it clear that until he delved further it was not set in stone in his mind. He frustrated the hell out of journalists and opposing politicians especially, because by being totally honest he could not be pinned down. Put simply, he was annoying to them because he was doing exactly what they all intuitively wanted to do themselves. As such he remained free in a world dominated by lies, spin, deception and the desire for personal gain and power, which stemmed from good old ego and fear. He truly was a centred, spiritual person, sent from God in the eyes of many in those troubled times.

Many tried to undermine and destroy him with a hostility beyond what had been seen in politics before.

Conspiracy theories abounded. However, today we know it was because his inner light shone so bright he was holding up a mirror to all those who engaged with him. Everybody understands today that when we see our faults reflected to us by another, we thank them at least mentally. We all embrace the spiritual truth that if somebody or some situation comes into our lives and presses antagonistic buttons, then they or it are there to help us in some way. We know we then have the choice to do something about it – or not.

It is madness to think that just a few years ago the world was thinking in terms of the 'good guys' and the 'bad guys'. The major attack on him was for not having the courage/intellect to speak on all subjects when questioned. He was frequently accused of 'cowardly ducking out'. His answer was that he was only human and had huge limitations, but was quite envious of some of his contemporaries who knew so much more than he and could speak on any subject. What was even more irritating was when he said this he actually meant it.

Harold, as he liked to be called by everybody, had managed to detach and live totally in the moment. He was still touched to his very core by the atrocities in the world – unlike a few of the blissed out New Agers around at the time. He planned for the future but had no expectations. This was because he knew that his Spirit/God knew better than he, hence when he was sidetracked or presented with the unexpected he accepted that this was 'meant to be'. He would then address and deal with the situation with all his energy and gusto as best he could, as usual leaving the outcome to the Universe.

His speeches are very well documented now and seen as one cog of many in a wheel of catalysts in assisting the global transformation. He regularly spoke of the simple spiritual truth and universal laws that flow through every living and inanimate human, animal, vegetable and mineral on earth. His delivery of the truth was in a charming matter-of-fact manner that could easily be embraced by the most cynical of humans if they opened up even in the smallest way. He never judged those who rejected him or his work, and no one could say he was as a priest in a pulpit looking down on a congregation. The people said that he sincerely looked at every other human being as more important than he and he was honoured to be in service to them where he could. However, being extremely sensitive, he felt the pain of others and the world very deeply, a pain that became etched on his face in a short space of time.

He spoke about the important issues of the day and never held back from speaking his truth no matter what ripples resulted. This he could do, being an independent. It wasn't as if all politicians were deceitful, dishonest liars shrouded in a sense of hidden agendas and spin – far from it. The problem was that if politicians did not 'toe the party line' and stepped outside the very narrow, rigid barriers, then they were moved sideways and downwards, or simply sacked.

He saw globalisation, and the 'one size fits all' policy, war, debt and a lack of love (a word politicians until then had been too afraid to use), as the facets in most need of addressing. This in the light of alleviating poverty and if the world was at least to try to avert a global environmental catastrophe beyond anybody's wildest dreams.

'I dream of a day when Christians, Arabs and all Islamic people, Jews, Hindus, Buddhists, New Age Spiritualists and the rest of us, worship the one God under the same roof. For this we in the West need to be a beacon – not of terror and fear, but of compassion, understanding and love of our brother and sister in each and every corner of the globe.'

This was a quote taken from his first ever speech. Ridiculed as he immediately was, nevertheless the juices were stirred up in much of the disillusioned non-voting public, as well as many who did vote. Many liked the fact that he put himself in the 'rest of us' bracket.

With regard to poverty, which was at an unnecessarily high level (as I hope is clear from this book so far), he stated that global policies were in fact opposite to what they claimed to be. The claim was they were pro poor when they were in fact pro poverty.

He goes on: *'The IMF talks of "actively combating World poverty"; the World Bank is "fighting grinding World poverty"; The WTO says it is "reducing poverty on a world-wide basis"; and George Bush and Tony Blair claim they are "attacking global poverty". So why do they make countries conform to a development and trade model that does the opposite? Trade negotiations and aid distribution by the West are simply tools of foreign policy to further national self-interest.*

'US and UK aid has historically mostly been tied to conditions that have serious negative consequences on the poor, democracy and the environment. Aid and debt relief are used to force crippling policies on developing countries, such as the privatisation of health, education, water and land. Had the UK been serious in its commitment to "Making Poverty History" in 2005 it would have returned economic sovereignty to developing countries and stopped using aid to bully them into unjust, unpopular and unworkable policies. The message from the World Bank is, "If you don't accept the conditions, you don't get aid."

'When the water system was taken over by the private sector in Manila, the capital of the Philippines, householders saw their rates rise by over three hundred per cent in six years as a result. The result was families were forced to cut back on expenditure on health, food and education. Poverty, debt, ill health, unemployment and suicides were a direct result. The same happened with privatisation of electricity in Karnataka in India, the rail network in Malawi – the list is endless.

'*Most staggering of all is that on average for every dollar the West gives in aid to developing countries, $6 is paid back by these same countries in debt repayment. Debt relief is only given conditionally – for example in exchange for controlling a country's foreign policy. With one sixth of the world's population undernourished with no consistent access to fresh drinking water, it surely is time for a new model.*'

Harold stressed above all a need for the West to win the world's trust. For this to happen it was action that was necessary not just more hollow, meaningless rhetoric. Debt relief was to him the first and most important part of the equation. In 2003, Africa alone was paying £23 million a day in debt to the West. Rose-tinted carrots had been dangled before to poor nations concerning debt relief, only to be snatched away as the grateful hands reached out. For example, the G7 decided in Cologne in 1999 to forgive debts to the tune of $100 billion. However, the huge street parties were soon cut short when those lovely bodies in the form of the IMF and World Bank stepped in to dot the 'i's and cross the 't's. As always, they demanded 'structural adjustments' such as opening markets to international trade before money was released. A year later, and just $2 billion of debt reductions had been made. The likes of Nicaragua, Zambia, and Mali – countries most in need, did not see a 'single penny of relief'.

Zambia, for example, in 2004 was paying thirty-eight per cent more on its debt than it was on health and education put together. To give him his due, the then Chancellor of the Exchequer in the UK, Gordon Brown, was doing his best to initiate some serious debt relief. It was becoming well known that the small amounts of debt relief given to some countries had made a significant impact. It hadn't been squandered, as the sceptics believed it would. For example, in Benin, forty-three per cent of debt relief granted under the HIPC, the Highly Indebted Poor

Country initiative, went into education in 2002, and fifty-four per cent to health and rural clinics, especially to anti – malarial and HIV/Aids programmes, immunisation and access to safe water. It was similar in both Mozambique and Tanzania, who were both let off tiny proportions of their debt. Here the funds saved on debt relief were used to finance free immunisation for children, and free primary schooling respectively.

Brown said he wanted a hundred per cent write-off of multilateral debts (he was never gonna be allowed to become PM). This he suggested could be paid off in part by the sale of or revaluation of the IMF's (a public institution, en passant) massive gold reserves. He believed that as an organisation the Fund didn't need the gold and could make more money by investing the proceeds in better performing assets. He even said any gold transaction could take place 'off market' so as not to depress the global market price, even though there was little evidence of this in the past at times of massive sales. He, like everybody else, knew US Congress would reject the proposal outright – which of course they did.

Brown was expressing these views in September 2004. The UK was due to take the Presidency of the G8 in 2005, and Brown knew nothing could happen until the G8 Summit at Gleneagles, Scotland, in July that year. He, like so many others, was acutely aware there were 30,000 preventable deaths per day. It was some two hundred days from the time he issued his statement until Gleneagles during which time some six million people (200 x 30,000) would die unnecessarily – a problem that could have been largely solved by the gold in the IMF's bank vault. 'The love of money...'

As an aside, money (debt) owed to commercial banks (who lent it carelessly or with ulterior motives, as mentioned) was miraculously converted in the late 1990s, by the G7, into debt owed to public institutions like the IMF. The IMF then passed the bill on to the taxpayer. Hence, ordinary people were picking up the tab for the malpractice of the commercial banks. The worst part of all this was that the then G7 were prepared to forgive (release) the debt owed by commercial banks, but not the HIPCs who had to divert money from education, health, agriculture and fresh water programmes.

In the light of this, Harold proposed a dismantling of the IMF, World Bank and WTO to be replaced by a body of democratically elected representatives throughout the world.

'I propose a new Global Constitution. This to be based on legislation to prevent excessive trade surpluses and deficits from occurring and thereby minimise debt creation. The Service Industry Bureau (SIB) would simply oversee global trade with the power to retract any trading companies' trading rights if either of the following two criteria were breached:

'The first law would be to allow developing countries to protect their industries against foreign imports until they were strong enough to fend for themselves. Every country would be required to openly declare their balance of payment details. The SIB would then vote on when a country's tariffs were to be lifted and thereby fully open up to global trade rules, or likewise be allowed to be re-imposed should a country run into difficulty.

'The second law would be that countries and companies will have to meet a set of criteria if they wished to trade globally. All trading companies would have to satisfy a simple set of rules. For example, that their workers were not being exposed to asbestos, banned pesticides or other toxic materials, and they were not employing slaves. Equally as importantly, companies would have to pay the full environmental cost of the fossil fuel it used. Aviation tax alone reflecting this would immediately stop low-value, high-volume goods such as fruit and veg from being flown around the world.

'This second law especially would encourage localisation. Countries would all have to have a policy of self-sufficiency. However, companies would still be able to make a profit, albeit not as huge as those made now, by trading in less bulky high-value products. This would also mean that companies would not be able to transport bulky raw material, even by ship, to processing plants in the West. They would have to set up manufacturing industry in the port of origin, thus creating jobs for the local people.

'The minerally rich Third World countries, especially in Africa, would directly profit hugely from this, but at the expense of the minerally exhausted West. It wouldn't be too long before some countries would be able to afford to buy up the manufacturing industry set up by the Western companies in their country. The balance could even eventually tip to the extent that Zambia, Malawi, the Congo and China would be giving aid to the US and UK somewhere down the line.

'The giving up of power and global dominance by the West to create a level playing field would be an act of love, on a scale never seen before in our history. However, if we are to save our planet and maybe even our souls, this is what we must do. Sadly, I cannot see the current breed of world politicians having the courage to open up their hearts and take this leap. There are though many around, primed and ready beneath the surface, who would. It is the duty of every one of us to seek these people out and put them into power. It is our only true hope of salvation.

'We have all heard the phrase, "Power corrupts, absolute power corrupts absolutely." Likewise Christ said: "No man can serve two masters: for either he will hate the one and love the other; or else he will hold to the one and despise the other. Ye cannot serve God and mammon (money)." For example, how will we be able to stop members of the SIB from receiving millions of dollars into a Swiss or offshore bank account from, say, the likes of Rio Tinto wishing to quietly chop down much of the Madagascan rain-forest to obtain minerals to make soaps and cosmetics? In this case we'd be no better off than we are now where everybody from the US President to members of local authorities accept bribes for anything from overthrowing countries rich in oil to building supermarkets and McDonald's.

'The answer again is faith. I would suggest that all members of the SIB not be paid a penny or allowed to have a bank account – at least at the beginning. The number of members from different countries would be based on some kind of global democracy index. Needs such as housing, transport, hotels (modest) would be met, but there would be no opportunity for personal gain. Only those with absolutely no bias towards their country of origin would be considered for the SIB. Also, nation states would not be allowed any control, hold or influence over fellow countrymen who are voted into the SIB. The point is that all members would join for the 'joy' of being in service to the world. Even in retirement from the SIB, they would not be allowed a bank account due to the risk of corruption. They would, however, be well cared for, respected as the 'elders' of a tribe. Throughout history, the world's most influential and fulfilled people have seen themselves as in service to others.

'Faith is the polar opposite of fear. World leaders, businesses and most individuals are nearly all operating from fear. Where there is fear there is no love – for ourselves or our brothers and sisters in different cultures and creeds across the globe. God has given us the precious gift of free will. This means that we can choose to do good or evil or sit on the fence. Without this we would be a world of automata with no potential for growth, expansion and spiritual development. The global powers are doing all they can via TV, media and so on to engulf us in a fog so thick that we feel helpless and scared, and thus conform to their will.

'We many of us, especially the better off, think we are "free". But I implore you to look around you at all the abundance and beauty of this world. Take a moment to reflect on your lives and listen to your hearts. Feel if your hard-working lifestyle makes you free and ask yourselves about the validity of what you're doing. It may be the eleventh hour but it is not too late. We must not blame or judge others such as our presidents, prime ministers and big businesses.

Coming from a base of fear, they are not truly happy inside no matter what face they put on. With compassion and love and understanding that they are operating from a place of the highest possible truth they have available to them, it is time to send them on their way. Whether you vote for me or one of the others adopting a similar line it doesn't really matter. A change, however, is vital – if we are to avoid becoming like robots with no free will and risk eradication of our planet in the process.'

It was well documented at this time by top scientists that the world was heading for a cataclysmic end, if not in our lifetime then certainly in our children's. This was due to our greed and fear-based attitudes. In the same vein, some religious and spiritual nuts, into the Book of Revelations and other such prophesies, were convinced they would be part of the 144,000 chosen to survive. Many were convinced that after a couple of years of 'Judgement' the selected (and very special) few would inhabit an abundant, fairy-tale world along the Garden of Eden lines. Such people had, sadly for them, utterly failed to understand anything about the workings of universal law.

During the Permian period, two hundred and fifty-one million years ago, there were a series of gigantic volcanic eruptions in Siberia. The huge amounts of sulphur dioxide and carbon dioxide released resulted in acid rain and rapid global warming respectively. The greenhouse effect warmed the world enough to destabilise the polar ice caps. This was then enough to release the frozen gas beneath, called methane hydrate. Methane is a far more powerful greenhouse gas than carbon dioxide. Life on earth was almost extinguished. It took a hundred and fifty million years to recover, and it was ten million years before coral reefs were again laid down.

The Intergovernmental Panel on Climate Change (IPCC) estimates the upper limits for global warming to range between seven and ten degrees centigrade by 2100.

Global warming of six degrees triggered the cataclysm in the Permian period. The IPCC have not taken into account the partial melting and release of methane hydrate under the poles. In 2002 an area of ice the size of Wales broke free and melted in Antarctica. The Wilkins and Larsen ice shelves in Antarctica are, according to scientists, 'in full retreat!' In just four months in 1998, 420,000 acres out of the 1.7 million acres of the Larsen B shelf gave away. The reason: temperatures in Antarctica have risen by three degrees centigrade since 1950, pushing summer temperatures above the critical freezing point of 0°C.

Harold, to give him his due, recognised the urgency of these issues (and the rest) and resolved not to hold back at all. At that time half the US Government's energy and half of people's taxes were devoted to war and weapons of mass destruction. Over $10 trillion had been spent on this over the thirty years leading up to 2002 after which this figure went up almost exponentially as the US sought to keep control of their crumbling empire.

One of their more alarming toys, which fortunately never got the chance to get off the ground, was their star wars program. The many billions spent on this was not even featured in the US Defense Budget, which itself rose from $1 billion a day in 2002 to nearly $2 billion in 2007.

The idea of Star Wars was to have satellites in space to collect information, concerning say incoming missiles, and then direct US anti-missile missiles. This would protect the US from any nuclear attack (it also meant the US could start a nuclear war without fear of being attacked back). For this Bush tore up the ABM Treaty with Russia which helped keep the status quo during the cold war. With the threat of Russia gone, the US based their case on the threat from rogue 'terrorist' states such as Iraq, Iran and North Korea – an extremely weak case.

Most alarming was those satellites would be equipped with lasers capable of attacking anybody, anywhere, at will – with no risks at all. Tiny hamlets in Pakistan, Saudi Arabia, Afghanistan and the rest; guerrilla bands in Indonesia or Colombia; anti-capitalist marches heading for a US Embassy; or simply individuals, could be 'taken out' at the push of a button. This would increase the terrifying aura of US power, and make mass movements hesitate. Most of the huge expenditure for this would, of course, go to a small number of US arms and aerospace corporations.

★

Midway through 2004 a nice surprise came our way. The German company, Bayer, said they would not grow GM maize in the UK. (This happened at the same time the Canadian campaigners amazingly managed to stop the planting of GM wheat worldwide. This would have contaminated all our native grass species with devastating consequences.) They had, as expected, been given permission by the UK Government to grow the crop commercially. However, the Government, nervous about civil disobedience in the countryside on a scale not seen since the peasants revolt in the 1300s, cleverly gave the go-ahead to appease the pressure from the US corporations, yet making it impossible for the growing of GM crops at the same time. This they did by not making any provision as to who would be responsible for contamination. No law or guidance was given as to who would pay for claims made by conventional and organic growers, and no specific distances were given between non-GM and GM crops. The enormous public resistance and threat of an uprising from the Green Gloves 'slashing' campaign seemingly won the day.

When the news broke, Dad, far from celebrating, went into a state of shock. He'd been talking for some time how he was going to go off with a group, slash some GM crops, get locked up, spend a couple of days with us on his release, then off with another group to slash more crops. It wasn't just that he'd mentally geared up to at least one summer of living this way (he admitted a week later he was quite relieved not to have to get arrested, though it didn't quite work out that way); but, most importantly, his dream of uniting city and countryside on a common cause was foiled.

There were many in the cities signed up ready to join in with those from the countryside to slash GM crops. The names were held on a data base, so when GM crops were forced in some years later, the troops were quickly rallied, even with the Civil Contingencies Bill up and running by then. This appalling Bill allowed the Government to confiscate property or goods 'with or without compensation' if people were breaking the law. They could then be 'tried without jury' if the deed was deemed a threat to state security. They were even locking up people by then on suspicion based on laughable phone taps, home video evidence and personal photographs.

However, Dad had worked hard back then, spending time with activists in London encouraging them to rise above the distracting fox hunting issues dominating the news at that time which was fuelling the divide between town and country. He didn't have to wait long before the perfect opportunity presented itself in a roundabout sort of way. 'God works in mysterious ways' was a much used phrase back then, but as we all know how, the Universe/Spirit/whatever will provide the opportunity using those most likely to 'take up the sword' to do the work.

As usual, Dad found an excuse not to address the fundamental issues affecting his flagging business – he never made any money from conventional methods. He and some others decided at the start of the summer of 2004 to have a big concert and launch the ambitiously named 'Save Our World' Trust Fund (they liked it because it shortened to 'SOW'). This was to raise funds to help other organisations especially to do their small bit to raise awareness and assist in the change over period. They had great speakers and top bands at the time such as Seize the Day, Kangaroo Moon, the Ozric Tentacles and the Fine Young Cannibals and... a wee bit of help from above. It had been the wettest July and August on record; however, the field dried up a treat in the sun and strong wind two days before the event – without which it wouldn't have stood a chance.

I was in the kitchen the day after the concert where some of the country's most passionate activists were lingering, discussing future plans and challenging each other's beliefs and methods. Dad looked like a Cheshire cat at this all going on under his roof. It was here that the 'plan' was hatched for a spot of something at the Labour Party Conference, which was just less than four weeks away. Best go again to Dad's diaries, since this event helped increase his involvement in the so-called Global Justice Movement:

We planned to get twenty of us into the Conference, scatter ourselves throughout the balcony, then start a loud slow clap in the hope others would join in and applaud Tony Blair out of the Conference and his job. Wayne, a leading light in the Global Justice Movement, felt it could work knowing most MPs are utterly fed up with Blair. We got straight onto the computer and downloaded the very tough forms off the Internet for the Conference and, ignoring the bitter taste in our mouths, we joined the Labour Party. We agreed to circulate the information and forms to close friends only, and not communicate at all about it outside our own homes or on the phone in case someone was 'listening'.

Friday week ago I rang the Conference Centre to find out about my pass. They said it was being inspected by the privately hired security firm. I mentally gave up knowing when they put my name into the

Internet they'd find 'activist' and convictions for protesting, including a short prison sentence, as long as your arm. Next day I received my pass and nearly fainted. Unbeknown to me I was the only one out of all of us to get in, a feeling I'd had from the start. It was then off to Barnardo's and a Cancer Research shop to get the boring, bland, nondescript look – a grey pinstripe suit and white shirt, costing £12 and £5 respectively.

Racked with nerves that I might miss something by arriving late on Sunday when 'Conference' opened, I rang the manager of my Sunday morning football team to cancel. However, on remembering Drake finished his game of bowls before tackling the Armada, I rang the manager back and asked if I could still play.

On arriving at 'Conference' on Sunday afternoon my pass was rejected – a 'security problem' – and I had to go to a special tent. This was hardly surprising, since an extra £2.5 million had been spent on 'security'. Here a lady apologised that my pass had gone to the Police for inspection. I thought, Oh well, I've got so far... It was a bit like being on the train to Genoa when the CRS got us off the train at 4 a.m. somewhere in the Alps and we were pleasantly surprised we'd nearly made it to the Italian border.

Forty minutes later a policeman gave me my pass apologising for a 'mistake their end', and buzzed right up in I went. It was weird walking past the demonstrators, many of the banners and people I recognised – SWP, Peace Activists and Trade and Justice Movement (it was great to see the Bideford Trade and Justice contingency at the fore). One person said as I went past, 'Hey isn't that Hector?' and their mate said, 'No, he's too smart.' Phew!

I got into the hall 'to case the joint' just after John Prescott's speech. I had been there ten seconds when the first announcement came that if we wanted to go to Blair's speech on Tuesday we had to get a special ticket from the Labour Party stand. There was a mad rush and I followed a couple moving swiftly and was fifth in the queue – it was meant to be.

I slept for half an hour on Monday night, mulling over every kind of worst-case scenario – I really felt like a wounded gazelle about to enter a lions den. I planned to get a front row seat on the eastern balcony, where there was a ten-metre drop, and threaten security when they approached to stop, or 'else I'd jump head first and break my neck for the poor Iraqi people and our soldiers being killed unnecessarily just so we could have their oil; and our ludicrously named "free trade" policy which results in billions starving and without water throughout the world'.

I got up early to go to Conference and was near the front of the queue, hamming it up with some passionate Blair fans. However, they started by filling up the south balcony first; so, having to think quickly, I lay down and pretended to have a bad back, waiting for the doors into the east balcony to open. Unfortunately, they'd filled the east balcony up from another way and I was last into the south balcony, afraid I'd have a more accessible aisle seat. Luckily for me there was one chair right dead centre of a block facing Blair, and as I clambered into it a guy said, 'I was wondering who would sit here, obviously it's meant for you – I was expecting the Conference nutter to turn up.' I said, 'You never know yer luck mate, there's always one.'

Blair came out to a fanfare worthy of a 1970s World Heavyweight boxing champion. Every song that most suited a hyped-up egomaniac except (amazingly) 'Simply the Best' was blasted out, strengthening my resolve. I was the only one who stayed sitting and told the guy next to me if Blair comes out in a dressing gown wearing red boxing gloves then I'll join in.

I was ready to start the clap when Blair got his compassionate look, tears nearly welling up in his eyes, and expressed his condolences for Ken Bigley and his family. Poor Ken Bigley was being held hostage by an extreme group of insurgents led by Abu Musab Al Zarqawi. Zarqawi was only extreme because he'd been held in a Yemen prison for five years, supported by the US, and regularly tortured, like the prisoners in the infamous Abu Ghraib prison. He was also forced to watch the assassination of members of his family; and the US wonder why so many are taking up arms against them...

Blair then cheered up enormously (showing how much he really cared about the Bigleys) and said, '…and now for my speech'. I started to clap and saw security mobilising rapidly. Plan B: rant. I asked people to join us in applauding Blair out of Conference and Office, that I was sick of his lies, spin and deception. I then said I was an ordinary socialist sick to death at his carrying on the work of the Conservatives by embracing privatisation and further selling our hospitals, schools and railways etc. to the highest corporate bidder who put profit before people, stating he truly was a clone of Maggie Thatcher. I then called him a terrorist, that if there was a democratic global vote (real democratic – not Blair's twisted version of it) he'd be the 'Ace of Clubs' – number two, maybe second equal with Bin Laden. Security was then on me so Plan C: angrily yell out the sound bites I had planned. 'How can you (Blair) sleep at night, with so much blood on your hands?' And, 'Do you know how much the soldiers hate you for sending them to war officially pronounced by Kofi Annan as illegal, where there's now officially no WMD and where you were warned a year earlier that things would disintegrate into chaos and anarchy? Shame on you, Blair! Shame on you!'

I was then dragged down the corridor with the police tightening the handcuffs the more I ranted (I've got the marks), but I must say the police were very good to me when they realised I wasn't a total nutter. I said that if Blair's family was blown up 'accidentally' by an occupying force, which was then casually brushed aside as 'collateral damage', would the word 'insurgent' be so hostile to him, or would he be tempted, like so many Iraqis, to get himself a Kalashnikov? I then said Blair talks about Africa being a scar on the face of humanity, and how he's going to alleviate poverty, but as in his promise to sort out climate change (it was the same promise a year before the last Election), does nothing. I said if he was serious about poverty he must demand to Bush that affordable generic AIDS drugs from India are allowed into Africa; and went on about 'free trade' and so-called Aid, and their dubious efforts to alleviate poverty.

Finally, Blair said as I was dragged off, 'Isn't it good we have democracy and free speech in this country, so this man can speak?' Hmm… Also, this when two million marched against the war last year and most of the country (in this so-called democracy) was

against it. Likewise, eighty per cent of people would rather not eat GM food, yet Blair continues to allow enormous shiploads of GM maize and soya animal feed to come in from the US and Canada. For the reasons above I will continue a life of Direct Action, whatever the consequences, until we can change the world currently fuelled by spin, lies, deception, war and power hungry greedy egomaniacs, to a world based on forgiveness, compassion and loving our neighbours independent of culture, creed and skin colour. I've got kids, and simply want to leave them a world fit for them and their children, but there ain't gonna be one unless we collectively rise up together, unite on issues of the bigger picture and enforce the change ourselves.

★

It was the third 'security breach' in as many weeks. The first was a 'Fathers for Justice' protest on the balcony of Buckingham Palace by 'Batman and Robin'. This was closely followed by Pro-Hunt members storming the House of Commons. All this when security was supposedly tighter than ever due to the so-called 'terrorist threat' because of the 'War on Terror'. It's incredible looking back now to see the extent the human race was lied to by the world's leading politicians, who fed a culture of fear to the masses to further their own self-interests. Al-Qaeda, for example, was simply a bogeyman dreamt up by the US intelligence agencies and then taken up by a few radical Muslims. September 11 was one man's idea who then approached the wealthy Osama Bin Laden who liked it and sponsored the event. There were no 'sleeper cells', massive networks, hi-tec caves in Afghanistan such as those described by the wretched Donald Rumsfeld. This culture of fear and bold promises to protect everybody against the (enormously exaggerated, mostly phantom) bogeymen, allowed the UK Government to pass through the Civil Contingencies Bill and have trials without juries for suspects.

The so-called neo-cons in the US, up there with Zeus and Neptune in their minds following Bush's re-election in late 2004, and Blair, believed everybody in the West to be so brain-dead they could continue to force parts of the world, who had something they wanted, into 'their' form of democracy. By this time things had gone from bad to very bad in Iraq. Bush, on re-election, immediately launched an all out attack on Falluja where the people were still reeling (surprise, surprise) from the US soldiers opening up on parents and children demonstrating against the military occupation of their primary school on April 28 2003, killing eighteen people in cold blood.

The literal flattening of Falluja, dramatically adding to the 130,000 civilians killed up to then, lit a torch of indescribable anger in the area against the West. The ferocity of the insurgency meant the US never got the chance to fulfil their wish of bombing Iran. Whilst most US citizens continued to be brainwashed by the right wing controlled media into thinking the war in Iraq was actually going well, and most Iraqis were Zarqawi-style hostage-murdering terrorists, Europe and the rest of the world were waking up. Bush and Blair were terrified of the Iraqi people voting for anti-occupation leaders in the forthcoming 'democratic' elections. The problem was they had built up so much blood on their hands, legitimising themselves through sham elections supervised by the occupation authorities, they never managed to wash it off no matter how hard they scrubbed.

The US was, when all was said and done, simply following a tried, tested and successful policy mirroring Britain's recent imperial history. In the 1950s alone, British forces brutally suppressed uprisings against colonial rule in Kenya, Malaya and Oman. The Mau Mau in Kenya represented a popular, nationalist rebellion, yet the British media continually expressed horror at their savage tactics.

However, not only did British forces kill at least 10,000 of them compared to the loss of 600 UK servicemen, but brutal 'resettlement' operations led to the deaths of tens of thousands more, and forced around 90,000 into detention camps. Officers who worked in these camps described 'short rations, overwork, brutality, and flogging' and, 'Japanese methods of torture' – the same tactics as were endorsed from the top at the infamous Abu Ghraib prison in Iraq.

In Malaya, the popular rebels were officially called 'terrorists'. In secret, however, a Foreign office correspondent described the war as being fought 'in defence of the rubber industry', which was controlled by British and European countries. British soldiers had photographs of themselves holding decapitated heads of the 'terrorists', and it was claimed the revolt was ended by winning the 'hearts and minds' of the nation. It was, however, simply crushed by overwhelming force, especially massive aerial bombing. Similar mass bombing, especially of water supplies and farms, was used to crush the rebellion in Oman in 1957. The message was 'resistance will be fruitless and lead only to hardship'.

Another common denominator between these events was keeping activities and the truth behind the military operations as secret as possible. As one British Army commando in Oman said, 'Great pains were taken throughout the Command to keep all operational actions out of the press.' Unfortunately for US and British imperialism, by the time Iraq was attacked in 2003, the internet and computer age meant operations could no longer be undertaken under the cover of darkness.

The second attack on Falluja not only bolstered the torchlight of resistance amongst the Muslim world, but, even more significantly, pretty much cut off the final stands of genuine warmth between the US and the rest of the world. Colin Powell, the last moderate in Bush's hawkish Government, politely resigned at this time, and even Blair stated he would no longer be Bush's pandering poodle (mind you, he had an election looming as well). As history had shown time and again, whenever a dominant superpower 'went it alone' they quickly found themselves on the scrap heap. The whole world now thanks God the Collapse happened as soon and as quickly as it did. The formidable suffering on a global scale has left us all scarred, yet we all believe had it been long and drawn out the impact on the planet of climate change alone would have been irreversible.

It wasn't long after this that the world started turning on the big multinational corporations. The US neo-cons had thought that it's constant emphasis on its 'war on terror', with Bin Laden being wheeled from one (fancy) cave to the next in Afghanistan (on his dialysis machine), would keep the masses blinded with fear. They hugely miscalculated the core of their problem – that the vast majority of the world and nearly half their own people had seen through their little game.

In its market position and political influence, modern corporate management, unlike the capitalist, had public acceptance. It was not the fault of those who worked in this field. The Western education system groomed the masses to be successful businessmen. The 'ultimate' was deemed to sit at the ritual meetings of directors and the annual stockholders' meetings, and work your way up to a senior Management position where respect and security were guaranteed. Corporate power ordained that social success is more automobiles, suits, TV sets and the amassing of consumer goods (including lethal weapons). The negative social effects such as pollution, the unprotected health of ordinary people, destruction of the countryside and the threat of military action and death, were deemed secondary issues. The irrefutable statistics of sub-Saharan Africa perfectly sum up the effects of enforced 'liberalisation'. Between 1960 and 1980, when these countries exerted more control over their economies, growth rose by thirty-six per cent. This sank to minus fifteen per cent between 1980 and 1998 when the IMF, World Bank and WTO were largely pulling the strings.

★

It was a week or so after the Labour Party Conference that Dad went to the European Social Forum in London. It was here he made contact with José Bove's organisation – *Confédération Paysanne*. Dad felt extremely tickled that one of the world's leading activists had selected him to help coordinate the mission ahead. Bove wanted Dad to rally British farmers especially to do joint actions together in the UK and France. It was the moment Dad had been working for during the past few years. His ambition up until then had been to unite city and countryside together on actions; however, moving into the international arena was a massive leap for the cause. Unbeknown to them back then, a seed had been sewn that would have big repercussions and embrace all of Europe.

They began by collecting petitions from UK farmers, and Dad's contacts in the city, in support of *Confédération Paysanne* plus other French locals who destroyed much of the GM trial plots in the summer of 2004, and were off to Court for their efforts. A database was collected and the fun began.

I loved going over with Dad on holiday to the South of France, where we stayed with the small French farmers. It was much more fun than the threatened trip, by Mum and Dad, for me to stay with some unknown French family to learn the lingo. Dad and I had to speak French because they spoke no English. There was a beautiful river outside Millau where I swam a lot, especially when Dad went off slashing crops. The holidays once extended into term time because the fed up French police took a while to release Dad and his mates on one occasion. The French police, often led by the CRS riot unit, were much more heavy-handed than the British equivalent. They would tear gas the slashers, and often beat them with truncheons – Dad was fortunate to get away with just a few cuts and bruises.

The French would then come and stay with us and return the favour. There were always more of them, probably having had a revolution more recently in their history than us, and 'revolution' in France was deemed good by the general public, whereas it was frowned upon by most in the UK. They would go and blockade depots supplying Tesco and Asda especially, and the ports where GM animal feed was flooding into the UK. This was a backdoor method the multinationals used to offload their wretched GM into our food chain. Their parrot-fashion response when challenged on this was that 'no GM BT toxin had been found during the [very limited] tests they'd done on milk from cows fed GM maize'. The anti-GM lobby's report was that the digestive process was a very powerful thing, giving the example of when cattle were fed sheep's brains in the 1980s and '90s, there was no trace of sheep brain found in the meat or milk when tested. However, a subtle molecular change had occurred which gave rise to the killer CJD some years later. In 1980 John Gummer, the Agricultural Minister, had assured farmers and consumers that it was 'perfectly safe' to feed sheep's brains to cattle.

Dad and the others always said that unless scientists knew specifically what they were testing for, they'd be as much in the dark as the rest of us unless they stumbled across something. They said there was enough of a threat from this, based on the limited testing done to that date, of the potential harmful effects of GM on human health. Sadly they have been proved right, and there are still those today paying the price from consuming food tampered with in some way by genetic engineering.

Dad and the others kept their hand in during the lead up to the crop slashing in France in 2005 by targeting the supermarkets. They began with Sainsbury's because in 2001, Sainsbury's promised to 'phase out the use of GM feed to the animals which produce their meat and dairy products'; then, as was par for the course for most big companies who made promises, they did precisely nothing.

I sadly missed the first – and best – demo on Sainsbury's in Barnstaple. However, I thoroughly enjoyed the photos. They had three beaten up old Massey Ferguson tractors and trailers occupying the whole forecourt by the main entrance. Dad was standing precariously on his cab, clad in a white boiler suit emblazoned with 'NO GM' just beneath the orange 'SAINSBURY'S' sign, ranting through his loudhailer. In the background were forty-odd others, mainly from our house, dressed as pantomime cows – genetically modified, of course, with melons, tomatoes and the rest, politely handing out information sheets and talking to the customers.

The local TV, radio and newspapers were in attendance covering proceedings. The TV showed the security behind the glass windows wondering what to do and customers saying, having read the bumph, they would not buy milk or meat from anywhere other than local shops after this. The one mistake Dad said he made was when the manager said he'd call the police, Dad said, 'Oh goody!' Being arrested on camera would have not done their cause any harm. Eventually, the manager asked Dad and Tom, the other organiser, into his office for some tea and biscuits and a tour of the store – desperate to get the demo called off. Dad said he quite respected what the manager did, plus he wanted to get back to watch the Ladies' Wimbledon Final because he quite fancied one of the women. However, he got a flat tyre on the way back and missed it – served him right!

They spent most of their time focussing on Asda and Tesco – the big two. The farmers were getting squeezed and squeezed. By then fifty-three per cent of dairy farmers were making the same or less than the cost of production – bottled water was even retailing at more than milk in the supermarkets. Eleven farmers (mainly small dairy farmers) were going bankrupt each day, and one a week committing suicide. Those farmers who did survive/manage to hang on were earning an average of just £2.90 an hour – almost half the minimum wage at the time.

A former dairy farmer from South Devon led a very potent campaign in which he won Tesco customers on side to lobby Sir Terry Leahy, the Chief Executive at the time, via a simple postcard. In this he stressed the points made above, plus the worsening animal welfare issue, as farmers were trying to squeeze more and more from their cows to try to make ends meet, and the severe impact on wildlife, as all the far more ecologically friendly small farmers were going to the wall.

Lots of small, peaceful demonstrations such as these won the sympathy vote, but with a society so in debt they were never going to win the war. It did, however, increase public anger against the corporations, and many extra recruits from all walks of life were gathered for the epic G8 Summit at Gleneagles in July 2005, when even Bush seemed overwhelmed at the depth of resentment from so many ordinary people. The squeeze on farmers by Tesco is summed up by the fact that turnover increased by sixty per cent in the five years to February 2003, yet group operating profit rose by 75.6%.

Cheap immigrant labour was equally important to keep the profits high and food cheap. Nearly two million immigrants were working illegally in 2004, many working double shifts seven days a week. The Government made a few noises to appease the masses, yet as usual did the bare minimum. Increased productivity and deflation in food prices (the direct result of cheap immigrant labour) helped hold down inflation while corporate profits soared, hence the incentive was not too great. The Monopolies and Competition Commission left supermarkets well alone, and the Office of Fair Trading simply set a watered down voluntary code for them. Nothing much changed until that huge rise in fuel costs.

★

When a journalist asked Harold what he would do if he became President, he said, '*Easy, I would honour Kyoto, pay for the next Earth Summit to be held as soon as possible and join the World Court. I'd immediately halve the US Defense Budget so they'd have to get by on a measly $300 billion for the next year, after which I'd dispense with it altogether, all being well. I'd stop subsidising all earth rapers such as Exxon, Dupont and Monsanto, thus saving $200 billion from corporate welfare. I'd then make them pay the full environmental costs for their activities via the SIB. I'd save another $100 billion by stopping the war on non-corporate drugs, and shut down all nuclear plants.*

'*With this approximately $1,000 billion of extra spending money, I'd give $300 billion back to the taxpayer and pay teachers and nurses, especially, what they deserve. I'd put $200 billion into alternative fuels such as ozone-friendly hydrogen fuel to drive cars, and renewable energy such as wave and wind power. I'd make the farmer the root of the economy, and pave the way for as many who want to return to working the land – plus I'd immediately ban all use of genetically engineered crops! Finally, I'd make paper and fuel from wheat straw, rice straw and hemp... oh, and immediately replace the IMF, World Bank and WTO with the SIB.*'

Of course, this would have just been the start of saving and redistribution of wealth. With the peaceful society we have now there is no need to finance a police force, solicitors, judges and the whole judicial system. Also with people eating properly – pesticide-free foods, for example – there are far fewer of us getting ill. It was, however, a fascinating time at Dad's eighteen years ago as he battled with so many others against the tide to create the positive alternatives that are now manifesting themselves today.

Part Three

CHAPTER VI: JUDGEMENT DAY

The dominant global emphasis and overriding focus at the end of the last century and start of this one was this: to voluntarily not consume, acquire, compete, dominate and through this grow, is in some way an admission of failure.

All advertising via TV (especially), newspapers, magazines and the rest was geared to titillate the human psyche into a perverse excitement about 'how much more fun and happy your life will be once you have acquired a fridge-freezer and traded the Ford Anglia and Robin Reliant for an Audi Quattro and Montego for the missus'. The Western world especially had become a culture-consuming monster. This self-centred, indulgent world was a marketers and Corporate heaven. Consumerism had become the dominant religion of the world. Most major religions had even insidiously replaced this as 'the way' over and above their old God or gods. In many ways, they couldn't be blamed for this. In that world, without power via money you were cast onto the scrap heap.

There were, however, many individuals who followed these religions who were still living and abiding by God's rules more than man's. They read and lived by writings of unadulterated truth, such as the Sermon on the Mount. They gave of their last farthing and practiced small acts of anonymous mercy. They, and many of the ever increasing vast numbers of those with no orthodox religious leanings, realised the Kingdom of Heaven was within them. They prayed in secret rather than ostentatiously in public, and didn't let anybody know about their acts of charity and good deeds. They did not acquire wealth, and if they had any extra would give it away to those in need. They forgave the past and didn't worry about tomorrow, working hard with what they were given in the day. If their plans were upset or shattered they knew God/Spirit/ the Universe had something else lined up for them. And if they suffered for whatever reason they *knew* this was an opportunity to help them, and often others, learn and grow spiritually. Put simply, they had *faith*.

By the turn of the century, science was well on the way to proving the existence of something it had once disproved: the interconnectedness of all things in a living Universe. Acceptance was creeping into science that 'when a butterfly moves its wings in one part of the world, a hurricane can sometimes be felt on the other side' – a concept that until recently had been much maligned and simply brushed aside.

The phenomenal power of thought was being explored, tested and accepted as real in potentially changing an individual's circumstances (or even a country's situation, with enough thought from enough people), by hitherto conventional and well-respected institutions. For example, Harvard University tested and proved that the healing process could be dramatically increased when an individual focused and prayed for another. This was so even when the two people didn't know each other or had never met. Likewise, it was demonstrated that when enough folk in a crime-ridden city meditated on this, crime would suddenly drop at a certain threshold, depending on number and intent of the meditators.

Examples of these shifts can be seen repeatedly through-out history. When the collective global consciousness reaches a certain point then something set in stone up until then will be shattered and a change occurs. One such example is the collapse of slavery (though only sadly in its official capacity). The legacy, however, of black people being treated as inferior carried on until the 1950s. It was then that the likes of Martin Luther King and Rosa Parks challenged the inferiority of black people in the US during the 1950s Civil Rights movement, which caused the shift to occur. (Bear in mind that with the world still in a mess back then there was always the ignorant minority who held on to the old thinking.) Likewise, it was the sacrifices by the likes of Steve Biko and Nelson Mandela who helped bring attention to and alter global consciousness with regard to apartheid, resulting in its collapse in the early 1990s.

The universal law that the greater mass will always overcome the lesser mass is shown up by these examples. It is only a great shame that so many great men and women throughout history had to sacrifice their freedom and lives to act as catalysts for change. What these wonderful people did was to change or sometimes initiate people's thoughts concerning a specific situation. Every bit of light generated by individuals or small groups had more power and influence than anybody could have possibly realised back then. What is also so clear now in this context, is that if you light a small candle in a dark room it will light it up. However, the equivalent of darkness in a room filled with light will not be noticed.

Most folk fifteen or twenty years ago were engulfed in a feeling of despondency and helplessness, brainwashed into the global corporate cult. Double standards, however, as per usual prevailed. In small cults worldwide, physical, mental and sexual abuse, brainwashing and death were frequently inflicted on cult members and sometimes innocent outsiders. This was widely and rightly condemned by all governments. A cult by definition is: 'any person or group who says that the way to divinity, salvation, enlightenment, happiness, freedom or clarity is only and exclusively available through them'. For those prepared to question, this provided a wholesome benchmark for anyone wishing to join a religious or spiritual group. At the same time the corporate-driven US 'one size fits all' form of freedom and democracy was being forced on every country in the World with any natural resources that could benefit the US economy. Those who tried to stand in their way, along with the ever more rapid destruction of the planet, were brushed aside like a minor irritant. The US global cult policy, wholeheartedly supported by its timid eager-to-please chum – the UK – put simply read; 'Democracy is government of the people, on behalf of the people, by the Americans.'

One (of many) consequences of American democracy at this time was a rapid increase in the number of 'Detention Centres' around the world where suspects could be 'processed'. The details of the horror taking place at Guantanamo Bay and Abu Ghraib were well documented at the time. However, these were just the tip of an unbelievably sinister iceberg.

The US set up their 'centres' in any country with poor human rights records, from Afghanistan, Syria, Pakistan, Uzbekistan, Jordan and Eygpt; to Thailand, Malaysia, Indonesia and the British island of Diego Garcia in the Indian Ocean. Even some boats at sea were converted into detention centres. President Bush was in the meantime publicly condemning the likes of Syria for harbouring terrorists and its human rights record at the same time as building prisons there for the sole purpose of torturing un-convicted suspects.

Away from any public gaze and with access granted only to specially selected military personnel – accountable to no one – anything went. Guantanamo Bay was almost made to look like a time share holiday camp. Detainees spent much of their time shackled and hooded. They were subjected to electric shocks, sexual humiliation, whipping, starvation and mock executions. A favourite example of the latter to the military was 'water boarding'. This was when detainees were shackled to a board and lowered into a tank having been told they were to be drowned. Many, of course, did die. Robert Baer, an ex-CIA case officer in the Middle East, said, 'We pick up a suspect or we arrange for one of our partner countries to do it. Then the suspect is placed on civilian transport to a third country where, let's make no bones about it, they use torture. If you want a good interrogation, you send someone to Jordan. If you want them to be killed, you send them to Egypt or Syria. Either way, the US cannot be blamed as it is not doing the heavy work.'

Many innocent Muslims, such as Naeem Noor Khan and Maher Asar, were scooped up in the net – like dolphins into fishermen's nets, because they were in the wrong place at the wrong time. After months of torture in solitary confinement, some simply gave the names of their friends or acquaintances to alleviate some of their own suffering, thus widening the net still further.

In November 2001, George Bush signed an order to establish military commissions to try 'enemy belligerents'. A 'foreign war criminal would have no choice over his defence council, no right to know the evidence against him, no way of obtaining any evidence in his favour and no right of attorney–client confidentiality'. Many prisoners were shuttled from one centre to the next, hence the US military expression 'ghost detainees' to vary how justice could be 'rendered' – much like a piece of meat hanging in a butcher's shop.

★

It is mind-blowing to look back now twenty years and less to see that man, knowing he was using up oil at a rate that would run out in his children's lifetime, seemingly did not give a damn. Events in early 2006 which sent oil prices spiralling upwards were, in retrospect, clearly a blessing in disguise. The consequences on the global economy at the time were, however, quite extreme, and gave a real taster of what was to come.

The rapid increase in the gulf between rich and poor was the worst thing to witness. In developing countries where subsistence farming had been replaced by the large-scale growing of monoculture (often GM) crops, dependent upon large machinery, the effects were devastating. With fuel prices too high to plant and harvest the crops with machinery, much of the land was laid waste. There were horror stories of displaced subsistence farmers returning from the cities to try and grow crops using the old tried and tested methods, being tortured and shot by big agribusiness employees. The starving ex-farmers only wanted to help feed their families and other people in the same boat. However, through fear of losing their land, the corporate farmers preferred to leave the land fallow and become taken over by weeds.

The shortage was due to many Arab countries, led by the Saudis, drastically reducing supplies to the West. The anti-American feeling in Saudi Arabia and increased tension forced the Saudi Royal Family, hanging on by a thread, to shut their country off from the outside world as much as they could. Had they not done this it seems an Islamic uprising to overthrow the Royal Family would have been inevitable.

The Muslim leaders knew that they sat on the most valuable single resource in the world. Projections in 2003 stated that the Muslim world would control up to sixty per cent of the world's oil production and ninety-five per cent of the remaining global oil export capacity by 2010. They also knew that due to the escalating Western gluttony with regard to this product, it would all be gone by 2040 or 2050.

The Taliban in Afghanistan, booted out because they would not allow the US to build a pipeline across their country, were forever blowing up the exposed pipeline. Likewise, Islamic freedom fighters were doing the same in occupied Iraq and neighbouring Pakistan. The American oil cartels had been frantically trying to open up oil reserves in Africa. However, their policy of exploitation and increasing poverty, thus creating political instability, slowed this process down. Thus American and European corporate business practices, based on personal gain and greed, backfired, as they did more and more over this period.

The effects on the world at this time were pretty devastating. Many industries reliant on oil, such as plastics, most of manufacturing and even the textile industry went into near or total liquidation. There were corporate oil wars over ownership of the oilfields still operating. Coca-Cola had for years been keen on having trade union bosses in Colombia, for example, murdered for trying to get workers a fairer wage and better working conditions. However, the world only became shocked at such behaviour when they knew business leaders were doing the same to each other. Travel suffered hugely, and hence commerce and the stock market went into free fall, taking three years to bottom out. It wasn't as bad as the Great Depression of the 1930s, but globally speaking it was.

Those countries who had oil and could be controlled by big oil companies suffered the most. For example, in the early 1970s the oil cartels had started moving into Ecuador to exploit the oil reserves. Companies such as OXY, BNL, OCP and Texaco Chevron had bought up most of the Amazon basin in the area. Pipelines had been built across ninety-four seismic fault lines, near to active volcanoes and through eleven protected areas.

The inhabitants of Ecuador were told this exciting find would help sustain the people and provide jobs. By 2002,

500,000 acres of forest had been destroyed, seventeen million gallons of oil had leaked, terminally polluting every river from fifty breaks in the pipeline, and incidences of cancer in the local people had increased exponentially. Global warming aside, the forests which once sustained the five main tribes no longer could. One tribe had been wiped out altogether and the other four were under serious threat.

The promise of riches for the country had proven to be totally false. Debt had risen from $344 million in 1972 to $20 billion in 2002. Eighty-five per cent of all income from oil went to the oil companies, the rest went into servicing their foreign debt. The IMF even threatened to bankrupt Ecuador if OCP could not get their deliveries on time, and they were told output needed to double from 350,000 barrels to 700,000 purely so they could service their debt. Here lies one of many examples, barely publicised in those days, of 'money screaming so much louder than the voice of the people'.

The positive outcome was that the whole Western world was at last woken up to the evils of global corporate capitalism. Those who were teetering or simply having the odd moan finally started to get off their backsides and take personal responsibility; they got out and did something. McDonalds, a typical disgusting corporate American fast food chain, went bankrupt. Even more amazing was that sales of Coca-Cola dropped dramatically, sending shares in the business to an all-time low. It didn't help the firm once everybody knew that Coca-Cola was a branch of the dreaded Monsanto.

Monsanto had by then sneakily become the major shareholder in nearly all the world's main seed companies. Europe especially was still livid they had had GM crops forced upon them against their will. The result was a huge upsurge in organic farming. Many landowners at last set aside large tracts of their land to those who wished to grow organic produce. The carcinogenic effects from the abundance of herbicides and pesticides used in monoculture farming was by then well documented. Doctors, struck off in the past for mentioning these facts, were openly shouting from the rooftops and getting away with it. This was because so many spoke out, and they had safety in numbers.

It wasn't until 2012 that this all really took a hold. In the meantime activists did a great job with many sacrificing their freedom (including my dad) in slowing down and disrupting the progress of GM for example.

The only thing that amazes us now is the extent to which the Western world had its head buried in the sand. The vast majority of people were too afraid even to peep over the parapet. Oscar Wilde once wrote, 'As long as war is regarded as wicked, it will always have it's fascination. When it is looked upon as vulgar, it will cease to be popular.' Certainly there were those waking up to the absolute vulgarity of war as shown by the massive demonstrations leading up to the 2003 Iraq war. In the same way the forcing of Western imperialism, both economic and cultural, in the name of free trade and modernisation, on developing nations was construed by many as equally vulgar. This in the light of the destruction of communities, human health and a way of life being a direct consequence.

In 2003 the vast majority in America, especially, chose to accept at face value notions such as 'Operation Iraqi Freedom' and 'Reconstruction'. They accepted that bombs were necessary to give birth to life, a new civilised society and *peace*. They even accepted that corporate rule would provide the foundation for freedom and democracy in that part of the world: at least 10,000 civilian deaths during the war itself, and even a few 100,000 afterwards as a direct result, was largely acknowledged as acceptable collateral!

This in the light of the threats posed by Iraq (false) and the wickedness of Saddam's regime (true).

What so many failed to realise was that bombs annihilate life. Reconstruction born out of destruction meant that a historical and cultural legacy of ancient civilisations could be destroyed in the process. It is now clear to all historians that this was the objective. How else could you make a culturally different society 'homogenised' and bulldoze them into your way of thinking without undermining their culture and re-orientating their spiritual leanings – in the case of corporate rule, this being to money? Secret documents from that time state it was for this reason US soldiers were ordered not to interfere with the looting of museums containing 7,000 years of Mesopotamian history after Baghdad was 'liberated'. At the same time, anybody trying to get within spitting distance of those oil wells was gunned down.

Most people accepted without question when the Bush administration awarded George Shultz's Bechtel Group the first big Iraqi reconstruction contract. This was worth $680 million over eighteen months and an estimated $100 billion in the long term. The deal wasn't even put out to tender. Most of the US population didn't care or see that the US first bombed the hell out of Iraq, including water supplies, electricity and sewage, then unashamedly went out to profit from this. A British MP was famously known to have said when other countries offered to help in Iraq's reconstruction that, 'those who didn't lose men in combat will not be entitled to a share of the spoils'.

War had become a convenient excuse for enlarging Corporate rule. If the World Trade Organisation (WTO) couldn't do it, then use war. As the Bechtel example in Iraq shows, war was not just for acquiring oil but also for control over vital services. Whether it was water privatisation contracts in India, Bolivia or China, 'reconstruction' in

Afghanistan and Iraq, or patenting basmati rice in India and even life itself, and the profits of big companies were at stake, anything went. Most were too afraid to see and acknowledge that 'free trade' was deceitful, corrupt and violent. They refused to see that Saddam's dictatorship was replaced by US corporate dictatorship. They refused to accept that governance had become 'of the corporations, by the corporations, for the corporations'. As the legendary Indian activist, Vandana Shiva, put it: 'The Western illusion of creation confuses destruction with creation, and annihilation with birthing.'

It was when oil prices shot up in early 2006 and the Western world was plunged into relative poverty that the vast majority allowed their eyes to open and see and question what was going on. This, of course, was a spiritual 'opportunity' provided for the world – even though it was not perceived as such by ninety-nine per cent of people at the time.

The realisation soon after this time that some American leaders, CIA and FBI *knew* about the hijackings before they happened on September 11 2001 raised the resistance levels a notch or two. The information was available to those who chose to look for it soon after September 11. However, it was only when people's lives were crumbling into poverty and the promises which had been made broken, that many chose to wake up. The poverty-stricken masses in developing countries had seen for years what was going on but never been a real threat. However, when the 'relatively' cushy existence of Westerners – some working thirteen to sixteen hours a day often just to make ends meet, became for many unsustainable in the then system, the powerful elite knew they had a problem.

Conversations in restaurants, pubs and people's homes across America and Europe abounded about the details of this historic event on September 11 in 2001. Americans in particular were understandably horrified when they discovered that their authorities had willingly sacrificed three thousand of their citizens to help further their cause of global domination under the guise of 'the War on Terrorism'. Donald Rumsfeld, and others, had been murmuring for years that 'the US needs another Pearl Harbor', so when the opportunity came their way on 9/11, they practically paved the way.

It is common knowledge now that at least eleven countries gave advanced warnings of the September 11 attacks. Mossad experts, according to the *Telegraph* newspaper on 16/9/11, had warned the CIA and FBI in August 2001 to prepare for a big attack. They even provided four of the hijackers' names, but they were not even questioned. It was standard procedure to scramble fighter aircraft even if a small aircraft went slightly off course or did not respond when contacted by air traffic control. Even more so, it was standard policy to automatically apply intercept procedures when a hijacking occurred. The first of the four hijackings (an unprecedented number) occurred at 8.20 a.m. Amazingly not one fighter plane scrambled from the US Andrews Airbase ten miles from Washington until the third plane had hit the Pentagon at 9.38 a.m. Bear in mind that the military launched fighter planes on sixty-seven occasions between September 2000 and June 2001 due to simply suspicious aircraft.

A quote by Tony Blair whilst addressing the Commons appeared in *The Times* newspaper on July 19 2002. It read as follows:

> To be truthful about it, there was no way we could have got the public consent to have suddenly launched a campaign on Afghanistan but for what happened on September 11.

The CIA spent endless amounts of energy on trying to prove a connection between the hijacking on September 11 and Iraq. Even when they came back empty-handed, still seven out of ten Americans believed Iraq was directly involved; such was the brainwashing of the world's most powerful nation. Put this with the fact that no serious attempt was ever made to capture Osama Bin Laden, and the so-called 'War on Terrorism' lights up like the bogus cover for the wider US geopolitical objective it so clearly was.

Evidence was printed even back then of these oh so obvious double standards. For example, *Time* magazine stated on May 13 2002, that the US airforce had complained in November 2001 that it had had Taliban and Al-Qaeda leaders it its sights at least ten times. Permission from on high to strike was delayed until these people had safely disappeared. Similarly, in October 2001 Pakistan negotiated Bin Laden's extradition to their country. The US blocked this offer, saying they wanted to capture Bin Laden for themselves. Yet General Myers of the US said that 'the goal was never to capture Bin Laden'.

Indeed, Bin Laden was never captured or obviously killed, even though the world had become a very small and exposed place. Powerful US satellites orbiting in space could quite literally locate the proverbial needle in a haystack. Having such global 'terrorists' at large helped keep the fear levels up in the US public to allow America to go round forcibly and systematically taking control of the global oil supplies.

★

It is so refreshing to see the 'live and let live' attitude of the world today. Different cultures and tribes are encouraged to thrive no matter how dysfunctional, weird and different they seem to others. The age of conquest and domination is, thank God, over. Mankind had for millennia been motivated by one innate, overriding fear – that 'different is dangerous'. Those countries keen to dominate and on a power trip ALL felt their way to be the only way. The gross misinterpretation by the Christian theologians of the words in John's Gospel – 'The only way to the Father is by me' – is one of many such examples. Many Christians genuinely felt that anybody who didn't worship God through Jesus was condemned to hell – how bonkers is that! Also what about the poor folk who had never heard of Jesus? Not forgetting that 'they'd' say in the next breath that God is a God of *love*? An extreme, yet sadly not uncommon, example of this fear-orientated judgemental behaviour was the mass slaughter of the Jews by Hitler during WWII.

The Western powers consciously herded native tribes into reservations. Here they were embraced into the modern, better and happier 'civilised' world. They were given 'job opportunities', fast food and a TV. Many lost their original spirituality, skills and knowledge. A homogenised society where people became dependent upon their masters was easy to control. The fact that tribal diversification could safeguard humanity over and above anything else, via knowledge of cures from jungle plants, to cultural and genetic diversity, was deemed totally irrelevant.

It is in this area that mankind has had his biggest kick up the backside. Many, except for the profit-driven big companies, knew that the loss of diversity in any system increased the risk of destruction by disease. A monoculture of crops or trees was far more susceptible to an attack from bacteria, viruses, fungi or pests, as well as minor localised shifts in rainfall and temperature. Hence man's constant battle against nature with his herbicides, pesticides and fungicides, giving rise to the now well-documented devastating effects on human health and the environment.

My dad was very aware of these points, as were a growing number of others worldwide. He knew that his 'community' for want of a better word (he hated the expression) was a microcosm of the new world. He endeavoured to study what was happening in the world and do the opposite where appropriate. For example, with regard to the dangers of homogenisation, he made sure his 'community' was as diversified in terms of people and the food grown, and as self-sufficient as possible.

★

Rumours abounded locally as to what was going on at Dad's house. They varied from a hippie commune sitting around naked smoking pot all day, to never ending raves, orgies and cocaine smuggling. Dad said it had been much the same during their New Age phase in the early 1990s. The rumours then centred on witchcraft, the dropping of live rabbits into cauldrons of boiling water, and Dad ceremoniously biting off live chicken's heads. It was also said that he was doing voodoo-style black magic and having sex with maidens on gravestones in the local churchyard.

It wasn't quite as exciting as this. However, Dad used to enjoy adding coals to the fires to 'give people something to talk about'. For example, he was once down at the local pub with a long-term friend and the friends' wife from London being grilled (and judged) about his dodgy spiritual practises. Dad, having heard the rumours suddenly put on a creepy African mask, got some bones out of his pocket, which he'd borrowed, and summoned up the spirit of some famous witch doctor of 'well renowned repute' in the Congo to ward off evil spirits.

Many looked at Tapeley as an easy cop-out of society where you could simply hang out and do as you pleased outside of the rules of the real world. Some were envious and others angry – hence the malicious rumours. Even so, Dad wrote almost daily letters to people wanting to come up and live with us. He always said 'he wished he could take the world in, but there just wasn't the space'.

Being open-hearted and trusting, he did get his fingers burnt fairly frequently. He found confronting people who went off the boil, and weren't sticking to the deal they'd agreed to, extremely challenging and draining. Dad normally worked a twelve-hour day and most of the others just had to do a twelve-hour week. This in exchange for a roof, electric, and basic food. Dad believed if he offered a good deal people would respect it, and do extra for the place out of love and respect. Many did; however, human nature being what it was, some took advantage. In doing so they would drag others down.

Dad had become impressed and even obsessed by the need for low-impact, sustainable housing. He was particularly inspired by Tinker's Bubble run by Simon Farely in Dorset. Tinker's Bubble was built in an area of woodland high up on a hill using natural or waste materials such as wood, straw, hemp and canvas. The water for the shower was heated using wood or home-made charcoal, for example. Dad liked the whole idea of community living in natural surroundings, working with nature and respecting it. Being more open to prying eyes though, he didn't fancy the approach of build first and go for planning permission later with the Sword of Damocles hovering over everyone's necks for years. Tinker's Bubble eventually got permission, but only after a huge struggle and much uncertainty.

The Tapeley posse (or 'Tapeleyban' from 'Tapeleystan', as they had become known) decided to approach the planners with openness, honesty and humility. They took them into the woods, explained their dream and told them they were completely in their hands. They stressed they wanted it to be a joint project and hinted that the credit would go to the Council, rightly, for allowing a greenfield site to be used in such a radical (for the time) way. The Council would have been aware of Dad's media contacts and some would not have been averse to some positive publicity and a pat on the back.

It was good for Dad to be doing something positive with what he had. Many friends were saying he needed to balance out his activism by demonstrating a positive alternative. This was all the more important in the light of nature programmes at the time, which painted an extremely distorted and misleading picture of how man was supposed to interact and integrate with his surroundings. TV programmes set in the Serengeti in Africa, for example, showed amazing panoramic shots of a landscape devoid of human habitation with 'nature living how it should'. Needless to say, many tribal folk indigenous to an area of land, nearly always coexisting and nurturing their surroundings (which kept them alive after all), had been ruthlessly displaced. This frequently happened so that white businessmen could make a healthy living from the likes of safaris and hunting, to agriculture.

One such example of the latter was Canada paying for the ploughing and planting of wheat on the Basotu Plains in Tanzania. Unlike cassava, maize or beans, wheat was only eaten by the rich in Tanzania. Canada's chemical companies profited whilst 40,000 members of the Barabaig tribe were displaced. When some tried to return to their land, they were beaten up and/or imprisoned and tortured with electric shocks. The women were gang raped.

The point was such programmes brainwashed people into thinking that man would always destroy nature if he lived in it. Yet it was nearly always the small farmer, as in the UK for example, who nurtured the hedgerows and left areas wild for the wildlife. The large businessmen farmers, on the other hand, often ripped out the hedgerows at the expense of all things natural to optimise the efficiency of their ever bigger machinery. On a smaller scale still, many thoughtful, intelligent yet disillusioned Westerners were opting out of society, getting a bus or truck and living on the road.

With regard to 'the travellers' there were, sadly as always back then, the reckless freeloading minority who spoilt it for the large majority. These few would park up anywhere, let their dogs chase the farmer's sheep, which if heavily in lamb would then abort their lambs or prolapse (push their uterus out), and help themselves to whatever they felt like. Most travellers, though, would set up small organic-style permaculture gardens, respect their surroundings, and tidy up after themselves and support the local wildlife. It was the latter that Dad had up at his house, and it was thanks to them I learnt so much, which enabled me to survive through those difficult times from food in the hedgerows, and catching rabbits and deer for my meat.

A beautiful straw bale hut built by the lovely Martin, using his Millennium Award funds of just £10,000, set the ball rolling. It was an educational project set up as a course for those who wished to learn how to build their own homes and become more self-sufficient. As was the way at Tapeley, a carpenter miraculously appeared during the preparation the week before. He sorted out a pile of planked ash from a fallen tree into perfect rectangular boxes which were used on the house. Without him, Martin said the whole project would not have taken off, or at least have been a mess.

The 'eco' village started to go up in the summer of 2006. Planning permission was granted on a temporary basis for five years. By the time the second rollover for planning was required in 2015, the conventional system had all but gone by the wayside. The police had their hands full. Cells were overflowing with the understandably rebellious underclass due to everything being in short supply. Hence, much of the work of the legal system, solicitors and the like had been sidelined. All the police could do was to keep some sort of law and order in the broadest sense, though sadly their tactics became even more desperate and brutal.

The warning signs had been around for many years before. Historians today write that many Western people had had things too good so they could choose to ignore the atrocities caused by global corporate capitalism throughout the developing world. Spiritually speaking they'd had their warnings, but the vast majority chose to keep their heads in the sand and fingers in their ears. The universal laws, being based on ultimate love and patience, are so clear and obvious in so much as we collectively (and individually) get little knocks to start with, to wake us up to something. These knocks gradually increase until it's so in our faces we have no choice but to react. However, by then it is just so much tougher. I remember Dad talking to a group of people about these global issues and seeing their eyes glaze over after a couple of minutes... such is the power of the mind.

The mirror, reflecting the devastating effects of modern day colonialism begun by the British, Spanish and French some six hundred years ago, had been shining blindingly bright for many years. However, even when such rape and exploitation of countries was actually increasing at the start of this century, most people pretended it was not happening. Examples of this have been given throughout this book such as the war in Iraq, Palestine and the objectives behind the pushing of genetic engineering on to the global markets. Yet another modern day example of greedy colonialism was the exploitation of Bolivia.

In October 2003 the whole population of Bolivia was in rebellion. A decade of neo-liberal, cost-cutting privatisations and pro-US policies advocated by the IMF and World

Bank, dramatically increased poverty to the extent that eighty per cent were living below the poverty line. A consortium of multinationals including British Gas, BP and Spain's Repsol had been given the contract by the Bolivian Government, a US puppet regime, to transport Bolivian gas to a Chilean port. Here it was to be converted to liquid form and shipped to the US.

The Bolivian people stated that all their natural resources had been stolen since colonial times began, and gas was their last remaining energy source. They also knew that not a penny of this would filter down to the Bolivian people, other than the minimum wage paid to locals working on the gas extraction until such time as the resource was exhausted. Hundreds of thousands of Bolivians took to the streets in La Paz especially. Many were shot and killed or wounded by the police. Bolivia was a country in revolt motivated by sheer and utter desperation.

Western people refused or couldn't see that this would be them in a few years. It was, however, awful to see friends and loved ones simply crumble when such circumstances set in. Nobody of course said, 'Told you so! You could have done something to prevent or at least lessen this.' Dad's friends especially had demonstrated how another way was possible, but there were too few of them to make any difference for the vast majority. Dad always said even if most people had simply refused to shop at supermarkets and buy local produce instead, this would have helped enormously.

The whole GM issue certainly helped raise the level of consciousness in many with regard to the food they were eating and where it came from. The increase in organic farming helped save many lives over this transitory period. However, I remember Dad, Martin and Biff saying in 2003 and 2004, on returning from London, how shocked they were at the ignorance of their close, intelligent friends on issues such as GM.

★

A section from a letter I received from Ishmael in January 2005, just before the elections, demonstrated the effect privitisation was having on his country:

> *Mother has left the house just twice in the past month. The lack of security and the very real fear of kidnapping is keeping her, and many other women, prisoners in her own home. She is now suffering from acute depression. She complains of the looting of our once beautiful country by Halliburton, Bechtel, US missionaries, mercenaries and local sub-contractors while we are denied electricity and clean water. Unemployment is now at seventy per cent further exacerbating poverty, prostitution and back street abortions. One of my sisters has just had an abortion and we're all worried about the infection she has contracted as a result. This combined with cousins of ours in other cities, some now suffering terminally from the effects of cluster bombs and napalm (yes, they did use this despicable substance again), dropped by US fighter jets, and is it a wonder Mother is on the verge of giving up?*
>
> *Fortunately my father still has his job in the bank. Were it not for this we'd be in real trouble. Let's just hope they don't intercept one of my letters to you or they'd be sure to sack him and we'd be in real trouble. This especially in the light of the group of western countries, known as the Paris Club apparently, plan for dealing with Iraq's un-repayable debt, unveiled on November 21 last year.*
>
> *The idea is for a three-year plan to write off eighty per cent of Iraq's debt. However, the IMF and WTO are insisting on a 'restructuring (privatising) of state-owned enterprises. A friend of my father, who's a Minister in Mr Allawi's puppet interim regime, says this will result in the laying off of a further 145,000 workers in addition to the 500,000 laid off when Paul Bremer was in charge. To cap it off, the IMF has said it wants to eliminate the programme that provides each Iraqi family with a basket of food. This will*

> *remove the only barrier to starvation for millions of us, all to pay for Saddam's disgusting debts 'generously' donated by Western banks and Governments.*

The morale of the US and British forces in Iraq was, quite understandably, also dropping all the time as a result of up to fifty attacks a day and frequent loss of life of their own men. Many of them were questioning why they were still out there and most had decided to sign out of the Army once they had the opportunity. It truly was a vicious circle. The worse it became, the quicker the troops resorted to blood-curdling massacres of anyone who remotely got in their way. It was worst-case scenario; the soldiers didn't want to be out there, and the Iraqi people didn't want them there.

I then received this letter from Ishmael soon after the Iraqi 'elections' in January 2005:

> *Well I'd like to say praise Allah those 'bloody elections' are over, were it not for the fact the violence is as unrelentless as ever because the British and US troops are still here. On the contrary, far from preparing to leave (as we nearly all want), the US are not only reinforcing their existing bases, but building yet more new ones. We all know the Americans will never relinquish control of this opportunity for unmetred oil to the West – 'who do ya think ya kiddin?'*

> *The elections were a farce. Just over fifty per cent of Iraqis who registered to vote went to the polls, but the percentage of us who registered no one seems to know – my Father was registered but few of our friends were. The United Iraqi Alliance (UIA) were the most popular amongst voters until the truth about their front man Abd al-Mahdi leaked out. The UIA said they'd 'adopt a social security system under which the State would guarantee a job for everyone and offer facilities for Iraqis to build houses; write off Iraqi's debts and use our oil wealth for economic development; re-nationalise the major industries back from the private companies;*

and… set a firm timetable for the withdrawal of all foreign troops'. However, once it was uncovered al-Mahdi announced to gatherings of US businessmen on two separate occasions that he 'planned to restructure and privatise Iraqi's state-owned enterprises', and that he had plans for a new oil law 'very promising to the American investors', confusion and despair again descended upon many of us.

Campaigning had been non-existent due to everyone's fear of the US troops especially – yes, my friend, they are continuing to kill three times more people than the insurgents kill. Father is disgusted at the elections here. He remembers the elections during the height of the Vietnam War in 1967 when the Americans were reporting they were 'surprised and heartened by the size of the turnout, despite a Vietcong terrorist campaign to disrupt the voting'. This as a US Vietnam puppet regime was being set up, just the same as is happening here. Father sometimes jokingly puts on a US military hat taken from a dead serviceman and imitating George Bush's voice (very badly incidentally) says: 'If your country does not serve our needs it is an enemy state. It will be occupied, its leaders removed and pliant satraps placed on the throne.'

The US now have a military presence in Iraq, Saudi Arabia, the UAE, Kuwait, Oman, Qatar and Bahrain. In not one of these countries did an elected Government invite them in. All self-respecting Arabs (some 99.999% – contrary to how many Western diplomats portray us) want an end to tyrannical regimes.

Father insists the US push for 'freedom and democracy' US-style will only increase the distress and resentment in this area. It's not democracy that's on the march in the Middle East, it's the US military that's on the march. The terrible Northern Alliance are only back in power in Afghanistan in place of the Taliban because they've done a deal with the US to allow them to build their oil pipeline and set up military bases (in return the US turns a blind eye to the Northern Alliance's favourite export crop – opium). Again here, because elections were held they claim this is democracy, but it's not; it's occupation and control.

The 'crusade' is now targeting the non-compliant Syria. The recent murder of Lebanon's former Prime Minister, Rafik Hariri, is being used by the US to increase the pressure on Syria to introduce 'democratic' elections in its country, and pull out its 14,000 troops from Lebanon before their May elections to ensure the elections are 'fair and free'. Yes, you may say, 'Then what about the 140,000 US troops ensconced in our country before, during and after our elections?' President Bush praised the middle-class, mainly Christian, demonstrations in Lebanon against Syria, saying that the US is 'on your side'. A few days later the group known as Hizbullah mobilised ten times the number of people in Beirut is support of Syria. Bush, as always, did not even acknowledge the mere existence of this latter demonstration dominated by the poor, suppressed, mainly Shia majority. The US are not calling for genuine democracy, but for elections under the long-established corrupt confessional carve up, which gives the traditionally privileged Christians half the seats in parliament and means there can never be a Muslim president. Pierre Gemagel of the far right-wing Christian Phalange party, whose militiamen once massacred 2000 Palestinians under Israli floodlights in Shatila and Sabra in 1982, recently said that voting was not just a mark of majorities but of the 'quality of voters'.

Hizbullah, as you may know, gained huge respect in the Muslim world for driving Israel out of Lebanon in 2000. Hizbullah is, as expected, labelled a 'terrorist' organisation by the Bush administration. However, not only is Hizbullah a legitimate political party with many MPs, but it pours vast sums of money into the poorest sections of society from income derived from its own fund-raising and from charitable foundations from its ally, Iran. Without Hizbullah the poor Shia South would be so much worse. Hizbullah wants to disarm, but fear the Israelis would move straight back in. In many towns people are happy to pay Hizbullah a voluntary tithe of one fifth of their income to keep the Israelis at bay.

How dare the West label such wonderful people as 'terrorists'? Saddam's secret police used to creep over our roofs into our homes at night; occupation troops simply break our doors down in broad daylight. Doctors, journalists and clerics are eliminated by western troops for speaking the truth, especially if they start counting the *dead civilians. For example, late last year US forces literally flattened the city of Falluja to the ground. The previous April insurgents had victoriously beaten back the mighty US Army from Falluja, but at a cost. That 'cost' had a human face put on it by al-Jazeera, al-Arabiya and the unembedded western journalists, whilst doctors reported the number of dead, and the clerics, seizing upon the appalling statistics, delivered fiery sermons rightly demanding an immediate withdrawal of all foreign troops.*

Second time round the US wasn't going to make the same mistake. The first major operation by US marines and Iraqi soldiers was to storm the Falluja General Hospital, arrest the doctors and put it under military control. Soon after emergency health clinics and makeshift medical centres were bombed to rubble. Likewise, al-Jazeera's Baghdad offices were bombed the year before by aircraft, killing reporter Tareq Aggoub; and all other reporters and clerics who'd spoken out during the first attack were either killed or arrested.

Even our cousins in Basra noted when the British troops stood back immediately after occupying the city, and allowed Basra's hospitals, universities and public services to be burned and looted whilst only defending the oilfields and oil ministry, they concluded then that we were dealing with a brutal, heartless force. The whole country was left in no doubt the US and UK had simply come to take control of our oil. The privatisation of our oil is simply neo-colonialism and an attempt to impose a permanent economic occupation to follow the military one. The West has deliberately fuelled a sectarian division between Sunnis and Shias – divide and rule I believe it is called. This when we most of us never knew of this sort of division. Our families intermarried and we lived and worked together in harmony. This disgusts us.

Please tell Blair, Bush and your countrymen that those who voted in our recent election are as hostile to the occupation as those who boycotted it. Tell them we do not want a timetable for withdrawal – this is just a stalling tactic. We are Iraqis and will solve our own problems. We know our country and can take care of it ourselves. We have the means, skills and resources to rebuild and create our own democratic society.

I pray this letter finds you in good health.

Your dear friend, Ishmael

This letter arrived at a time when the Western press were talking about the 'ripple of change' now spreading through the Middle East. 'Because' the allies invaded Iraq and 'because' of the 'successful' election in Iraq, everybody from Libya and Egypt to Saudi Arabia was supposedly talking about free democratic elections. This on the back of the recent 'orange' revolution in Kiev which replaced the pro-Russian regime with a pro-Western Government, and the new peace orientated Palestinian President Abu Mazen elected on the back of Yasser Arafat's death. President Bush bragged (much as he had on that big boat when he declared 'military operations in Iraq are over' after Baghdad fell), 'the untamed fire of freedom' was spreading through the Middle East.

The rosy exterior had a shady, sinister underbelly few in the West were aware of at the time, but the history books are clear about now. Fundamentally, the countries at stake were not going through some idealological conversion, but were simply hoping to get America off their backs. It wasn't just the threat of invasion of non-compliant regimes such as Syria and Iran, but financial destitution. Not only were countries first threatened with (then dealt) arms embargoes, the freezing of their assets in the US and Western Banks and the banning of US companies from working in the country, but the under-the-table deals and bribes that have now come to the surface, defy belief. The behind the scenes wrangling and manipulation of the Iraqi election results which maintained American objectives sums it up.

The UIA, despite Al-Mahdi's blunders, easily won the election. However, Washington, terrified at the prospect of Iraq being run by Iraqis, had set up an electoral system 'less than democratic', to put it mildly. Former Chief US Envoy,

Paul Bremer, had written election rules that gave the US-friendly Kurds twenty-seven per cent of the seats despite the fact they made up just fifteen per cent of the population. The rules dictated that all major decisions must have the support of two-thirds or, in some (the important) cases, three-quarters of the assembly. This gave the US, via the Kurds, the power to block any new rules that could (a) be added to the constitution, (b) change Bremer's economic orders and (c) demand a withdrawal of any foreign troops. The Bush administration had thus given itself a veto over Iraq's democracy. To consolidate the US stronghold even more, the pre-election, pro-US puppet President Allawi was persuaded to join the new National Unity Government instead of going into opposition. With his party's extra forty seats (out of two hundred and seventy-five), the US had the extra leeway they needed and could relax.

As a further safeguard, after much wrangling and 'negotiation', the US managed to secure Kurdish control over Kirkup (the home of a massive oil field – surprise, surprise). This meant that if foreign troops were eventually kicked out of Iraq, Iraqi Kurdistan could be separated off giving Washington a dependent, oil rich regime – well... there wouldn't have been much point of Kurdistan without it.

The much vaunted collapse of the Arab (Berlin) wall never quite materialised. How naïve were Western powers in thinking they could overthrow, control and change a whole culture dating back many millennia killing nearly one and a half million people in one country over fifteen years by using the only weapon they knew... *fear*?

So called 'reconstruction' had become the popularist term to replace the outdated, offensive antagonistic words such as colonialisation and crusade – though President Bush would sometimes get them all mixed up. A 'reconstruction and stabilisation' mandate was drafted in the White House in late 2004, headed by former US Ambassador to the Ukraine. By mid-2005 post-conflict plans had been drawn up for some twenty-five countries in which there wasn't, at that time, any conflict going on. The mandate stated that the US could coordinate three full-scale reconstruction operations in different countries, each lasting between five and seven years, at the same time.

It didn't really matter to corporate America and England, whether 'reconstruction' was necessary as a result of bombing a country half to pieces or a massive natural disaster, such as the tragic tsunami on December 26 2004 in the Indian Ocean. The latter was preferable to the Neo-Conservatives because they could play the knight in shining armour coming to the plight of the needy without too many finger-wagging protestors moaning about killing people – though either way, however, they didn't seem that bothered. Sophisticated colonialism had replaced vulgar colonialism and more than half the world was blind as to what was going on in the early part of this century.

'Reconstruction' revolved around a cast of engineering companies, consulting firms, mega-NGOs, Government and UN aid agencies and financial institutions. However, complaints from Aceh to Afghanistan, and Haiti to Iraq, that 'nothing seems to have been done with regards to rebuilding and repairs' many months after the catastrophe or bombing, were all too common. This was because it was not reconstruction that was the priority, but re-shaping. Whilst the devastated nation was focussed on corruption, incompetence and overall inaction, a sinister form of disaster capitalism was at work. This meant mass privatisation and land grabs occurring before the country even had a chance to recover from the shock.

The Governments left in charge of the countries were told by the US, via the World Bank and IMF, that they'd only be given desperately needed aid if they abided by the above criteria. They quite literally had a gun held to their heads. Many war-torn countries were considered too unsuitable to manage themselves so aid money was put in a trust fund managed by the World Bank, such as in East Timor. The bank only gave such governments funds provided they demonstrated funds were spent 'responsibly'. This normally meant slashing public sector jobs and giving aid money to foreign consultants on massive salaries. For example, Bearing Point, who advised governments on selling off a countries' assets to foreign corporations, reported in 2005 that revenues for its public services division had quadrupled in five years.

Condoleezza Rice summed up the Neo-Con philosophy when, barely one month after the tsunami, she blurted out, 'The tsunami is a wonderful opportunity, that has paid great dividends for us.' The Thailand tsunami Survivor and Supporter group stated that: 'For businessmen/politicians, the tsunami was the answer to their prayers, since it wiped these coastal areas clean of the communities that had stood in the way of resorts, hotels, casinos and shrimp farms.' Halliburton had engineering and supplies contracts in Iraq and Afghanistan worth some ten billion, and Bechtel had similar for its water contracts (which were shoddily built and always leaking – to maintain profits and growth), but the curtain, unbeknown to them and the rest, was rapidly coming down. The scandalous appointment by Bush of Paul Wolfowitz, the ruthless warmongering Neo-Con US Deputy Defense Secretary, to the President of the World Bank in early 2005, hastened the demise of disaster capitalism rather than tightening its grip. The global masses were waking up.

The US Government whilst giving increasingly generous tax cuts to the super-rich – to win friends – became even more hypocritical (yes, it was still possible – just) with regard to its foreign policy. Whilst imposing free trade and denying Iraq the right to impose tariffs, America was protecting its airlines and media with foreign membership restrictions. Even more obvious was its subsidising of farmers and imposing massive import duties on steel; this in direct contravention of WTO policy. During one glorious presidency the US had witnessed corporate scandal and deception, Enron being the biggest example, on a level never seen before. ('Lost funds', such as an incredible $9 billion in money for reconstruction for Iraq – funded mainly by the seized assets of Saddam's regime and Iraqi oil money – were similarly all too common.) It had torn up the ABM arms control treaty with Russia; risen above human rights issues (e.g. Guantanamo Bay) and UN policy and all it stood for (Iraq); disempowered any form of democracy in the WTO, and abandoned the Kyoto Protocol. This combined with its illegal pre-emptive strikes against Afghanistan and Iraq and its continued support – both financial and military – of Israel's illegal occupation of Palestine, and it managed to destabilise the whole world. Judgement Day, unbeknown to the vast majority, was just around the corner.

★

The deck of cards with regard to food was thrown well and truly into the air with the collapse of the WTO talks in Cancun, Mexico, in September 2003. Not even the most optimistic politician or economist was giving the talks much hope.

It quickly became clear that the West's concessions on farm subsidies, much vaunted before the talks, amounted to little more than a reshuffling of money paid to European farmers in particular. In 2001 at the WTO summit in Doha, both Europe and America officially agreed they would cut the subsidies paid to farmers. The following year Bush then directly *increased* farm subsidies by $180 billion; likewise the EU decided to keep the Common Agricultural Policy going with its increasing subsidy payments at least until 2006. Again it must be stressed that the direct beneficiaries of this were not the smallholders but the huge multinational agribusinesses – the supermarkets alone managed to squeeze out every penny of subsidy paid to farmers for themselves.

The EU's trade negotiator, Pascal Lamy, supported to the hilt by the US, even looked to go a step further into the existing archaic system. He strongly hinted that the 'Investment Treaty', which was part of the old multilateral agreement on investment, should be reintroduced. This would in effect allow the corporations to force a government to remove any laws that interfered with their ability to make money. Hardly surprising then that potentially money-losing issues such as biodiversification were booted off the agenda before the talks began.

The West knew damn well that any remote evening up of the trading ballpark would result in a rapid shift of power to developing nations. As such they were going to continue dumping their subsidised goods on developing nations and impose tariffs on imports. At the same time they tried to spin and twist words and persuade the world that they were actually trying to do the opposite. Unfortunately for them, the developing nations had heard it all before. It was once too often.

Led by Brazil, China and India, more than twenty countries, called the G21, stood up to the powerful West. For the first time they refused to be bribed, bullied and blackmailed. These countries happened to include the countries with not only the largest populations, but with the fastest growing economies. China's growth for 2003, for example, was nine per cent.

The US and EU had up until then always got away with the tried and tested 'divide and rule' approach, whereby concessions were given to compliant nations and massive tariffs imposed on the awkward ones. Again at Doha in 2001, the US and EU negotiators actually called for the dismissal of so-called 'unfriendly ambassadors' to the WTO from poor countries. These countries were threatened with trade embargoes and cuts in aid if they failed to toe the line. It truly was a case of 'You liberalise, we subsidise, or else...'

Getting China on board the WTO and thus Western corporations into the country, would have been seen as a jewel in the crown by Western politicians and businessmen. However, this jewel turned out to be a massive thorn, and another example of frenetic greed and the need for growth and domination backfiring.

Things were not helped when Lee Kyoung-Hae, a South Korean farmer, plunged a knife into his heart outside the checkpoint in Cancun that separated the luxury hotels for the delegates from the masses. He did this in protest at WTO policies which forced the opening of Korean markets to rich countries to allow the dumping of rice and other foods. He and most of his fellow farmers had had their livelihoods destroyed, and could do no more than watch, helpless, as their rural communities were destroyed.

The same had happened in the West African countries of Chad, Mali and Burkino Faso. Here the predominantly cotton producing farmers were going to the wall. They were more efficient growers than their Western counterparts, but couldn't compete with cotton – mainly from Mississippi – subsidised to the tune of $4 billion a year. For these reasons and countless others the world over, the G21, representing a massive sixty-three per cent of the world's farmers, decided enough was enough.

The US had seen this coming and resorted to Plan B: ignore the WTO and simply set up bilateral agreements with individual countries who would play ball with them. The added incentive of a tasty arms deal carrot proved too much for many countries in the developing world, especially those who had historically high tensions with their neighbours – which meant most of them. However, what surprised the Americans was that it was far from the vast majority who jumped on their seemingly lucrative bandwagon. Anti-American feelings were running at an all-time high, and the people in even the poorest countries with the least education had sussed out their motives. The corrupt governments, who had relatively easily been bought out before, were becoming more afraid of their people than the US if they sold out to their Western 'allies'.

With world domination slipping away from the US rapidly in 2007, they played what they felt to be a trump card. It was well below the belt, even by their appalling standards. However, the justification for it – yet another hijacked plane in 2007, that, missing the White House by a few metres, careered into the expensive houses beyond. They began calling in the debts of Third World countries who wished to govern their own people rather than being governed by the caring global peacemakers!

History states that the US was geared up to commencing this abomination in early 2005, but then that first (sadly of many) modern day massive natural disasters struck on December 26 2004. Mother Earth had been finding it ever more difficult to shield her people from the pain she was suffering due to mankind's overall persistent spoilt, greedy, selfish, egotistical ways. Forest fires, mudslides, a record four enormous hurricanes hitting Florida alone in late 2004, storm damage such as the one in Boscastle, Cornwall, were rapidly increasing almost exponentially in ferocity. Even so the vast majority of us refused to open our eyes and continued to buy gas guzzling Hummers and other SUVs, and take advantage of bargain price air travel to get that little extra 'much needed sun on our backs.'

The tsunami in the Indian Ocean is now widely regarded as a desperate plea to mankind from the Earth's Spirit to wake us up to what we were doing to the planet. We were then (and still are now, but there are glimmers of hope) on the cusp of irreversible damage. Our overall attitudes were no better summed up than by the newly re-elected US President who initially offered (reluctantly) $15 million in one hand to the tsunami victims, whilst demanding an extra $82 billion with the other for the war in Iraq. Blair was not much better and both deemed the 'incident' not important enough to return from their luxury holidays.

Donations given by ordinary people rapidly shamed Governments to dig deeper into their pockets (of loose change) and Bush upped US aid to $350 million – much of which was not paid as usual. Indeed Thailand initially refused the UK's offer of a year's respite in debt relief due to the conditions imposed – more control of Foreign policy, allowing multinational companies in to take over from local industries etc. etc. The phenomenal generosity of ordinary people also shamed the big corporations and shed light on their sole motivating force. Vodaphone, for example, 'announced' it was donating a generous £1 million plus would match all staff donations – pocket change to the £10 billion profit it made the previous year. Tesco proudly announced it was sending water, hygiene products and food (presumably some of the tons of past sell by date stuff dumped and destroyed before the homeless and hungry could help themselves) along with an anaemic £100,000. This, when its profits were nearing £2 billion.

It seems crazy to us now that companies announced what they were giving. Everybody now understands you don't give to receive, but until the collapse, most

Companies and Governments had no concept of this fundamental Spiritual Truth and would at least 'cast their alms' (brag about their 'generosity'). The sacrifice made by the spirits of the 300,000 who gave their lives for the future of the human race and planet is now viewed as the catalyst the world needed for a change in values. It sounds awful to say now, but had it not been for the death of tens of thousands of white holidaymakers nothing much would have changed. At this time 1000 people were dying each day in the Congo as a result of disease and conflict – the equivalent of a tsunami every ten months – and the psyche/conscience of most Western folk was barely touched. The sacrifice stemming from an act of pure, unconditional love for mankind and the planets, made by the spirits of the 300,000, woke billions up to the issues of war, wealth distribution, poverty and debt (plus it helped greatly to reduce the amount of debt the US tried to claw back from 2007 onwards). It also acted as a massive spiritual wake-up call for many.

The outpouring of emotion - love especially, in the form of physical help and unconditional giving to our fellow man, was on a scale never seen before. This, combined with the behaviour of the animals, provided the catalyst for millions to embark on a deeper spiritual search/quest. Barely any animals died during the tsunami having 'sensed' what was happening and moved to higher ground. This was the cue for many to look at and work on their own very powerful and important intuitive faculty, which had all but been snuffed out by the then unnatural dominance of the intellect over the centuries. The polarisation between those holding on to the 'old way' and those who chose to embrace the 'new' increased markedly following this historic event.

In calling in those debts in 2007, the US bankrupted several countries. With many countries still paying more in interest on their debts than on health and education put together, it wasn't hard to foresee the outcome: the global bailiffs, in the form of the IMF and World Bank, moved in. Much as had happened in Indonesia and in so many other countries, the natural resources – mineral rights, forests and the rest – were carved up and sold off to the highest bidder. A US corporate puppet was then put in to run things 'temporarily', and the people were made to oblige until further notice – a corporate-financed police force ensured this with an iron fist where necessary.

This in effect was what had happened in Afghanistan and Iraq under a seemingly different umbrella. The American wheeze was: following the attack on Washington where more 'innocent Americans' were killed, the policy following the September 11 attack of ' hit them before they hit us' needed reiterating and taking up a level. These countries were said to be 'harbouring terrorists'. America playing hurt and wounded, claimed to have been playing the global policeman and in simply trying to help the world had become the innocent victim of hatred and terror. They had had enough; it was now a policy of 'zero tolerance'. Having 'given, given and still given', they had no more in the chest to give…

Ironically, this last point was fine provided you replaced the word 'chest' with 'bank'. The US quite simply was in desperate financial straits. It needed to grab every penny from every available quarter if it was not to forego its power to the likes of India and China. Here the cheaper wages and good education of the people meant they were a far more attractive proposition to the large corporations than the overpriced West. Put simply, America and Europe had become victims of their policy of globalisation.

It was only when they started calling in their debts that the world realised how desperate the US had become. The whole debt issue and process is now recorded as one of the biggest cons in history. It was a 'legal' weapon used by the

West to take control of weaker nations. The fallout in terms of loss of life of the aggressors was nil compared to many millions in the nations conquered. The numbers 'killed' far exceeded those who died as a result of the two World Wars in the twentieth century – yet the vast majority of Westerners simply sat back and accepted this.

The argument that life expectancy in the Third World was far lower before than after colonisation, so why all the fuss, has been well and truly kicked into touch by all today's main historians. There is no doubt the West could have helped on a large scale. The only time it did help was when it stood to make a profit out of something, and as such it was simply exploitative help. The ecological destruction left behind by oil companies such as Texaco Chevron in Ecuador with the accompanying rise in cancers, and the holding back of cheap, affordable generic drugs from reaching Africa, are two of many such examples.

On the surface it looked as if the West was doing the best it could. There were many unbelievably corrupt governments in the Third World and in Africa especially. Their materialistic corruption was largely born as a result of colonialism. The combination of a lack of education and seeing the opulence and wealth of their Western conquistadors was understandably too much for most.

Quite simply, the eyes of the vast majority lit up and they wanted as much of it as they could get. The boost to the ego via the adulation given to those with massive wealth had been the spiritual undoing of many throughout history. Even most educated wealthy entrepreneurs in the West were self-indulgent, arrogant, egomaniacs right up until the final shift two years ago. How much harder must the trappings of a lavish lifestyle, endless mistresses and ostentatious parties have been for the sometimes less educated man or woman in the Third World.

Western powers and psychologists had worked this out long ago. A typical example was Mobuto, the dictator for the Republic of Congo (then Zaire) in the 1990s. He became a 'friend' of the West and the West lent him money – lots of it. He was known as a 'Kleptocrat' because of his lavish lifestyle and palaces. He died in 1998 leaving $13 billion of debt. The West then wanted their money back, and demanded that every individual repay $260 in debt, which of course they didn't have. Again the West had given the money, knowing it was being laundered with not a penny going to those who needed it. The huge debt created was the weapon used to control the new government and its policies.

Many countries, such as India, had paid more in interest by the year 2000 than their original debt. At this time the financial assets of Western banks was growing at a rate of $2,500 billion a year. This was the amount of the entire Third World debt. In 2002 US and EU taxpayers forked out $400 billion to subsidise their farmers, a figure eight times that given in aid; this in spite of the fact that between 1503 and 1660, 185,000 kilos of gold and sixteen million kilos of silver had quite simply been stolen from Central America and taken to Europe. Had Central America deemed this a 'loan' and charged minimal interest, we would have been having to repay them interest on that debt hundreds of times greater than what they were expected to pay us. Back then 'we' were rich because 'they' were poor. That was the long and the short of it.

The sickest thing was that the West made only token gestures in actively building hospitals and schools as aid, and setting up efficient water and energy supplies in poor areas. A developing country, with vast amounts of natural resources compared to the West, becoming educated, healthy and self-sufficient would have been far too great a threat.

The massive brainwashing of the majority of Western people into thinking that Africa (especially) was a hopeless, tragic mess due to the corrupt mentality of those in government along with the primitiveness of the people, *and* that without Western kindness and aid things would be so much worse, lasted until 2012. Dad, having lived in Zambia and Malawi for some time, said he came across numerous Africans with intelligence, integrity, and the ability to farm at least as well as the white settlers. They were also acutely aware that Western businesses had taken most of their good land for cash crops for export. A Zimbabwean activist who stayed with us said the same about his countrymen.

The whole Live Aid issue in 1984 didn't help this mentality. Sure, it helped in the short-term and brought attention to the ecological catastrophe in this part of the world (even though the then dodgy Ethiopian Government had been warning the West for some time of the impending tragedy, and as such it could have been averted). A BBC programme twenty years or so on reinforced the brainwashing by talking about 'Iron Age farmers', a place 'without trees', and a government that 'wants its people to remain peasants'.

History books and psychologists today state clearly that this was an appalling lie designed to con Western people that there was no other way. The reformed Ethiopian Government, barring a ridiculous war being waged with Eritrea, had become a well organised, sensible, 'pro-poor' model for what could be done. It had tens of thousands of health clinics and schools built, and had millions of trees planted. Far from 'just being able to feed themselves for five months', in 2003 they had an abundance of food due to exceptional harvests. The problems they had harked back to the 1984 tragedy, ecological disasters over many generations and international control over internal policy.

As the twenty-first century progressed, information such as this and the imposing of Western puppets, such as Mobuto in the Congo, was more than just seeping into the consciousness of Western people. Films were being made for mainstream cinema bombarding people with the horrific facts. The following example comes from the film *Bowling for Columbine*:

1954:	US overthrows democratically elected President Arbenz of Guatemala. 200,000 civilians killed.
1963:	US backs assassination of South Vietnamese President Diem.
1963–1975:	American military kills four million people in Southeast Asia.
Sept. 11 1973:	US stages coup in Chile. Democratically elected President Salvadore Allende assassinated. Dictator Augusto Pinochet installed. 5000 Chileans murdered.
1977:	US backs military rulers of El Salvador. 70,000 El Salvadorians killed.
1980s:	US trains Osama Bin Laden and fellow terrorists to kill Soviets. CIA gives them *$3 billion*.
1981:	Reagan administration trains and funds 'Contras' in Nicaragua. 30,000 Nicaraguans die.
1982:	US gives $1 billion in aid to Saddam for weapons to kill Iranians.
1983:	White House secretly gives Iran weapons to kill Iraqis.
1989:	CIA agent Manuel Noriega (also serving as President of Panama) disobeys orders

	from Washington. US invades Panama and removes Noriega. 3,000 Panamanian civilian casualties.
1990:	Iraq invades Kuwait with weapons from the US.
1991:	US invade Iraq, and Bush Sr reinstates dictator of Kuwait.
1991 to 2001:	US planes bomb Iraq weekly. UN estimates that 500,000 Iraqi children die from bombing and sanctions imposed in 1991.
2000–2001:	US gives Taliban ruled Afghanistan $245 million in 'aid'.
Sept. 11:	Osama uses expert CIA training to kill 3000 people.'

As barrages of information such as this hit the public, attitudes were insidiously changing from apathy and helplessness to outright anger.

The single factor that made most people in the West sit up and take notice that something was 'maybe' wrong, was something no politician or analyst had foreseen. Broken promises by then were not only an acceptable pastime, but a tried and tested morale booster. Everything from aid for those in need to hydrogen-based cars were promised, temporarily appeasing and lifting the spirits of the people, only for nothing to materialise.

The attitude of most Americans was summed up in the words of Ronald Reagan's staunch ally and supporter of Western energy interests called Gale Norton: 'The earth was put here by the Lord for his people to subdue and use for profitable purposes.'

Most Americans believed global warming was a myth put about by lazy, work-shy greenie hippie types. Even when Hurricane Isabel destroyed most of the luxury houses on the shifting sands of the Outer Banks in North Carolina in 2003, locals were convinced the government would sort out the problem. These people genuinely felt safe in the knowledge that the US not only had the means to control all the people in the world but nature as well. However, when supplies of coffee nearly dried up and failed to reach the breakfast table in many households, there was chin scratching and gnashing of teeth in Middle America.

Coffee is as good an example of the evils of corporate capitalism and the damage this does to indigenous people as anything else. Western corporations took the best land, by fair means or foul, from Brazil to Ethiopia and Kenya, and on to Asia.

For much of the 1990s farm workers on coffee plantations in Africa were earning around £70 a year. This figure fell to nearly £10 a year in early 2000. The big multinationals began colonising more and more land for coffee and created a global glut of the stuff. There is now a well-known story of a Kenyan mother, who worked on a coffee farm, having to take her ten-year-old son out of school. She couldn't afford the £3.72 a year school fees – the price of barely two cappuccinos at Starbucks.

Starbucks was a massive multinational chain making truckloads of money as a result of many families dying of malnutrition. To redeem its dodgy image it announced, in a blaze of glory, the introduction of 'Fair Trade' coffee. This guaranteed growers decent wages and conditions. However, like any promise from a government or corporation, this largely proved to be a lot of hot air. Far from all of their coffee was bought from Fair Trade products. I remember going into a Starbucks with Dad to suss them out. He asked for a cappuccino with Fair Trade coffee; 'Sorry, we don't do Fair Trade cappuccinos,' came the reply. The same happened when he asked for a 'Café Latte'. He then asked what Fair Trade coffee they did sell. The lady behind the counter said they 'did do Fair Trade espressos, but they had just run out of Fair Trade coffee'.

Dad said every Starbucks he past, he repeated the same experiment and met with the same response. Most had 'Fair Trade' coffee advertised on their counters. Does buying Fair Trade make much difference? many were asking. In 2004, when western folk bought a jar of instant coffee, they were often paying 7,000% more than the farmers received for growing it. Some folk in the middle were making an awful lot of money. Now we can see why Starbucks were not really that interested in stocking any more Fair Trade coffee than was really necessary.

The US-run World Bank had a lot to answer for in creating mass poverty. It, via the New York global development Bank, encouraged poor nations who had never grown coffee to enter the market. Within ten years Vietnam became the second biggest producer of coffee behind Brazil.

As was the norm for all commodities and raw materials, it was uneconomic for poor countries to process the coffee. This was because of the tariffs imposed in Europe and America. The markets back then had been shamelessly rigged to favour the rich and they still had the audacity to talk about 'free trade'. The West knew damn well that had, for example, Africa been allowed to process its coffee and other commodities it could have started to haul itself out of poverty. *But...* at a cost equal and opposite to us in the West. This was *not* the reason globalisation was introduced.

In the lead up to the devastating failure of the coffee crop of Brazil in 2006, other countries were growing less and less due to the glut and lack of profit. Coffee quickly became the 'caviar' drink to start the day. The outcry, in the US especially, shook politicians to the core. People en masse demanded to know how things had been allowed to get so out of hand. The fuel crisis and increase in so-called terrorism were bad enough, but when the vast majority's favourite energy boost and crutch was no longer freely available, their foundations were rattled.

Drought, disease and political instability had destroyed a whole nation's harvest. Maybe 'those' scientists were wrong? Maybe global warming was real? Maybe their culture of consumerism was destroying the planet after all? Maybe the odd billion dollars here and there couldn't simply patch up the increasingly destructive power of nature?

The increasing political instability in South America was largely as a direct result of South American countries joining the North American Free Trade Agreement (NAFTA). Mexico joined in 1993, and within ten years 215,000 workers in the 'Maquiladora' factories lost their jobs. This was because many contracts were lost to China – big companies had no loyalty; if they found a better deal they'd up sticks immediately. The same happened when privatisation and deregulation of the financial sector in Argentina happened in 2001 – an economic collapse accompanied the loss of jobs here.

Even when the left-wing reformist, 'Lula' da Silva, was voted into power in Brazil he appeared to be powerless to make any real changes. Such was the hold the Western powers had. However, as also happened in Ecuador, many people in those countries rose up and took the law into their own hands in 2005 and onwards. The powerful Landless People's Movement in Brazil led the way simply by taking their land back and farming it to feed their families. Corporate farming of things like coffee became a dangerous occupation. The numbers of undocumented immigrants flooding into Florida reached one million in twelve years by 2006. This was due to global corporate capitalism driving families to despair and even starvation in many cases. Everybody was fed up at the unalleviated poverty created by ruthless and hypocritical Western policies.

Elsewhere in the world things were not much better. George Bush's road map for peace in the Middle East in 2003 all but collapsed in just six months. Ariel Sharon's highly unchristian lust for revenge meant, even with his assassination by his own people, it wasn't until 2012 before things calmed down in the Middle East.

The escalation in numbers of US soldiers killed in the run-up to so-called 'democratic elections' in Iraq early in 2005 saw the tide in the US turn against Bush and the neo-cons for the first time. The poor US troops were, increasingly against their will, made to stay in Iraq. To the freedom fighters it was like shooting metal ducks at the fair. The Americans were now desperate not to let go of their control of the oil. It was five times cheaper for them to get it from the Middle East than Russia, for example. Also they knew if they lost control of this source and the greedy gas-guzzling SUVs couldn't fill up, they would have a revolution in their own country. The sudden increase in fuel prices caused when the Saudis drastically reduced supplies nearly caused this anyway.

In the UK, Tony Blair squeezed in for a third term, and most people didn't bat an eyelid. It had got to the stage when it didn't matter which party got into power. They were all controlled to a very large degree by big business. None had the courage to stand up to a multinational, even when their products were killing people, through fear they'd up sticks and move to a country with 'less restrictions'.

★

In 2007 Dad took me to meet the legendary Harold Smith who was by now under house arrest in Italy. He hadn't done anything wrong other than speak the truth. He was a mixture of European and American by origin, and it was as if he had just walked out of the woods one day. The strength, directness and humility of his delivery many said would not have been seen since the days of Jesus Christ, Buddha or Muhammad. It became too much for the American authorities since his following had gone from nothing to many millions overnight. Had he not gone into exile he would certainly have met with a mysterious accident.

It was to be our last trip abroad. Our passports were about to expire. To get a new one you had to give the authorities an iris scan and be fingerprinted as if you were a common criminal. The main arguments were that this would reduce terrorism and fraud. However, the cards didn't prevent the Madrid bombing or September 11 – where the hijackers all had ID papers – and the single document made life easier for those committing fraud doing away with a multiple check system. The result was DNA samples were introduced in place of fingerprints as many had been saying it would. As the authorities became more desperate, leading activists were 'taken out' by, for example, smearing a dead body in the trouble shooter's DNA. ID cards became known as the 'Racist Card' as 'foreign-looking' people were routinely stopped and checked under the constant suspicion of being 'illegal immigrants/terrorists'.

ID cards initially carried up to fifty items of information about you, including medical history, bank and mortgage details and personal details. Many felt the cost of £5 billion could have been better spent elsewhere.

They tried to make them compulsory after the huge terrorist attack in London in 2005. However, thanks to civil rights campaigners and the press they only got voluntary status – not that it made much difference. Those of us though who didn't hold one found life much more difficult. Access to healthcare, education and basic services were made so hard for most who refused to get one that they eventually capitulated. It was also made nigh on impossible to renew your passport or driving licence without one, and if you were stopped in the street not carrying one you were sometimes treated like a criminal.

I had never seen Dad so nervous and in awe at the prospect of meeting anyone. Harold's location was kept secret to protect him from the masses, so he only saw people by appointment, for which Dad, being a well-known troublemaker by then, qualified. The Italian authorities had struck a deal with Harold and his friends that they wouldn't give him any grief, provided he remained in the confines of the house. He hadn't committed a crime himself, so they couldn't legally lock him up in prison. Many in the West were by then ready for a full-scale revolution, and had they locked him up they knew they risked triggering the masses. Likewise, the same could easily have happened had they allowed him to roam the streets and speak. Hence, an uneasy compromise was reached.

We arrived on a hot summer day at the village where Harold was being held. It was a fairly remote village in the beautiful rolling, hilly landscape of Tuscany. My dad was no culture vulture but even he seemed moved at the peaceful, unspoilt nature of the lovely old houses and cobbled streets, with a thriving market in the village centre. We walked down a side street off the market square to where Harold was holed up. We knew Harold's precise whereabouts from a good hundred metres away. The 'undercover' police attempting to mill inconspicuously around his front door and blend in with the locals, as usual, stood out like sore thumbs.

It was with a mixture of trepidation and enormous excitement that we approached the door. The undercovers and friends of Harold at the door checked us rigorously for weapons – the police in case we were smuggling in weapons for Harold's bunch of followers; Harold's friends in case we were on an assassination mission. It was a spacious house on the inside with a lot of new, freshly varnished beams reaching up to high ceilings. The place seemed out of character with its surroundings. There was also a surprising number of people hanging around, smoking and drinking, playing card games, dominoes and chess.

One elderly man came over to me and started putting his hands all over me. This was not what Dad and I were expecting at all. I warned the man if he persisted I'd smash the glass he was holding in his face – I might have been only fifteen but could look after myself. I didn't have to worry because Dad hit him hard in the chest with the palm of his hand. The other people in the hallway, mainly men, simply roared with laughter. Any delusions of spiritual grandeur we may have harboured for the supposed 'great man' were immediately dispelled. How could such an incredible messianic figure surround himself with such idiots? Dad's disappointment was tangible and it became even more so as we descended the stairs into the sitting room, which was brimming with more of the same type of people.

In the middle of what could only be described as a bunch of freeloading degenerates was Harold himself. He was immediately recognisable to us from behind from the pictures we had seen of him, with his small, skinny frame and shortish blond hair. When he turned to us he was laughing rather raucously, but I was immediately struck by something in his piercing blue eyes. Any awe and respect rapidly dissipated as he chased us round the room, giggling, firing Brazil nuts and walnuts from a toy catapult. We ran round the room to get away from him because it hurt when he hit us.

Dad had said before arriving that he was having a personal spiritual battle/challenge. He said he felt a need to tell Harold about himself – his deeds and achievements during foot-and-mouth, and his successes with supermarkets and GM. He said that he thought he had gotten over his ego needs and insecurities about what others thought of him, but the reputation of this man showed him he wasn't quite there yet.

Dad was speaking to him whilst dodging the nuts fired in his direction. It was when Dad was talking about the massive nuclear leak some months earlier that triggered the most radical, almost terrifying, instant change I'd ever seen in a human being. Dad never spoke about it after we left that house, and something changed in him for ever after the experience.

★

We had been putting the finishing touches to our eco homes in the woods and testing the reed bed sewage system, when we received an urgent call from Globalise Resistance. It concerned a rapidly organised Direct Action protest in one of the UK's major cities in response to a rumour of a nuclear leak. I'm ashamed to say I don't remember the name of the city, and the national news was banned from including such information through fear of encouraging more to 'join' us. Dad was going off with his band of merry men on many of these actions, which had largely taken over from simple street protests. He rarely told me where he went so as to protect me from being labelled an accomplice when questioned by the police, which was happening ever more frequently. However, I often managed to overhear his tales.

This particular action took them to an enormous hangar close to the city centre. The hangar had had an enormous fence put around it a few weeks earlier. This was at the same time as rumours started circulating about an explosion or leak of some kind in one of the big ageing nuclear plants.

Large military lorries were then seen going in and out of the hanger in the early hours, and the word was they were coming from the nuclear plant, which itself had just been further fenced off. Hence the call to Dad and the other members of the Resistance countrywide.

Dad said the fences were not only high, but had razor blades on the top, much as in a prison. In addition he said there were portable huts spaced out around the fence where military personnel kept a round the clock eye on the floodlit fence. Dad met up with the GR brigade, about 2,000 of them, at the only entrance. It was heavily guarded and the atmosphere was very tense indeed. People were getting searched and taken away under the by now much used Section 44 of the Terrorism Act. Dad felt very afraid because he'd refused to have an ID card. In such a situation anyone without an ID card was a terrorist and treated as such.

All of a sudden the air was thick with tear gas. The protesters, as they were still called, had been surrounded and were being attacked. They fought back bravely, so much so that the young military personnel at the entrance of the gate temporarily left their post to help out a particularly violent rumpus some ten metres away. It was then that Dad and two others walked through a small gap in the entrance.

Dad said he made a dash for the one open doorway across some forty metres of open ground from the entrance. He said he expected to hear the shots ring out, but fortunately all eyes were temporarily on the violence. He burst through the door and saw machines all around the side of the room. There was nowhere to hide other than under a table in the middle of the room; however, he felt this was pretty hopeless because it had no sides.

Before he had time to think further, he heard footsteps and ladies' voices coming down a corridor he hadn't noticed at the end of the room. He was convinced they would see him if they turned the lights on, but hoped the daylight coming through the door would be enough and they'd simply pass through.

The ladies arrived, two of them, and turned the lights on with Dad playing dead under the table in full view – resigned, he said, to a long, miserable, indefinite stay in a high security prison without a trial or access to a solicitor. This was the fate that befell any activist for often the most minor of misdemeanours deemed by the authorities to be a 'threat to state security'. The purpose, of course, was to scare and quash civilian opposition and exposure which might undermine their control and objectives. Dad had only been to prison the year before, so he knew they would throw the book at him this time.

Fortunately for Dad, a large Alsatian came in through the door by which he had entered. It initially went over to the two ladies, who stroked him and pulled at his head whilst saying, 'Who's a lovely boy then, Derek?' in a doggy-type voice. Derek then spotted Dad and went over to him.

Dad didn't feel afraid. He loved dogs, especially the more aggressive breeds. We had at home a black Labrador called Phillip, an Alsatian called Soul and a crazy but lovely English bull terrier called Bryan. Derek, even though he was a guard dog, must have sensed the love in Dad for dogs and simply stood over him wagging his tail, blocking him from the gaze of the two ladies.

He cautiously looked up when he heard a machine door opening and saw one lady putting a load of filthy clothes into it from an enormous trolley they had steered in. He realised they were all washing machines and the ladies were laundry women. He said that they were talking about one guard who had noticed that two or maybe three men had broken into the compound. Two had been arrested and they were searching for a possible third, however, fortunately for Dad, not too hard due to the uncertainty. The two ladies then left with Derek in tow.

Dad had noticed a door at the end of the corridor when the lights were on and headed towards it. He said that he had a huge sense of trepidation, even foreboding, at what he might find the other side – provided it wasn't locked. It wasn't, and on entering he literally got the shock of his life.

Initially he saw what he thought to be a couple of hundred makeshift beds with people lying on them. The lighting was dim, but after his eyes acclimatised a minute or so later he realised there must have been more than 1,000. Of the faces that were not bandaged, many had open wounds like burn marks and some had large patches of hair missing. He said the worst thing was the terrible noise. It was a cacophony of groaning, which from being relatively constant would suddenly get louder at random. Dad said it reminded him of when he was a teenager working on an intensive turkey farm (not his idea of fun), where from a few constant brrrrrrs it was as if someone suddenly pressed the group soul button, and they'd all burst out as one in a resounding, 'Gobble-gobble-gobble-gobble-gobble...!'

In the far distance of the hangar there were four or five orderlies working their way slowly down the line of beds, feeding the patients, and emptying the urine bags and the buckets of faeces and sick. Having got over his initial shock, Dad announced that he was from the outside and he was there to get their stories, and report to the world and see if he could get them some real help. He said the groans turned to noises of excitement, and he hissed at them to shut up. He made them swear on their mothers' lives not to give him away. If they did he was as good as dead and they would be condemned to this disgusting, filthy existence probably until they died. Quietly, Dad was surprised that the powers that existed then hadn't gassed the lot, Gestapo-style (many inmates said they wished they would do this), but he felt if that got out the whole world would have risen up.

The world by then was fed up with big companies poisoning and killing thousands then using highly paid legal eagles such as Burson Marsteller (Monsanto's, Dow Chemical's and Exxon's chosen favourite), to mop up their mess. One of many typical examples was the explosion at the Union Carbide chemical factory in 1984 in Bhopal, India. Here a cleaner accidentally triggered the catastrophe whilst cleaning the pipes with water. Union Carbide had by then pulled out, having made their money, leaving their toxic time bomb to an unsupervised skeleton staff with not even a safety manual. The death toll exceeded 20,000 with a further 500,000 terminally debilitated by chronic illnesses. These included skin, lung and gastrointestinal cancers, impaired immune systems and pulmonary oedema (the latter also being the main cause of death by drowning from collapsed fluid-filled lungs). Even miscarriages in Bhopal were seven times the national average. Burson Marstellar managed to restrict compensation to victims to a paltry £300. Union Carbide was bought out by the equally despicable Dow Chemicals. Dow Chemicals were the manufacturers of napalm/Agent Orange and was the world's number one producer of highly carcinogenic dioxins.

Dad got his pad and pen out from his rucksack. Everybody carried a rucksack to Direct Action gatherings. They contained everything from waterproofs, a space blanket to sleep in and a toothbrush, to tear gas protection gear and wire cutters and – most important of all – a good book in case you were banged up.

The stories about the leak/explosion were horrendous. The speed with which the lorries arrived, and men in alien spacesuits and hooded gas masks piled those still alive and fleeing the scene into the trucks, was the most creepy thing of all. Everyone was told over a loud PA system not to panic and to make for the lorries as quickly as they could. They were not given gas masks. The announcer kept stressing the most dangerous thing they could do was to run away. If they went to the lorries they would be fine.

Some noticed a cordon of hooded men forming a ring around the outside in case the workers cut through the fence and disappeared into the undergrowth. They were clearly under strict instructions not to let one person escape and start shooting their mouths off concerning the hideous happenings at the nuclear plant. The whole nuclear industry had an appalling reputation by then, following a series of minor leaks at home and abroad. It had also become a popular target for terrorists and everyone was amazed they had not had a successful hit in the UK before.

Even though wind farms and wave energy plants were gradually spreading, the Government, who had on many occasions baled out the nuclear industry, still continued to support it over and above the ecologically friendly alternatives. As in the States, France and much of Europe, Government ministers had a very close relationship with the nuclear industry. Many ex-ministers got to sit on the Board of Directors at the various nuclear plants, picking up enormous directors' fees. It was the very well paid up members of the nuclear industry who, posing as ordinary caring civilians, had successfully brainwashed the nation with well-written articles and letters to newspapers. They stated that wind farms were ugly, very destructive to wildlife – birds especially – and devalued the price of any house nearby.

All the time while Dad was getting people's stories and dodging the orderlies – he had huge trouble controlling the excitement of the patients – he was thinking how on earth he was going to escape. He said he drew heavily on his faith and spiritual knowledge. He was very aware that Spirit/God or whatever had paved the way giving him the opportunity to break in – the violent fight at the entrance, plus the extraordinary timing of Derek's arrival, for example. It was because of this he knew that if he was meant to be caught and imprisoned, it was for some karmic reason. He also knew damn well that if he didn't listen to his intuition and act when it felt right, or if he relaxed and lazily felt God would look after him come what may, he would be caught. Free will was what it said it was. If you didn't 'listen' and put huge amounts of effort and energy in yourself to a situation, then your life path could dramatically change. The only thing that was 'meant to be' (as people used to say) was the opportunities or set of circumstances that came your way. The choice as to how you responded was down to you and you alone.

Dad felt that they hadn't entertained the arrival of a possible third activist too seriously. After a few hours he started to think he had enough information to blow the lid wide open and it was time to leave. At this moment he heard the sound of keys in the door he had come through. The thought passed through his head that he'd been very fortunate that the door hadn't been locked some hours earlier.

The two laundry women entered the huge hanger and started collecting some of the clothes drenched in sick, faeces and urine – Some job these poor ladies had, Dad thought. Then bingo! Surely with so many washing machines in one room there were some clothes belonging to the military also being washed. He noticed the big trolley being pushed by the two ladies was not even half full. It was time to go. Without a by your leave, Dad rushed to the door, which just had a latch on the inside, and quickly but cautiously approached the laundry room.

The smell was terrible compared to when he arrived. There were piles of clothes everywhere, but no sign of any military gear. He was terrified about a soldier coming in or seeing him through the window. He was also aware that the laundry ladies would soon return, and there was no sign of Derek this time. In desperation Dad started looking through the piles of clothes, in case there was a soldier's jacket and trousers buried beneath. He was heaving all the while and sick twice. Sheep prolapses, foot rot and maggot-ridden carcasses, and burying pig and cattle heads, offal and smelly colons were one thing; but he couldn't deal with human excrement and the rest (I hear he used to heave whilst changing my nappy).

He was starting to panic when he heard a machine stop. He took a chance and opened it, and found it full of (wet) military clothes. He did a quick change and stuffed his rucksack at the back of the machine, keeping the notepad in his underpants. Then, when the coast was clear, he took a few deep breaths and walked boldly and purposefully into the open air.

It was night-time but the yard area was lit up brightly with huge spotlights. Fortunately the rain was coming down quite hard and the khaki military cotton camouflaged just how soaking wet he was. He walked around for half an hour saluting, trying to have the odd laugh at the universal English scapegoat, the weather, with other soldiers. He then saw a group of soldiers getting into the back of a transport lorry and got in last just before the canvas was shut, apologising for being late. Freezing cold, wet and tired, he pretended to sleep on what felt like a long journey. When the lorry pulled up at a service station to allow the soldiers to get food and go to the toilet, he slipped away.

★

When he sat down with Harold, it was about the fifth time I had heard him recount this story. Harold had stopped playing around at last and sat there appearing disinterested throughout. However, when Dad was talking about his frustrating attempts to get the story publicised I noticed Harold stiffen slightly. Dad had given the story, via friends and acquaintances in the media, to get the message out there and something done to help the poor inmates in the hangar – he understandably wanted to keep anonymous himself. However, not a squeak was allowed out. Some of his friends were threatened by the secret police, and a few who became particularly incensed and vociferous were locked up.

At this Harold leapt to his feet and spoke with an intensity that turned everyone in the house as white as sheets.

'Now is the time! We spread the word through the streets, across the countryside, from the ports to all the sprawling suburban outposts throughout Europe and America. It is time for… *revolution!*'

Dad and I left quite literally blown away by the man's power. The debauched aura of every man and woman in the house was instantly transformed to one of intense focus and readiness for any action they were asked to do. They calmly looked at us in complete silence as we went from the relatively cool house into the hot cobbled streets of the village.

Dad knew he had been 'used' as a catalyst. Harold had been waiting for a signal to fire into action. Clearly, intuitively, he knew this was it – not to say it was or wasn't anything to do with the plight of those suffering radiation burns back in England. Dad felt deeply humbled to have been used in such a way. He also understood why Harold had played the buffoon whilst in the house up until then.

It wasn't long before the news reported pockets of intifada across all of Europe and into the States. They called it a peasants' revolt. However, looking at the pictures and hearing the comments of those involved it was clear folk came from every corner of the social and cultural spectrum.

The targets were, quite simply, the earth-raping, profit-loving, smug multinationals. Also, within the green belts, the number of people moving into these areas and other common and private land around the cities especially, went up enormously at this time. The authorities had just about managed to control this exodus up until then.

Most people, especially those in the UK, had never broken the law. Millions in the UK alone had lost their jobs and their houses because they couldn't pay their bills and the mortgage. Many once respectable people had for some time been squatting in houses, doorways, subways and Tube tunnels, trains, wherever they could put their head. However, inspired by the words of Harold they felt bold enough to flout the law. Harold gave them the inspiration to break the shackles that they'd been educated to accept and abide by since the day they were born. He also explained clearly, succinctly and (most importantly) very simply, the evils of the by then crumbling system which never cared how much suffering it caused so long as the masses were kept subservient and helped them achieve their goals. Harold lifted the veils from their eyes and showed the world precisely how unnecessary the stress, strain and needless illnesses and deaths were.

It was an extraordinary sight, seeing so many cast off their chains and go out into the metaphoric wilderness and build new homes with whatever raw materials they could get hold of. Some built beautiful 'benders' using flexible ash with a canvas over it and windows in the sides. Others simply drove a van as far as it could go before it ran out of fuel, then stayed in it but built a lean-to on the side. Many developed their own little permaculture gardens and set up trading cooperatives with their neighbours.

Naturally, it wasn't all sweetness and light by any means. It made a huge difference with Harold encouraging, even demanding, cooperation, sensitivity, patience, forgiveness and the need to give without expecting anything in return (in contrast to the old system). However, even so lawlessness was rife and many lost everything. Most communities set up round the clock vigils to mobilise everybody if they came under attack. It was going to take time to break down the freeloading mentality of many from the old system along the lines of 'the world owes me, I can take whatever I like'- not helped that this was the example shown by most of big business.

Fortunately there was not a complete collapse in society back then, or else there would have been total chaos and anarchy. Spiritually – as always, thank heavens – the knock on the door was just loud enough to show everybody what they could expect if they continued down this path for too much longer. There was, of course, an escalation in violence towards people's property and towards the corporations especially. This was because as in any readjustment there was much fear, uncertainty and sheer desperation. Pension plans had all but gone to the wall, many investing in the stock market had lost all or much of their money, and some of the banks were closing down.

At home there was damage inflicted on our property. However, this was not from local people, but the establishment. It was designed to try and scare us into backing off activism against the system.

Harold disappeared without trace some months after our meeting. There were endless rumours about how he was dragged out of his bed in the early hours, beaten senseless and taken off in one of the ten armoured trucks that came to get him. His faith was such that he never bothered with bodyguards. He knew he would be taken out at some point. We heard the one thing he prayed for was not to go before he had completed his work. This he did. Dad said it was a miracle he was not removed before – which indeed it was.

His words had spread around the world and inspired many in all four corners to take up their swords. It was thanks to him and other activists that in the lead-up to 2012 so many rich individuals gave their savings and land to help save the planet. They realised there was not much point having lots of cash stashed away and material goods if there wasn't going to be a planet to live on. With the polar ice caps and glaciers melting at an ever increasing rate, hurricanes and huge tornadoes ravaging areas they had never touched before, and massive tidal waves wiping out much of the lowlands of the Eastern American coast especially, plus so much more, the signs were there for all to see.

Dad, of course, had set up a 'Not For Profit – Save Our World' Trust Fund in the summer of 2004. Funds went to non-government and non-corporate sponsored organisations who exposed the damage done by corporations using a variety of methods and tricks, and who put people before profit. The 'Buy Local, Boycott Supermarkets' campaign was a major outlet for funds.

Individuals started giving so much money to established funds and organisations such as ours, that money was used to buy up land and give it to people who wanted to live and work on it. Sure things were chaotic and there were food and water shortages, and the rich barricaded themselves in, but even so there was still some structure.

There is no question that 2012 proved to be the turning point. At last there really seemed to be genuine bright white light at the end of the tunnel. The Palestinians and Israelis voluntarily choosing to pull down the barriers separating them and live in harmony together was the most powerful single symbolic gesture in recent history. If they could do it, there really was no excuse for the rest of us…

America was furious. They were booted out of the region with their tails between their legs when it came to light that they had been fuelling the feud for their own ends. The arms deals to the Israelis alone would have been enough to keep many ordinary countries' economies in the black. Also, you couldn't beat the good old tried and tested 'divide and rule' technique. Both the Palestinians and Israelis (and the world) were so disgusted when they discovered they had been pawns to further the political agenda of the US. Ordinary people on both sides had lived their lives in fear and terror – no doubt brushed aside as mere collateral damage by the Pentagon and CIA.

The US were not, however, going to give up their ways and global dominance lightly. The world was still far from out of the woods. The US Government had done very successful under the table deals with China and other countries to keep them in the fold. It also made sure that all oil continued to be traded using US dollars rather than the Euro, as Saddam Hussein and a few others had sometimes threatened to do – to their cost! Equally as important, they successfully managed to keep Europe's global significance to the minimum.

An unbelievable amount of work was done in those eight years from 2012 to 2020 to irreversibly change the power base of the planet. This is another long story all of its own. The US and Western governments generally, and the enormous multinational companies, were not going to give up without an almighty fight. Bear in mind it was they who paid the Army and police.

*

The worldwide riots of 2020 will go down in history as creating the biggest ever change in human consciousness since the beginning of time. Considering the enormity of the change, the number of people who died was surprisingly small. However, sadly the violence seemed necessary to bring down the curtain on the old way once and for all.

The shameless violence meted out to anyone or group even hinting at standing up for their rights (going self-sufficient was included in this bracket) was disgusting, such was the desperation of the authorities. The prisons everywhere in the world were quite literally bursting at the seams. Simple warehouses and old shipyards were converted to hold millions more. This, of course, made organising and coordinating the final push for freedom a piece of cake.

I went to London with Dad, Biff and a few others from here for that extraordinary, mind-blowing uprising around Trafalgar Square. Similar events were happening in most other major cities across the UK and the world simultaneously. The authorities were instructed to do all they could to prevent it. When we arrived in London you could feel the tear gas burning your eyes on the outskirts. The helicopters hovering above were dropping the stuff on people as they arrived – Dad said this reminded him of Genoa in 2001.

Once the police realised they were outnumbered a thousand to one and had no chance of stopping us, *The Moment* arrived. It brings tears to my eyes as I write about this. The police and Army, who had been instructed to be so brutal towards us, dropping their weapons, removing their visors and bullet-proof vests and coming over to us with tears streaming down their faces, apologising and begging our forgiveness, I don't believe had ever happened before in history. I think most of us had forgotten, and so had they, that they were our fellow countrymen, our brothers and sisters.

Over the previous twenty and thirty years it must be remembered that a massive spiritual awakening had occurred. Everybody by now was keen to live and work together, give of themselves freely and experience the joy of this, and pray that it is just not too late for the planet to heal herself. Dad died shortly afterwards with the biggest, happiest, radiant smile on his face any of us had ever seen.

AMEN

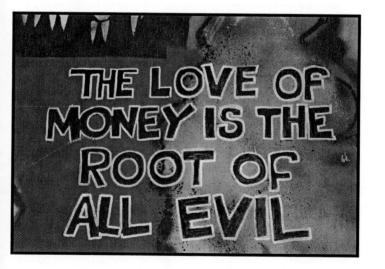

PROTECTION AGAINST TERROR

Tune in, turn on, believe...

Trust no-one, spy on your neighbours...

Raise your flag, lock your doors, pray...

Stay safe, stay inside, do not go out....

...ever again....

OR...

LISTEN TO
BOB MARLEY.

Fear Trade

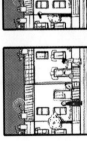

Fear Trade

www.mau-mau.co.uk